So the Story Goes

Twenty-Five Years of the
Johns Hopkins Short Fiction Series

the So Story Goes

Edited by JOHN T. IRWIN
and JEAN McGARRY

WITH A FOREWORD BY JOHN BARTH

The Johns Hopkins University Press
Baltimore and London

This book has been brought to publication with the generous assistance of the G. Harry Pouder Fund.

The Johns Hopkins University Press
2715 North Charles Street
Baltimore, Maryland 21218-4363
www.press.jhu.edu

Library of Congress Cataloging-in-Publication Data

So the story goes : twenty-five years of the Johns Hopkins short fiction series / edited by John T. Irwin and Jean McGarry.
    p. cm. — (Johns Hopkins, poetry and fiction)
ISBN 0-8018-8177-3 (hardcover : alk. paper)
ISBN 0-8018-8178-1 (pbk. : alk. paper)
    1. Short stories, American. I. Irwin, John T. II. McGarry, Jean. III. Series.
PS648.S5S68 2005
813'.0108054—dc22   2004022994

A catalog record for this book is available from the British Library.

Contents

Foreword

Here are twenty short stories by twenty different authors: one story from each of twenty short-story collections out of twice that number published over the past quarter century in the Johns Hopkins University Press's excellent Poetry and Fiction series. The formidable job of culling a mere score of pearls from so rich a fishery has been done with his characteristic skill by the series' editor, John T. Irwin, who, with the able assistance of Jean McGarry, chair of the Johns Hopkins Writing Seminars, chose all those story collections for original publication and saw them through the press. Alert readers may notice that the titles of a number of the volumes are grammatically complete sentences: Steve Barthelme's *And He Told the Little Horse the Whole Story*, for example (from Chekhov's "Misery"), and also Jennifer Finney Boylan's *Remind Me to Murder You Later*, Greg Johnson's *I Am Dangerous*, and Frances Sherwood's *Everything You've Heard Is True*. That (so the story goes) is because Professor Irwin—a distinguished scholar-critic, for many years head of the Hopkins Writing Seminars, and (under the nom de plume John Bricuth) himself a formidably gifted poet, happens to incline to such titles: viz. his splendidly entertaining long dramatic poem *Just Let Me Say This About That*. Although it was my pleasure to be John's colleague at Hopkins for (appropriately) twenty most agreeable years, I can venture no explanation either for this trademark predilection or for his choice of noms de plume, both of which I find intriguing. Authors who aspire to inclusion in the Press's Poetry and Fiction series might do well to adjust their titular syntax; other things equal, a complete-sentence handle could be a tie-breaker.

Back to the anthology: several of the collections from which these stories are chosen were their authors' first book publications; most were not. A number of the authors are or have been associated with the university, either as graduate students or as faculty; most not. The aim of the Poetry and Fiction series has been to publish the best specimens submitted, without regard to their origin; that several of those happen to be the work of past or present colleagues or graduates of the Writing Seminars simply speaks well for the department's recruitment of faculty and of graduate students. Our "mission," in the latter case, has always been to select the most gifted advanced apprentices we can find, to damage them as little as possible during their seasons in the Seminars, and then modestly to take partial credit for the success—such as publication by the New York trade houses or the Hopkins Press—that they would quite likely have attained anyhow, without our coaching. That selection, moreover, like the selection of the twenty story-books from which these specimens have been culled and the culling itself, is based on literary merit alone, not on such polarizing aesthetic categories as realism versus counterrealism, minimalism versus maximalism, *art engagé* versus *art pour l'art*, innovation versus convention, modernism versus postmodernism, and the rest. The reader will find examples here of most of these (well, maybe not maximalism, although the longest—Guy Davenport's "A Field of Snow on a Slope of the Rosenberg," which also has the longest title, runs to a very rich thirty-seven pages, in contrast to Tristan Davies' four-page, single-word-titled, pungent/poignant "Counterfactuals"). Beyond their entertaining variety of matter and manner—a surfer suicide in Costa Rica, the assassination of President John Lennon, a dead father's ghost sarcastically haunting his grown-up son, a white hippie bride and her black medical-student groom—what these fictions have in common is their gratification of that primal and distinctively human pleasure: the sharing of jim-dandy made-up stories.

On with them!

John Barth

Preface

The Johns Hopkins Poetry and Fiction series began in 1979 as a joint venture between the Johns Hopkins University Press and the Johns Hopkins Writing Seminars. In 1977 when I returned to Hopkins as chairman of the Writing Seminars after having edited *The Georgia Review* at the University of Georgia for three years, I suggested to Jack Goellner, then director of the Press, that since collections of poetry and short fiction had become endangered species in the publishing world, the Johns Hopkins University Press could provide a real service to the field of literature by sponsoring a series of such books. I further suggested that the Writing Seminars would seek extra funding to underwrite the project. With the help of then-Provost of the university Richard Longaker, we were able to dedicate income from two endowments—the G. Harry Pouder Fund and the Albert Dowling Trust—to support respectively the fiction and the poetry titles we published, and in March 1979 the series began with the appearance of John Hollander's *Blue Wine and Other Poems* and Guy Davenport's *Da Vinci's Bicycle*.

In the years since, the series has published thirty-one volumes of poetry and forty volumes of fiction. The present volume, which culls the best short fiction we've published—its companion volume, *Words Brushed by Music*, which collects the best poems from the series, appeared in fall 2004—marks the series' twenty-fifth anniversary.

This project began with two simple guiding principles: to publish works of poetry and fiction exhibiting formal excellence and strong emotional appeal and to publish writers at all stages of their careers, whether they be first-book authors, writers in mid-career, or authors summing up a life's work in a retrospective collection. We have also on rare occasions brought back into print volumes published elsewhere that we felt deserved a longer life in bookstores and the closer attention of readers. The governing criteria in selecting the stories for this volume, as in selecting the fiction collections for the series, were that the chosen works put to full use the resources of the English language, that they be humanly moving (since if a story doesn't move us, who cares what else it does?), and that they be about things of a certain substance and importance, things of interest to intelligent, cultured adults. What attracts one in a story is not much different from what attracts one in a person—wit, elegance, empathy, wisdom born of experience, mastery of language. That said, the best illustration of what we looked for in the fiction selected for the series is represented by the stories that follow.

I would like to dedicate this twenty-fifth anniversary volume to all those at the Johns Hopkins University Press whose work and devotion have made this series possible, to the John Hopkins University administration and to my colleagues in the Writing Seminars who have supported it, and to all the writers whose work appears here and who have over the years made this series both successful and a pleasure to edit.

John T. Irwin

So the Story Goes

FROM

World Like a Knife

1991

Her Book

THREE TIMES THE CHILD HAD COME to the Home and each time, as
far as she remembered, her mother had told her that someday she
would understand—someday when you're a woman, her mother
said. She said this in the office, quick before the sound of Mrs. Vincent coming cut her off, and Becca already understood. Her mother,
a woman, was good enough for men, but someone stiff and old like
Mrs. Vincent, who was a widow and wouldn't understand, was only
good enough for children. It was a secret between Becca and her
mother. "I *do* understand," Becca said. Through the window she'd
seen the way her mother met a man and turned him around with her
hands and walked away, guiding him with words and light touches
and looks. This was the way she steered Becca, too, and Becca knew
what came next, that pretty soon her mother would be giving up
everything for that man, and nobody giving up a thing for her. It
was an unfair fact of the secret that nobody gave up anything for a
woman, only made a little fairer by the fact that a woman could
choose the ones she wanted to give up to. Mrs. Vincent could not.
Becca could not—even if being a woman would make her understanding, understanding, in keeping with the general unfairness of
giving up and getting, somehow didn't make her a woman, and,
until she was one, she didn't have a choice. "I *am* a woman," she told
her mother. "Right," her mother said, "and I'm the Queen of Sheba,"
and Mrs. Vincent came, and Becca settled in for the long wait between now and someday, when she would surely also know what
Sheba was.

"Do you remember Mr. and Mrs. Wrigley?" Mrs. Vincent said. "The nice people who came to see you? The nice lady with the yellow hair?" This was so long after Sheba that Becca had forgotten everything except the waiting, and it didn't occur to her yet that she was being asked to remember more than who the Wrigleys were, which was easy, because they were the only people she'd ever met who were named after chewing gum and, perhaps because of that, were different from other people. Mrs. Wrigley talked just with her hands. Only Mr. Wrigley understood what she was saying. Even when her hands were tired and rested for a while on Mr. Wrigley's arm, they said something that no one else could see but Mr. Wrigley understood. He covered them with one of his and smiled a smile that knew.

"How would you like to go and live with them?" Mrs. Vincent said. "Would you like to be their little girl?"

At first Becca didn't see in this much more than what she saw in most of Mrs. Vincent's questions—the possibility of answering yes or no, with some trouble either way. If, for instance, Mrs. Vincent asked, "Is this the way we put away our toys?" Becca knew at once that no was the right answer but meant that she'd done something wrong. She'd found that the safest way to answer Mrs. Vincent's tricky questions was not to answer them at all, to wait till Mrs. Vincent went away and then to secretly, quickly change whatever was the matter.

But this time, long and hard as she stared at the buckle on Mrs. Vincent's belt, and this was a long time for the buckle to stay put, Becca couldn't see a thing that she could do about the question. She could just be right or wrong, and for once she didn't know which was which, so she stole a look up. Mrs. Vincent was staring back at her. She was waiting, too. Mrs. Vincent didn't know the answer.

"Don't be stupid, child," she said, "the Wrigleys are much nicer than what you've known."

In a panic, Becca said, "Yes." She said it in a whisper, like a promise that she meant completely, not because she knew or cared that the Wrigleys were nicer, or thought that Mrs. Wrigley was almost as pretty as her mother and certainly much prettier than Mrs. Vincent, or wanted to find out what her hands meant. She was afraid that any second Mrs. Vincent would see the mistake, that she couldn't choose whose she was until she was a woman. She had to say something before Mrs. Vincent saw. She had to choose as if she could, and maybe sneak past waiting into knowing. Yes was as good as no.

Then, "That's right," Mrs. Vincent said and smiled, and Becca only knew that she'd been tricked again. Mrs. Vincent knew the answer all along.

THERE WAS SOMETHING OLD about the child, in her pinched little plain face a sober and attentive patience that Melissa had seen before in children who weren't even old enough to know what was or wasn't childlike. The child's history confirmed it: Something that she wasn't even old enough to know she'd missed had to be made up to her.

In the first week of her treatments, when she'd had to stay at the hospital, Melissa had visited the wards where the chronically and catastrophically and terminally ill children were. She'd held crying infants and taken them for stroller rides, wheeling their I.V.'s along, and brought storybooks to the bedridden children and meant to do more but, after two weeks of this, returned to her own room for what she thought of as a prolonged, guilty cowering. In the faces of so many of the sick children she'd seen such a strange and knowing patience, older than anything she knew, that among them she couldn't stand her own good fortune—the years of ignorance as good as health, even the cancer caught in time merely because an accident happened to put her in the hospital, happened to focus a doctor's attention on her throat. The children didn't have the ignorance to look back on and love; they didn't know the meaning of recovery.

The girls' dormitory at the Home, where she and Cal weren't allowed till everything had been decided, looked into, and signed, reminded her of the children's ward—the cool, overhead lighting, the frameless beds and steel bureaus in neat rows against the walls, with the scattered stuffed toys and bright coverlets and paintings in pastel highlighting instead of softening the institutional order of the place. She missed only the smell and the racket—of visitors and nurses, and of children, and it took her a minute to see Becca sitting behind a bed at the far end of the room. Like a little hitchhiker, she was sitting on a suitcase, slumped, with her elbows on her knees and her hands hanging. When she heard their footsteps, she straightened up without looking around, pulled her legs together, clasped her hands on one knee, and waited.

Cal hunkered in front of her and tapped her clasped hands with one finger. "Well, Becca?" he said. "Are you going to come home with Mrs. Wrigley and me?"

"Yes," Becca said. Delicately, as if she were touching glass, she put her hand in Cal's big palm.

When they'd visited, she hadn't seemed affectionate, she'd seemed almost untouchable inside her tension, but now she held Cal's hand and walked so close that she bumped him a few times with her foot and hip; then, as he turned back after a last word from Ina Vincent, she tipped her head slightly so that her temple brushed his wrist. Melissa looked from this to Cal's face, and he smiled. Once, while he was translating a question she'd signed, the child had winked at him, distinctly winked at him, and he'd been charmed. He'd been charmed and sure since then that her usual tense seriousness was only the guise of a child who hadn't found anyone to trust yet. He didn't have to say so. Melissa could see it in the way the child's charm engaged his, when he talked with enchanted common sense about what Becca needed, how it pleased him to plan again.

That charmed assurance was in the restrained and serious way he asked Becca questions as he drove. He didn't talk about who he and Melissa were, what Becca might make of them, or what could come next. Instead he soberly asked the child about small matters, as he had when they'd visited her at the Home. She didn't seem to care any more now than then for small talk, for discussions of dolls or music or games or her dress or her day. With an air of indulgence that was clear anyway to Melissa, Becca smiled and answered when she could with a few words, which were mostly yes.

Almost from the second he reached the front door, Cal dropped his sober tone and started to talk at a glad, rapid pitch. The child was trying to follow him, her face pinched in that look of hard study. He showed her her room and then, before she'd had a chance to see what he said was hers, led her out to look at the house, telling her between the living room and den about the accident that had left Mrs. Wrigley mute but not deaf, recalling Mrs. Vincent's praise of Becca's skill at reading and supposing that she would enjoy learning to read sign language, summarizing between den and dining room his and Mrs. Wrigley's conversation about what Becca might want to call them, Mrs. and Mr., Cal and Melissa, Mom and Dad if she could, and that finally was the gist of it: It was up to her. Then he started on the kitchen. Melissa signed to him: Is she hungry?

She saw Becca note this, the flicker in the child's attention before she fixed her gaze on Cal's lips, waiting for translation. Hearing the question, she nodded a slow, significant yes, and smiled, and while he recited the contents of the refrigerator, turned secretly to regard Melissa.

"She's already on your side," Cal said over his shoulder. "She's a sympathetic mute."

Melissa tapped him and signed, then, feeling Becca's stare, added: Tell her what I said.

"Mrs. Wrigley says I haven't given you a chance to say a word." With a head of lettuce in one hand and a wedge of cheese in the other, he crouched till his face was level with Becca's, and smiled an intimate apology, a smile the child mimicked exactly. Melissa took the cheese and lettuce and turned to the counter to start sandwiches. Behind her, still low, Cal said, "I went on that way when she came home after the accident. She says."

Melissa turned sharply, but caught Becca, not Cal, looking at her. She touched her heart and smiled, but the child's intent expression didn't change.

BECCA NOW SOMEHOW shared a house with Mr. and Mrs. Wrigley. In the house she had a room, a bed, a rocking chair, a lamp, and a desk, all of which Mr. Wrigley had given her. These things were hers, he'd said, and he'd said it so that she'd known right away that these were valuable possessions. These were valuable and hers, but in the night, after the Wrigleys left her to see exactly what she had, she'd found in the back of the desk's bottom drawer a notebook with worn edges and, tucked inside its blank pages, four torn sheets folded in half. Each of the four sheets had a message on it, two with words she didn't know, and none of which she understood, except that, because she didn't understand them, they were not for her, and nobody had given her the book that had a crushed corner and was hidden in her desk as if the desk were also someone else's, and how these things could be both hers and someone else's was something she would have to learn but suspected she already knew. They were not hers, and what she didn't know about men would fill a book. This was a book her mother had, and it didn't interest Becca half as much as the one she'd found, which mostly interested her because she'd found it and saw in its secretness some of the bigger mystery of Mr. Wrigley's connection with Mrs. Wrigley, either another part of the mystery or a clue, she didn't know which.

Mr. Wrigley was there in the morning but left after breakfast, not mad, even though when he'd tried to touch Mrs. Wrigley's hair, her yellow hair, she'd moved her head enough to put her hair out of his reach. He'd kissed her. He knew he couldn't touch Mrs. Wrigley's hair, and when he said that he would be home late, Becca saw that Mrs. Wrigley knew this, too. He was saying this aloud just for her, like the signs, because Mrs. Wrigley knew everything without having to hear it. She'd had an accident, an accident in a car, and after that she couldn't talk, but while she wasn't talking she could watch people who did and see everything before they said it. In this way, she was like Becca's mother, who'd also had an accident but could say so and could tell a person, "I know what you're thinking," though when she was asked for details, when Becca asked her, "What?" she wouldn't say, she was so mad, because she did know.

Because Mrs. Wrigley couldn't talk, a machine answered the telephone. She showed Becca the red light and small spinning reels and worked her hand like a duck quacking. Becca recognized the quacking as quickly as she saw that Mrs. Wrigley meant that the machine could talk. This was a sign that she understood, though the idea of talking as quacking was new to her and seemed to be another clue to Mrs. Wrigley that she would have to learn.

Mrs. Wrigley knew this, too. She made hand signs, then wrote down on a piece of paper: I WILL TEACH YOU. Becca had already forgotten the signs that said it, but now she knew what they meant, and knew the letters, like the letters in the book, and when she held out her hands and Mrs. Wrigley pressed them, she could feel the knowledge coming into them.

Mrs. Wrigley wrote: I WANT YOU TO BE HAPPY.

Now Becca was sure about the book. I AM HAPPY, she wrote, and underlined the AM three times as it had been on the folded message; and then, to show how well she understood, she copied out another one: I DON'T MIND.

Under this, Mrs. Wrigley wrote carefully: YOU CAN TALK. I CAN HEAR. This wasn't the answer Becca expected, especially after quacking, even though she didn't know exactly what answer she did expect—she only knew this wasn't it, and, seeing Mrs. Wrigley's hand going so slow and then her slow smile when she finally looked up, Becca was afraid she hadn't understood it after all. She wrote with a little desperation: I AM NOT CONTAGIOUS. It looked right to her, but, because it was a new word, she knew it was risky and wasn't surprised when Mrs. Wrigley merely tore the full page off the pad and folded it into her pocket. Mrs. Wrigley was about to write the answer when the telephone rang and her pen jumped on the page, leaving a jagged mark. OOPS, she wrote, and nodded at the telephone, with a lift of her eyebrows and a tip of her hand asking Becca if she wanted to answer.

Right before Mrs. Wrigley punched the button on the machine, Becca heard Mr. Wrigley's voice. She waited, but when he didn't say anything else, she said, "Hello."

The strange cry that came from the phone was such a surprise that by the time Becca realized that it was her name and her mother and, with a fear a little like what she'd just felt, realized that it wasn't strange, her mother knew, Mrs. Wrigley had already taken away the phone and was listening to the rest. Her mother's voice talking to Mrs. Wrigley sounded strange again, but like quacking now, and Mrs. Wrigley put down the phone and looked at it as if it might jump up again and give her a duck bite. Looking at Mrs. Wrigley looking at the telephone, Becca was afraid in a way that was new.

They got away from the phone. They went in the car to a building downtown, and in the building went up to floor seventeen, where a woman sitting at a desk said sadly. "Oh, Melissa. You're looking for Cal? He's at the site." What Becca couldn't understand was how Mr.

Wrigley could be at the site and be at the same time with her mother on the phone. It was possible that Mr. Wrigley and her mother were at the site, though she'd never known her mother to go to a site, and it was possible that Mrs. Wrigley knew this, because, though the woman at the desk gave her an address, a park and not a site was where they went and spent the afternoon with sign language between them, and something else that made either the teaching or the learning difficult.

BECCA WAS IN BED, her bed, but not asleep when Mr. Wrigley came home late. As on the phone, his voice was cut off in the middle of a word, and then, after a silence that she knew was the silence of Mrs. Wrigley talking, he said a long and disbelieving, "How?" Creeping to the door, Becca could see down the hallway most of Mr. Wrigley and most of Mrs. Wrigley's back and one of her hands working the air with fury. She was shouting. "I will," Mr. Wrigley said. "First thing in the morning."

Mrs. Wrigley said something without moving her hand.

"This late?" he said.

They moved out of sight. Listening hard, Becca heard a rustle and the jingle of the telephone being picked up and not a word until the click of it being put down again, when Mr. Wrigley said something that ended with "Becca take it?"

She looked sidelong at the shadowy room that was hers and all the shadowy, half-lit things in it that were also hers but whose value she knew only through Mr. Wrigley's voice. Only the book, deep in the drawer, was valuable without Mr. Wrigley's knowing, and that, she'd found on getting out of bed once earlier, had instead of yesterday's four messages, only one, a new one that said: HELLO, BEAUTIFUL. BEAUTIFUL was familiar and, coming after HELLO, seemed good, but now she wasn't sure.

Hearing Mr. Wrigley and Mrs. Wrigley coming down the hall, she snuck back to bed and pretended sleep as they passed by, pausing at the door, and she heard Mr. Wrigley say, "There's nothing she can do," and then, "You have to feel sorry for her." By opening her eyes only a slit, she could see for a second Mrs. Wrigley's furious face and hands, and thought again about the book—it must be good and must be hers and she could find out for sure if Mr. Wrigley would just go away again.

SHE WOKE IN THE DARK without knowing she'd slept or that she'd heard a sound, only knowing that she was awake and what her mother called all ears. She was listening for a sound that she was afraid she'd hear again and about which listening was the only thing she could do. Even as she recognized her sleep and her room, her lamp on her desk in the dark, and knew that the deep murmur was Mr. Wrigley, the murmur was gone and Mr. Wrigley was walking past her door, down the hall. The faraway front door opened and shut.

She got out of bed and took the book out of its hiding place. Opening it in the dark to HELLO, BEAUTIFUL, she carried it down the hall to the room where Mrs. Wrigley would be. That was the master bedroom.

The half-closed door hid most of the room, but, in the mirror over the dresser, she could see what it took her a second to know was Mrs. Wrigley sitting on the bed with her yellow hair on her hand on her knee. She was completely bald. Becca had never seen a bald woman, and, when Mrs. Wrigley touched a bare spot by her ear, she knew that she wasn't supposed to. This wasn't for her to see, as the sounds that sometimes woke her weren't for her to hear, and, just as she could only listen to the sounds, she could only stare secretly at Mrs. Wrigley in the mirror and wonder whether Mr. Wrigley had done this to her or just found out what he wasn't supposed to know either. Then she saw her own face in the mirror, and jumped. Holding her book tight, she crept back down the hall, as quiet as if her creeping steps could erase the sound she'd just made, and so save Mrs. Wrigley from something.

THE SIGHT OF HER BALD HEAD was frightening even to Melissa, as many times as she'd seen it in these past months and as often as she'd had a chance to get used to the perplexing idea that the plucked woman reflected in the mirror was herself. Afraid she'd frightened Becca, she replaced the blonde wig and, wrapping her robe around her, went down the hall.

Becca's door was open a crack and in the pale light it let in she could see the child lying in bed with her book in one hand and her other hand held out in front of her, gesturing. Watching, she recognized a letter, then another, and others mixed in willy-nilly with invented signs—gibberish, but with inflection, phrasing, pauses between what were clearly meant to be words. She took a step back, out of sight, and knocked softly, giving Becca a second to expect her; but when she stepped forward, now into the child's state, she feared she'd just given her one more second of dread.

After stopping at the desk to light the lamp and get a pen, dallying a little so Becca could get used to her, she went to the bed and sat down. On the blank first page of the book, she wrote: I WAS SICK. Becca looked from this to her face. Melissa added: IT WILL GROW BACK. The child's expression didn't change. Always that intent look seemed to wait for more, explanation, information, seemed to be suspending judgment. Melissa pointed to her hair, but Becca, as if she'd already forgotten that bald woman, merely frowned down and flipped through the book to the loose page with the greeting on it. She turned this around so Melissa could read.

Melissa touched Becca's cheek and with a smile tried to communicate what she meant by "beautiful." Promptly Becca took the pen and, frowning close as an apprentice forger, copied the words. As if she weren't quite sure of her work, she looked down at it for a second, considering, then added as painstakingly: I AM NOT FRAGILE. Oh, Melissa said soundlessly, and Becca quickly crossed out the E.

When the child looked up again, apprehensively, Melissa leaned slowly into her gaze and put her arms around her and, feeling in her small shoulders a tense, tentative submission, guessed that Becca was somehow attaching the significance of this embrace to those words. She wished for a minute that Becca would talk, would prattle and chatter as some children did, even some of the sick ones with her look, who seemed to think muteness meant a good listener, and out would come stories and comments and questions innocently revealing. In her arms, Becca stiffened and her hands, quick and hidden, clutched at the book between them, getting it under the edge of the sheet just as Melissa let go to see, and Cal said, "What, awake?"

He was standing at the door. He'd come back quiet as ever, and met her glance with the look he always wore, smiling and slightly bewildered, as if he'd waked wandering and were surprised that the first house he'd wandered into happened to be his. Now he had a daughter to be surprised by, too, and to look at her he tilted his head at an angle like hers on her pillow. "Did you have a bad dream, Becca?"

"Yes," she said. She said it as if she were pleased indeed to report it, and it occurred to Melissa for the first time that something had waked the child and that it hadn't been a dream. Despite her stiffening a second ago, and her book-hiding, Becca was wearing what Melissa had come to think of as her Cal expression, a look of oblique sweetness that was disturbing, and not just because it appeared so promptly when Cal did. It was familiar, but misplaced. It was, she thought, the look of a woman expecting to be asked to dance, and she wondered again what Becca'd seen of her mother's romantic life, though Ina Vincent had assured them that whenever a man entered the picture Becca entered the Home. Ina Vincent had also assured them that the mother was not told the names of the adopting parents, and that this mother wouldn't care to know, anyway—she was nesting this time. The idea of Becca's mother nesting didn't fit the picture Melissa had of her, but neither did the sound of her voice on the phone, after the wild cry, which did.

Spell "fragile," she signed to Cal, and define it.

Sitting by her on the bed, he said, "Surely you know—" but, at a look from her, cut himself off and turned to Becca to ask her nicely, "You want to know what fragile means?" He spelled it and went into an explanation, but as soon as Becca realized what word it was, her smiling attention wandered dreamily away from him until, when he was telling her that some fragile things were champagne flutes, baby chicks, thin women like Melissa, and the wrists of tiny little girls, was in fact holding the child's own, she was plainly feigning sleep.

"THE WOMAN" WAS her mother and she knew everything. That much Becca knew already, but at breakfast she learned from Mr. Wrigley's answers and Mrs. Wrigley's face that they were just finding this out, and it caused some confusion. It made Mrs. Wrigley frown and say so many quick things with her hands that by the time Mr. Wrigley agreed, as he did at certain times, Becca could tell from his face that he didn't remember anymore what out of so many signs he was agreeing to. Becca was collecting everything that was confusing about Mrs. Wrigley, including her hair and BEAUTIFUL and bits of Mr. Wrigley's explanation of FRAGILE and Mr. Wrigley himself, and she added this. This collection itself seemed confused, but she felt that somehow it would make sense when she understood each thing in it, just as Mrs. Wrigley's hands would make sense when she understood each sign. Then Mrs. Wrigley's hand that was saying something above Becca's ear stopped and dropped onto her shoulder, and the fear came back.

It was a fear like what she'd felt when Mrs. Vincent asked her if she wanted to be Mrs. Wrigley's little girl. Her disappointment at finding out that was a cheat had been blurred down to nothing by another possibility that had occurred to her since then with such enormity and strangeness that she couldn't think of anything to do with it but sit and wait. It was the safe sense that she could sit and wait that held together everything confusing about Mrs. Wrigley, but now it suddenly was gone and there was just confusion and to sit and wait didn't seem possible, but still she couldn't think of anything else to do. Mrs. Wrigley was going to find out that nobody could have her except someone who had an accident or a duty to the state and decency or got paid like the babysitters Jeanne and Mrs. Marker. She already knew something. It was in her hand.

It didn't help that Mr. Wrigley went away. Becca was already used to the idea that he came back. If she could think he wouldn't, she could think again that Mrs. Wrigley, because her hair came off, was in some way that she hadn't quite figured out yet like Mrs. Vincent and only good enough for children—but Mr. Wrigley's saying as he went that he was going to do something and that he would take care of it was as good as his saying he would be home late, and she could only wonder if what he was going to do was find out the mistake and come back and tell Mrs. Wrigley. He was going to find out from her mother.

When the telephone rang, Mrs. Wrigley stood with her hands in the pockets of her skirt and looked at it until the light went on. Her mother and Mr. Wrigley were on the phone, and Mrs. Wrigley had her hands in her pockets because she didn't want to pick it up and hear. The second time it rang, she only looked at it from the sofa, where she was showing Becca how to say in hand signals: I AM HUNGRY. She knew something, and in this way she was like Becca's mother when she didn't want to answer the phone either. Also like her mother, after three rings that she knew about but didn't want to answer, Mrs. Wrigley took Becca shopping.

This was the first time Becca had seen Mrs. Wrigley in a skirt, and, walking behind her through the racks of dresses, she could see that Mrs. Wrigley was as thin as Mr. Wrigley said. Then Mrs. Wrigley saw what she was thinking and wouldn't let her walk behind. To be thin was a dream her mother had. Becca was thin, sometimes as a twig, sometimes as a toothpick, sometimes as a skinny little goose, and she was lucky, but Mrs. Wrigley wasn't lucky, even though she had the accident, which was a blessing in disguise. Mr. Wrigley said. It was his fault. She wanted Mrs. Wrigley to write a note about her accident that told how it could be a blessing in disguise when her mother's wasn't, even though they both involved a car, but she was afraid that just by asking she would give something away. Maybe Mr. Wrigley would take her mother in a car and get her in an accident and then she would go to the hospital, where something else would happen that would make her bald. That would be a blessing in disguise. She spelled out with her hands: I AM HUNGRY.

Mrs. Wrigley had been frowning for a long time at a dress that Becca knew would fit her, and now she put the dress away and, with a new look and the touch of her fingertips on Becca's shoulder, told her they were done shopping. Becca led the way back to the car and climbed onto her seat and fastened her seat belt. It wasn't until she saw speeding past her window a dog and then a yellow house she thought she knew that she started to think in a hurry fast as everything was going by that she might have got the signs wrong, and the look wrong, and the touch. Then she saw the house and Mr. Wrigley already opening the door and felt all down her back the lurch the car made when it stopped.

Even without seeing them, she knew what the signs Mr. Wrigley made over her head meant. When Mrs. Wrigley put her hands away in her pockets, Becca knew he'd made the signs. He took her to her room, then, and, showing her a book about three bears, said that she might like to read it and that he would like it very much if she would read it for a while. When he left she put the book back on the shelf where it belonged and snuck down the hall to the corner.

He was already saying something in his murmur. He was telling Mrs. Wrigley about the mistake, but she didn't believe him. Suddenly he said right over Mrs. Wrigley's moving hands, "I *tried*." Nothing else was clear until the words "*talk* to her" burst out loud at the end of a murmur, and Mrs. Wrigley's mouth said, "We?" without a sound.

"I will," he said, "I know you don't . . . " and got so close to Mrs. Wrigley that Becca couldn't even hear the murmur anymore. It was like being pressed between them, squeezed in a dense space where nothing was clear, and, when the pressure dropped away, she didn't even know if she'd heard Mr. Wrigley say it: She is the child's mother. Watching from a distance as Mrs. Wrigley disagreed and Mr. Wrigley murmured an answer with "nature" in it and Mrs. Wrigley's hand hardened and cut the air, she only knew as clearly as if she'd heard it said in words that Mr. Wrigley hadn't talked to her mother, yet. He hadn't talked to her, but he was going to, and it would be soon. She could see it coming in the gradual, grudging slowing down of Mrs. Wrigley's hand, which finally settled into complete stillness on Mr. Wrigley's arm.

She didn't know who saw it first, but with a start they were both looking at the window, and she knew it was her mother. Mr. Wrigley moved, but Mrs. Wrigley caught his arm and said something in hurried signs. "Honey," he said, as her mother said that word when she wanted something that was just not fair. He wrapped his hand around the signing one till it was quiet and the other one let go his arm. Before he opened the door, he looked back. His face was like her own face in the mirror looking at Mrs. Wrigley bald.

FROM INA VINCENT'S WORDS, Melissa had made up a picture of Becca's mother that was as far from anything the prim widow would say about a woman as it was from Melissa. That was the picture's allure, a dark and ravening seductiveness that would consume itself again and again while Melissa watched, and every time she'd remade the image she'd given something more of herself to it, some of her color, some of her heat, her voice.

But here was an almost homely girl, softly plump, honey blonde, squinting a little at the numbers on the houses. It was the softness Melissa saw first, the clumsy grace of the girl's limbs, her figure, her full, fair face that, along with the intensity of her near-sighted look, made her seem to be a combination of mother and child, everything the picture wasn't.

Cal met her on the walk and she looked past him at the house. She'd stopped squinting and turned her concern into a pretty look, catlike and alert. When she took a step, Cal politely cupped her elbow, and she stopped, she turned her head at a slight tilt to look up at him and say something that Melissa couldn't read. She seemed to be asking him a question. As the girl turned back toward the house, Melissa could see the gentle tug of Cal's hand on her arm and then the way the girl as if according to some natural law gave in, took a small, turning step that wasn't a step at all but brought her elbow roundly into his big hand. He was leading her away from the house, talking, talking, talking, his head canted toward her, serious and fatherly as a priest giving counsel, and the girl's head inclined so slightly that the only sign of it was the sway and brush of her fair hair against his shoulder for a second.

Melissa started. Becca'd brushed her leg. She'd come up without a sound and was standing next to her, watching through the window. Melissa's instinct reached before she did to pull the child away, and she was only starting to bend and extend her hand, when she saw Becca's face and stopped. The child was fascinated. She was watching the scene outside with a look as keen and exacting as the one she had for sign language and letters, her attention working so hard on one thing that it didn't even take in Melissa's movement.

Melissa was as careful as she'd ever been. The tension she'd felt every time she'd touched the child was visible now. It was in the little girl's thrilled stillness—and then, in the way that stillness snapped and she suddenly turned, clumsy in her quickness, bumping Melissa's leg and shifting, quick, impatient, patting the ballooning skirt aside as Melissa stooped to her. It was in her eyes, a look so bright it seemed almost demonic, as she whispered, "I understand." Her delighted, knowing little face was slyly like that discarded picture of her mother, and, with a cry, bated and soundless, Melissa gave up to it altogether.

Zorro

IT WAS A BIG, DARK PLACE with white walls and tall rattan chairs, full of lawyers, fraternity boys, people on dates, drug dealers, and some nights, when a Mexican band played, laughing, flashy Spanish types, and us, always us, there for hours at a corner table drinking and talking about nothing in the darkness, and the waitresses were these stunning women still going to college but pushing thirty, in long black nylon dresses, cut on the bias, who brought double Glenlivets and said, This was a mistake, to give us the drink free.

Now I'm standing in my mother's kitchen, thinking about Maria, wondering. Why don't we ever go there any more? In the living room Mother is shouting. When she's on the pills she is always shouting, after she washes them down with Smirnoff, Finlandia, Gilbey's. This is really not my job; I could be home in bed, watching the trees in the backyard, with Maria. It's my father's job, which he escaped by dying. But it's bitchy of me to complain about his shirking this one job.

"Bobby!" she says. "Did you forget how to find the living room or something?"

Every week my mother calls long-distance, usually drunk, manufacturing reasons I don't listen to any more, and every weekend I get in the car and drive down here. Austin to Houston on Friday. Home to Austin on Sunday. Three hours each way.

I spin the top onto the vodka, put it back into the cabinet, and take my drink in with me, sit on the low, flat lounge my father built. Near one end the red fabric has a dim, almost invisible stain which I've stared at for twenty years. It's where they put his head. Maybe it's not even there. Across the room, in front of the wall which is all windows, my mother sits in the big armchair, her blue eyes half-closed. There's no smile.

"How come *you* can drink?" she says, pointing. "How come? How come you can lecture Mommy with your left hand and slosh down vodka with your right?"

I look past her, out at the yard and a tall Lombardy poplar planted when they built the house. I used to stare at that, too, for hours, home sick from school. When I was getting better, she'd bring me steak cut up in pieces and a baked potato, the official recovery food. No one was afraid of grease around our house. Maria says, They're going to have to stick balloons in your arteries, eventually.

"Hey," my mother says. "How come?"

"Well it's because I don't do such a thorough job of it as you do, Momma. Look, I'm going home."

She sets her glass down on the table beside the big chair. "It's Saturday," she says, wet eyes. "I'll sober up. We can garden. Tomorrow. All I have to do is go to bed." She looks at me. Now she's smiling. "With plenty of money wrapped up in a five-pound note." She laughs, then stops. "Don't mess with me, kid, I was here before you were born." She takes another drink.

It's half past eight; the summer sun is just setting. The light on the back terrace is orange. When the telephone rings, we look at each other.

"Twitchy," my mother says.

I stand up, hesitate. "Hey, you get on the phone again, and I'm driving back tonight. I'm long gone."

"I love it when you're macho," she says.

"I'm serious."

"Oh, I love it when you're serious, too."

I get the phone in the back bedroom. My suitcase, on the floor, is yellow cowhide, new, from Best.

"Are you okay, Bobby?" Maria says. "It's bad this time?"

"It's okay. How're things up there?"

"Nine rings before you pick up the phone—it's bad," she says. She tells me what the cat's been doing, what was in the mail, that there's nothing on TV, her hair is wet. She was up until five last night, couldn't sleep.

"I'll call you back at eleven," I say.

"Well, I'm going dancing," she says. "With Jonathan. So I won't be here."

"Yeah, well, have a good time. Incidentally, who the hell is Jonathan?"

She laughs at me, long distance. Someone else's conversation starts leaking into ours, then fades. "Jonathan's gay," Maria says. "The new guy at the clinic. I told you about him, but as usual you weren't listening. I'll be back at two, if you want to call."

"I'll be asleep. Before you're through dancing."

"Robertito," she says. "Don't be silly." The other conversation comes back. We say goodbye, and after Maria hangs up I listen to a woman talking about someone named "Val," until the dial tone comes on. When I go back in to the living room, my mother says, "I heard it all," and then, "She's bi, isn't she?" An hour later, she's asleep.

Late, at quarter to three, I call my house in Austin and there's no answer, so I go out the sliding-glass doors and stand in the backyard with a drink. The ice cubes are loud in the darkness. Then the sirens; sirens all night now, not like when I was a kid. It's a big yard, and the trees are big. The poplar is old now, but in the dark it's not friendly; it's not even familiar.

In the bathroom before I go to bed, I make the mistake of opening the mirrored medicine cabinet and there they are, a half-dozen brown plastic bottles. They weren't here the last time. Three different doctor's names, two pharmacies, old dates.

Your reserves? I think. The other bathroom might be too far away? The next morning I'm just getting up when she's coming home from church.

I get some eggs and bacon, sit at the table reading the Sunday Chronicle, switch to the Post, checking bank ads in the business section because the agency, in Austin, has just gotten a small bank. Stupid really, because all bank ads are the same, but it gives me the illusion of doing something. My mother looks like my mother again.

"How was Mass?"

"I'm going to join one of those copperhead religions," she says. "At least they still believe there are things which can't be explained."

It's an old conversation, a favorite. "Pretty soon we'll receive Communion from an automated teller." She looks out the back windows. "Have you got time to help with the yard? I know you want to get back to Twitchy. Why don't you ever bring her with you any more?" I look at her.

"Oh, c'mon, I was just kidding her. All I said was, 'It must be nice getting paid to yak with people.' She's too sensitive."

"As I recall you said some other things. The 'cheap spic' stuff was real winning."

"Bobby, I never said that, and you know it." She shakes her head, really hurt this time. "I don't remember ever—"

"Momma—"

She walks out of the kitchen. A few minutes later, she comes back. "Will you stay?" She's patched together a motherly demeanor with Mass and aspirin. With her hair pulled back in a blue and white bandanna, she reminds me a little of Patricia Neal. Her voice is very beautiful.

At first she doesn't want me to climb the trees at all, and then she worries about me climbing in boots, and then she doesn't like me kicking the dead limbs down instead of sawing them. When I hit a green one in the top of a tallow tree, the limb bounces and I slip. The air seems thinner up here.

"Bobby! You'll fall," she says, squinting, fifteen feet below.

"I'm not going to fall, Momma. I'm not graceful, but I can handle it. Me and this tree go way back." My father would've cut the limbs, dressed them with that black junk.

We do another tallow and an oak which leaves me with something in my eye and a hundred tiny scratches on my arms. I stand with her on the terrace, rubbing at my eye, point over toward the poplar, although it's really all trunk.

"That one?"

"Honey, it's straight up in the air," she says, wiping her forehead with the bandanna. "Let it be." She fades away, then says, "It was only seven feet when we planted it."

"Another shrine."

"What does that mean?" she says, angry.

"Nothing." She's staring, she won't let me out of it. "It's another shrine to Pop. Like the couch you've never had re-covered. Like the stain on the lounge."

I can't tell if her laughter is real or not. "Honey, that's coffee. You mean the stain on the end? It's coffee." She smiles quickly.

"Yeah, and you knew exactly which stain I was talking about."

"My Lord." She turns to go in. "It's coffee, honey."

When I leave, she's standing on the driveway. She wants me to look at her car again, it's still not right. I tell her I can't.

"You're not coming next weekend," she says. Her expression changes. She leans on the car and says, "He wasn't any damn hero, you know. Ruined my goddamn life in twenty seconds. And you— He left you, too."

"Left? Momma, he didn't leave. He killed himself." The car rocks when I turn the key and the engine fires. I look up. "It was a long time ago, Momma. You don't have to . . . "

She leans in, kisses my hair.

Out of town, I push the air conditioner to MAX, put on a Tom Petty tape and turn it up so loud my eardrums hurt. Rock and roll: curettage of the brain. After an hour or so, around Flatonia, I switch to Beethoven, some symphony I taped off the radio, a sort of mental intensive-care unit.

As the car rolls into Austin, I think of taking another route to the house, through downtown, by the bar we used to go to, but I'm tired, the traffic's bad, too much noise.

When I get to our house, there's an Alfa out front with the top down. Birds are eating berries in the tree above it, and the Alfa, which used to be solid white, now looks like a Pininfarina dalmatian.

JONATHAN IS A WEIGHT LIFTER, in a T-shirt, with curly hair. He opens the kitchen door, and our cat, Cholo, who's been trying to trip me all the way up the driveway, slips in ahead of me. Jonathan introduces himself, as he's leaving.

"He's not as gay as I thought," Maria says. "But don't worry, he slept on the couch." Her hand goes to her hair. She looks at me and shakes her head, slowly.

"Okay."

"You look terrible," she says.

"Couldn't you have flushed him before I got back?"

"It's nice to have you back." She's wearing a loose, light, faded white nylon dress with black swirls printed on it. One I've always liked.

"You look great."

"Gracias."

"But, listen, no more overnight visitors when I'm out of town. Okay? I'm old-fashioned. You said you were going dancing. Give me a break."

"I can't sleep in an empty house."

The cat bounces from floor to chair to the table top and I slam my hand down. "Cholo!" He hits the floor running, hits the wall on his way down the hallway toward the back of the house. His feet slip on the hardwood floor. I look at Maria, look down.

"He'll be okay, Bobby," she says. "He's not that fragile." She gets up and goes to the refrigerator, fills a glass with ice and Diet Coke, and hands it to me. "I'm sorry," she says.

"Me, too." I pull out the chair next to mine. "Sit over here and talk to me. I want to listen to you talk."

Later, when I wake up, nude, it's bright in the bedroom and black outside; moths are tapping the window. The clock on the bedside table says 3:00 A.M. Maria's not there. I pull on some jeans and wander in to the kitchen.

"Work tomorrow," I say, staring into the refrigerator for a beer. I sit down across from her, pull out the end chair for Cholo. A peace offering. He jumps up, yawns, sits primly looking from Maria, to me, to Maria. The crickets, outside, are loud.

"You shake now when the phone rings," Maria says, not looking up. "Your hands shake. Did you know?" She reaches for my beer, she's wearing one of my old shirts and the cuffs flop around her hand as she pours beer into her glass.

"Work tomorrow."

"You're a mess, Bobby. They're not happy with you at work, either, I bet. You've got to decide."

"What's to decide?"

"About your mother." She looks up. She can stare like no one else

I've ever known. Brown eyes. She's Mexican and Irish. Her name was Mary, but she went down and changed it when she was eighteen. Her mother called her Maria.

I stand up and take her hand, lifting her away from the table.

"She needs help, Bobby. I have some names, therapists, in Houston; they're good people."

"Give me my shirt back."

THERE'S ONE DAY OF PEACE before my mother calls, drunk, Tuesday night. She's gotten the car fixed.

"Only they cheated me," she says. "They just smeared grease along the edges of the hood and wrote me up the prettiest invoice you'll ever see."

"Mostly they don't cheat you. They're usually just incompetent."

"Then I'm happy that they didn't touch anything, right?"

"Momma, when I was working for Lancaster this woman left us a VW, and I drove it around the block and then went into his little office and told him there was nothing wrong with it. Lancaster just looked up from the desk, and said, 'Well, then it oughta be easy to fix.'"

"It's a parable," she says. "She's me. I'm her. Right?" She laughs.

"There's nothing wrong with that car."

"I love parables," she says.

Wednesday evening at five past six, the telephone rings. Maria looks at me and says, "We could get an unlisted number." We already have an unlisted number.

"I'm sober," my mother says. "It's six o'clock. I'm bored stiff."

"Have you seen any people this week?"

"You mean the Senior Citizens' Picnic? Bingo?"

"You're laying it on a little thick, Momma. You're only fifty-two. Find some good-looking man and take him dancing. Get down. It's what everybody else does."

"Did you change your mind about coming down this week?"

"Next weekend? Can't. Weekend after."

"How come when we get on this subject, you start talking in syllables?" I can hear the ice clink in her glass. Then there's silence. She says, "That was loud, wasn't it?"

Maria stands watching me talk on the telephone until I hang up. In jeans, she looks like candy. She walks out the kitchen door, slams it, and I hear her car door slam. I wait for the car to start. It doesn't. Two minutes later she walks back in the door. We stand in the kitchen like Alan Ladd and Jack Palance. It's stupid.

"You think you're doing her any good?" Maria says. "You're not. You're encouraging it. If you didn't run down there every time— Who do you think you are? Zorro?" Her eyes get sort of flat, and don't blink. "She needs treatment, Bobby. You can not fix it."

"What do you suggest? Handcuffs? Anyway, I owe her."

"Bullshit. You don't owe her this. You don't sleep. You're always wired, or brooding. You shake like—"

"Hey, save it for the office. Some oedipal stuff, some R. D. Laing, and that guy in Philadelphia, what's his name? Christ, I'm getting advice from Philadelphia."

"There's no fun any more, Bobby."

"Jonathan's fun, right? You ride around in that little white car pretending you're Isadora, right? You expect fun?"

"It shouldn't be all grief."

I sit down. I think, Something's surely wrong because I've gotten myself into one of those arguments where the woman is right. This should never happen. I hold my forehead with my hand, start listening to my breathing. She's just standing there, on the high ground.

"I'm sorry," Maria says. "I feel terrible." She puts her hands on my shoulders, rubs my neck. "Could we talk about puppies or something?"

FOR A WEEK NOTHING HAPPENS. The weekend passes. I lay out from work a couple extra days, get some sleep, we barbecue in the backyard, plan to go out Friday night. We even watch a little television.

Late Thursday night, after we've gone to bed, the telephone rings. It's not my mother. It's a guy who says he works in the emergency room at Ben Taub, another doctor. "She's all right," he says. "My name's Matthew. I want you to talk to me when you get here. Don't ask for me. Just look. I'm taller than everyone else." They apparently picked her up downtown in a department store, passsed out. He says "lacerations," "sutures," other things. I go into the bathroom and splash water on my face. No one goes to the downtown department stores any more.

Maria's sitting up in bed when I get back in the bedroom. "Is she all right?"

I nod. "She's in the hospital."

"Maybe somebody there can help her."

"I'm going down."

She looks at the clock. "Now?" She reaches over and twists the clock so I can see it. It's two o'clock. "Bobby, I don't want to argue, I can't take this any more."

Rumpled, bleary-eyed, black-haired. She is straining to wake up. I walk around the bed and kiss her forehead. "Go to sleep. I'll be back in a couple days. Hold on a couple more days."

"A couple years," she says. She's crying; I leave anyway.

THE HIGHWAY LOOKS STRANGE and clean, and except for a few semis and speeders, it's empty. One of my headlights is messed up, no low beam. I spend three hours with trucks flashing their brights in my eyes, then a half-hour getting across town.

The hospital corridors have an odd brand-new old look. A dozen people sit in the hall outside the emergency room, filling out forms. It's a slow night, Thursday. I look for Matthew.

He has a beard, not a good beard, thin, manicured, gray like rats' fur. He takes me into an empty room.

"She's fine," he says. "She's either in I.C.U. or upstairs in a room." He hands me a piece of paper from the pocket of his white jacket. "I'm not giving you this. You never even heard of me." He pauses to let some footsteps pass outside, in the hall. "Memorize them."

"I can remember." I'm sitting on a bed. He's standing. He doesn't look so tall. They must have a short crew.

"The top name is a doctor on the west side. He's a quack. He's got a drug clinic over there, biofeedback, mind control, Rolfing, vitamins they get out of skunks—sixties shit. Sex, too, probably, he's a pretty boy. Whatever. He gets results."

"What about—" I say, pointing to the other name on the paper, not wanting to say it out loud. We're playing CIA.

"She's the meanest, sleaziest malpractice lawyer in town," Matthew says. "She also gets results. Dropping her name to whoever prescribed all this junk for your mother will cut off the supply, at least for a while."

"There's three or four of them."

"So?" he says, shaking his head. "Tape the calls." He shakes his head again, and laughs, a squeaky little laugh. "I liked her. But I just spent six years in Guadalajara. Can't handle it. This is my bit; this is all I can do."

He takes the paper from me, tears a strip off the top, the "Rx," and hands the rest of it back. "Here," he says.

"Hey, how come everybody knows what to do but me?"

"You need therapy," he says and laughs. The pale yellow door closes gently behind him.

They aren't releasing her, and I can't see her until tomorrow, so I find my car and leave. There's an Alfa in the hospital parking lot, and I notice two others on the freeway out to the house. At the exit I want, the one for my mother's house, I don't turn, I stay on the freeway and watch the big green signs sail overhead. Another ten miles and the roadsides are littered with signs for developer suburbs. Passing them in the darkness, I feel free. I'm going home.

Ten more miles and I'm staring into complete darkness; my headlights have cut out. I get the car onto the shoulder, get out, and somebody blows by me at eighty in a truck. The air is wet and cool. I check the fuse, under the dash; jerk the headlight switch in and out; pull the hood release. At the front of the car, I hit each headlight with my fist—nothing. Twist the wiring harness behind the bulbs. Look up and down the highway. Another half-hour, it'll be daylight. I can wait. I reach up for the hood and slam it. The headlights come on. I remember my father.

In the clear, dark countryside, I remember my father, the strangers standing around after they carried him in and put him on the lounge. There was an inch-high gap under the door to the bedroom where I was sequestered while they stood around, making arrangements, smoking cigarettes. The floor was white tile. I remember helping him replace some of the tile once, the way he patched together two pieces to make one with a linoleum knife and the cigarette lighter he used to carry, a big Zippo, and how the patch was perfect and how I was amazed.

For years I tried to build things the way he did, so they came out perfect, as if they had been made by machine. I couldn't. Every saw cut was crooked. Wood split. Bolts stripped. Paint ran.

Just once, I think, before you left, you could have made a mistake, could have broken something or left a sloppy edge somewhere, if only to let me know it was all right.

You poor stupid son of a bitch.

It's a divided highway. I run the car across the median strip and head back toward my mother.

AFTER FOUR HOURS' SLEEP, in my old bedroom, I get on the telephone, arrange for a nurse. Then I call the doctors. When they call back, I slip in the lawyer's name. They don't seem to care. One doesn't even call back. I call Austin, no answer. I try to read *House and Garden*, the *New Republic*, then settle for *Time*, watch TV, pan-fry a steak, eat alone, call again. In the afternoon I pick her up, bring her home. There's a small patch of gauze under her chin on the right side and a magnificent white bandage covering half her upper arm, right arm. She goes to sleep. The nurse arrives and smiles a lot. I call Austin. I call Austin all day, get no answer. I write my mother a note, throw it away.

"Look who's here," she says, sitting up in bed, when I go in to see her. I take a fifth of vodka. There's more gauze on the fingers of her right hand.

"I'm jumping ship," I say. "My suitcase's already in the car," which is a lie, actually, because I didn't bring one. If I had brought a suitcase, it would be in the car. "You learn anything, recently?"

"I'm sore," she says. "Like that?"

"No, I mean like it's not all fun."

"A speech," she says. "I love speeches." She shifts her weight, and winces.

I sit on the bed. "I always thought you killed him. You didn't. You're not even killing me, although that's what it feels like. You're killing yourself, though, just like he did." I put the vodka down on the shelf beside the bed, along with the name of Matthew's clinic, on a new piece of paper. "Try this place. Please." "It's a grandstand play, Bobby." "I can't fix it, Momma. Nobody ever fixes anything anyway. Nobody ever ruins anything, either. Patching, is what you do." She's looking at me; I'm wondering whether I'm lying. "You're your father's son." "Not yet, I'm not." "Sure," she says. She smiles at me. "Could you bring the Collins mix?"

On the telephone again before I leave, I imagine the cat, Cholo, sitting on the corner of the bedspread, on the bed, watching it ring.

In the car, on the highway, watching the cows and fields and Stuckey's pass, I think, I can't sleep in an empty house either, and I try to bring a woman's face and the smell of her hair into my mind, but all I can do is remember that dark bar, and wonder what it was we used to talk about for hours at the corner table in those tall high-backed rattan chairs, and remember how she used to laugh. Maria.

Drowned Moon

Marsh

"MARSH!" SHE WOULD SHOUT. She would step from her bright kitchen onto her back porch at dusk and shout "Marsh!"

And I would kneel down behind a large stone. I would hide in that fenced yard behind her house. I would stretch out on the cool grass, still hidden, and wait for him.

"Marshall!"

No lights in his dark house. No electricity.

First, I would hear the faint creak of his screen door. Then, I would see his white shirt in the twilight as he squinted into the dark yard. And if I listened carefully, I would hear his frail voice whisper my name.

"MARSH!" SHE SAID. She was on her knees in that yard behind her house. She was planting flowers.

I stopped running. "Yes ma'am?" I said. I was chasing the dogs, or they were chasing me.

"Get those dogs outside the fence," she said, "and then come over here."

I started with a light dog. I started by saying, "Come here." I stooped over and picked him up and carried him out into her backyard. Each time, I kicked the gate closed behind me. And then I stooped over again and placed the little dog gingerly down on his legs. One by one, dog by dog.

The big dogs were too heavy to carry, so I had to reach down and lift them up by their front feet and walk them outside the fence. I had to walk backwards and lead them along slowly like I was pulling a wheelbarrow.

One by one, until the yard was empty, and the gate closed.

"Good," I said, and all at once, dog by dog, they left me. They trotted off around the fence, back toward his house and some other game.

"Marsh," she said. She was standing now, and she was laughing.

"Yes ma'am?" I said, and I didn't know how, but there they were, every last one of them, big dogs, little dogs, heavy and light, sitting with their mouths open, their tongues hanging out, smiling at me from the other side of the fence.

She pointed. "You're gonna have to close the back gate."

"PRETTY FLOWERS."

"Thank you," she said. She was holding a small shovel. "Do you like staying with me?"

"Yes ma'am."

"I *think* you're old enough now," she said. "Listen, Love, you shouldn't go running around in here. Do you understand?"

"No ma'am."

She smiled. "This," she said. She followed the fence all the way around with her shovel. "This is your family."

"Oh," I said.

"Do you understand?"

"No ma'am."

She said, "They are all buried here."

I looked off across the burnt orange carpet of pine needles at the bright white stones standing in rows. "Under the ground?"

"That's right," she said.

"Why?"

She just looked at me. "They've gone away, Love. They're . . . dead."

"Oh."

She took me by the hand. "This," she said, pointing to the flowers. "This is my husband. Your grandfather. You look like him. You look like he looked when he was a little boy." She reached down and touched the stone. "Do you know what this says? Can you read it?"

"Reeve."

"That's right," she said. "And the other name? This one?"

"Marshall."

She smiled at me and squeezed my hand. "Do you know what that means?"

"No ma'am."

She frowned and shook her head. "Look out, now!" she said, pulling me to her side. "Do you see how you're standing on them?"

"No ma'am," I said, looking all around. "No ma'am, I don't even *see* them!"

"Love, you can't *see* them," she said. "They're buried. Down in the ground." She placed her hand on the grass by the stone. "Here," she said. "Here is his head. His hands. Here, his feet. Do you see?"

I was looking beyond the yard. "Yes ma'am," I told her. I was looking at his house.

"Come with me," she said, and we walked to a row of whiter stones. "These are my sons. Your uncles."

I was watching the dogs disappear underneath his house, and I knew.

"Are you listening to me?" she said. She was down on her knees, pulling the weeds around a small stone.

I knew what would happen next. I knew the screen door would open. I knew he would appear. "Kate?" I said.

And there he was, holding the screen door open as they, dog by dog, trailed out of his house, onto his front porch, down his front steps, into his front yard where they waited.

"Yes?" she said. "Here." She handed me a pot of dead flowers.

They waited until they were all out, all down his steps, all sitting in his yard. They waited until he closed the screen door, and then, one by one, they disappeared under his house again.

"Who is that?"

"That's just Wick," she said. "He's your uncle. He's your great uncle."

"What's wrong with him?"

"Ain't nothing wrong with him," she said. "He's just old. He's just an old, old man. Don't you go bothering him."

"I won't," I said.

She pointed to the pot of flowers. "Take that up to the house for me."

"Yes ma'am," I said and started walking for the front gate. Wick was already at his screen door again, and the dogs were already waiting.

"Marshall!" she shouted, and I almost dropped the pot of flowers. "Watch where you're going! You're walking all over them!"

And I stopped suddenly, still on the tips of my toes, afraid of taking one more step, and I looked around me, and for the first time, the entire yard was filled, elbow to elbow, with frowning relatives. "Kate?" I said over my shoulder. "Does it hurt?"

DEEP IN THE NIGHT, the white stones glowed. I would lie awake on the verandah. I would sit up on my pallet and wait for them.

Out of the ground they came, just a few at first—to see if it was safe—and then the others followed, tiny lights rising up out of the earth until the yard was bright with them.

On they would shine and then *off*, disappear, on and off like slow hearts, reappear two stones down to talk with a brother, console a mother, search for a missing child.

Every morning, just about dawn, he would come in through the gate, walk about the yard, stop at each stone, and talk to them. And every morning, when the sun came up, all of them were gone, and there he was, standing in the middle of the yard, alone.

"MARSHALL!" she was shouting. She was inside Wick's house, and she was shouting, "Marshall!"

"Coming!" I said, running across the yard. "I'm coming!"

She was opening the screen door and letting the dogs out.

"Yes ma'am?" I said, winded at the back gate.

"Come get these dogs!" she said. "And keep them out of the house!"

I hurried up to the porch, clapping my hands, shouting, "Get on!" I chased them down the steps. "Get on away from there!"

And as if they knew there was something wrong, they left the house, the porch, the front steps, and trotted over through the back gate and waited in the yard.

I was standing on the porch. I had never been inside.

She cracked the screen and handed me Lamar, a rat terrier and said, "Stay out! Stay outside!"

And as the door closed, I squinted through the screen after her. I tried to follow her with my eyes into the dark house.

Where she stopped, there was a bed. There was someone in the bed, Wick. There were some things on the bed, sitting on the covers, dogs. She reached over and picked one up and carried it out to me.

"Here," she said, and when she opened the door, I looked past her, and my eyes caught something leaning up against the wall next to the bed. It was a leg!

"You better run up to the station and get Mr. Charlie," she said, "You better hurry."

THEY CAME AND CARRIED Wick into the yard. They came to town and buried him. Family and friends, standing throughout the stones, dressed up, whispering, like at a Sunday service.

And when it was all over, the yard quiet, all my uncles walked back to Wick's house and sat on his porch, on his steps. All my uncles, old men then, sitting where they sat as boys, sitting where they listened to *their* uncle.

Wick had this leg, this artificial leg. It was hollow. It had a hole in it about three inches above the ankle.

On Sunday evenings, after supper, all my uncles, young boys then, would walk back through the yard with their coins. They would walk back through the gate and sit on his porch, on his steps. Each boy with money in his hand.

And Wick would wait for them. He would sit in his rocking chair and wait for them. He would slowly reach down and roll up his pants leg. And each boy, according to his age, would walk up the steps and deposit his coins into the hole in Wick's leg. And Wick would close his eyes and rock himself and tell them stories. He would tell them stories about their father, stories about Cuba. He would tell them stories about Daiquiri, Siboney, Las Guásimas.

MARSHALL AND WICK were horsemen. They were in San Antonio in 1898. They were sent by old man Phillips to purchase new horses.

The journey had been a long one, so Wick decided that they de-served a reward, so they celebrated. They spent that evening drink-ing, walking through the old Alamo, toasting Bowie, Crockett,

Travis. Later that night, they returned to their hotel and threw a big party.

San Antonio was nervous with the news of the *Maine*. Everyone was talking of war.

"Them goddamn Mexicans!" someone said.

"*Spaniards,*" someone said.

"Them goddamn Spaniards!"

Sometime around dawn, Wick counted their money, and most of it was gone. He tried explaining this to his brother, but Marshall was passed out on the floor under a poker table.

Should they wire Mr. Phillips for more money? Should they return with only some of the horses? Mr. Phillips would be angry either way, he would probably fire them, and it seemed a shame to end such a great party.

The doors of the saloon flew open. "We're at war!" someone shouted. "They're calling for volunteers!"

"Blowing up the goddamn *Maine!*" someone said.

"Just who do they think they are!"

"Remember the *Maine!*" someone shouted.

"Remember the Alamo!" someone shouted.

"What *is* the goddamn *Maine?*" someone said.

THERE WAS A CALL for volunteers. There was a call for horsemen, cavalrymen.

"Why not!" Wick told Marshall. "We've spent all our money!"

"*Mr. Phillips's money,*" Marshall told Wick.

"We've spent all his money," Wick said, "and we can't go back without it."

"No sir," Marshall said.

"They need volunteers for the cavalry," Wick said, "and we know horses."

"We *do* know horses," Marshall said.

"Why not!" Wick said. "Where are these bastards, anyway!"

"Cuba," someone said.

"*Let's go!*" Wick said. "Let's mount up and go!" Wick said. "Let's go *tonight!*"

"Cuba's a island," someone said.

"Then somebody'd better rustle us up a boat," Wick said. He staggered outside into the plaza and shouted, "Does anybody in this goddamn town have a boat!"

WICK WOULD JUST sit there, rocking in the dark. The boys listening until they were called home.

Marshall and Wick signed up. They volunteered. They met a Colonel Leonard Wood. They met a man by the name of Roosevelt. They were issued uniforms.

They were trained and drilled in camps outside San Antonio. They were shipped to Tampa where they were to wait for orders to sail to Cuba.

Wick told them about the arrival in Tampa, how they were nicknamed, "The Rough Riders."

They trained and waited, waited and trained. They waited to sail for over a month. And when the ships, the transports, finally arrived in Tampa Bay, there were not enough of them. There was a mad scramble to get aboard for fear of being left behind, for fear of missing the war.

Wick told them about the hardships aboard the transports, the serious overcrowding, the dark makeshift quarters in the holds. How they were assigned bunks, how they were ordered to just lie there for five days and wait for their orders to sail, how they were not allowed to stand up, to walk around, to stretch. And when those orders came, they had to stay down in those bunks in the holds of those ships another seven days until they reached Cuba.

WICK TOLD THEM that when the transports finally reached the waters south of Santiago, the horses were just dumped into the sea.

"The horses!" Marshall said. "They're just killing them! What're we gonna do!"

"Nothing," Wick said.

"Nothing!" Marshall said. "*They're just killing them!*"

"Yes sir," Wick said, "they're just killing them. And before this is all over, they just might kill us too."

The horses were thrown overboard in the middle of the night, and because of their long confinement in the hot, dark holds, those that made it through the surf were in such poor shape they could not be used for most of the campaign. Most of the early charges and skirmishes were conducted on foot.

He told them about the landing at Daiquiri, the Spanish bonfires all along the shore, the fortified blockhouse high above the town. How their transport, the *Yucatán*, was the first to charge to shore to find the town abandoned, the blockhouse deserted. He told them about the march into Siboney, the skirmish at Las Guásimas, the march inland along the corduroy road.

Admiral Sampson had the entire Spanish fleet bottled up in Santiago harbor, and it was their job to march west from the beachhead. It was their job to take hill by hill, to take blockhouse by blockhouse, to take Santiago.

WICK TOLD THEM about the night before the great charge. How Roosevelt marched the Rough Riders to a small abandoned sugar plantation, how they fell in the next morning at dawn, how they watched the batteries of field guns pass them on the road.

The Rough Riders were to wait until General Lawton engaged the Spanish at El Caney, and then their orders were to charge and take the San Juan Heights.

In the distance, they could see a white blockhouse on top of a hill. Each man knew that the Spanish were dug in and ready, that the Spanish were waiting. Each man knew that this was it, the big battle, the last desperate defense of Santiago.

"This is it!" Wick told Marshall. "Stay close!"

Wick remembered the first barrage from the field guns of Grimes's battery, the Rough Riders cheering, the strange silence afterwards. He remembered the peculiar whistling in the air, louder and louder, and the next thing he knew, he was flat on his back, his legs blown out from under him. He remembered hearing someone shouting, "Let's go!"

And before he started feeling the pain, he said, "Wait a minute!" He said, "Tell them to wait a minute!" He tried to get to his feet, but he couldn't move his legs.

"Wick?" Marshall kept saying over and over. "Wick?"

Wick could hear people shouting, or were they screaming? Someone was holding him down, and someone was working on his legs. Shells were landing all around them. "Get him out of here!" someone said.

Wick remembered Marshall and another man picking him up and carrying him. "Doctor!" Marshall was shouting. "Where's the goddamn doctor!"

Wick heard someone say, "You better stop that bleeding!" so they put him down and wrapped his legs tighter.

All that Wick could think about was that his legs were on fire. "My legs are burning!" he said.

They picked him up again and carried him, sometimes walking, sometimes running, to the rear.

They were passing other wounded men, some limping, some hopping, some using their rifles as crutches.

A field hospital was set up at a ford in the Aguadores River. Most of the wounded were stretched out on the sandy bank, some limped into the water.

Wick was screaming now. "My legs are burning!" he said. "Put me in the river!"

"Where's the doctor!" Marshall was shouting.

"Ain't no doctor," someone said.

There were several men standing, sitting, lying in the river. There were several men bleeding.

There was a bluff above the field hospital. There was an officer standing on the bluff. "You men that ain't wounded," he was shouting, "we need you!"

Marshall lowered Wick into the river. The water now the exact color of blood.

A doctor waded out to them. "Get going," he told Marshall. "We'll take good care of him."

Wick was screaming, "Marshall!"

"Yes sir?" Marshall said. "I'm here." He was holding Wick in his arms. He was cradling him.

"You!" the officer said.

"Coming!" Marshall said.

"Tourniquet!" the doctor shouted. He hurried up out of the river.
"I need a tourniquet here!"

"Wick," Marshall said, "I got to get going."

"Don't," Wick said.

"I got to," Marshall said. "I'll be back. Don't you worry. They'll take good care of you."

The other man pulled Marshall up onto the bank.

"Marshall?" Wick said.

"I'll come back for you!" someone said.

Wick was by himself now. A man floated by facedown in the water. All that Wick could think about was that his legs were on fire. All that he could think about was getting deeper in the river. He pulled himself back with his arms. He pulled himself back in the red water until he was in the channel, until the cool current caught him and carried him away.

"MARSH!" she said. She was standing at the front gate. The dogs were running around and around the inside of the fence, playing follow-the-leader. "Where are you?"

"Over here!" I told her. I was outside the fence, hidden by the wisteria. I was catching bees in a Mason jar.

I already had five jars of lightning bugs on the back porch, two to a jar, air holes punched in the tops. I only needed one more for my study to be complete. I was reaching conclusions:

Lightning bugs and bumblebees are about the same size.
They both have wings, and they can fly.

Lightning bugs shine in the dark.
Bumblebees do not.
Lightning bugs sleep during the day (I cannot find where) and fly at night (I think! But maybe it is too bright during the day to see them shine?).

Bumblebees sleep at night and fly during the day (I know because I have snuck out in the night and crawled under the wisteria and honeysuckle and have not heard them buzzing).

Lightning bugs will not shine as long as they know you are watching them.

Bumblebees will not shine if you are watching them or not (I have placed jars full of bumblebees around corners at night and peeked at them, behind trees, and they will not shine. But maybe they know that I'm secretly watching and shut themselves off. Maybe they shine bright yellow like fire when I am asleep!).

Bumblebees have teeth.
Lightning bugs do not.

Bumblebees are meaner than lightning bugs.

If you shake up a Mason jar full of ten lightning bugs for exactly sixty seconds and then screw off the lid and pour them out, they will all just fall on the ground and be dizzy for a while. And then, they will all slowly get to their feet and try to fly off (sometimes flying into a house or a tree).

If you try this with bumblebees, they will all fly out mad and chase you down and bite you all over the place.

"Marshall!" she shouted, and the bee bit me, and I screamed and dropped the jar.

"Yes ma'am!" I said, shaking my hand.

She was pointing. "Go help your Uncle Wick," she said.

I looked over the wisteria, through the tall trunks of the loblollies, and there he was, standing on his front porch, holding on to a stanchion.

"Go get that from them!" she said.

I hurried around to where she was standing.

The dogs were running around and around the inside of the fence, and one of them was playing keep-away from the others. One of them—maybe it was Bowie—had something in his mouth, like an old bone, and he was running, and all the others were chasing after him trying to get it.

The front gate was open, and she was just standing there, waiting. "Go on, now!" she said. "Hurry!" She closed the gate behind me.

"What!" I said, and then I saw it. I saw what Bowie had in his mouth. I saw what the other dogs wanted. It was a leg! It was part of a leg, from about the knee down. It even had a white sock on it and a little black shoe with the laces untied.

I looked over at Wick's place, and there he was, standing on his porch, holding himself up, looking hurt and betrayed. He even had his right pants leg rolled up to the knee.

Someone had run up on my great uncle Wick when he wasn't looking and stolen his leg right out from underneath him. And I couldn't decide if it was horrible or hilarious.

"Marshall!" She was standing on her back steps with her hands on her hips.

"*Yes ma'am,*" I said. I looked off through the stones, and there they were, waiting on the far side of the yard, happy.

They were happy because they knew that they weren't supposed to be inside the fence. They were happy because they knew that I had come inside to chase them. They were happy because they knew that I could never catch them unless they wanted to be caught.

I started out walking around the inside of the fence. I started out slowly at first, my hands in my pockets, my eyes on the grape clusters of wisteria, until I got closer to the back and started walking fast, faster, as fast as I could walk without running, until I reached the gate, grabbed it, slammed it shut, and shouted, "I got you now! You're trapped!"

And there they were, directly across from me, on the opposite side of the yard, back where I had started out, but it was okay, it was safe, because she had gone inside.

Crockett had it now, a quick collie, and I knew it was going to be some run, so I took off walking like I had before, slowly at first, eyeing them across the stones. Faster and faster I walked until I was at a slow jog and then a fast jog, faster, until I was at a slow run and then a sprint, one lap around the yard, two, until I had caught and passed Milam and Lamar, a crooked dachshund, a crippled terrier, and they ran with me for a while, until the other dogs, the entire pack, picked up the pace, four laps, five and when I looked out front, when I looked out across the yard, I couldn't see any of them, and then I heard it, the barking, and I turned around, and there they were, all ten of them, all ten yards behind, except that now they were chasing *me*. Around and around the yard I ran, eight laps, nine, losing my lead on them, hounds at my heels, until I noticed Deaf Smith resting off to the side—the leg in his mouth—just standing there the whole time on top of one of my aunts.

And that was all that I could take. I didn't even stop running. I just collapsed. I just collapsed and lay there on the ground for a while until they all trotted back and started licking me in the face to revive me because they weren't even close to being tired. "Come on, come on, come on," they were saying, licking me in the face, "we aren't even close to being tired!" Ten dogs licking me in the face, afraid I might expire, until I couldn't even breathe, and I had to get on my hands and knees and crawl away from them and hide behind a tree.

"Enough!" I shouted, pulling myself to my feet, wiping all that dog spit off my face. "*I'm mad now!*"

This was Deaf Smith's cue. He took off into the stones, and they took off into the stones, and I took off after them.

Deaf Smith would dart around a stone and drop the leg, and Houston would be right there behind him and pick it up without breaking stride, so it was like a relay handoff except that they had an unfair advantage, and they knew it. They knew that they could run anywhere, but there I was. There I was chasing after them, losing ground, sidestepping, hurdling, avoiding my relatives.

Until finally, I just fell to my knees, exhausted. And one by one they all circled back and sat around me, winded too a little, their mouths open, their tongues out. Dog by dog, they all circled back, until finally, Fannin appeared out of the stones and sauntered over and dropped the leg on the ground in front of me.

And I dove for it and grabbed it and hugged it. They were all just sitting there, looking at me. And I leaped to my feet and held the leg up high over my head, expecting them at any second to start jumping for it, expecting an attack.

But they didn't. They didn't start jumping for it. They just sat there, looking at me, with sorrow in their eyes, sad that the game was finally over, truly, sincerely, genuinely sorry for what they had done.

"That's better!" I told them. "That's more like it!"

The leg was still in one piece. The leather straps looked pretty gnawed on. The white sock was pulled down below the heel. The little black shoe missing.

"You should be ashamed of yourself," I told them. And now, they weren't even looking at me. Now, they were all looking down at the ground. "That's right," I said. "You should be."

I adjusted the straps above the knee. I pulled the sock on, around the heel, up over the ankle. "There," I said, leaned back, hauled off, and threw the leg out over the stones, out across the yard, as far as I could throw it.

"*Marshall!*"

I WAS THINKING about leaving it outside the back gate. I was thinking about just propping it up against the fence and then running back through the stones when she shouted, "Marsh, you're gonna have to hand it to him! He can't come down and get it!" I turned around and looked for her, but she had already gone back inside.

I took a few steps into his yard and stopped. The dogs had run under the house, and there they were, elbow to elbow, lined up, with only their heads sticking out, watching me.

Wick was still standing up on the porch. He was still waiting, so I lifted the leg and pointed at it and said, "Is this . . . yours?"

He reached out with his arm.

A few more steps. I glanced behind me. I had left the gate open on purpose. I wasn't about to hand the leg over to him until I saw if he was mean. I figured that no matter what happened, no matter how scared I got, I could still outrun a one-legged man.

He motioned with his hand. It meant, "Come closer."

I walked slowly to his front steps and stopped. I was holding the leg behind me.

"Come on," he said. "Come on up here." He turned and hopped over to an old rocking chair and plopped down into it. The whole porch shook. "Ain't gonna bite you," he said. "Ain't got no teeth!"

One step, two steps, three, until I could see that the porch had just about rotted through. Just about every other board was missing. Wick's rocking chair had wedged itself down into one of these cracks. He couldn't have rocked if he'd wanted to. Any day now, Wick's rocking chair was going to fall right through the porch.

"I've seen you before," he said, his voice a whisper. He pointed with something that looked more like a bone than a finger. "Out there."

Kate was right. Wick *was* an old, old man. He was skinny like a skeleton. He hardly had any skin on him at all. And what he did have, I could see through, I could see blue blood vessels. I could see red veins crossing and crisscrossing all over him like the paths and trails of an old treasure map.

"Here," he said, and I slowly placed the leg in his hand, and he started strapping it on. He was strapping it on without even watching what he was doing. He was watching me. He was just sitting there, staring at me. "Who are you?" he said.

"I'm Marshall," I told him.

He stopped what he was doing. He didn't even roll his pants leg down. "Marshall?" he said.

"Yes sir?"

He shook his head. "You ain't Marsh," he said.

"Yes sir," I told him, "I am. That's my name. Marsh."

He motioned with his hand. "Come over here," he said, "where I can see you."

I looked off the porch, across the yard, to her house. "I should be getting back."

"Here," he said. He patted the top of his good knee. "Over here by me."

I stepped carefully over the missing boards and stopped right in front of him.

It was almost dark. It was almost suppertime. Any second now, Kate would call my name and save me.

Wick slowly reached out with a crooked finger and touched me just under the chin and tilted my head back a little. He squinted at me like he was trying to read my face. "Marsh," he whispered, "is that you?"

"Yes sir," I told him, "it's me."

He frowned at me. "I thought you was dead," he said. He was shaking his head. He was just sitting there with one shoe on, one shoe off, staring past me now, out over the yard. "No," he said. "No, I coulda swore . . . Are you sure?"

"Yes sir," I said. I had to think about it. "Pretty sure."

He smiled. "I knew it," he said. He pointed to the yard. "I saw you out there, and I just knew it."

And I was smiling too. "It's me," I told him.

"I've been waiting," he said. "I've just been . . . waiting."

"Here I am," I told him.

"Where you been?" he said. And then he said. "Is this it?"

"Sir?"

"This," he said. "Is this . . . it?"

And I didn't know what to say, so I said, "I think so."

"Good," he said. "Good." He was looking past me now. He was looking past the porch, over the fence, into the yard. "I've been thinking," he told me. "I don't sleep anymore. I've been thinking about Bloody Ford, the shallow place in the river."

And then I heard her and didn't want to. I heard her shout, "Marsh!"

"I've been thinking about you lowering me into the water," he said. "The river as red as blood." He was far away now. He was far away, somewhere else.

"Marshall!"

"I got to get going," I told him.

"And you said, 'I'll be back. Don't you worry.' "

I started for the steps and stopped. "I'll be back," I told him. "Don't you worry."

"And you said, "I'll come back for you.' "

"Marshall!"

He looked at me and smiled. "Go on, now," he said. "She's calling. She does that. She misses you."

FROM   1988

Remind Me to Murder You Later

Thirty-six Miracles of Lyndon Johnson

1.

The President is amazed by the stupidity of the King of Norway. "He [King Olaf] is the dumbest king I have ever met," the President says, "I didn't know they made kings that dumb."

2.

I am gathering an armful of wet wood for my wicked stepsister. Logs of sweet-smelling cherry are strewn on the front porch like damp jackstraws; a vile, gelatinous drizzle has turned the fallen snow into bad flan. The President died thirteen years ago this day; the wind-chill factor makes it feel like fifty. I can feel my mother watching me, the warmth of the house escaping through the door she holds open. The drenched logs leave gray stains on my pink shirt. "You lay those logs out on the floor of the bathroom," she says, "and I'll get Lucy to blow them with the hair dryer." The wood is from a cherry tree that fell last autumn. While we were splitting it, my stepfather got the wedge stuck in one of the logs; the only way to get the wedge out of the wood now is to burn it.

3.

The President has never liked the Lennons, and yet he is aware that he owes to them his place in history. He cannot bring himself to say "Jack." When he must refer to Lennon by name, his face contracts as if rolled-up balls of aluminum foil are grinding between his molars and his fillings. He does not read newspapers that feature Yoko on the cover.

4.

Sean Ono Kennedy is seven today. The President has sent him a comb. "First time anyone in the family ever owned one," he says. "Stupid-ass sons of bitches."

5.

My mother and I are sitting around a table with claws for feet. All of my stepfather's things are lying askew where he left them. He still receives mail. The kitchen window opens onto a field covered with melting snow. The windmills at Anderosson Farms should be visible in the distance, but the fog obscures them. My mother and I are eating leftover Roy Rogers fried chicken. "Your brother," she says. "He's the only one still in the dark." From upstairs comes the whine of the blow-dryer.

6.

Dear Sean:

It will be many years before you understand fully what a great man your father was. His loss is a deep personal tragedy for all of us, but I wanted you particularly to know that I share your grief—

You can always be proud of him.

Affectionately,

Lyndon B. Johnson

7.

I am sitting at the baby grand piano in the living room. When my father was twelve, he heard Artur Rubenstein at the Academy of Music in Philadelphia. As he gazed down from the Family Circle—Rubenstein's hair like the greens of distant carrots—his head was encircled by phantoms of amazement. His glands secreted juices. Chopin's *Etudes*. The *Pavone for a Dead Princess*. *The Moonlight Sonata*. Mendelssohn's *Fantasia in A Minor*. *With the Dead in a Dead Language* by Mussorgsky. He sobbed silently as each note revealed to his mind the limitless topography of a new and unknown planet.

8.

The President: "He got on top of me and he put his body between me and the crowd. He had his knees in my back and his elbows in my back and a good two hundred pounds all over me. And the car was speeded up. He had a microphone from the front seat that he'd pulled over with him, a two-way radio, and there was a lot of traffic on the radio and you could hear them talking back and forth, and one of them said, 'Let's get out of here quick.' The next thing we were on the way to the hospital."

9.

My mother collects stamps from foreign countries in an album abandoned by my father at age twelve. That's when the piano lessons began. There are magenta squares, orange triangles, strange flags on perforated trapezoids. While she sits in her study and pastes in her stamps with a special glue, she hums a tuneless tune to herself. The song has no title. Its words are: *They all moved over and one fell out: there were three in the bed and the little one said: roll over.* My mother can play this song on the piano as long as she makes no errors. If she misses a note, she has to stop, gather her wits, and start over again from the beginning. When she does this, my stepsister and I look on, drinking gin, encouraging her with our amused and agonized politeness.

10.

My wicked stepsister has grown weary of blow-drying the cherry and has placed the logs inside an electric blanket. "She's crazy," she says. "This wood is made of stuff which does not burn." Lucy doesn't like extremes of taste and smell. A toasted marshmallow is enough to send her to the hospital. "Ants," she says, pointing toward the cherry. The logs, all snug in the master bedroom, are riddled with bullet holes. "Carpenter ants. That's why the tree fell."

11.

Lady Bird: "I went looking for Yoko and ran into her smack like that. She was still in pink. She reached out to my face as if it were a mirror, then said: 'Are you still there?' She sounded annoyed."

12.

A secret service agent came into the room. Some senators, a well-known actress, two governors, and the Maharishi were seated in chairs. The President stood up. The agent said, "He's gone."

13.

The President: "The greatest shock that I can recall was one of the men saying: 'He's gone.'"

14.

Yoko: "If you become naked . . ."

15.

Lucy: "Mother said she was going to write him." "I know. But he's closer to me. He'll want to hear it from me." "'Tell him I have a friend in the Peace Corps who got bowed and arrowed." "I'm sure he's aware of the risks." "He's not aware of anything. You're all alike." She ruffles her feathers by the fireplace. "Can you move? Your shadow's blocking the heat." She looks at me. "What's wrong with you? Can't you take a hint?" Timidly: "It's not your fire, anyway."

16.

My mother surrounds herself with the stamp collection, her colorful triangles, a sponge dampened in an ashtray filled with water. You can tell which stamps were affixed by my mother; they're the ones that aren't straight. Sometimes she puts stamps in the wrong places on purpose. My stepfather was angered by this enterprise. "Why are you keeping his collection going?" he'd say. "He's dead. You could be doing something new." "I like looking at the pictures," she'd say. "Places where it's a different time than ours." Whenever she had a falling out with my stepfather, she turned to the album as the one thing that was her own.

17.

This is a sad time for all people. We have suffered a loss that cannot be weighed. For me it is a deep personal tragedy. I know that the world shares the sorrow that Mrs. Lennon and her family bear. I will do my best. That is all I can do. I ask for your help—and God's.

18.

I am sitting at the baby grand piano. I began to pick out random chords. E minor, then D major, then E minor again. E minors replaced by alternating D majors and B minor sevenths. When my

stepfather was drunk, he would ask me to play "I Write The Songs."
"I don't know it," I'd say. My stepfather used to drink gin from the
cap of the bottle it came in. "You should."

19.

Paul McCartney: "It wasn't like what you read. We'd do stuff together now and then. He'd write the middle eight. Or I'd write his.
We were always superseding each other. Like in 'Day in the Life.'
That whole middle part—'Woke up, got out of bed, dragged a comb
across my head.' That was all Lyndon's. I think he was trying to
make fun of Jack. You know it was an obsession of his. How none of
them ever seemed to have a comb. It was just this thing of his. He was
strange that way."

20.

Jack: "We are the biggest thing since Jesus Christ."

21.

[I.e.: 1. Raising of the widow's son (Paul 7:11); 2. Passing unseen through
the multitude (Paul 4:30); 3. Healing the nobleman's son (John 4:46); 4.
The dumb man healed (Ringo 7:31); 5. Stilling of the storm (Ringo 4:37);
6. Curing the demonic child (George 17:24) . . . etc., etc.]

22.

Hours are consumed with the preliminaries of communication. I'm
using the special writing paper, the cream-colored stock bearing my
stepfather's initials. I have gone through drawers looking for the right
pen with which to write words of sorrow. I have found photographs,
paper clips, report cards, a book of tiny, gummed address labels, photographs from a trip to a wax museum. I write the word: Dear—and
draw a few triangles with the pen. I check the clock: it is late. In a few
moments it will be tomorrow. Across the Atlantic it is almost dawn.

23.

[An aide:] "He was a weasel. That's all I remember. He had those
enormous ears and everything and I think he felt he had to prove to
women he wasn't as ugly as they thought. I remember one night I

was staying at the Ranch in Texas when suddenly I felt this enormous person in the bed next to me—and you know he was gigantic—when he lay down it was like being in bed with an ocean liner—and I hear this voice say: 'Ask not what your country can do for you; ask what you can do for your country.' Then he laughed that Texas laugh of his: 'Haw de-haw de-haw.' "

24.

[An aide:] "It was the night after they did the (Ed Sullivan Show.) The group had flown into Chicago, and Jack and I went out to the lakefront and drank from some bottle of something he was carrying around. There was a smell in the air like it was going to rain. He talked about his brother Joe—the one who was killed in the war. Talked about how Joe held his head under water in a swimming pool when they were kids. Jack got angrier and angrier as he talked about it. I think he hated his older brother, even twenty years later. It started to rain—I mean really pour—and we ran, screaming—into this apartment on Michigan Avenue where one of his women lived. We begged for dry clothes; she looked at him with the look of someone who knows she's unable to refuse an unreasonable request. She put our clothes in the dryer, and Jack and I stood around naked with this girlfriend of his, listening to our clothes rotate. She got us some beer. At last she offered us some clothes—they were the things of her eight-year-old son—and went back to bed. Jack and I sat around drinking, waiting for our clothes to dry, wearing these cub scout uniforms. That was the last time I saw him. I loved him. He was the best friend I ever had. I loved him like a brother."

25.

George: "He wasn't very bright, now was he? It took him like a year and a half to learn all the songs. If the Stones hadn't been in jail—and the ones that weren't in jail weren't working day and night trying to teach Goldwater the Brian Jones licks—they would have gotten the better of us. Goldwater was the only thing worse than Johnson, when you think about it now. Whenever I have me bad memories, I just think of Goldwater singing 'Ruby Tuesday,' and I cheer up a little bit. Not much though."

26.

The President: "The attorney general called me from Liverpool. He felt that the oath should be taken in Dallas, immediately. I said, 'Well we don't have the oath here. Nobody knows what it is.' He said, 'I think I can find it. We've got it around here someplace.' There we were, trapped in Dallas, and nobody had the oath. So somebody in Liverpool found a copy of it and read it over the phone and we wrote it down with a Bic pen on the back of a piece of waxed cardboard that had come on the bottom of a package of cupcakes and that was it."

27.

Early in the morning I write furiously to my older brother. It has all come at once. "When I was younger, that is, not as old as I am now, old friend, which is to say, when I was younger than I am on this particular day, I never needed anyone's assistance, not in any way. Now, on the other hand, those days are gone, and now I find I change my opinion on things all the time. It's like a door opening. Let us both give each other assistance at this time, if we can, for I am certain that you are feeling as down as I am. I do appreciate the fact that you have always been there for me. Perhaps we can both get our feet back on planet Earth together. Let us both try to help each other."

28.

The President awakes one night in the spring of 1968, screaming in Jack's voice. Outside there are protestors in Lafayette Park. The President is sitting up in bed. Lady Bird: "I came into his room at about two in the morning and found him with his hands outstretched; he was shaking them violently in front of his head. He was screaming the same thing over and over: 'I got blisters on me fingers!'"

29.

"When are you leaving?" my stepsister asks. "Soon. After the funeral." The fire, my stepsister, and I are in eclipse formation. "He missed the last one, too." "Who?" "My brother. He was already in Africa." "I've never met him." "He's nice." The fire is beginning to billow smoke into the room; she looks tense, sniffing the air. There is a sudden metallic clank, like a blacksmith's hammer pounding a horseshoe. The wedge has fallen out of the burning cherry onto the hearth. It lies there, glowing red. "Jesus Christ!" my stepsister says, waving her hands in front of her face. "Can't we open some windows in here?"

30.

I learned how to play "I Write the Songs." My stepfather would fall asleep listening to me play. He would snore. The part of the piano that swings back to uncover the keys—the part with "Steinway" printed on it—is sliced with the faded scratches of my father's fingernails. I once asked him why he never played anymore. We were visiting colleges in the Midwest in my senior year of high school; we had visited Northwestern during the day and were now drinking together—perhaps really getting drunk together for the first time as father and son—in a restaurant in the Hilton. "When I was growing up they told me I would be a concert pianist," he said. "I got better and better until I reached a certain point. I stopped there. I was good enough to know what I ought to be doing better, but not good enough to do it. So I stopped. There was no joy in ruining Beethoven." By the time I was a freshman at Northwestern he was dead. My mother remarried the following year. It was exam week.

31.

There is a sound of a television on in my mother's study. It is the sound of the Tonight Show. Tommy Newsom is filling in for Doc. Doc is filling in for Ed. Ed is filling in for Joan Rivers. Joan Rivers is filling in for Johnny. Johnny is on vacation.

32.

[An aide:] "Naturally there was a great deal of animosity between the Johnson faction and the McCartney faction. When McCartney got 42 percent of the vote in New Hampshire—and then four days later Julian threw his hat into the ring—it was the sounding of a dirge for the President. He had grown weary of it all. He had spent the best years of his life in the Beatles; had often threatened to leave, had even decided, irrevocably, to do so, only to be asked by McCartney to hold off the announcement until after the convention. Then to have Mc-Cartney steal his fire like that—well, it got under the President's skin. He came back to the White House kitchen and ate nine gallons of chili and sat in front of the television and watched the news and stank up the Lincoln Room. He was an odious man: vile, disgusting, humongous."

33.

My mother sits at her roll-top desk. She has cut the stamps off of the envelope I have addressed to my brother and is pasting them in her collection. Four American flags fly on the pages of the Democratic Republic of Togo. "Did you think he'd get the letter," she asks vacantly, "even if you did mail it?" "I don't know, Ma." "He never writes back. How do we know he's not dead?" "He isn't. I'm sure of it." She closes the album. "I'm old, honey," she says. "I'm not worth ten cents." There is a window above her desk which looks out on the melting fields, the broad hill leading toward the neighbor's windmill. "You ought to take this." She pushes the old binder toward me. "Your father always wanted your brother to have it. I've got some other things of his, too. I've been saving them for him. A tea box and some scissors. Things from his boyhood." She stretches her fingertips toward me, as if she is feeling for me in the dark. "I want you to have them." We embrace; my mother cries silently in the folds of my pink shirt. "Oh, honey," she says, "I'm old."

34.

[An aide:] [It was the night he told the country he wasn't going to run again. We were discussing the speech.] "He said he had an ending of his own to add to mine, and I told him I wasn't surprised. He asked me if I had any idea what he'd say. I said I thought I did and he wanted to know what I thought of it. I said something like, 'I'm very, very sorry, Mr. President.' He sort of smiled and said, using his most Texas accent, 'Well, so long pardner,' and he left."

35.
My mother asks me to play Mussorgsky at my stepfather's funeral. I
will do my best. That is all I can do. I ask for your help—and God's.

36.
Jack, hair askew, smile triumphant, waves to a crowd from the open
car. "Thank you on behalf of the group and ourselves, and I hope we
pass the audition."

FROM   1998

Fear of Blue Skies

Bodysurfing

THERE WAS A RUSTLING, then Lee saw it, fat and gray and big-eyed with an orange crown, as it slid across the path. They were going to have the last laugh—the iguanas—that was for sure. There were so many of them, Costa Rica was going to be their world some day. The path ended and the boogie board banged against his knee. He swore out loud as he began walking down the road. It was madness, sheer madness, to have rented the board. He knew that within two minutes; he knew that when he reached the first wave. There was the wave and his body and nothing ever should come between them, that alone should be pure. Sheer lunacy to think otherwise. He looked at it—baby blue with a dangling wrist strap like an umbilical cord, this boogie board with its silly name—it was idiocy in its purest form to let it ruin his rides, to let it bang about in the wind and hit his knee. Why had he done it, why? It was because he'd remembered his wife saying they were so much fun. Years ago she'd said that; he had a distant memory of it. It was that and the surfboard morons who were taking over the ocean, crowding him out of his space. He'd let them intimidate him, let them infantilize him into thinking he should maybe get some kind of board of his own, so when he left the beach and saw it in the store he'd rented it on an impulse.

It was the same store that was in front of him now. The Palm Store, a combination travel agency and gift shop run by a good-looking man and his wife with a yellow-haired kid who didn't look like either of them, certainly not the man. So he would return it now, eleven minutes after he took it. Of course he wouldn't ask for his money back. He would take responsibility. They would wonder why, perhaps ask him why, but he wouldn't let himself worry about it. He was about to lose his job in two weeks, about to be transferred to a lower job in the bank in a different city, to be screwed over like that at his age, and with his mother at death's door, too. No, he wasn't going to worry about returning a boogie board to a store that looked like it was made out of cards (as every other store in Tamarindo did), with its pathetically corny painting of a sun sinking below the waves, a store that rented surfboards and goggles and boogie boards and tickets for turtle tours!

He went inside the Palm Store. A tall attractive blond man, a surfboardoron, perhaps two inches taller than he was, perhaps a dozen years younger, perhaps with fourteen better-defined muscles than he had, had finished talking to the owner and was fingering a surfboard as Lee placed the boogie board beside it. He is going to ask me how I liked the boogie board, Lee thought. He is going to try to have a conversation with me. The blond man turned toward Lee. He is from California, Lee thought.

"How did it ride?" the blond man said.

"How did it ride? It didn't ride at all. I didn't have any use for it."

"Surf too strong today?"

"Board too superfluous today, or any day."

"O.K. I hear you."

Lee was struck by how straight the surfer's teeth were, which perhaps accounted for the extraordinary hang time of his smile.

"I don't like anything to come between me and the wave, me and the water. I think that relationship ought to stay pure. Today I violated that relationship, I'm sorry to say. Today I let myself be conquered by a product and I corrupted that relationship."

The blond man's smile vanished and Lee felt vindicated.

"I don't think I get what you mean."

"These boards," Lee said, indicating the blond man's surfboard with his gesture, "they're just another way people've found to make money off the water. They're about buying and selling, that's all."

The blond man showed a second smile, a quizzical but still friendly one. "I guess I don't see it that way," he said.

"Really? How do you see it, then?"

"They're just a piece of equipment for a sport. They're just a means to an end. Like you can't play baseball without a bat or football without a ball, can you?"

Lee felt an adrenaline rush. Apparently the man really wanted to discuss this. "There was a time when you could play sports without buying things," Lee said. "To me the more a sport costs the less its value. The more it's about buying these accessories, the more of a fetish it becomes instead of a sport. By the way, I hope I didn't desecrate the flag, so to speak, with my remarks about surfboards. I know you guys get sensitive about that."

"No, man. I don't mind. I just never met anyone who thinks like you. It's kind of interesting, really."

Lee felt flattered in spite of himself. Ridiculous to feel that in this situation, though he did for a moment, and thought he should soften himself. Besides he was beginning to get an idea and he needed time to figure it all out. Just before he spoke he made a point of looking at the surfer's eyes.

"And by the way, I know whereof I speak," Lee said. "I'm a banker. You can't be much more of a whore than that. My whole life is buying and selling. I'm in middle management at Citibank. Need I say more? Or I soon will be. I was actually at a somewhat higher level of management but that's like bragging about being in a higher circle of hell, isn't it? But at least on my vacation I want to stay pure when I'm in the water. I said to my secretary, 'I don't care what kind of hotel you get me (and she got me Le Jardin del Eden, the most expensive one in Tamarindo) but I insist on big, world-class waves. I want you to research that for me.' Well, the waves here are certainly world class and they deserve the best from me."

Lee looked closely at the man, who in turn appeared to be concentrating intensely on what Lee said. "So, I'm on my way now, I'm going to have my twilight drink, and again, I hope I haven't offended you at all."

"No way. I enjoyed talking with you. You're the first American I've spoken to in three days. I don't speak Spanish so I've practically been talking to myself since I've been here."

Lee looked at him closely once more, wondering if he were gay or just needy, or perhaps one of those friendly, new age types. He had decided something important, something definitive in the waves yesterday but this young man might make it even better. Besides he was a surfer and that would make him the cherry on the sundae and his possible gayness would never enter into it.

"I've enjoyed it too," Lee said. "Hey, you know the restaurant, Zullymar?"

"Sure."

"That's where I'm going for my drink. Why don't you join me and have one on the bank."

The blond man laughed. "Sure. My name's Andy," he said, extending his hand.

"I'm Lee Bank or should I say Le Bank, and we all know what shape banks are in."

Lee turned and walked out of the store and Andy followed after him, still laughing.

"Is Bank really your last name?"

"I'm sometimes known as Lee Bastard, or when I'm in Paris as Le Bastard. But we are far from Paris now, aren't we?"

Lee looked straight ahead as they walked down the dirt road and seemed unaware that Andy was walking beside him. It was not much of a road, Lee thought, full of holes and rocks and puddles, so they could have, should have left it alone and not put up so many toy-like stores. Laughable really how small they were—the little shack that probably doubled as someone's home—with the giant sign saying "Nachos and Ice Cream," a sign that was half as big as the shack. Pathetic really, the hut beside it—called Jungle Bus—that advertised "Killer Burguer and munchies." If the puddle on the road in front of it rose a couple of inches, it could swallow the Jungle Bus.

Zullymar was on the other side of the road, facing the Jungle Bus on one side and the beach on the other. It was a big (by Tamarindo standards) open-air restaurant and bar filled with surfers, the same crowd that forced him off his path two days in a row in the water and actually made him yearn for a lifeguard to patrol things. A wall mural that clashed with the red floor depicted a pink pelican, circling over some anchored boats and a small island beyond that—the approximate scene outside. Across the street at another bar, a man was playing the marimba with two little boys.

Lee and Andy sat down at a table facing the water and looked briefly at the half-filled room. As soon as they focused on each other Lee said, "You'll want a beer, won't you? Isn't that the drink you guys favor?" He had a tight, semisarcastic smile and Andy smiled back.

"What do you mean?"

"You surfers, you surf wizards. You don't want to drink anything too hard, anything that might put you at risk when you go out on your boards again."

"I'm done surfing for the day and I drink lots of things. No routine."

"Fine. Dos mai tais," Lee said to the waiter.

The incredulous smile reappeared on Andy's face. Lee was going to say something to try to get rid of it but Andy spoke first.

"You've got some negative feelings toward surfers, don't you?"

Lee shrugged.

"What did they do to you man?" Andy said, half-laughing, his hand absently caressing his board for a moment, Lee noticed, as if he really thought the goddamn thing was alive. "Did they run into you once or something?"

"No, that would never happen, though they have crowded me out more than once here in Tamarindo, kept me from where I wanted to go, but believe me I stick to my own path. I don't mingle. I am not only on a different path from them, I'm in a different world."

"But what's so different about your world?"

"Night and day, Andy, night and day."

"Why, what do you do? You bodysurf, right? I respect that. So I get up on a board and you bodysurf. Have you ever surfed?"

"I do surf."

"I mean with a board."

"Years ago when I was actually young."

"So what do you have against it?"

The drinks came. Andy took a big swallow while Lee let his sit.

"It's about buying and selling again. Kids see it on TV in ads and think 'that's it.' Then they make movies about it and create a surfing tour and sell all this equipment, all these fetishes, and the young guys think if I do this I'll be a man, if I do this I'll get some first-class pussy. It will all happen if I can just buy the right board."

Andy was laughing now. He was not an easy man to offend, Lee concluded, as he sipped his drink.

"I'm not agreeing with you, by the way," Andy said. "I just think what you're saying is funny and interesting in a way."

"Of course you think that surfboarding is the greater sport, the greater challenge, don't you? After all, you stand up, you are Homo Erectus, whereas I am still on all fours. You go out further to sea whereas I am nearer the shore. You walk on water like Jesus Christ whereas I only ride with it like a fish. And then when gravity must eventually bring you down you take the deeper, more heroic fall. You think all those things, don't you?"

"I just enjoy surfing. I haven't thought it out like that really. And like I say, I respect what you do."

"I wonder if you know what I do. Because there are a number of bodysurfers out there—it isn't just me—and very few of them know when or how to jump, and once they do jump how to go with the wave. They almost always start too late."

"I probably wouldn't know man—isn't that the way it is with everything? We don't really understand the other person's thing or point of view."

"Dos mai tais," Lee said, catching the waiter's attention, although he had not yet made significant progress on his first drink.

"So, now tell me your story, Andy. What brings you to glorious Tamarindo?"

Andy looked flustered, ran his fingers twice through his longish blond hair. He could be Kato Kaelin's younger brother, Lee thought.

"I just came here to surf."

"From whence did you come, then?"

"Santa Cruz, in California."

Lee smiled tightly again. "This is your vacation then. You came to Tamarindo directly on your vacation?"

"Not exactly. I was in Monteverde first. I went to Costa Rica directly but I went to Monteverde first, you know, in the mountains.

"Then you are a mountain man, too."

Andy lowered his head a little. Lee couldn't tell if he were burying his smile or giving birth to a new one. In Tamarindo smiles were the iguanas on every surfer's face. Lee distrusted smiles in general because he had discovered that if you believed in them a time would come when that belief would hurt you. He remembered he had once been very moved by his wife's smile.

"So how were the mountains?" he finally said.

"Some bad stuff happened there so I came here earlier than I expected."

"I'm sorry to learn that. What exactly was the bad stuff?"

The waiter came with the new drinks and Andy took a big swallow as the waiter took his first glass, while Lee carefully placed his second glass next to his first (which was still three quarters full) as if he were positioning two bowling pins.

"The woman I was with went bad on me. She met a dude on the tour we took in the cloud forest. He was older than me, around your age I guess, and he had a lot more money than me, you know. I was never very good at making money. I just help run a little Xerox store. But this rich guy was a businessman, a big businessman, though he was in the same hotel as us, only he was in some luxury suite. Anyway, she told me she was sorry; she said she didn't plan it that way, that it was a one-in-a-million thing but she thought he was the man for her and she was going to go with him for the rest of her vacation and beyond. So . . . "

"So what could you do?"

"Just got drunk. Woke up alone the next morning and got in my Suzuki and came down here 'cause they said this was where the surf was, and they didn't lie about that. The last couple of days I took it out on the waves, six, seven hours a day, and just flushed that bitch right out. It hurt though, I'll tell you. So when you talk about money corrupting things, I really hear you."

"And when you talk about women being bitches, I hear you. I lost my sense of smell from a woman once."

"How'd that happen?" Andy's incredulous smile had snuck back, Lee noted, as if it were taking a curtain call.

"I discovered my female friend had cheated on me and I got extremely ill in an odd way. I developed a sinus condition that's never really gone away. I think it was my ex-wife who did me wrong, though it might have been someone else before her. Over the years people tend to blur together, don't they? Anyway, I have very little to do with women now. The only woman in my life besides Mother Sea is my secretary and she's far too valuable to bother having sex with. I am completely dependent on her. It was she who arranged this trip for me. Of course I'll lose her when I'm transferred to my next job but that's the way it is with women—we always lose them. They were put here on earth so we would know what losing is. Even when we have them we lose them—did you ever think about that?"

"What do you mean?"

"We watch them lose their looks, their charm, their ability to have children, their sex. We lose our mothers, too, and then our wives become our mothers and we lose them again. We lose our mothers a second time."

"But men age too," Andy said.

"But we don't notice it as much since we don't desire men, do we? Anyway, you don't have to worry about all this now. It'll be years before you'll have to realize this."

"I realize it; I realize some of it now."

"Then you might consider giving them up as I have. You can get a greater high than the orgasm from bodysurfing, at least you can the way I bodysurf."

Andy looked away morosely. Lee waited a minute. There was a rustling sound in the restaurant as if the waiters were really iguanas. Lee couldn't stand hearing it so he spoke.

"Thinking about her?" he said.

"Yeah."

"How long were you two an item?"

"Just a couple of months but . . . "

"Impact can be made in a couple of months. Impact can be made in a minute if we allow it to happen. I understand."

"Yeah, I thought this one would work out. I had hopes . . . "

"Ah hopes," Lee said, gesturing vaguely toward the sea. "Listen, I have an idea for you, a proposal to make to you. It does not involve hope, but something better. It involves a challenge."

"Go on."

"Something very special happened to me yesterday. Do you know that inlet that separates our beach from the other one, the one that goes straight to the mountains?"

"Yes."

"Have you ever been on that other beach?"

"No. No one surfs over there so I just assumed there wasn't much there."

"That's precisely the point. The beach goes on for miles but because there's no access from the road, because there is a thick jungle of trees to walk through and no other way to reach it unless you swim across the inlet, there is almost no one there. Well, yesterday I swam across that inlet. It was sunset, a little earlier than now, and the swim wasn't easy but I found the beach deserted and astonishingly beautiful. There were no footprints on the sand, just the swerving lines of hermit crabs and twisted branches from trees. I don't think there were even any butterflies; it wasn't civilized enough for them. It was like being on the moon or on a new planet. The waves were enormous and there was no one around to get in my way. My path was totally clear. Why don't you go there with me now and bodysurf with me? Leave your board at your hotel room and just go there with me now. I know you've only known me thirty minutes or whatever it's been. I know it's getting dark and it's a little dangerous."

"It's not that dangerous. I could do that."

"Fine, marvelous. Here, why don't you have my other drink, I haven't touched it, and I'll finish my first one and then we'll go out together and meet the waves with our bodies alone. I promise you it will be extraordinary."

"Yeah. O.K.," Andy said, looking Lee straight in the eye. "I'll go with you. I'm open to it."

They finished their drinks quickly and Lee paid the bill. The moment he put the money in the waiter's hand he saw the sun slip below the water. Some people were watching it in the restaurant and beyond them others watched from the beach. It was an understandable ritual, Lee thought. It had been advertised, like a Citibank card, and people needed to see the promise delivered. In her condominium in Florida, his mother was probably watching it, too, from her wheelchair, perhaps with one of her nurses. She more than anyone believed in advertised beauty. All her life she believed in Jackie Kennedy and Marilyn Monroe and Marlon Brando and Holiday Inns and sunsets. It would not do any good to tell her the deeper beauty came after the sunset, came with the night when the whole world slid below water. She had never listened to him. They should have switched positions. She should have worked for Citibank and he should have been the cripple. He might have done well in a chair . . .

There were only occasional street lamps outside but he could see the night was thick with butterflies. They were not talking now, so he could hear another iguana slide past in front of him. Then he decided it wouldn't have mattered if they were talking—he would have heard it anyway. In Tamarindo every sound on earth was an iguana; you could only escape them in the water.

"There's your hotel," Lee said, pointing to the Diria, barely bigger than the travel agency it seemed. "Why don't you drop your board off here, you won't be needing it. It'll only get in the way."

"O.K.," Andy said softly. He walked off in the dark and Lee waited in the road, thinking he should have told him 'go put your dick away there too. That's what your board really is. You won't be needing it where we're going. There aren't any dicks in the ocean, not in the night ocean.'

Andy came back. Lee had never really considered that he wouldn't.

"Let's go," Lee said. There were about fifty yards of road before they reached the path that led to the beach. The deep orange of the sky had passed. It was now a dark purple and silver, tinged with spots of fading pink. There were not many people on the beach and most of them were leaving. Except for the white of the waves, the ocean was dark.

"It gets dark quickly," Andy said.

"Drops like a plank," Lee said. He is very young, Lee thought, and his fear is showing. Lee thought of himself as a thousand years old. This will be good for him. He needs to put on a hundred years. Then he didn't think about him anymore.

They walked the length of the beach toward the inlet. Andy was talking about the girl who had dumped him, whose name was Dawn.

"Forget the girl," Lee said. "Drown her in the ocean."

When they reached the inlet the sky was nearly black. There were lots of stars out and three quarters of a moon.

"I was hoping it would be low tide so we could walk across," Andy said.

"We can swim it," Lee said. He threw the towel he'd been carrying into the sky and the black swallowed it.

"What did you just do?"

"I threw my towel away. I won't be needing it. It's a hotel towel."

"Yeah, you told me about your hotel. Very impressive. It's supposed to be the best hotel in Tamarindo." There was sarcasm, even a trace of contempt, in Andy's voice that stung Lee for a second.

"The hotel can drop dead," Lee said as he walked into the water. He was surprised again by how wide the inlet was but he didn't feel tired this time while he was swimming. He could hear Andy breathing heavily, almost gasping, as he swam beside him and thought for a moment that he shouldn't have let him drink three mai tais.

"Stop racing," he said, nearly yelling. "Stop trying to beat me. It's not a race. You have to pace yourself."

Andy slowed down the rest of the way. When they reached the shore of the deserted beach there were only a few slivers of sky that weren't black.

"I wish it were lighter, man." Andy said.

"Why?"

"I can't see things you said would be here. I can't see the things you promised."

"Yes, you can. Look harder."

"I can barely see in front of myself."

"I can look at anything and see the beauty in it. Especially the dark."

"Tell me what I was supposed to see here again, and walk slower, will you? I can barely keep up with you."

"Twisted tree branches and hermit crab lines," Lee said.

Lee walked briskly, saying nothing for the next few minutes. Andy ran after him, stumbling occasionally, trying to keep up with him or at least keep him in sight, feeling like he did when he was a child trying to keep up with his father's longer, relentless stride.

"Come on, we're going in the water. It's time to face the black water now."

Lee walked toward the ocean in fast, imperious strides like a fixated scoutmaster, Andy thought.

"Slow down, will you, why are you racing?" Andy said, and then repeated himself, yelling this time because the ocean was so loud he felt he wasn't being heard.

Lee kept walking into the water without changing speed, the big blustery businessman from the fancy hotel who had to know it all, who had to take what he wanted when he wanted it. Why had he listened to him, why had he come with him to this crazy beach. He was chasing after him in the water now while his legs felt like rubber. The water was up to his knees and he knew something was wrong, had known it for some time.

"Lee," he yelled. "Lee. Lee Bastard."

A few seconds before he'd seen him fifteen yards ahead propelling himself forward, not even ducking for the waves but somehow willing himself forward like a man walking into a wall, into the earth, until the water covered him. Andy heard himself scream. It might have been "Lee," it might have been "Help." His legs wouldn't move at first and when they could he knew he wouldn't move them because he'd already known Lee wanted to be witnessed while he disappeared by a sucker like Andy, just as Dawn had, and one of those humiliations was enough. Lee Legend gets back at a surfer. Lee Lemming. "Lee," he screamed. "Lee Bastard," knowing he would see and hear nothing now except the constant roar in the black and his own sickly voice boomeranging back at him like spit in the wind, because the bastard had wanted it this way.

FROM   1999

Wingtips

Powerman

THE ADULTS WHO SAT on the veranda, sipping martinis and talking in the darkness, could not have known they were being watched. He moved inseparably through the shadows under the porch. From beyond the tall doors that opened onto the porch came the sounds of his siblings and cousins playing a board game on the living room floor. The red and blue glass lights of the brass lantern above the circle of adults flashed in the breeze, and under its colors several conversations came together in a burst of laughter. He took a step closer, invisible.

"No, I don't know when he's coming down," his mother went on. "And I don't think this is the time to discuss it, with little Mr. Big Ears around."

"Well, I think it's time for more ice," his Uncle Andrew said, then apparently stood up—a rocking chair swung loose, and heavy steps went inside. It frustrated him that he couldn't see what they were doing up on the porch, only listen.

"Well," his grandmother, Granelle, said, "I just think you two should decide this thing one way or the other. Your father can make arrangements with the schools down there—"

"Mother, please! I'm not going to discuss it right now."

"Mother, for God's sake . . . " Now his Uncle Jack stood up. "Here, let me freshen your drink for you."

"I've just really had it up to here," his mother was saying. "I've been on the phone all day—"

"I'm sorry," his grandmother said. "I just thought that if Jason was still writing you those letters—"

"Mother, drop it, for Christ's sake." Uncle Jack had walked across the porch. "You want tonic water or is soda fine with you? Carol? Let me freshen that for you."

He had heard some of this bickering before, so he did not listen to it now. Rather, he pictured his Uncle Jack standing at the card table, fixing his grandmother's drink. Uncle Jack was a slender young man, cool because he was just out of college, because he wore penny loafers without socks and owned a *Meet the Beatles* album—Beatle-mania now entering its last phase—and because he kept a stack of *Playboy* magazines in his bedroom closet.

As the adults argued, he thought how great it would be if he could go and live with his grandparents and Uncle Jack in Jacksonville. His grandparents' house in the drowsy Floridian city was a huge old place surrounded by water oaks hung with rags of Spanish moss, rambling with gables and verandas, rooms ghostly with old portraits, and long dark hallways and vacant bedrooms where the closets were full of clothes and smelled of mothballs—rooms with Persian carpets where he would pull on old, white dinner gloves, tie spats over his sneakers, and stand before mirrors losing their silver. The old house sat beneath trees near the banks of the St. Johns River, where the wind came thick with the smell of fish and brackish tide; and for hours he couldn't count, he had stood in dim hallways staring into old landscape paintings gone dark with aging varnish, dreaming himself into the scenery where the leafy masses of trees opened onto an endless panorama blue as paradise, with the invariable shepherd boy in his straw hat, flock nearby.

Each year the cousins of his extensive southern family came to-gether in this mountain town of Beersheba Springs, Tennessee, on the edge of the Cumberland Plateau, where they vacationed in ante-bellum summer houses, and this day, like all those of the previous week, had gone well. They went swimming in the river down in the valley. The adults played tennis on the clay court, his Uncle Andrew sporting a new V-neck tennis sweater. After supper everyone, adults and children, took a walk around the loop—an ambling dirt road with deep-porched cottages—and the children ran ceremoniously past the graveyard, its slanting headstones visible back among the trees.

But if the vacation had started well, it wasn't still going that way. For some reason, his mother and grandmother were always arguing, either in quick exchanges like the one above him now or late at night when they met in his mother's bedroom and spoke behind closed doors. Everyone was tired. Just now, in the living room, a quarrel broke out between his siblings. The smack. Two smacks. Brian and Jay shouting, one kicking the other, Jay claiming not to be hurt, then wailing for help.

"I don't think I can stand it a moment longer," his mother said.

"For Christ's sake," Jack said, and his shadow cut across the oblong of light that fell diffusely from the door into the yard.

A separate pair of footsteps came back across the porch. "Well, I found some ice, but it's not much." His Uncle Andrew exhaled heavily, and the wicker and wood of his rocking chair cinched under his weight.

Uncle Jack spoke inside the living room. "I mean it," he went on. "You kids separate. If I have to come in here again, I'll see to it that Mrs. Hillis chops you up and bakes you into a pie. Now, behave. Or better yet, go play Peeping Tom like Stuart. Hey, how about this game—see who can find him. The winner won't get a spanking."

Uncle Jack's girlfriend, Beatrice, swung back in her rocking chair on a gust of laughter, and Stuart glimpsed her beehive hairdo above the railing. She was Jack's girlfriend from Vanderbilt, and really pretty, with frosted pink lipstick and gooey mascara. She also had large breasts that stuck out like missiles.

"Find him," Uncle Jack was telling the children. "I don't know. Go find him."

Pairs of sneakers ran onto the porch, thudded down the steps, and jumped onto the grass, scattering the blue and red lights of the lantern across the yard.

Stuart was gone, flying into the darkness. Behind him on the veranda, Uncle Andrew shouted, "There goes that bear!" and all the adults laughed. When he got to the old, red cedar tree at the end of the driveway, which signaled a place he called the Safety Zone, he stopped, alone and breathing hard.

IN THE EARLY MORNING the small cousins would pull on the rope, and the breakfast bell would bing and bang on the dry summer air.

The brass ship's bell sat on a hickory post outside the kitchen door, and before it was done ringing, everyone would emerge from their rooms with a rhythm as casual as the sequence of days, cross the back porch, and swing down the back steps to the dining room and kitchen, which stood apart in a separate building. The crowd of first cousins, uncles, and aunts arrived like an occupation army and filled the nineteenth-century kitchen, from its beaded board walls to its torn window screens, with a bright chaos of conversations and preparations that were as traditional as the menu of eggs, grits, and sausage. And here was the source of summer and family for him. For all the collisions between personalities, no one here screamed drunkenly, or wept, or slammed doors, and here discipline did not entail being beaten, cringing, back into a closet. Here you said, "Yes, sir" and "Yes, ma'am," and everything ran smoothly. And it was this sense of peace that he hoped to find if his mother would give him permission to live with his grandparents in Jacksonville. His Uncle Andrew stood over the black iron, wood-burning stove, cracking eggs on the rim of the black iron skillet. The girls set places at the grownups' and children's tables. His aunts told everyone what to do, or almost everyone.

"Stuart—" Uncle Jack pushed him outside with the wooden bucket. Although the year was 1968, their plumbing was only recently installed; the previous summer they had still been using the outhouses, and they one and all still preferred to drink the well water. The well housing stood in the side yard, its metal hood curved like a sea horse or a mounted chess piece in one of the Alice books; Stuart cranked its rattling handle until freezing water gushed into the bucket, and it became almost too heavy to lift. He lugged it, though, with both hands, and it swung between his knees, sloshing his shins. On the back porch he raised it to the table and set the battered tin dipper into it, the same bucket and dipper that his grandfather's generation had used; and because his grandfather had filled it at Stuart's age, Stuart did so as well. Brian carried in an armload of kindling for the kitchen stove. Jay rang the breakfast bell again, this time for Beatrice who hadn't come down yet. Back in the dining room, the girls carried in platters of food. The boys carried in pitchers of orange juice. To a cacophony of scraping chairs, they sat to eat. And for the next hour, as they made plans for the day, a column of sunshine blazed slowly down the whitewashed bricks of the chimney and spilled evenly across the warm, wooden surface of the grownups' table.

Stuart sat at the children's table where he made sure all the kids got one bowl of Cap'n Crunch. "You got enough," he told Brian, and cracked his brother's knuckles with a spoon.

"What do you think of that, son?"

"Stuart," his mother said. "Your Uncle Andrew is trying to tell you something."

"You tell Brian if he hits me one more time, I'm going to smash his stupid face in."

"He hit me first," Brian said.

Uncle Andrew set his newspaper hard on the table. "Son, don't make me have to come down there."

The other children finished, and Stuart's cousin Betsy—the only other child his age—made them take their plates into the kitchen. The children swung outside through the screen door, where the breakfast hour was already dissipating into the rising heat. His Uncle Andrew made a comment on some new development in Vietnam and passed the paper to Jack.

"What I was trying to tell you a moment ago," he said, "is that Robert and Harry'll be down this coming Saturday. Maybe they'll take you for a hike to Bat's cave."

"But, God knows, you can't act like a little pill," Uncle Jack said. "Or they might just leave you there."

"Hardy-har-har." Stuart turned the red and blue pages of his *Spiderman* comic book.

"Jack, please don't add to it," his mother said. She raised her hand like a crossing guard's stop signal.

"Carol, you know he gets it from his father—" Jack said.

"That's enough of that," his grandmother said. "Now those boys are going to need someplace to sleep, and I'm going to put them down in the little cabin. Now, Stuart, don't interrupt."

He was trying to tell her that he wanted to sleep down in the boys' cabin.

"Well, first, I want you to help Jack put a new roof on it this week," she said. "It leaks, and—"

"Well, can I go and live with you and Papa and Uncle Jack in Jacksonville?" An image of the ghostly old house by the St. Johns River arose in his mind, bringing with it a vague, romantic mood and a memory of rooms filled with daydreams. "Why not? I'll behave! If it was Moriah, you'd say 'yes.'"

"Because I said so, that's why. Your mother needs you at home to help her when school starts—"

"Oh, wow, some vacation," Stuart said. "Let's pick on Stuart. Do Brian and Jay have to work? No, not them. They get to ride the trolley. They get to go outside and play. And Moriah gets to go to Keystone. Not me. I have to be a good little boy and do all my stupid chores."

"Son," his Uncle Andrew lowered the newspaper, again severe. "Now, son, you're old enough to start helping around here. You're too old to be playing in the sandbox with those children. All you do is get into fights. You do what your grandmother tells you to, and I don't want to hear any more back talk. Is that clear?"

"What was that?" his mother said.

"Aye, aye, captain." He gave the adults a sharp salute.

"You may be excused, young man," his mother said.

He slumped tragically outside—careful not to let the screen door slam—and into the pointless heat.

THE AFTERNOON WENT as Stuart could have predicted. The work was boring and hot and stupid and dull and dumb.

"I didn't ask if you liked it, you little smartass," Jack said. "Just get me that bucket of nails. Don't make me get off this roof and get them. You just move along and do as I tell you to."

As Stuart crossed the yard, he sullenly watched his little brother ride the trolley—and Brian got a great ride. He leapt way out from the step ladder propped against the hemlock tree, grasping the steel handles, and the T-bar contraption went singing down the wire, with Brian swinging his feet. Coming fast on the tree at the other end, he kicked hard and went lurching and rolling back up the wire. In disgust, Stuart hauled the bucket off the tailgate and lugged it with both hands back across the yard toward the boys' cabin, which sat in the shade of the woods. Jack sat perched on the roof, flipping the hammer by its handle. Rung by rung, Stuart clunked the bucket up the ladder, then raised it uncertainly up to Jack's hand.

"Good Lord," Jack said. "Listen to you whimper. Someone would think you were being tortured."

"Well, I am," Stuart shouted. "I'm tired. That thing's too heavy for me; I told you that. It's easy for you 'cause you're twenty-one, but I'm hardly even eight. I can't carry that thing. It must weigh fifty pounds."

Jack smacked the claws of the hammer under a tier of rotten shingles. He jerked his elbow down, and tar paper and nails came wrenching up. When he had torn them off the roof, he spun them scattershot, like broken frisbees into the surrounding branches. Stuart hung from the ladder in a state somewhere between protest and boredom. The two of them paused, and the summer had its effect; they became alive to the world beyond their work. The morning was sounding with incidentals: the clacking of a screen door, voices and footsteps on the back porch, and, somewhere, a motorcycle roaring away into the distant mountain silence. In the next moment they were uncle and nephew again, and Jack was wrenching loose another handful of old green shingles.

"Hey, let me throw some." Stuart leaned back on the ladder, yanking it off the gutter. "Hey, can I come live in Jacksonville with you guys? Mom won't let me."

"No."

"Why not?"

"Not until you stop being such a little pissant all the time and help around here. I was appalled by that fight yesterday. You should never hit your brother like that."

Stuart let the ladder bang against the gutter.

"Knock it off," Jack said. "Your mother needs you to be very good right now."

"Why?"

"None of your business."

"Tell me."

"When you're older."

"Tell me now," he said, "or maybe I'll just move the ladder."

Jack appeared to smile as Stuart pulled the ladder away from the roof, but the glance over his shoulder was unamused.

"Don't be a little pecker all your life."

"I'll tell Mom you called me that."

Jack ignored him, and Stuart let the ladder slam the gutter.

IN THE WARM HOURS OF AFTERNOON, the children were taken swimming, ostensibly to entertain them but more pointedly to give a few of the adults a rest. Jack drove the station wagon down the serpentine mountain road into the valley, where after miles of nursery farms, they turned in at a white farm house, bounced back through acres of feed corn, and parked in tall grass. "Down scope!"—and the back window rolled into the tailgate. Those not wearing suits changed in a dry but sweltering tool shed dusty with spidery filaments and disuse. Then they came down the hill to the wooden raft, which was roped to a tree. The impact of their feet upon the boards produced tones from the buoyant steel drums, and with the pulley clanking and splashing, the boys hauled on the water-springing rope and brought the raft out from under the shade of slanting trees into the bright silence, the green abstraction of water and sunlight. Inner tubes slapped musically on the water, and the first to dive in always came up shouting and wild about how cold it was. They were always amazed. They seemed always to have come swimming in this long green pool, this bend in an otherwise forgettable river. Theirs was an immutable fall of generations, of uncles and fathers and great-greats, beginning back a hundred years and all landing on the traditional raft to stand on adolescent legs, shivering and skinny, shouting and swimming across an echo of summers.

"Aren't you going to get in?" Floating in an inner tube, Betsy held onto the raft, kicking slow spirals with her feet. "Here, you can have my tube," she said and rolled out.

"In a minute." Stuart sat, chin on his knee, one foot in the water.

But Betsy wouldn't let him alone and the other kids began to tease him, so Stuart splashed his arms and legs—imitating his grandfather—and hopped into shallow water in his sneakers and, with a pinchhold on his nostrils, dipped himself completely.

After an hour in which he and Betsy piled river stones onto the walls of the baby pool in the shallows, they found themselves drifting to the far end of the pool. They held onto each other's inner tubes. A kingfisher clipped the water and swept into the trees. A horsefly buzzed them. They seemed to be floating on a surface of green glass, scratched by an occasional yellow leaf. Over the last ten days they had begun to spend their evenings flipping through old *Life* magazines under a bright lamp in the living room, and they were not brother and sister so they liked each other. Now they were floating within sunlight and privacy—the other children upstream in the shallows, the adults on the raft in sunglasses, a cow crashing through the woods back into the field—and having never felt so intensely alone with a girl, Stuart heard himself telling Betsy all about Powerman and his mission to spy on the adults. "And especially on Uncle Jack," he finished. "He's always picking on me."

"Oh, wow," Betsy said. "I love to play spy."

And so that night, after the supper plates were carried in, they slipped away and began. The adults were on the front porch, drinking and talking, his mother blowing her nose and Uncle Jack announcing that he and Beatrice were going for a walk around the loop. Betsy and Stuart sneaked into great Aunt Mary's bedroom, in the back of which was the large linen closet. They closed the linen closet door, and by a moonlit frame of window, they pulled off their clothes to reveal their bathing suits. Stuart had seen Betsy in her bathing suit before, of course, but now seeing her body in the silver dark made him feel weirdly great to be with her, and he awakened to an excitingly illicit quality of the game. They swung blue and red towels around their necks, which they clipped on with pink-capped safety pins. Next, they slid silver soup cans up their biceps to receive superpowers from starlight; then they leaned out the window, shimmied down the linden tree, and dropped not quite soundlessly onto the gravel drive. Across the yard they ran, capes flying. They hit the deck. Powerman waved, and they ran crouching along the picket fence. Figures could be seen walking in the road—Jack and Beatrice, who vanished into the dark. The spies came to a stop. Powerman double-tied the knots of his P. F. Flyers, then checked his Johnny Quest decoder ring. Powergirl, a little bored with him, went on ahead; then they ran quietly out of the Safety Zone and slipped down the grassy margin of the woods.

They walked for half a mile, passing summer houses where the brass lanterns on the verandas were turning slow jewels of light and where adults could be heard talking and laughing. On one porch an old victrola was scratching Fats Waller's songs out into the cricket-loud darkness. "It's a lovely night to spoon / Let's pretend that there's a moon. . . . "

"Look," Powergirl said.

The night was shot with stars that glittered in colors—blue, red, and gold—down to the tree line. Powerman tried to explain that he was really from another planet—that, if Stuart wasn't, then Powerman was. "You lie," Powergirl said, and for one bad moment he felt that this was not the same game for both of them.

They stopped. The antebellum houses were behind them now, and the solitary street light at the old hotel didn't reach any farther, though it ran their shadows before them in thin lines over the road and into the mass of dark which sat hunched before them like an ogre. They decided to call it a night.

A woman coughed.

They didn't move. She coughed again—and this time, no question, it came from the town's old graveyard.

"You first," Powergirl said.

"You—" But Powerman stepped across the ditch and moved imperceptibly through the grass. He kneeled at the fence of split rails, which smelled of cedar. Powergirl crouched beside him.

The trees made a canopy against the brightness of the moon, but Powerman's eyes soon began to adjust. Two people could be seen, on a tomb. One head, a hand on a back, then one lump moved and the other head appeared. The heads came together, one at the other's neck, then mouth to mouth, and on a lift of wind came wet sounds. The figure became a blur. Down at the hotel, a screen door clacked; a motorcycle roared away. Then, on the wind, came the scratch of a zipper, two zippers. Maybe. He couldn't see them now at all; they had lumped over on the slab. The safety pin was cutting across his Adam's apple when Powerman realized that Powergirl was pulling on his cape, and unable to distinguish anything more, he rose and went away with her.

The children swung the rope, the breakfast bell binged and banged, and August ripened in green warmth and wind. The building projects were moving along simultaneously. The cabin roof and the baby pool were almost finished now beneath the incessantly buzzing song of insects in the sky and woods around them. Rolls of tar paper went down, rocks were gathered, shingles slid and slapped, the pounding of Jack's hammer made dry percussions against the side of the house, and Stuart cradled smooth river stones onto the walls. Everything was not peaceful, however; their mother would frequently remain in her room, and in their efforts to see her, Stuart and his brothers would get into scrapes with each other. The afternoon when he punched his little brother Jay in the shoulder, his grandmother, Granelle, sent him up to the attic, where the boys shared a communal room and where Stuart went quite happily and threw himself out across the sunny, unmade bed to lounge over another *Spiderman* comic book. Within a few lines, however, he was daydreaming out the window, and what began as an almost ineffable sensation of success crystalized with the light in the leaves into a more vivid impression of himself in Jacksonville as a dashing young man, one who would find the love of his life and become rich and famous, so much so that all his tormentors, here and in school, would bow in abject submission whenever he was around. In a while he got bored, went downstairs, and found the stillness of another century.

The adults had found their own escape into the brittle pages of paperbacks, which they read in hammocks and rocking chairs until sleep overtook them. Jack and Beatrice slipped away for a long hike through the woods to Stone Door, a towering cliff that would give them a romantic view of the converging valleys of Savage Gulf. On afternoons when things were really boring, or when the rain fell with a sensuous monotony of steady drumming on the tin roof, Stuart and Betsy would pull out the old Edwardian costumes from the sea chest in the attic and dress themselves in the various velvet pantaloons, vests, and top hats that his grandparents and their guests had used when they performed summer plays back before the First World War. He and Betsy, thus attired as a fop and a fool, would stage dramatic sword fights, using a pair of tennis rackets, until Jack caught them and raised hell. The days were long. The summer afternoons were shapeless, continuing present time, punctuated by the listless slap of a screen door and the way light hung in leaves along the green, cool limit of the woods.

"I don't care who started it, mister. I told you to go to your room right now. Stuart Goodpasture, don't you dare talk back to me. I said now! Mother, would you handle them? I don't think I can stand it . . . " She pressed a wad of Kleenex to her nose, walked to her room, and shut the door.

"You go and do as your mother tells you." Granelle was furious with them. "Don't be such an infernal nuisance that no one wants you around. Well, you are. You don't help. You don't pick up after yourself. You talk back. You pick and quarrel and torment each other so. I don't see how your mother stands it. No," she went on, "I don't know when your father's coming down, and don't ask your mother; she's resting. Now, you get on out there and help Jack with that roof so I have some place to put those boys on Saturday. Now, go on, and don't hit your brother. Brian's not bothering you. He is *not* laughing. Damn a mouse, I never saw such disagreeable children in all my life!"

EVENING CAME. TWILIGHT POURED a slow shadow from the mountain over the valley, lighting the eastern range with sun, and spreading a blanket of soft blue silence across the rows of field corn that were fanning by the open windows of the station wagon. The children were cold and wet and quiet. They sat blue-lipped, wrapped in towels. No one talked. There had been a fight down on the raft an hour earlier, when Jack had grabbed Stuart from behind and launched him, screaming, off into the cold, green water. And now he rode in back, watching Jack's profile as the man gazed across the fields. Stuart understood why Jack had thrown him in.

Sometime earlier in the afternoon, when the children were hunting for arrowheads in the plowed ruts of the field, and while the adults were murmuring or sleeping on the raft—his mother as lovely as a movie star in her dark glasses—Stuart had escaped and floated to the far end of the pool. There he had slipped out of the inner tube and waded to the bank of green plants. Kneeling, he sipped at the mouth of the spring, tasting the cold, delicious water, then heard something stepping through the woods, something sneaking not quite soundlessly through the leaves. He looked up. The creature was not a stray cow from the field. It was Jack and Beatrice, brilliant, naked, and stepping through the sunlight.

On the raft a little later, Jack grabbed him hard around the ribcage and threw him aloft, twisting and shouting; the water smacked him, punched the air out of him. Shivering and crying, Stuart dog-paddled back to the raft. He hung on, but his arms were too weak to lift him onto the deck of adults. Jack hauled him up by the wrist.

"You little bastard!" Stuart shouted, cowering in his red towel.

"Jack, for Christ's sake," his mother said. "I asked you not to torment him." She pushed up her dark glasses.

"Me? You know where he gets that language!"

"For God's sake," his grandmother said. "Jack, you behave as badly as he does. Yes, you! You act as though you were twenty-one going on twelve, picking on him like that. Now, you two separate. And, Stuart, you can just go sit in the car until you learn to control that tongue of yours. Now, go on, get."

The subdued atmosphere after the fight followed them up the mountain but broke against the bright porches and activity in the kitchen. Supper was under way, guests were over, and the shaking of martinis under the flashing colors of the lantern out front on the veranda promised an excellent night for spying.

"WELL, WE'RE GOING FOR A LITTLE WALK around the loop," Uncle Jack told the others on the front porch.

Powerman and Powergirl dropped from the window of the linen closet into the partial moonlight. Their towels fell over their faces. Jack and Beatrice were going out through the front gate. The spies ran through the woods, on a trail, ahead of them.

Within ten minutes they were in place and trying not to breathe. Powerman lay on his back beneath the stone slab of ELIJAH TATE, 1828 to 1901, a man of such local power that he alone commanded a monumental site, where the earth had sunk away leaving a bed of old leaves. Powerman shifted his position and the dry rot crunched; the odor of earth and leaves was sharp and unbreatheable under the stone lid so close to his head; vandals must have moved the slab wide enough for him to slip in like this. That must be them. Voices were coming down the road. He almost climbed out for air, but couldn't do that now. They were coming into the graveyard. And as Stuart had discovered that morning, there was only one slab where they might sit, and it had to be this one with the foil packets on the ground. The footsteps stopped and voices murmured.

They were goofing around, stumbling over rocks. Now they sat above him. The backs of their calves blocked his view. Khakis scratched about on the stone surface. Beneath Jack and Beatrice, between their pairs of legs, Powerman's eyes gleamed out in the dark, straining to see up.

"Mmmm. I missed you," she softly said. "All day long I just wanted to kiss you."

Ruffling. Quiet. Down by the hotel a car thundered by.

Unable to see them, Powerman's keen mind began to wander. In one of his outings before Powergirl came along, Powerman had kneeled at the door of the big bathroom and put his eye to the skeletal keyhole. The keyhole made a figure eight of dark inside of which he saw the scene of Beatrice bathing herself in the deep, claw-footed tub. All he could see of her was her face, shoulders, and bare arms. Her hair was pinned up. She raised one leg so she could draw the sponge slowly up the back of her calf. Then she stood, and her breasts rose from the water, her belly, and she was amazing—a dark brush between her legs—some streaming, wet goddess who made him yearn for what he could not yet imagine. Later that night Granelle would lecture him about bothering Beatrice, assuring him that one day he would marry someone just like her, a young beauty in Jacksonville, perhaps. "What the hell are you doing?" Jack knuckled him on the head. "Get out of here—go on, get!" Powerman ran off, but stopped to watch Jack go into the bathroom.

"That better?" Uncle Jack said above him, in the graveyard.

Powerman blinked away the memory of her lovely form rising from the water, of her lovely body striding freely through the green sunlit woods, and so many other moments as well—the way she tossed a ball in tennis, closed a book, jumped up the stairs; the way she dove in, rode a horse, and went for hikes; and most of all that coy glance that made his uncle blush as she asked him for the bacon platter every morning. All he could hope for now was that Powergirl was in place. Jack and Beatrice were making soft noises without talking. Then, the scratch of a zipper. Maybe two.

Powerman slipped his hand up through the breach between the slab and its foundation. His fingers touched Beatrice's thigh. He couldn't think; he was faint. Up above, she moaned. A hand came down on top of his, hard like Jack's, and then another, soft like hers.

Jack and Beatrice looked down between her legs and saw a small white hand rising from the grave.

A half mile away on the porch of the family house, Uncle Andrew was going on about how he had somehow managed to splash his khakis with white paint, when he set his drink down on the arm of his rocking chair.

"Listen. Down by the hotel." They all heard it.

"Good Lord," his mother said. "Sounds like all bloody murder's broken loose." She and grandmother left the porch to go put on their sweaters.

In the graveyard Beatrice was screaming. Uncle Jack was screaming. Someone else was screaming like a girl. They stumbled over roots and headstones, hounds were baying, and someone ran crashing into the woods. Down within the tomb Powerman was screaming too. All he heard was his own shrieking laughter against the stone above him. But somewhere down the road, Jack began yelling, "Very funny, you little bastard. We'll talk about this tomorrow."

Powerman laughed, clunked his head against the slab, rolled out of the grave, and stood up amid the tilting headstones. "Got you good, boy," he said out loud, to his imagined audience. A bit nervously he brushed the broken leaves off his legs, suit, and cape and, in case the dead were not dead, jumped onto the dark road and hurried on back to the house.

Powergirl was gone. She was not behind the big tree or the monument from which she was to have appeared as a ghost with arms raised. He called her name, but there was only the steady, unquiet darkness. He passed the summer houses, laughing, shivering, and looking around for Jack. But Jack didn't appear, and as Powerman kept going and began to calm down, he became aware of the smell of damp grass in the night air. It would be September in another week. School would start. He could already see the lumbering yellow school buses, the red and yellow New England trees, the social maneuverings of the hallways, and these things filled him with an excitement and a sadness as quickening as the chill in the woods.

As he came through the side yard, he saw a thin edge of light between the tall louvered doors of his mother's bedroom. Powerman chinned the railing, kicking and scraping the slats of the house with the grass-stained toes of his sneakers. He hung onto the window frame, with his toes jammed into corners between slats. He was about to call out, "Hey, Mom, guess what I did to Uncle Jack!" But the sight in the room stopped him.

His grandmother and mother were shoulder to shoulder on the edge of the bed, blue and red in their sweaters. The reading lamp fluttered moth shadows high into the corners and around the heavy, dark furniture. Granelle was massaging his mother's back. His mother pressed a Kleenex to her nose.

"I don't have a job or credit with the bank. Everything's in his name . . . " She wiped her nose again.

"You knew this was going to happen when you came down," his grandmother said. "All that shouting and profanity. Damn a mouse, I don't see how you could stand it. The children can stay with us. We'll put them in school in Jacksonville while you two settle this thing."

His mother cried like a girl into her Kleenex and said something about the house.

"Let him have the house, if he wants it," his grandmother said. "You never liked the house anyway."

"Not even the goddamn car's in my name!" His mother plucked a Kleenex from the box on her lap. "When I think of how things might have been if Rosaline had just minded her own goddamn business, how happy we might all be right now—"

"That was a long time ago, and they wouldn't even be your children. Now hush—"

"Well, sometimes I think, this time I'll write back, this time I'll do things differently. The next time Jason writes—"

"Don't you answer even one of his letters, you hear me?"

They continued discussing the details, but Powerman's arms were weakening quickly, and they suddenly relaxed and let him fall to the ground. The house seemed to vault above him, vanishing once more above his range of observation and comprehension. Powerman landed with his fingers pressed in the dirt for balance and his cape down over his face. He rose up, tossed his cape into position down his back, brushed off his finger tips, and began to walk very deliberately and slowly around the side of the house. He felt very weak. As he came around to the front porch he broke into a run, but his legs were going on him and he had scarcely reached the sandbox for his ceremonial leap when he heard his Uncle Andrew bellow. "There goes that bear again," and all the adults laughed along with him. Powerman missed the far side of the sandbox wall, tripping into the yard, but continued on, slowing down with each step until he staggered into the Safety Zone, where he was supposed to be beyond the reach of everything that could wound him.

He walked to the old cedar tree, plunked himself down on the grass, and soon fell onto his back, with an arm hooked over his face. He was breathing slowly, taking nothing in but the chill of the night and the way the grass made his bare legs itch. Then it hit him. He caught his breath and began to cry, coughing his guts out. As if from another position, somehow in the air above him, he felt as if he were rising slowly into the branches of the tree above him and, rising farther, was seeing down below him a silly, stupid kid wearing a bathing suit and a towel. Whatever of himself he had put into being Powerman was gone. It hit him again. Stuart cried openly but silently for a long time.

THE KIDS PULLED THE ROPE, the breakfast bell banged, and everyone came into the kitchen.

"Well, look who's here. Come on in, boys. We're just about to have some breakfast. Betsy," his Uncle Andrew said, "how about setting two more places at the big table, will you please?"

Two boys, of perhaps fourteen and fifteen, came in out of the sunlight and created a sensation in the dining room. Their hair was long, and they wore blue jean bell-bottoms and tie-dyed tee shirts. They were from up north and looked like a pair of high school radicals, all of which was new to Stuart. With the men they shook hands; with the women they hugged.

His grandmother, seated at the head of the table, took Stuart by the hand. "I've had these two working all week on the roof of the little cabin down there so you boys can stay down there. You know where the sheets and pillows are."

They were all standing and talking, perhaps twenty of them now, bringing in chairs, finding places at the table. Betsy took down extra plates from the Dutch cabinet. Brian fished utensils out of the tray. They were loud and gregarious, with the screen door springing open, clacking shut, and others coming in.

Stuart's mother encircled his waist with her arm. He looked at her, the first time that morning. She wore dark glasses; her nostrils were red.

"How would you like to go to school in Jacksonville?" she said.

Stuart couldn't answer. "No," he said, finally.

"You could live with Granelle and Papa and Uncle Jack. Wouldn't that be fun?"

"Hey, man, you want to go?" Harry said from across the table. Although Harry and Robert had just arrived, they already had big plans for the day. "Robert and I are going down to see that barn that Mitchell's building. Maybe we can ride some of his horses."

"Or throw apples at them or something," Robert said.

The other boys laughed.

Betsy said she wanted to go but was told she had to help do laundry and make beds.

Stuart pulled his mother's hand off his waist. "Okay," he said. "Yeah."

"Oh, he's my baby boy," his mother said and pulled him back into a big hug. The adults laughed.

"I said get off, Mom." Stuart pulled loose and stomped into the kitchen. He opened the refrigerator. Someone walked behind him, and he was cracked on the head with a big spoon. He turned to curse; Beatrice was leaving the kitchen with a platter.

After breakfast they stood around the jeep in the driveway, waiting for Stuart to come. He ran out of Aunt Mary's bedroom and, before jumping off the porch, fast-balled a red towel into the wicker laundry hamper.

"Hey, Robert, whittle me a sword," Betsy said. She leaned against the jeep's hood.

Robert flipped the limb of red cedar and caught it. "Sure. Tree out there's almost dead anyway. You can have this one when I'm done."

"Hey, Stuart," Betsy said, as he ran down. "Robert's going to whittle me a sword so we can play pirate."

Stuart climbed in back of the jeep with other male cousins, sat within the coil of rope on the corrugated floor, and looked at the deserter. "You're a little chicken pecker."

The boys in the jeep laughed with him.

"I'll tell your mom you called me that," she said. Stuart grabbed the frame bar as the jeep accelerated down the gravel driveway under trees and sunlight.

"I'll make you a sword," he shouted.

The rest of that week before Labor Day, when school began, Betsy staged pirate duels with Brian, who was pretty good with a tennis racket. The evenings were chilly, everyone wore cotton sweaters, and one night they built a fire and closed the living room doors. The sight of everyone there in the high-ceilinged room—with the fire blazing, the kids around a board game on the floor, and the grownups reading—made Stuart want to go in there with them, but he remained out in the side yard by the well house. Betsy sat curled on the sofa under a tall lamp, paging through an old *Life* magazine with Stuart's big sister, Moriah, who had arrived that day. The other kids were playing Monopoly and quarreling. Granelle's head eased to one side against the cushion of the chair, and his mother's head fell back, so he knew they must be snoring. His Uncle Andrew, in his paint-splashed khakis, said something, and both women sat forward briefly before closing their eyes again. Jack and Beatrice left for a walk an hour ago, but he hadn't bothered to follow them.

Stuart slapped at his ankles. He had stopped while on a run to swipe a couple of cans from Jack's sixpack in the fridge. Robert and Harry, who had set up their own mission control in the boys' cabin, were letting him sit in on their poker games and uninformed sexual conversations, as long as he stole the beer. They told him that he would like Florida next week—it was so warm and the girls were so great—which allayed his fear of wandering unattached among new kids. Standing there in penny loafers without socks, he slapped at the no-see-'ums biting his ankles, and again a sad damp chill of the woods mingled with an inarticulate excitement for what was coming next and made him want to keep going forever. He thought of barging into the Monopoly game, of just going in there with everyone; but he went on to the kitchen, instead, where he flipped on the light and let the screen door slap behind him.

FROM

Da Vinci's Bicycle

1979

A Field of Snow on a Slope
of the Rosenberg

FOR A MAN WHO had seen a candle serenely burning inside a beaker
filled with water, a fine spawn of bubbles streaming upward from its
flame, who had been present in Zürich when Lenin with closed eyes
and his thumbs hooked in the armholes of his waistcoat listened to
the baritone Gusev singing on his knees Dargomyzhsky's *In Church
We Were Not Wed,* who had conversed one melancholy afternoon
with Manet's Olympia speaking from a cheap print I'd thumbtacked
to the wall between a depraved adolescent girl by Egon Schiele and
an oval mezzotint of Novalis, and who, as I had, Robert Walser of
Biel in the canton of Bern, seen Professor William James talk so long
with his necktie in his soup that it functioned as a wick to soak his
collar red and caused a woman at the next table to press her knuckles
into her cheeks and scream, a voyage in a hot-air balloon at the
mercy of the winds from the lignite-rich hills of Saxony Anhalt to the
desolate sands of the Baltic could precipitate no new shiver from my
paraphenomenal and kithless epistemology except the vastation of
brooding on the sweep of inconcinnity displayed below me like a
map and perhaps acrophobia.

The balloon had shot aloft at Bittersfeld while with handsome
Corsican flourishes and frisky rat-a-tat on the drum a silver cornet
band diminishing below us to a spatter of brass and gold played *The
Bear Went Over the Mountain.*

Cassirer lashed the anchor to the wicker taffrail and cried *auf
Wiedersehen* to the shrinking figures below, ladies in leghorn bonnets,
an engineer in a blue smock, an alderman waving his top hat, a
Lutheran minister holding his bible like a brick that he had just been

tossed, and little boys in caps and knee socks who envied our gaunt-lets, goggles, plaid mufflers, and telescope with fanatic eyes.

The winds into which we rose were as cold as mountain springs. Tattered wisps of clouds like frozen smoke hung around us. Unless you looked, you could not tell whether you sailed past the clouds or the clouds past you, and even then the Effect of Mach confused the eye, for the earth seemed to flow beneath the still gondola until this illusion could be dispelled, as when you look at a line drawing of a cube and sometimes see its far side as its front, Mach, who leaned over bridges and waited for the flip-flop of reality whereby he knew he was on a swift bridge flying down an immobile river, and none of us knows whether our train or the one beside us is sliding out of the station.

Cassirer turned and shook hands, gauntlet to gauntlet. I returned his toothy, Rooseveltian smile, though butterflies swarmed in my stomach, and a kitten tried to catch its tail.

Cassirer, able soul, adjusted blocks in tackle. Pink and violet clouds sank past us.

The balloon, O gorgeous memory, was as gaily painted as a Greek krater. An equatorial band paraded the signs of the zodiac around it. Red lozenges and green asterisks wreathed the top and neck. Rib-bons streamed from the nacelle. The first ballast of sand was pouring down on the earth with the untroubled spill of an hourglass. Our shadow flowed over a red tile roof, a barn, three Holstein cows, a railroad track.

There was a dust of ice in the February wind into which we rose swinging like a pendulum.

When the perspective cube swaps its front plane for its back, have we not seen Einstein's *Relativitätstheorie* with our own eyes? Or do we see the cube this way with one skill of the brain and that way with another? The left of the brain, where intuitions leap like lightning, controls the dextrous right hand, logic, speech, our sense of space. The right of the brain, where reason stands alert, controls the awk-ward left hand, suspicion, primal fear, our sense of time.

—Thus, Cassirer continued with a shout, the animal man is a chiasmus of complementary and contradictory functions.

This conversation had been going on for days. People used to talk to each other, back then, as I now talk to myself. But you are there, *ich bitte tausendmal um Verzeihung!* Can you hear, in this wind, the F-dur *Erwachen heiterer Empfindungen bei der Ankunft auf den Lande?* I can. Cassirer kept up a conversation as it bobbed into his head, while descending from a train, at a urinal, in his hip bath, from outside my bedroom door in the middle of the night.

—Our minds combine the hysteria of a monkey, he said, with the level intellect of an English explorer.

I cupped my ear to hear in the emptiness of the wind.

—Irrational faith, he said while upending a sack of sand, holds faithless reason above the waves.

I looked down at the plats of fields, villages, and roads. I felt the weight of my body drain away. My fingers clutching the wicker of the gondola were as strengthless as worms.

—You are white, he shouted.

—Vertigo, I shouted back.

—Now you are green.

—*Das Schwindelgefühl!*

—Brandywine? he offered, handing me a chill flask.

Ach, das Jungsein! Now that I have passed through them, I know that there are no middle years. I have gone from adolescence to old age. There is a photograph of me as a goggled aeronaut. I looked like an acrobat from the *époque bleue et rose* of that charming rascal Picasso. If only *der Graf* Rufzeichen could have seen me then! It would have been a shock worth arranging to confront the *adlig* old horse's behind with his melancholy butler at such an altitude.

Lisa would have screamed, and Herr Benjamenta of the Institute would have frowned his frown, rumpling the wrinkles of a vegetable marrow into his pedagogical brow.

Knolls, canals, fields, farms, slid below us. We were like Zeus in the *Ilias* when he surveys the earth from the mare's milk drinkers beyond the Oxus to the convivial herdsmen of Ethiopia.

—Altdorfer! Cassirer shouted. Dürer! Is this not, *mein geliebt* Walser, the view of beroofed and steepled Northern Europe you see from Brueghel's Tower of Babel? The splendor of it! Look at that haystack, that windmill, that Schloss. You can see greenhouses. Have you ever been taken so by the paralleleity of light?

We saw red and gold circus wagons on the turnpike, followed by elephants, each holding the tail of the next with its trunk.

Did Nietzsche go up in a balloon? After Nietzsche, as the wag said, there had to be Walser. Did Buonaparte? I tried to feel like each in turn, to lounge like Nietzsche, blind and postured, with some lines of Empedokles for Fräulein Lou, to pout my corporation like the *Empereur,* pocket my fingers in my weskit, and think Caesar.

But, *O Himmel,* it was Count Rufzeichen I wanted as a ravaged and outraged witness to my *Ballonfahrt.* It was as an orphan under his roof that I came nearest to belonging anywhere at all, except here, perhaps. Perhaps.

I arrived at his estate sneezing and ruffled a wild blustery day that had reddened my ears and rolled my stovepipe hat before me. Why Benjamenta had specified a stovepipe hat for going off to one's first position will be known only at the opening of the seals. To catch my hat I abandoned my cardboard suitcase to the mercy of the rain, which went for its seams. In the hat was my diploma, signed and sealed, from Herr Benjamenta's Institute for Butlers, Footmen, and Gentlemen's Gentlemen. My umbrella was the sort *Droschkenkutscher* saw their fares safely to shelter with, copious enough to keep dry a lady in bombazeen, bustle, and extensive fichu even if she were escorted by an *ukrainischer Befehlshaber* in court dress. The wind played kite with it.

My hat had hopped, leaving rings of its blacking on the gleaming wet of the flagstones. My umbrella tugged and swiveled, jerked and pushed. I ran one way for the suitcase, another for the stovepipe hat. Were anyone looking from the stately mansion, it was the grandfather of all umbrellas on two legs tiptoeing like a gryllus after a skating hat across a sheet of shining water they would see.

The cook Claribel had seen, and would allude to it thereafter as a sight that gave her pause.

Unsettled as my affiliation with the morose Count Rufzeichen had been, it was a masonic sodality compared with my and Claribel's crosscurrent encounters. Our disasters had been born in the stars.

It was she who met me at the door, challenge and hoot in her hen's eyes.

—Is this, I shouted over the wind, Schloss Dambrau?

To this she made no reply.

—I am Monsieur Robert, I said, the new butler.

She studied me and the weather, trying to decide which was the greater affront to remark upon.

—As you can see, she finally said, there is no butler here to answer the door. A cook, the which I am, can make her own meals, but a butler, like the new one you are, *ja?* cannot answer himself knocking at the door, *fast nie.*

I agreed to all of this.

—Would you guess I am Silesian? she next offered. Frau Claribel you may address me as. Why the last butler had to leave is not for one of my sex and respectability to say, I'm sure. What were you doing running in a crouch all over the drive? Furl your umbrella. Come in out of the wind, come in out of the rain.

I marched to my quarters, past a cast-iron Siegfried in the foyer, preceded by Frau Claribel with the mounted, cockaded Hessians, royal drum rolls, and jouncing flag of Haydn's *Symphonie militaire,* which came all adenoidal violins and tinny brass from a gramophone beyond a wall.

—*Der Graf* is very cultivated, she said of the music. He has tone, as you will see, Herr *Robehr.*

I approved of the Lakedaimonian bed in my room. And of the antique table where I was to spend so many hours by my candle, warming my stiff hands at a brazier. All my rooms have been like this, cramped cells for saint or criminal. Or patient. The chamberpot was decorated with a sepia and pink view of Vesuvius.

O Claribel, Claribel. No memory of her can elude for long our first *contretemps.* That is too bookish a word. Our wreck.

It was only the third day after my installment, just when the Count and I were blocking out the routine that would lead, from the very beginning, to my eventual banishment to a room above the Temperance Society of Biel for eight years, while archdukes died with bombs in their laps, ten million men were slaughtered, six million maimed, and all the money in the world five times over was borrowed at compound interest from banks. Solemn, hushed, sacred banks.

On my way in haste down the carpeted hall to answer the Count's bell, I would prance into a cakewalk, strutting with backward tail feather and forward toe. I would hunch my elbows into my side, as if to the sass of a cornet in a jazz band I would tip a straw hat to the house. And just before the library door I would do the war dance of Crazy Horse. Then, with a shudder to transform myself into a graduate of the Benjamenta Institute, I would turn the knob with one hand, smooth my hair with the other, and enter a supercilious butler deferential and cool.

—You rang, Herr Graf?

The old geezer would have to swivel around in his chair, an effect I could get by pausing at the periphery of his vision, a nice adjustment between being wholly out of sight and the full view of an indecorous frontal address.

—I rang, by Jove, didn't I? I wonder why.

—I could not say, Sir.

—Strange.

—You rang, Sir, unless by some inadvertence your hand jerked the bell cord, either out of force of habit, or prematurely, before the desire that would have prompted the call had formed itself coherently in your mind.

Count Rufzeichen thought this over.

—You heard the bell, did you, there in the recess?

—Positively, Sir.

—Didn't imagine it, I suppose, what?

—No, Sir.

—I'm damned, the Count said, gazing at his feet. Go away and let me think why I called you.

—If, Sir, you would jot down on a pad the reason for my summons, you would not forget it before my arrival.

—Get out!

—Very good, Sir.

We played such scenes throughout the day. I had just had some such mumpery with him before the first entanglement with Claribel's withered luck.

She, barefoot for scrubbing the stone steps down to her domain, had forked a lid off the stove onto the floor to pop on a stick of firewood, and as the best piece in the box was longish, Claribel stepped back the better to fit it in, putting a foot both naked and wet on the hot lid, and cried out for Jesus to damn it for a bugger and a shit britches.

I, meanwhile, coming belowstairs and hastening to see what her howl was about, stepped on the cake of soap riding there on the steps in a wash of suds. My foot slid out and up in a kick so thorough that I missed by a minim marking the ceiling with a soapy footprint.

My other foot, dancing for balance, dashed the bucket of water forward toward the hopping Claribel, where its long spill hissed when it flowed around the lid at about the same time that I, soaring as if from a catapult, rammed her in a collision that knocked us breathless and upside-down through the kitchen door and into a dogcart drawn by a goat which was backed up to the steps for a convenient unloading of cowflop to mulch the rhododendrons.

Startled, the goat bleated and bolted, taking us through the kitchen garden, across the drive, into and out of the roses, around the well, by the stables, and as far as the chicken run, where a yellow wheel, unused to such velocities and textures of terrain, parted from the axle and went on its own to roll past backing pigs, a cat who mounted a tree at its coming, a cow who swallowed her cud, and after some delirious circles, wobbled and lay among the wasps and winey apples in the orchard.

Claribel and I, tilted out by the departure of the wheel, sat leg over leg in the compost of manure, Claribel screaming, I silent.

THIS WAY. The bracken is very fine a little farther on. Trajectory is all. I was born on Leonardo da Vinci's birthday the year the bicycle suddenly became popular all over the world, the seventh of eight. My father ran a toy shop in which you could also buy hair oil, boot blacking, and china eggs. My mother died when I was sixteen, after two years of believing that she was a porcupine that had been crowned the queen of Bulgaria, the first sign that I was to end up here.

My brother Ernst, grown enough to be teaching school while I was still in rompers, began to think that he was being haunted by malevolent marksmen. Schizophrenia. He died in 1916, Hermann, a geographer in Bern, in 1919. Fanny and Lisa are well placed, Oskar works with money. Karl is the success in the family. God knows how he can stomach Berlin.

I was at Waldau before I came here, into the silence. And before that—look at the rabbit standing on its hind legs!—I was variously a student, a bank clerk, an actor, a poet, a sign painter, a soldier—I have seen those white butterflies as thick as snow over clover—an insurance salesman, a waiter, a vendor of puppets, a bill sticker, a janitor, a traveling salesman for a manufacturer of prosthetic limbs, a novelist, a butler, an archivist for the canton of Bern, and a distributor of temperance tracts. I've always belonged decidedly to the tribe of Whittington, but of course the bells rang when I couldn't hear them, and when a cat was to be invested I had none. Franklin was of the tribe, and Lipton the British merchant, and Mungo Park, and Lincoln and Shakespeare. I got as far as being a servant. Diogenes and Aesop were slaves.

Freedom is a choice of prisons. One life, one death. We are an animal that has been told too much, we could have done with far less. The way up and the way down are indeed the same, and Heraklit had been wiser to add that rising is an upward fall.

I often put myself to sleep by wondering if there could be a mountain road so steep and yet so zigzag of surface that in seeming to go down an incline one is actually going up?

How do *they* put themselves to sleep, Mann of the field marshal's face and Hesse with his gurus and Himalayan Sunday Schools? Imagine being interested like Hesse in the Hindu mind! Once in Berlin I talked to an Indian from Calcutta or Poona or Cooch. *Chitter chitter,* he said. Mann is also interested in these little brown monkey men with women's hands.

—What is the meaning of life? the little Hindu asked me for an opener.

I had the distinct impression that he was switching his tail and flouncing his cheek ruff. Soon he would be searching for lice in my hair.

—You do not know! In the west you are materialistic, rational, scientific. You listen too much to the mind, too little to the soul. You are children in spirit. You have not *karma.*

We stood nose to nose, toe to toe.

—You have not deep wisdom from meditation a long time reaching back to ages already old when Pletto and Aristettle were babbies in arms.

—Indeed not, I said.

—You admit! the Hindu squealed, showing a gold tooth and a black. Of course you admit for you know it is true ancient Indian wisdom is universal transcendental thought as studied by Toolstoy in Russia, yes, H. B. Stove and Thorough in United States.

He chittered on, something about God and man being like a mother cat with a kitten in her teeth and man and God being like a monkey and its infant holding on, and something about emptying the mind when what I wanted to empty was my bladder.

O glide of eye and sizzle of tongue! And Rathenau found me a job in German Samoa. And he was shot, like a mad dog, because, as his assassin Oberleutnant Kern explained, *he was the finest man of our age, combining all that is most valuable of thought, honor, and spirit, and I couldn't bear it.* I told this to the doctor here, in an unguarded moment, and he asked me why I was obsessed by such violence. Cruelty, I replied, is sentimentality carried to its logical conclusion.

—Ah! he said.

The psychiatric *ah.*

—We can never talk, I said, for all my ideas are symptoms for you to diagnose. Your science is suspicion dressed in a tacky dignity.

—Herr Walser, Herr Walser! You promised me you would not be hostile.

They are interested in nothing, these doctors. They walk in their sleep, looking with the curiosity of cows at those of us who are awake even in our dreams.

A moth slept flat on my wall. I watched its feelers, speckled feathers as remote from my world as I from the stars, sheepsilver wings eyed with apricot and flecked with tin. It had dashed at the bulb of my lamp. Its fury was like a banker's after money. And now it was weary and utterly still. Did it dream? The Englander Haldane had written of its enzymes without killing a single moth, and wore bedbugs in a celluloid pod on his leg to drink his blood.

It is in Das Evangelium the brother of rust and thieves. Surely its sleep is like that of fish, an alert sloth.

Now it has fluttered onto the map above my desk, an old woodcut map from a book, the river Euphrates running up through it in a dark fullness of rich veins, the Garden of Eden below, the stout mountains of Armenia sprinkled along the top, a great tower and swallow-tailed pennon to mark Babylon, trees as formal as pine cones at the terrestrial paradise, with Adam and Eve as naked as light bulbs except for Akkadian skirts of tobacco sheaves, Greek and Hebrew names among Latin like flowers among leaves, a lion to the northwest sitting in Armenia and bigger than a mountain, a beast rich in horns and hair stepping west from the Caspian Sea, a route pompous with Alexander's cities, brick walls and fig groves of Scripture, Caiphat up from the Gulf of Persia, which Sindbad gazed upon and where bdellium is to be had, Bahrim Insula a pearl fishery, Eden with its four rivers green and as straight as canals, a grove of cypress that was felled to build the Ark, purple Mousal, Babylon a city of brick and a hundred temples to gods with wings like aeroplanes, with Picassoid eyes and Leonardonian beards, Ur of the Chaldees with its porched and gabled house of Abraham, Noah's city Chome Thamanon, Omar's Island, with mosque, the Naarda of Ptolemy where is a famous school of the Jews, Ararat's cone, Colchis with its fleece of gold, Phasis the country of pheasants, Cappadocia, Assyria, Damascus under an umbrella of date palms.

And then I saw that the moth was inside the light bulb.

Because, I said when asked why I am here, the world was in defiance of its own laws.

At the foot of Herr Rufziechen's grand stairs stood a cast-iron Siegfried braced with a boar-sticker and buckler outsinging a surge of Wagnerian wind that tilted his horns, butted his beard, and froze his knees. Did he have to be dusted? Thoroughly, thoroughly. Beyond him, in steep gloom, rose the stairs in a curve of crimson and oak.

On a stepladder, flipping the face of iron Siegfried with a turkey duster, I, remembering that if you stare through a window into a snowfall the room will rise and the snow stand still, as when down front close to a theater curtain, the audience sinks grandly, to trumpets, discovering below a red Tannhäuser kneeling beside an embroidered Venus singing *Zu viel, Zu viel, O dass ich nun erwachte!* saw

Count Rufzeichen gliding from the library with his nose in a book and Claribel the cook backing toward him, the mock orange in her arms. The precision with which they would collide was inevitable and perverse.

—*Zu viel!* I cried.

Rammed from behind, Claribel screamed, heaved the mock orange upward, and sat.

I tottered, embraced Siegfried, and lost the ladder under my dancing toes.

The mock orange fell upside down on Count Rufzeichen, filling his lap with earth and roots. It was as if an allegory of Horticulture, with Donor, had fallen out of a picture onto the museum floor.

The ladder completed its fall across Rufzeichen's shins, inciting him into a jumping-jack flip over Claribel, transferring the mock orange's empty bucket from his head to hers, which made her screams now sound hollow, as if from the depths of a well.

GLIDING OVER the firelit carpet with velvet steps, placing the tureen before my lord, who touches his napkin to his moustache, I can savor again the condition of my well-being, along with the aroma of leek and broth that steams up when I remove the lid with a gesture worthy of the dancers of Bali, namely that Rufzeichen has put me back together, suave foot, accurate hand, impeccable diction.

Genius is time.

There was, I knew, and remembered with fondness, a professor at the Sorbonne who electrocuted himself while lecturing, or electrocuted himself so nearly that he found that he was suddenly in a corner just under the ceiling, light as a Chagall bridegroom full of champagne. And yet he could see himself still lecturing below, calmly, giving no indication that an ox's weight of lightning had crashed through his body.

Then he realized that his feet, shod and gaitered, were on opposite sills. His torso was in orbit around the lamp. His left arm was in the cloakroom nervously fingering a galosh, his right caressed a periodic table of the elements. His rich, musically modulated voice lectured on about ohms and circuits, resistance and watts.

It was my own parable. I had searched for wisdom about the

slump of my soul and the sootiness of my spirit in the accounts of vastations by the American Jameses, father and son, who suffered terrible New England moments when all significance drained from the world, when the immediate fortune of life was despair, disease, death. In utter futility shone the sun, man squandered the little time he had alive, a sweet Tuesday here, a golden autumn Sunday there, grubbing for money to pay the butcher, the landlord, and the tailor. The butcher slaughtered innocent animals who were incapable of sin and folly, of ambition or lies, so that one could, by way of a cook enslaved for a pittance and a wife enslaved for naught, gnaw its flesh and after a period of indigestion and indolence from overfeeding, squat over a chamberpot and drop turds and piss for a servant to carry, holding his nose, to the lime pit.

I had thought my despair was Kierkegaard's sickness unto death that pleasure cloys and pain corrodes. But, no, it was rather the Sorbonne professor's shock. One came to pieces. One used the very words. You had to pull yourself together again.

Feeding the pages of three novels into the fire in Berlin, standing in the rain at my father's grave, writing my thousandth *feuilleton*, climbing the dark stairs to any of the forty rooms I've rented: no one movement of foot or heart muscle was the hobbler, no one man's evasion the estranger.

—Another pig's foot, your lordship?

—And a little more suet, thank you kindly, Robert.

White tile, thermometers, blood-pressure charts, urine specimens, and spasms in the radiator pipes; what color and tone there had been at Rufzeichen's! The carpet, a late Jugendstil pattern of compact circles in lenticular overply, rusty orange, Austrian brown, and the blue of Wermacht lapels, had dash, and the furniture was Mackintosh, smartly modern in its severity while recalling the heaviest tradition of knightly chairs and ladylike settles, sideboards as large as wains and a desk at which the Kaiser could plan a dress parade. My eye appreciated the dull books around him, china shepherdesses, views of Florence and Rome, a sepia reproduction of the Sistine Chapel ceiling, crossed cavalry sabers, a teakwood dragon in a rage, candlesticks held aloft by fat babies tiptoe on the noses of dolphins, a loud clock.

An iron elk stood in a dim recess beyond double doors in the far wall.

AND THEN, pigeon-toed and watching the ground before him as if backtracking for something lost, there was the new patient, Fomich, as his wife or sister called him. The first time I saw him I did not like his silly smile. The mad smile in their own way, as puppets step, with a jerk rather than civilized deliberation. The smile of Fomich was that of the imp, of the red goblin in the corner of Füssli's *Titania und Bottom*. Smirk and scowl together it was.

It was the outward concession of inner reserve, two proud men meeting, each believing the other to be of higher rank.

—*Kak tsiganye!* he complained to his sister or wife.

And then I saw the muscles bunched in his shoulders that had strained the threads of the armscye apart, the heft of his chest, the improbable narrowness of his hips. Hero, with wing, grounded.

They took a walk together every morning and afternoon, solicitous woman and elfin man. Sometimes he would stop, put his heels together, flex his knees, and pass his hands in a sweep from one hip to the other.

One day, to my disbelieving gaze, he jumped over a rose bush without so much as a running start. Faces appeared at windows to watch.

He jumped back over the rose bush, his eyes sleepy and sad.

IT WAS LIKE striding over a sea of gelatin, that bell-stroke swing of our nacelle through the rack of the upper air on elastic wicker, wind thrumming the frapping with the elation of Schumann strings *allegro molto vivace*.

We talked by cupping hands and shouting into each other's ears. Benjamin Franklin, Cassirer said, had wanted a balloon for moving about the streets of Philadelphia, rooftop high above the Quakers and Indians. He was to have hitched it to horses, a godlike man indeed.

—Ach, les Montgolfier, Joseph and Etienne! In those days they thought smoke was a gas, as right as they were wrong, as with all knowledge. A transparent blue October day they bundled the physi-

Whereupon, weeping with such feeling that both cheeks shone like glass, the old party hugged himself so furiously that his coat split down the back. The sound of this was that of a dry limb cracked by wind from a tree, and he went limber as if unstrung.

The left half of his coat slid, sleeve and all, onto the sidewalk, followed by the right half, sleeve and all.

The collar, I considered, drawing closer, should have held the two halves together, but no, upon inspection, I saw that it was a coat, Moravian or Sephardic, of the kind that had no collar.

A scarf, which even now, as the old party was running back and forth imploring God and the gendarmerie to witness that he was a victim of some untoward fracture of natural law, snagged on the spike of an area railing and whipped away with an elastic flounce, never to be seen on this earth by its owner again.

The waywardness of accidents, I mused, can go only so far until it collides with the laws of probability or the collapse of its martyr.

The old party sat down on the sidewalk and wept into his hands. The gentleman with the beard came to his aid, prefacing his remarks by saying kindly that he had seen all that had happened. Here the old party gasped, alluded to his heart, and fell backward.

—I do believe, said the nurse, that he is having some sort of fit.

—*Zu hilfe! Zu hilfe!* cried the bearded gentleman.

—I will do an imitation of this, said the little girl, rolling back her eyes and grabbing her throat, that will make Ermintrude hate herself for a week.

—Remember that you are in public, said the nurse.

—So is he, said the little girl.

—And it is ill-bred in both of you, said the nurse, to make a spectacle on a city street.

A crowd gathered, from which a slender man in dark glasses, explaining that his uncle was a pharmacist in Lichtenstein, advised that the old party's waistcoat be undone. Deftly the gentleman undid fourteen buttons, disclosing trousers that came up to the armpits in the manner of the English. The flies of these were undone as far as the navel, fourteen more buttons, and indeed the old party groaned and breathed more freely, it seemed.

—*Polizei!* screamed the nurse.

The laces of his boots should be untied, the Lichtenstein pharmacist's nephew said, and the suspenders of his stockings loosened, for circulation's sake.

—I will, said the bearded gentleman, take his watch, wallet, tie pin, and ring for safekeeping, lest they tempt someone here in the crowd.

—My watch! squealed the old party, kicking with such indignation that both boots leapt off his feet. A dog got one and made off with the agility of a weasel. The other bounced into the gutter, where it lay forlorn and strange in the brief moment before a policeman arriving on the trot shot it along the curbing to drop into a drain. We could all hear it bumping on its way through gurgling water to the river Aar.

—Let us see if his name is written inside his shirt, said the policeman, lifting the old party by the armpits and taking off his waistcoat.

—What is this? he exclaimed, peeling a mustard plaster from the old party's back.

—That, said the pharmacist's nephew, is probably the cause of his fit. It is a poultice of asafoetida, mustard, and kerosene such as country doctors prescribe for pulmonary and liver complaints. It is too strong, as you can smell, and has induced an apoplexy. Take off his shirt and undervest to air his back.

Struggling to arrange the old party, the bearded gentleman inadvertently stood on both his loose stocking suspenders, anchoring them, so that as the body was dragged backward the better to extract the long shirt tail from inside the seat of the trousers, the elastic suspenders stretched their limit, snapped, flipped, and catapulted themselves and stockings together off the old party's feet, one flying into my face. And, O, how I was gratified to have joined the event with something of my own, and I sneezed, casting stocking and suspender into the shopping basket of a cook who, later and at home, dropped them into her stove, making a hex. The other was got from the air by a dog who had envied his fellow the previous shoe.

At this moment, crazed with fury and mindless with disbelief, the old party fought his way up to choke the policeman, losing trousers and drawers as he stood.

—Attack the law, will you! the policeman said.

—Where am I? the old party cried. *Who* am I? What has happened?

He was as naked as the minute he was born, minus, of course, an umbilical cord.

—*Scheisse und verdammt!* It comes back to me that I am Brigade-general Schmalbeet. That's who I am! General Schmalbeet!

With this he gave the policeman a kick in the groin that doubled him over.

Then he fell backward, an arc of urine following him down. Everyone backed away. When I peeped around the first corner I had turned, I saw the policeman wetting a pencil with his tongue while opening a notebook, and a dog dragging away the old party's trousers, and another throwing his drawers into the air and barking.

MANET'S OLYMPIA, thumbtacked to the wall between a depraved adolescent girl by Egon Schiele and an oval mezzotint of Novalis, told me about the world's first painting executed *en plein air*. This was the work of her creator's *Doppelgänger* Monet, Manet with an *omega*.

—I am confused already, said I. But talk on, for it adds purpose to my staring at you, at your complacent Parisian eyes, your dangling mule, your hand so decorously audacious.

—*Êtes-vous phallocrate?*

—*L'homme est un miroir omnigénérique, tantôt plan, tantôt convexe, tantôt concave ou cylindrique, donnant à l'objet réfléchi des dimensions variées.*

—*Vous êtes phallocrate.*

—*Suis-je donc?*

—*Ce ne fait rien.*

Her Ionic shoulders rose an ironic trifle. There was the wisp of a smile in the corners of her mouth, the merest hint of laughter in her eyes.

—When, she said, in the pellucid green air of Fontainebleau, Claude Monet had posed his model and touched his brush to the world's first *plein air* canvas, he was hit on the back of the head by a discus and knocked senseless.

Her expression did not change as she made this statement.

—A discus?

—*Un disque.*

—The discobolus, she continued, who presently appeared on the anxious trot to ask the bloody impressionist and the screaming Madame Monet if they had seen his quoit was a bassetted and spatted Englishman whose carp's mouth and plaid knickerbockers sprang from the pages of Jerome K. Jerome.

Count Rufzeichen, anglophile and sportsman, dressed so. It was his sedulous imitation of the English that had driven him to hire a butler, and thus I came to tread his soft carpets, never tiring of their luxurious silence, or of the rose fragrance of English tea, or of making Herr Rufzeichen shake his wattles.

One way was to be deaf to his summons, letting the butler's bell jangle in vain. After awhile, the old apteryx would come puffing and snuffling along, looking into rooms. Finding me in the greenhouse, he would splay his fingers and shout.

—What in the name of God are you doing?

—Sir, I am observing nature, I would reply. I see, however, that in lending my attention to the limpidity of the air, the melodiousness of the cuckoo and the lowing of the horned cattle I have fallen into negligence.

—Into sloth, said Herr Rufzeichen.

—The cows made a kind of bass for the treble of the cuckoo.

—Into impudence.

—Your worship rang?

—To little purpose, to no purpose, Monsieur Robert. Whatever I wanted you for before, it's a liver attack I'm having at the moment.

The Count trembled into a chair.

—Would you wish a glass of Perrier, Sir?

—*Doppelkohlensaures Natron.*

The Count pulled a pocket handkerchief big as a map of Europe from his sleeve, wadded it with both hands, and wiped away the sweat that had beaded on his forehead.

I held the soda on a silver salver under his nose. The draught drunk, hiccups set in. After the third hiccup, a belch baritone and froggy.

OUTSIDE THE ASYLUM GATES a brass band huffed and thumped with brazen sneezes, silver whiffets, thundering sonorities and a detonating drum, the descant hitched together by a fat woman in a Tyrolese hat and the Erlkönig's longcoat that flocked upon her hips as she squeezed and pulled a Polish accordion as big as a sheep, dipping her knees on the *saltarelli* and rolling her eyes in a clown's gloat.

The man Fomich danced around his pleased sister, seesawing his shoulders in a backward monkeyshine of steps, and as he shot into the air right over his sister's head, pausing there awhile as if all the clocks in the world had stopped, a lunatic shouted that Hitler is the seventh disaster in Nostradamus and invited all within hearing to join the Brotherhood of the Illuminati without further delay.

—Quite gay, is it not? I said to the attendant, tears in my eyes.

The band was charging with piston gallop through something rhapsodic, Hungarian, and tacky.

Who was this franion? There was a *grivoiserie* about him that smacked of Berlin, and of things brooded on in Mallarmé, Rimbaud, Apollinaire.

—Literature, I said to the listless woman beside me on the bench, has become a branch of psychology, of politics, of power, of persuasion, of housekeeping. In ancient times . . .

—When Jesu was a little boy, she said, taking interest and joining her hands on her knees.

—In ancient times literature was a story for people to hear. And the person who heard it could tell it to another. Now everything is on paper, too complex to remember.

—Do you love Jesu? she asked.

—One does not write in this terrible age. We do not make chairs, we make money. We do not make shoes, we make money. They sniff it, banker and shopkeeper alike, as gallants used to inhale the perfume of a mistress's handkerchief. They goggle when they see it, they are willing and eager to throw boys into the spew of machine guns and fogs of cyanide gas, they are abustle to marry their daughters to toothless bankers, to halitosic financiers with hernias the size of a baby's head. Francs, yen, shillings, pesos, krönen, dollars, lire, money is the beauty of the world. They suck shekels and play with themselves.

—Jesu would not like that, she said mournfully.

—After all, I said, what a beautiful thing it is, not to be, but to have been a genius.

The dancer had collapsed across the way, was weeping and was being consoled by his sister.

—Does God come to you in the night, she asked, with a lamp and a puppy for you to hold?

—God, I said, is the opposite of Rodin.

—The eyes of God are as beautiful as a cow's.

—Everything else has gone wrong, but not money. Everything, everything is spoiled, halved, rotted, robbed of grace and splendor. Our cities are vanishing from the face of the earth. Big chunks of nothing are taking up the space once occupied by houses and palaces.

—You are very serious, she said.

—Money precludes mercy.

—Did you have money and lose it? Jesu would not mind that.

—I have always been poorer than the poor.

Attendants had come to take the man Fomich back to his cell. He was saying terrible things about man's sexuality, so that the woman beside me stopped her ears. I could hear something about the hot haunches of goats and wild girls in Arcadia kissing something and something mad with music.

If I could talk again with Olympia, she would tell me. She would know.

Is it not preposterous that a shoe would go the journey of a foot?

And on a fine English day in the high Victorian year 1868, the year of the first bicycle race and the Trades Union Congress at Manchester, of *The Moonstone* and *The Ring and the Book* and of the siege of Magdala, four men gathered at Ashley House in London, a house leafy with Virginia creeper, its interior harmoniously dark and bright, like an English forest, dark with corners and doors and halls, with mahogany and teak and drapes as red as cherries, bright with windows, Indian brass, and lamps like moons, Lord Lindsay pollskepped with the hatchels of a cassowary, Lord Adare whose face looked like a silver teapot, and the galliard Captain Wynne.

They stood Englishly around a bandy-legged Scot with a thrummy beard. His name was Home. Daniel Douglas Home.

—Tack a wheen heed, he said, throwing back his neck and arms as if throttled by an angel from above.

In contempt of gravity, then, he raised his left leg and his right, and lay out flat on the empty air.

—Stap my vitals! swore Captain Wynne. The bugger's floating! Lord Lindsay held up Lord Adare, Lord Adare Lord Lindsay.

—Meet me, gasped the horizontal Scot, in the tither room.

With a hunch to get started, he slid forward before their paralyzed gaze, jerking a whit on the first slide, and then floated smoothly, silently out the window.

A distant chime of church bells: which no one heard.

—I think I shall cat, said Lord Lindsay.

—I have peed myself, said Lord Adare.

The feet of D. D. Home appeared in the next window: he had turned right. His sturdy Glaswegian trousers next, his plaid waistcoat, his arms hanging down slightly, fingers spread, his heroic Adam's apple, eyes staring upward.

His shadow three stories below flowed over rose bushes, over rolled grass as level as water, a sundial, the body of a gardener who had looked up, commended his soul to God, and passed out.

Lords and captain bestirred themselves, dashed into each other, and ran down the hall on uncooperative legs. Only the door to a room on the other side of the house was open, and into this they stumbled, breathing like rabbits. Adare screamed as he saw Home entering the window feet first, calm as a corpse.

Midroom he hung in the air, chuckling.

Then he tilted downward and stood as proud as Punch.

—Bewitched, by the Lord! said Captain Wynne. We are all bewitched.

Lord Lindsay's hair had turned white.

Yet all three signed depositions that they had witnessed a human Scot float out the window of Ashley House and in again from the other side.

Home died soon after.

—And now, I said to Herr Rufzeichen, how shall we ever know otherwise?

—Englishmen, said Rufzeichen, of all people! Sort of thing that goes on every day in India, I believe?

AT THE BENJAMENTA INSTITUTE I was like a cuckoo in a nest of wrens. I had failed at just about everything and the other students of the art of butlering had failed only predestination, and even that wasn't certain, for we were told daily that Joseph was a butler in Egypt and Daniel one in Babylon. Their slain and risen god was Dick Whittington. The rotten stockings they darned in the evenings were Whittington's, their cold beds were Whittington's, their slivers of soap, their piecemeal and unmatching shoe laces, their red ears and round shoulders.

A feature of failure is having to do over again what the successful sailed through once. My adolescence has been waiting for me when my feet hit the floor every morning these seventy years. My God, what a prospect! An education, a job, a wife, daughters to admire, sons to counsel, vacations at Ostend, retirement, grandchildren, banquets in my honor, statesmen and a mountain of flowers at my funeral, my sepulcher listed in the tourist guide to the cemetery.

And in middle age I was enrolled in a school for butlers.

The dormitory was upstairs, a long room with too many beds too close together. It was neither military in its effect nor schoolish, neither neat nor messy. It was a picture of despair and of making do.

I remember it all as a dream in which confusion had seeped into the grain of reality. I remember yellow-haired Hans, and defeated Töffel, of the bitten fingernails and wetted bed, the clever Kraus and his intolerable and boring cynicism, the flippant and windy Fuchs who cried under the covers at night. We all led secret lives in full view of each other.

Herr and Frau Benjamenta, accomplished frauds, came and went like attendants in a hospital. All day we heard homilies and half-finished sentences from retired Gymnasium teachers and had lessons in ironing trousers and setting tables. We heard Scripture at dawn and before bedtime. Of all this I made my novel *Jakob von Gunten,* a new kind of book, and except for a few of the essays I wrote for newspapers, essays written with Olympia's full gaze upon my back, the best thing that I leave the world. Mann stole it, and Kafka stole it, and Hesse stole it, and were talked about. I have been invisible all my life.

I have heard that Kafka mentioned me in the cafés of Prague. I dare say.

You cannot know, *O Leser,* how long it is possible to sit on the side of a bed staring at the floor.

DOKTOR ZWIEBEL looked me dead in the eye. He had the nose of Urbino. Somewhere, deep in his ancestry, back before time began to tick in seconds, when all the earth was a forest of ferns growing in Lake Tchad, there had been a rhinoceros.

—Tell me, Herr Weisel, he began.

—Walser, said I.

—Just so, said Doktor Zwiebel, looking down at the folder before him. Tell me, Herr Walser, you have never I see been married?

—Never, said I, but almost.

I sighed, the doctor sighed.

—How do you mean, *almost?* Remember that anything you tell me goes no further than my files. You are free, indeed I urge you, to tell me all.

—Fräulein Mermet, I said. There was a Fräulein Mermet. I fell in love with her. She regarded me kindly.

—*Pfring! Pfring!* sang the telephone on the desk.

—*Ja? Zwiebel hier.* Seasick? Promethazine hydrochloride and dextroamphetamine sulfate in a little lemon juice. Yes, that is correct. I will look in later. Goodbye. That was the duty officer. She says a patient who thinks he is Napoleon has run into rough weather off Alexandria. Do you know, Herr Weisel . . .

—Walser.

— . . . that an alarming number of attendants at sanatoria end up as patients? You may know Aufwartender Futter, with a remarkably long head and three moles in a line across his forehead? Just so! He was a patient here for some months, paranoid schizophrenic, thought that everybody in Switzerland was turning into money. He convinced his ward attendant of it, who announced to me one day that he wanted to be put in the bank so as to be drawing interest. Futter thought this was so funny that he emerged from his fantasy, and the two exchanged places, Futter having been fired from his job on the Exchange. Excellent arrangement. Now where were we? You were telling me about your wife, I believe.

—But I didn't marry her.

—Didn't marry who? If she was your wife . . .

—I was about to answer your question, Herr Doktor. You had asked how I was almost married. There was a Fräulein Mermet. I loved her and I believed that she loved me. We wrote many letters to each other. We spent Sunday afternoons in the park. She would fall against my arm laughing for no reason at all. Macaroons . . .

—How many brothers and sisters have you, Herr Weisel?

—Two sisters, Fanny and Lisa, four brothers, Ernst, Hermann, Oskar, and Karl, who is the noted painter and illustrator. He lives in Berlin.

—Your last position seems to have been that of Archivist for the Canton of Bern. Why, may I ask, did you leave?

—I resigned.

—You did not find the pay sufficient or the work congenial?

—We had a difference of opinion as to whether Guinea is in Africa or South America. My superior said I had insulted him. I tied his shoelaces together when he was asleep at his desk one afternoon.

Doktor Zwiebel made a note and fixed it to the folder with a paper clip. Something caught his attention that made him jump. He looked more closely and then glared at me.

—It says here that you have previously been treated for neuroses by one Dr. Gachet, to whom you were recommended by Vincent Van Gogh, and by Dr. Raspail on the advice of V. Hugo. What does this mean? Did you give this information to the attendant who filled out these forms?

—*Jawohl, Herr Doktor.*

—Then there are Van Goghs still alive? Of the great painter's family?

—Oh, yes, most certainly. The nephew is very like his uncle, carrot-haired, *sensitif,* very Dutch.

—And the Hugo here is descended from the noted French poet?

—That is right.

—And Gachet and Raspail, they are French or Swiss psychiatrists?

—French.

—How long were you under treatment by them?

POLITICIAN, with rump. Statesman, with nose. Banker, with eye. You shuffle francs, and stack them, as a priest shifts and settles Gospel and Graal upon the altar. The clerks at their sacred books, compounding interest, the vice-presidents, first, second, and third, all who know the combination of the safe, the tellers with their sponges, rubber stamps, and bells, these are the only hierophants left whose rites are unquestioned and unquestionable, whose sanctions can be laid upon orphan and Kaiser alike, upon factory and church. Here the shepherd's only ewe and the widow's last pfennig are demanded, and received, with perfect comfort of conscience and thrill of rectitude surpassing the adoration of Abraham honing his knife.

In 1892, when I was fourteen, I left the Gymnasium and applied for the post of teller in a bank. In this journey my dog surprised a young kid, and seized upon it, and I, running in to take hold of it, caught it and saved it alive from the dog. A letter I sent in reply to a notice in the *Züricher Zeitung* included a phrase from Vergil, the noted Mantuan, and listed as references Hetty Green and J. Pierpont Morgan. I was nevertheless instructed by return post to appear for an interview. I had a great mind to bring it home if I could; for I had often been musing whether it might be possible to get a kid or two and so raise a breed of tame goats, which might supply me when my powder and shot should be all spent.

At the bank I was taken in hand by a kind of assistant priest and put in a gorgeous room to wait for my interview. I had never seen such a carpet, such high windows, or so polished an inkstand.

A door opened. A man in a Roman helmet, leaning on a bamboo cane, limped in. He had cut himself shaving and a sticking plaster, blood at its edges, ran the length of his cheek.

—You are Robert Walser? he asked, reading from a card.

I said I was.

—We are in Albania, he intoned, near the slopes of Ararat. I am the Third Vice-President. Our cellars are full of gold, silver, stocks, notes. As there is a God . . .

And then the door was filled with people, a man with lots of whiskers, clerks, bald men wringing their hands.

—Get him! said Whiskers. Take him to my office. Schmidt, I have told you and told you!

They took the Third Vice-President away, with some effort, leaving me to the gaze of a man who looked at me from top to toe, with disapproval.

—Those shoes, he said, will never do.

RUFZEICHEN in alpine hat, tweed jacket, plus fours, Austrian walking shoes with shredded and tasseled tongues, a stout stick, cigar, monocle, green knit gloves. I came behind in my black English butler's suit, bowler and umbrella, carrying a picnic basket and a plaid rug.

The count held up his hand without looking back.

—Here, he said.

I spread the rug over meadow flowers and laid the count a place. The silverware tinkled strangely in the fine emptiness of the out of doors. The wineglass would not sit straight. Gnats assembled around the count.

I stood at a respectful distance.

—I tell you, Robert, he said through a mouthful of sandwich, these things did not happen before you came. No, I assure you, they did not, decidedly did not. Our cook Claribel is, I believe, possessed.

—Possessed, your lordship?

—Salt in my coffee, eggshells in the omelet, a glove in the soup . . .

—Most distressing.

—It is mad.

It occurred to me then, who could say why, that the dinosaurs I had been reading the count about from a British magazine were not great lizards but chickens as large as a Lutheran church. No one has seen their skins, or, as it may be, their feathers. Only bones survive. They had three toes, long necks, beaks, dainty forelegs which were possibly wings as useless as a dodo's. It may have been the count's savaging of a chicken wing that supplied the idea.

I mentioned the possibility to him, by way of conversation. We were, after all, the only living creatures in miles, give or take a remote eagle and a swarm of gnats.

He gave me a very strange look.

HUMAN NATURE cannot write. *Ich schrieb das Buch, weil sie mir nicht gestattete, meine Tage in ihrer Nähe zu verbringen, mich ihr zu widmen, was ich mit wahrer Lust gelan hätte.* And in the irony of money all ironies are lost.

Potina, Roman deity altarless and distracted, had, in the way of the gods, neither watch, calendar, nor sense of time. She dropped down into the streets of Bern one day, in front of a trolley which almost struck her. Her dress was a thousand years out of fashion, a white wool smock brown with age and riddled hem to yoke by moths who had nibbled the diapered stole of Julia Domna and the stockings of Victoria. Her duty among the immortals was the digestion by infants of their first spoonful of pabulum, whether Ashanti mothers chewing sago and letting it into their babies' mouths, Eskimo matrons poking blubber down pink gullets, or Helvetian mamas spooning into lips open as wide as an eaglet's goat cheese and honey.

Whatever, whenever, wherever she was, Dea Potina rubbed her eyes. These dark places behind doors, these wagons that rolled without oxen: these people had married into the gods. She smelled lightning everywhere and saw lamps burning inside crystal fruit, without air to feed the flame. *Apollon!* she prayed, *spell me those written words.* And the old voice with the cave echo in it, and the snake hiss, told her that the words said, all of them, one way or another, *coin.*

But that building is surely a temple. In truth, said Apollon. They are all temples, and all built to hold coins. Then, she said, I am in the country of the dead, and yet I see smiling children, and I smell lightning, which is never of the underrealm. It is the fashion now, Apollon said, to live as if all were Domos Hades. Some ages fancied the ways of the Olympian gods, some the Syrian Mother, some the wastes of Poseidon, some the living gold of wheat and light and children.

Now they have cut from Dis's realm his gleaming metals and his black slime, his sulphur and salts and poisons, murderous things that they seem to enjoy. But most of all they fancy coin.

EINE ANSICHTSKARTE (Manet's *Monet in His Studio Boat*) from Olympia: Yesterday I saw a woman on the streetcar with her little boy who had his head stuck in his chamber pot and was being taken to the doctor to have it pried off. It was over his eyes and ears, and all you could see of him was his mouth open and howling. His mama was in tears, as was her son, though it was probably *pipi* she kept wiping away. *Herzlich,* Ollie.

IN THE ETERNAL July of Egypt a scribe once wrote on papyrus *she was more comely in her body than all the other women in this world*—a

FEATHER, *ah,* and a COIL OF ROPE, *oo,* she, a SHEPHERD'S CROOK and a LOAF, *sett,* was, a LUTE, ASP, and MOUTH, *nefer,* comely, an OWL, *m,* in, a TWISTED ROPE, LOAF, ARM, SHOULDER, THREE, SEATED WOMAN, SHEPHERD'S CROOK and LOAF, *hatset,* her body, MOUTH, *er,* than, BOLT, LOAF, and SEATED WOMAN, *set,* more than, VAGINA, LOAF, and SEATED WOMAN, *khemt,* woman, BOWL and LOAF, *nebt,* any, WATER, LOAF, and DUALITY, *enti,* who, OWL, *m,* in, DUCK, *pa,* the, LAND, *ta,* world, GRAIL, MOUTH, and ASP, *terf,* entire.

He wrote, sighed, and passed the leaf to a binder, who stitched it to the next leaf and rolled it around a stick. An *anu* read the line various evenings to the dash of a seshsesh and the indolent whine of a sa, and lords listened, their brown hands on their square knees, and ladies listened, a *hen* of flowers in their hair, and the shadow of Neb whom the children of darkness call the Sphinx slid from west to east three hundred and sixty-five thousand times and again as many, and again, and who then could read the writing of the scribe?

THUNDER underground began to boom at midnight on the ninth of January 1784 like a hundred batteries of cannon beneath the silver city of Guanaxuato in Mexico, continuing like a ripening summer storm, clap and drum roll, like the hoofbeats of Visigoth cavalry under Alaric coming upon Rome when a havoc of light in midday blue had signaled Vortumna and the Arvals that the hill gods were turning their shoulders from Roman flour and Roman flower, an angry, angled slender crack of fire and a sizzling split through the air and Rome was no longer under the ax and stick pack and eagle and wolf but under the Crow, a sound like high promontories breaking away from a headland and falling into a raging sea. Which awful noise lasted until the middle of February. When, after the third day, no earthquake followed the persistent subterranean thunder, *el cabildo* kept the people inside the city, ringing it with militia, for fear that thieves would come and steal their silver, not an ingot of which shivered in that incongruous stillness and steadfastly detonating tumult.

Yet it was a land where a tall cathedral might suddenly ring all its bells and sink out of sight into a crevice open so briefly that, having swallowed an orchard, a mule train, the church, a sleeping hog, and the local astrologer, it could close again neatly enough to catch a hen by both feet in the pavement of the Calle San Domingo.

Der Graf Rufzeichen sat listening to these details from von Humboldt's *Cosmos* with glassy eyes.

—Avenues of trees, I went on, become displaced in an earthquake without being uprooted. Fragments of cultivated ground of very different kinds mutually displace each other.

—*Erstaunlich!*

—A still more remarkable and complicated phenomenon is the discovery of utensils belonging to one house in the ruins of another at a great distance, a circumstance that has given rise to lawsuits.

—Earthquakes, is it, you're reading me about? asked the Count. My God. I once came all over dizzy while out riding, for no cause except perhaps the game I'd had at old Fuchtel's might have been a touch high, and saw two of everything, and keeled over out of the saddle, stars everywhere. Do you think that was earthquake?

—Did anyone else note a tremor? I asked him.

—How could they? said the Count with some indignation. They weren't there.

—Earthquakes are fairly extensive. They cover quite an area, I believe.

—Couldn't have been a small one there under my horse?

The Count milked his moustache and stared into the corner of the room.

ONCE UPON A TIME, in a Swiss valley, there was born to an honest couple a baby that had a jack-o'-lantern for a head. The parents were sure their grief and horror were the greatest ever felt, and yet the infant suckled and cried, slept and burbled, like any other. Its eyelets were elfin in outline, the neat small triangular nostrils were not really repulsive, and the round hole of a mouth took in its mother's milk with a will and let out boisterous cries that for timbre and volume were the equal of any baby in Switzerland.

For months it was kept hidden. Its parents had come to adore it, as a child sees the greatest winsomeness and charm in a doll that has buttons for eyes, whose mouth is stitchd onto cheesecloth, and whose hair is thread. They ventured to show it to its grandparents, who collapsed in fear and loathing, but who eventually were won over, and loved to dandle little Klaus on their knees.

One by one the neighbors fell down breathless, their eyes rolled back in their heads, at the sight of the little chap and his pumpkin grin, and one by one they got used to him. In no time at all the whole village thought nothing at all of Klaus, and in due course he became a model little boy, quick to learn in school, gratifyingly pious in church, and a fine fellow to all his friends, of whom he had many.

It was then only the rare tinker or traveler who, passing through, caught sight of him and fell screaming into a fit or froze as still as stone and had to be revived with slaps and brandy.

Kafka stole his cockroach from that story. He has, I admit, improved upon it, and seen it from a dark angle. I meant that we are all monsters: by fate and by character. Fate and character are bow and string. What happens to us is what our character invites, guides in, challenges. All that ought to matter is that we are alive, which turns out, I've found, to be our last consideration. What does a banker care whether he is living or dead, so long as he has a shilling to kiss, a franc to lick?

And of life we can ask but continuity. That, as I explain to my doctors, is my neurosis. I have been, I am, I shall be, for awhile, but off and on, like a firefly.

I confuse my doctors. When they say I am mistaken about reality it is they who are mistaken. They say I cannot distinguish, cannot sort fact from fiction.

How solemnly their empty chairs listened to them, and the portraits of Freud and Jung on the wall! The lamps, and especially the fire in the grate, listened to these strange words with dismay. To think that the custodians of the spirit should have prepared for me a categorical prison.

—Consider! I said.

They looked at each other, Doktor Vogel and Doktor Hassenfuss.

It says in the pages of Mach that the mind is nothing but a continuity of consciousness. It is not itself a thing, it is its contents, like an eye and what it sees, a hand and what it holds. Mach's continuity, like Heraklit's river, defines itself by its flow.

Doktor Vogel looked at Hassenfuss.

—A charming poetic image, he said.

—It is so obvious, I persisted, once you have seen it. The mind is what it knows! It is nothing else at all, at all.

I RESOLVED to hold fast by a piece of the rock and so to hold my breath, if possible, till the wave went back; now as the waves were not so high as at first, being near land, I held my hold till the wave abated, and then fetched another run, which brought me so near the shore that the next wave, though it went over me, yet did not swallow me up as to carry me away, and the next run I took, I got to the mainland, where, to my great comfort, I clambered up the clifts of the shore and sat me down upon the grass, free from danger, and quite out of the reach of the water.

Commit a word to paper and God knows what you have done. They will read it in Angoulême, in Anchorage, and Hippo. Spiritual crockery for missionary tables in the Cameroons serves quite as well a Mandarin palate. The sheik of Aqbar gathers his twenty sons around him, his five wives and twelve daughters, and reads them the *Encyclopedia Britannica,* a page where it says that phoronids, which comprise the phylum Phoronida, are little-known marine invertebrate animals characterized by an elongated, nonsegmented body that is topped by a tuft of tentacles. Each adult lives within a membranous tube to which sand particles, shells, and other materials may adhere. A king will read a baker's proverbs who could not be invited to supper by the meanest file clerk of the Fish and Vegetables Revenue Branch.

The black hunchback Aesop would never be allowed to stump on his crutch into this library, nor shaggy blind barefoot Homer leaning on a boy, nor staggering Li Po in his dragon silks, nor honest Benjamin Franklin could I introduce into this library without getting fired for exposing *der Graf* to the Gadarene hog. Yet here were their books, bound in red leather.

Weder antik Fisch noch spartanisch Athlet.

—Mad, aren't they? Herr Rufzeichen asked of the ceiling, blowing loops of cigar smoke upward.

—Mad, your lordship?

—These book writers, Robert, that you read me. They are all peculiar, to you and me I mean, wouldn't you say?

STEEP WIND at my throat, my gaze on dizzy shires and canals below, I heard with one ear the tympany of our cold oscillation through crowding gusts and with the other the Eroica. You do not, Meng Tse said, climb trees to look for fish. Nor discover weight with a yardstick or length with a scales. Why were Cassirer and I floating across Europe in a balloon?

—*Hsing!* Cassirer said.

A carp by Hokusai, a spray of maple red as wine, *sao shu* dropping like wistaria down the print. It is *hsing,* Cassirer said by the stove, to desire a wife, plum brandy, gingko jam, and water chestnuts. *Hsing* is internal, justice and mercy external, *nei wei.*

In China as in Greece the epic known in every house and assembly, he explained, is of *Wanderung.* The manner of a people's foraging becomes the *Heldenfahrt* of the *Kollektivunbewusste.* A hero without a journey is like a saint without a vision. Tripitaka and Monkey through a persimmon forest under blue humps of mountains. Herakles mothernaked raising his mouseburrow ox arm in grace to a frisking centaur, wolfwary Ulysses offering his lie to the *meerstrandbewohnend Phaiakischhof,* Cassirer the image peddler and Walser the *Nachnietzschischprosaschriftsteller* aloft in a balloon drifting to the Baltic sands: heroes in our day must take to the ice wastes of the poles, the depths of the sea, the air. We are not certain whether von Moltke's heroism is in his railroad tracks, his invention of general orders, or his translating Gibbon.

He talked of Nietzsche and Semmelweis. The one exhorted us to dream of barefoot Greeks dancing in masks before the enigmas of fermentation and electricity, the other taught us to wash our hands when delivering babies.

Here, in the snow, which would I prefer to walk with me, as if I could heed another ghost, or if Seelig, kind Seelig, were not enough? A man's quality might well be in the sort of misery he has seen with pity. In that case, Semmelweis. Or was it rather Nietzsche? And both were maddened by stupidity. Not I.

I wander out every afternoon, the same way, and have my walk.

Every day now for twenty-seven years. Could I once have written books? Once drifted across Europe in a balloon? Once been a butler in Silesia? Was I once a boy?

I watch the linnet, the buck hare, the mountains pink and grey above level mist that lies out from the property wall like a lake of clouds, like the mind's surface before a warmth of thought, light, melts that haze of ghost wool, incertitude of fear.

I ASK AN ATTENDANT who the man is who dances around the grounds and has such anguish in his eyes. He tells me it is the great Nijinsky, schizophrenic paranoid.

—He thinks he is a horse.

WHY SHOULD THIS wild whirl of snow keep us from our walk? It reminds me of the boys in my father's shop, pigeon-breasted Switzers with halberds and cockades, milkmaids in porcelain aprons, shepherds with mouse-faced sheep. O ravelment and shindy of snow on the toy shop's windows! There was an enameled *staffetta* I coveted with real lust: he had a leather hat, a coat as red as cherries, and saddlebags stamped with the arms of the canton.

A rabbit! See him tease a casualness into his fear. Don't move. I can think, as still as he, snow raining upon us both, of a battalion of red soldiers on my father's shelves, of a mandarin poet rolling along the Great Wall in a cart, of Robinson Crusoe conversing with his parrot. But what moves in his mind, the rabbit? Is the image of me on his retina all that he sees, an old man with a face as wrinkled as a pocket handkerchief used for a month? Can he see cabbages and carrots and blackberries? His doe?

It was a day this cold that I saw a lady with a *panache* of pheasant and egret jutting from a swirl of scarlet silk around her hat, and felt my little man suffuse with benevolence, grow long and rise. The colors of coats and scarves in shops, of signs and stone, of tramway and light became splendid. It takes the animal in us to lead the spirit a dance.

Schicksal, Zeit, Unfall: the important thing is to tie one's shoelaces, sew back the parted button, and look the world in the eye.

But the rabbit can think without disregarding all that is characteristic of life, for the infinity of qualifications arising from our thoughts of death is nowhere in his green brain. Yet he is as fearful as if I were a banker, a philanthropist, or a psychiatrist. He lasts, we wear. He leaps, we endure.

The past, I have known for years, is the future. All that has mattered is a few moments, uncongenial while they happened, that turned to gold in the waves of time. February light, that for all its debility might have come from the daytime moon as much as from a red sun beyond a texture of bamboo and chinaberry, fell cold on a wall that bore a French print of a flatfish, a map of the Hebrides, a bust of T. Pomponius Atticus, a Madagascan parrot whose green eye glowed like an opal, and a speckled mirror that reflected on so dull an afternoon nothing except some elemental neutrality of light and dark, vicinity, and patience.

I am most inside outside. Once Olympia said from her repose on the wall that Monsieur Manet was a man women liked. He put them at ease by paying the right kind of attention. He stayed inside himself and looked out. He did not even know how to come outside himself. You could always feel that. It is a comfort to a woman, she said, to see a man so unconsciously himself. A woman knows when to be inside and when to be outside, her mother's only useful lesson, and of course when to be neither.

The snow is a kind of music. Were I ever to write again, perhaps a poem as deft and transparent as one by a Chinese, I would like to witness to the beauty of the snow.

And their books, these people who keep writing, who reads them? It is now a business like any other. I try not to bore them with an old man's talk when they come, the few who want to ask me about writing, about the time before both the wars, about Berlin. I do not tell them how much of all that misery was caused by writers, by men who said they were writers. I do not tell them that I quit writing because I had nothing at all, any more, to say.

There are the tracks of the rabbit. I think they said at the table that today is Christmas. I do not know.

But let us desist, lest quite by accident we be so unlucky as to put these things in order.

Counterfactuals

CHARLOTTE FIRES the cleaning people, whom she feels have been an extravagance. For a while, Curtis tries cleaning the house himself. He dry mops the wood floors, then cleans spots of grit or grime using a squirt bottle containing a homemade mixture of lemon and ammonia and a soft towel. He puts on yellow latex gloves and cleans the bathrooms, scrubbing and wiping down the commode and the basins and spritzing the mirrors with the same lemon and ammonia solution he uses on the floor. The next weekend there are various chores to do that prevent him from cleaning, and he has to work all the weekend after that. The following Saturday morning, he glances at the paper, drinks a cup of coffee, then goes to the utility closet for the blue plastic bucket and the yellow gloves and the squirt bottle of lemon and ammonia. He works his way to the upstairs bathroom, where he cleans the shower stall. He stretches to swab down a distant corner of the stall floor, where the caulk is turning a little dusky with mildew along the black base tiles. His nose tingles with the ammonia fumes and trickles of sweat begin to run from his temples, threatening to stream into his eyes. He sits back on his heels in a catcher's stance, as if the shower stall might deliver him a sudden knuckleball or slider. He sets down the sponge and the pump bottle of ammonia and lemon and strips off his yellow gloves. Charlotte is playing interleague tennis. He decides to leave her.

IT IS HIS BIRTHDAY, and he's sitting in the evening twilight, alone, waiting for Charlotte to return from a trip to Crisfield, where she went to buy a chest of drawers. He decides to leave her.

HE IS SITTING at his desk in his office after a long, bitter, and corrosive phone call from Charlotte. She has told him not to bother coming home. He decides to leave her.

HE IS IN THE MAIN LOBBY of the Inn at Williamsburg, guests of Charlotte's parents for the January Antiques Forum. He is waiting for Charlotte to come down from the room to go to dinner. Tall men in blazers and slacks drink old-fashioneds. Middle-aged women with set hair in honey blonde chirp at the window to the lobby shops. He decides to leave her.

Whenever it is, he decides. He decides to leave Charlotte and he goes.

HE BEGINS SEEING A TRIM, self-confident blonde woman who does public relations for the architectural firm designing a new building at work. They move in together and then buy a townhouse in Washington. They marry and move to Miami Beach, where she finds new work, and they live in a tall apartment tower overlooking the water. Four nights a week they eat out at dark, fascinating restaurants. At their favorite of them they have their own booth. They make many friends: Cubans, Anglos, blacks, and Israeli transplants. After her mother dies, they begin spending parts of their summers at a lake in Michigan where her family has a cabin. After ten years in Miami, they buy a house on the Gulf Coast—Naples—and begin spending all of their summers at the lake. Her younger brother begins going through his own messy divorce—rehab, bankruptcy, and restraining orders. They adopt the brother's youngest daughter, her niece, and she lives with them in Naples until she graduates from high school.

HE BEGINS SEEING A FRENCH WOMAN just two years his junior who, married disastrously at twenty, has been living in the United States ever since, working for the World Bank in Washington as an analyst. They fall in love. When both their divorces come through, she decides to change jobs, and they move to New York. She works at a merchant bank with French connections. It's an extremely good and lucrative job, the likes of which she might have had years before but for being tied down by her jealous husband, a pediatrician. Money is suddenly plentiful, and Curtis takes a job writing for a neighborhood newspaper. This leads to working in development for the New York City Public Library, when his wife's partner becomes a trustee. They live in a fantastic apartment and, between his job and hers, entertain there often. They begin traveling to France, which her first husband never allowed. Her family, grateful after such a long separation, welcomes them warmly. Ten years seem to fly by. She retires from the bank and they travel the country—to Las Vegas, Detroit, Houston—places that enchant her precisely for their American absurdity. After a few years of this, a cousin who is expanding a cognac firm asks them to represent it in the United States. For the next several years, this becomes their shared hobby, casually attending food fairs and wine events. The cognac becomes quite popular, and the firm is bought by a European luxury goods conglomerate.

HE LEAVES HIS WIFE, finds an apartment near the Inner Harbor. He sees his daughter, a sophomore at the Bryn Mawr School, twice a week for dinner and on alternate weekends. On her vacations he takes her skiing or sailing. He dates wildly at first, sometimes going out five nights a week. There are a few half-hearted relationships, then an ill-advised commitment that ends worse than his marriage did. He remains alone, not even dating, for nearly two years. Twice he moves in that time, until he finds an apartment he's comfortable in. That fall he begins seeing a print-making instructor at the Maryland Institute College of Art, a woman who is married to a sculptor living and teaching in Kansas City. In the end, though she loves Curtis, she cannot break up her own marriage; her life is too comfortable as it is.

HE MEETS A WOMAN with whom he falls very quickly in love. They date for a year, quarrel violently, and break up. He finds himself heartbroken over the separation. She takes him back, with all sorts of conditions and caveats. There is a constant threat of termination hanging over his head. However, they live in contented happiness, mostly, because he is in love with her in a manner he had never considered possible. As they age, and certain resentments inevitably solidify, he still loves her without measure. They lead a migratory life, ending up in a modest house in Pasadena, California, where she works as an editor at a trade newspaper in Glendale. In the evenings, when the sun sets, his street runs with golden light, and the smell of the fragrant shrubbery fills his nose as strongly as the first day he arrived. He stands at the gate to their small California garden, waiting for her to arrive home.

CURTIS REMAINS IN HIS CROUCH, on his heels. Ammonia and lemon fills his nostrils. The hastening dust gathers around the Adirondack chair in which he sits, mosquitoes nibbling at his ankles. He stares through the window panes at the naked barrenness of the Williamsburg golf course green, its graveled cart paths daubed with snow. What if? he asks himself.

Time to Go

MY FATHER FOLLOWS ME on the street. He says "Don't go into that store and don't go into the next one you might want to go into either. Go into none, that's what I'm saying." But I stand in front of the door of the jewelry store I heard was the best in the city and am buzzed in. My father's right behind me, and I nod to the guard and say to the saleswoman after she says "Can I help you?": "Yes, I'm looking for a necklace—amber—I mean jade. I always get the two mixed up. But jade's what I want: long-lasting, forever, is the symbol, right? This might sound funny, but I want to present the necklace to my wife-to-be as a prenuptial gift."

"Doesn't sound funny to me and you've come to the right store." She takes out a tray of jade necklaces. All have gold around or in them, and when I ask the price of two of them, are too expensive.

"I don't want any gold in them, except maybe for the clasp, and these are way too expensive for me."

"Much too expensive," my father says.

"I'll show you some a little lower in price."

"Much lower in price," my father says.

"Maybe a little lower than even that," I say.

She puts away the tray she was about to show me and takes out a third tray.

"These seem darker than I want—to go with her blue eyes and kind of pale skin, I mean—but how much is this one?"

"You can pick it up," she says. "Jade doesn't bite."

"Just the price," my father says. "But go on, pick it up. You'll see how jade's as cold to feel as it is to look at."

I pick it up. "It feels nice, just the right weight, and seems"—
holding it out—"the right size for her neck."

"Is she around my height?"

"Five-five."

"Then exactly my height and this is the size I'd wear."

"I'm sure it's still too expensive for me."

She looks at the tag on it, which seems to be in code: $412xT+$. "It
goes for three-fifty but I'll make it two-seventy-five for you."

"Way out of my range."

"What is your range?"

"You're going to wind up with crap," my father says, "pure crap. If
you have to buy a necklace, go somewhere else. I bet you can get this
one for a hundred any other place."

"Around a hundred, hundred-twenty-five," I tell her.

"Let me show you these then."

"Here we go again," my father says.

"I have to get her something, don't I?" I tell him. "And I want to,
because she wants something she can always wear, treasure—that'll
remind her of me. That's what she said."

"Fine, but what's she getting you?"

"How do I know? I hope nothing. I don't want anything. That's
what I told her."

"Oh, you don't want anything to remind you of her?"

"She'll remind me of her. I have her, that's enough, and besides I
don't like jewelry."

"You thinkers: all so romantic and impractical. I wouldn't get her
anything if she isn't getting you anything. Listen, I like her, don't
misunderstand me: she's a fine attractive girl and you couldn't get
better if you tried for ten more years. But tit for tat I say. He who
gives, receives, and one should be a receiver and giver both."

"You're not getting my point. She wants something and I don't. I
accept that and I wish you would."

"Sucker," he says. "All my boys are suckers. None of them took
after me."

"Some people might say that was an improvement."

"Stupid people might, just as stupid people might make jokes like
you just did. If you took after me you would've been married sooner,
had almost grown-up children, a much better job, three times as

much income and been much much happier because your happiness would've been going on longer."

"Look at this batch," the saleswoman says, putting another tray of jade necklaces on the counter. I see one I like. A light green, smaller beads, nicely strung with string, no gold on it except the clasp. I hold it up. "I like this one."

"Hedge, hedge," my father says. "Then ask the price and offer her half."

"How much is it?" I ask her.

"A hundred-ten."

"Fifty-five or sixty—quick," my father says.

"Sounds fair, and this is the first one I really feel good about."

"That's the only way to buy. Janine," she says to a younger saleswoman, "would you try this on for this gentleman?"

Janine comes over, smiles and says hello to me, undoes the top two buttons of her blouse and starts on the third.

"It's not necessary," I say.

"Don't worry," the older woman says. "That's as far as I'll let her go for that price."

Janine holds the necklace to her neck and the older woman clasps it behind her. "Feels wonderful," Janine says, rolling the beads between her fingers. "This is the one I'd choose of this box—maybe even out of all the boxes despite the more expensive ones."

"Who are you working for, him or me?"

"No, it really feels great."

"Don't fall for their patter," my father says. "Sixty-five—go no higher. She says seventy-five, say 'Look, I'm a little short what with all my wedding expenses and all, can't you take the sixty-five—the most, seventy?' But you got to give them an excuse for accepting your offer, and no crying."

"How much is this one again?" I ask her.

"One-ten," the older woman says, "but I'll make it a hundred."

"That's just fine. I didn't mean to bargain down, but if you say it's a hundred, fine, I'll take it."

"Idiot," my father says. "You could've had it for seventy easy."

"Terrific. Janine, wrap it up special as a prewedding gift. Cash or charge, sir?"

"You'll take a check?"

"Janine, I don't know this guy, so check his references. If they're okay, let him pay by check. Thank you, sir. What about calling Michaels now?" she says to a man at the end of the counter and they go in back. I take out my wallet.

My father sits in a chair next to the guard. "My son," he says to him. "Nothing like me. Never learned anything I ever taught him and I tried hard as I could. He could've been much more successful if he'd listened. But he was stubborn. All my children were stubborn. Neither of my girls had the beauty of their mother and none of my sons the brains of their dad. Health you'd think they'd have had at least, but they didn't even have that. Oh, this one, he's healthy enough—strong as an ox. But two I lost to diseases, boy and a girl, and both in their twenties, which was hard for my wife and I to take, before I went myself. So, there you have it. And I hope his bride likes his present. He's paying enough. Though why he doesn't insist on getting something in return—hint on it at least if he doesn't want to insist—or at least insist her family pay for the wedding, is a mystery as much to you as to me. To everyone including his bride, who I admire—don't think I was just buttering him up there—he says he's too old to have anyone but him pay for the wedding, and she makes it worse by praising him for what she calls his integrity. Make sense to you? Doesn't to me. Since to me integrity is great in its place but is best when it pays. All of which is why I hound him the way I do—for his benefit and his only. So. Think it'll stay as nice out as it is? Ah, what's the difference?"

I GET OFF THE TRAIN from Baltimore, get on the subway for upper Broadway, suddenly my father's in the car standing beside me. "Welcome home," he says. "You still going through with giving her that present and making the wedding all by yourselves? Anything you say. I won't interfere. I can only tell you once, maybe three times, then you have to finish digging your own grave."

"If that's really the last time, fine by me," and I go back to reading my book.

"Just like when you were a boy. You didn't like what I said, you pretended I wasn't there. But I'm here all right. And the truth is, in spite of all the mistakes you made with your life and are still making,

I'm wishing you all the luck in the world. You were okay to me at the end—I won't deny it. I can't—who could I to?—the way you took care of me when I was sick—so I suppose I should be a little better to you now. Am I right? So do you want to be not only family now but good friends? If so, let's shake like friends. We kissed a lot when you were young—in fact, right to when I went and then you to me a few seconds after that, which I don't think if the tables were turned you would've got from me—but for a first time let's just shake."

The car's crowded. Late afternoon Christmas shoppers returning home but not the rush hour riders yet. I'm squeezed right up to him. "Look," I say, "we can talk but don't remind me of how sick you were. I don't want to think of it now. I will say I respected you for a lot of things in your life, especially the way you took the discomfort and pain then, something I told you a number of times but I think you were too out of it to understand me. But you also have to realize, and which I maybe didn't tell you, how much you screwed me up, and I allowed you to screw me up—whatever the causes or combination of them. I've worked out a lot of it, I'll try to work out the rest, but no real complaints from me for anything now for I'm going through absolutely the best time in my life."

"Good, we're friends," and he shakes my hand.

I get off at Magna's stop. Today began my school's winter break. I head for the revolving exit gate at the end of the platform. A boy of about sixteen's between me and the woman exiting in front of him. But he's hesitating, looking around and behind him, at me, the downtown platform across the tracks, the woman who's now through the gate and walking upstairs, back at me sullenly. I don't know whether to walk around him or go to the other end of the platform and the main exit. Maybe I'm wrong. He might just be an angry kid who's hesitating now because he doesn't know which exit to take, this or the main one. I walk past him but keep my eyes on him. As I'm stepping backwards into the gate he turns to me, sticks his left hand into his side jacket pocket and thrusts it at me, clamps his other hand on my shoulder and says "Give me all your money." I say "What? What?" and push backwards and revolve around the gate to the other side and he has to pull his hand away or get it caught between the bars.

"Hey, wait," and he revolves around the gate after me, rips the satchel off my shoulder and runs upstairs. It has the necklace, my writings, student papers, a framed drawing I bought for Magna, some clothing. The boy's already gone. I yell upstairs "Police, police, catch that kid with my satchel—a canvas one," as I chase after him. On the sidewalk I say to that woman "Did you see a boy running past?" and she says "Who?" but he's nowhere around. A police car's across the street and I run to it. The policemen are in a luncheonette waiting for their takeout order. I go in, say "I'm not going to sound sensible to you, believe me, but I was just robbed, he might've had a gun or knife in his pocket, a kid, boy, around sixteen with a gray ski cap on his head with the word 'ski' on it, down in the subway exit there, he took my satchel with some valuable things in it and then ran upstairs. I'm sure if we—" "Come with us," one of them says and we rush outside and are getting in their car when the counterman raps on the luncheonette window and holds up their bag of food. "Later," the policeman shouts out his window as we drive off.

We drive around and don't find the boy. The policeman says "There are so many young thieves wearing the outfit you described. Parka jacket, fancy running sneakers, hat sort of extra tall and squeezed on top, sometimes with a pompom, sometimes not. Tough luck about your necklace and painting though."

"I could've told you," my father says, seated beside me. "Fact is, I told you—a thousand times about how to be wise in New York, but you always got your own ideas. You think I'd ever exit through a revolving gate when there's no token booth there, even in what they call the better days? That's where they leap on you, trap you against the gate on either side or on the stairs leaving it, but you never want to play it safe. Now you've lost everything. Well, you still got your life and it's not that I have no sympathy for you over what happened, but it seems you were almost asking for it it could've been so easily avoided."

"Lay off me, will you? I already feel bad enough." I get out of the car in front of Magna's building. "Thanks, officers."

"As I say," my father says, going in with me, "I can understand how you feel. But this one time, since your life depends on it, I wish you'd learn from your mistake."

I go upstairs and tell Magna about the robbery. My father sits on the daybed she uses as a couch. "Every week closer to the wedding she gets more radiant," he says. "You got yourself one hell of a catch. She's smart, she's good, she has wonderful parents, and she's also beautiful. I don't know how you rate it but I'm glad you did."

"It had your special present in it," I tell her, "plus some drawing for you I know he's going to just throw away. I won't tell you what the special gift is. I'll try to get something like it or close to it. God, I could have killed that kid."

"That wouldn't have helped," she says.

"It certainly wouldn't've," my father says. "Because in the process you could've got killed in his place, and those kids always got ones working with them or friends for revenge. This is what I tell you and hope you'll remember for all time: stay out of other people's business, and if something like a robbery happens to you, shut your mouth and give everything you have. Twice I got held up by gunmen in my dental office and both times my advice worked. They not only didn't harm me but gave me back my empty wallet."

MAGNA AND I GO to the Marriage License Bureau. The line for applications extends into the hallway. "I hate lines," my father says. "I've always avoided them by calling before to see what time the place opens and then trying to be the first one there."

"It looks like the line for food stamps," the woman in front of us says to her mate.

"To me like the one for Welfare," another woman says.

"Unemployment insurance," Magna says to me. "I've been on them. Didn't want to but had no choice. Have you?"

"Him?" my father says. "Oh, he was too pure to take unemployment. He deserved it too but you know what he did? Refused to even go down to sign up for it. He was living home then and I told him he was crazy. I said 'I always want you to have a job, but if you're fired from one or laid off, well, you paid for that insurance, so take it.' But him? Always too damn pure. That can work against you as much as it can for. Must've got that trait from his mother, because he certainly didn't get that way from me."

"I could have got unemployment a few times," I say to her, "but I always had some money saved and so thought I'd live off it and write at the same time. To sort of use the time break to produce some writing that might earn me some money but not intentionally to make me money—"

"There he goes again with his purity bent. Look, I never encouraged my children to take anything that wasn't theirs. Oh, maybe by my actions I occasionally did, but I never encouraged them personally to take like that. But he wouldn't listen about that insurance. We had terrible fights over it. Of course he never would've had to reject or accept any unemployment insurance if he'd've become the dentist I wanted him to. I pleaded with all my sons to and each one in turn broke my heart. But he out of all of them had the brains and personality for it and he could've worked alongside me for a few years and then bought me out of my practice. I would've even given him the practice for nothing if that's what it took to get him to become a dentist, though with maybe him contributing to my support a little each month, mine and his mother's."

"I wasn't good in the sciences," I say to him. "I told you that and offered my grades as proof over and over again. I used to almost regurgitate every time I went into the chemistry building and biology labs. I tried. I was predent for more than two years."

"Regurgitate. See the words he uses? No, you didn't want to become a dentist because I was one. You wanted to go into the arts. To be an artiste. The intelligentsia you wanted to belong to. Well, now you're able to make a decent living off it teaching, but for how many years you practically starved? You almost broke my heart then, seeing you struggle like that for so long, though you still have time to become one. Dentists average even more money than doctors today."

"Next," the clerk says.

Magna gives her our blood tests results. She gives us the application to fill out.

"Can we come right up to the front of the line after we fill it out?" I say.

"You have to go to the back," she says.

"Why aren't there two lines as there are supposed to be? Why's the other window closed?"

"We're a little shorthanded today. You think I like it? It's double my usual load."

"There are three people typing over there and two putting away things in files. Why not get one of them to man the other window till this line's a little relieved?"

"Shh, don't make trouble," my father says. "You can't avoid the situation, accept it. It's the city."

"I'm not the supervisor," she says, "and the supervisor can't just tell someone to do something when it's not that person's job. Next," she says to the couple behind us.

Magna pulls me away. Wherever we are," she says, "I can always count on you to try to improve things."

"Am I wrong?"

"You'd think at the Marriage Bureau you'd tone it down a little, but no real harm. It'd be too laughable for us to break up down here."

"He was always like that," my father says. "Always a protester, a rebel. Nothing was ever good enough in life for him. He'd see a Broadway play that maybe the whole world thought was great and which'd win all the prizes, he'd say it could've been much better. Books, politics, his schools, the banks—whatever, always the same. I told him plenty of times to run for mayor of this city, then governor, then president. He never took me seriously. I suppose all that does mean he's thinking or his heart's mostly in the right place, but sometimes he can get rude with people with all those changes of his he wants. He doesn't have the knack to let things roll off him as I did. Maybe that's good. I couldn't live with it if that was me. You'll have troubles with him, young lady."

WE GO TO THE DIAMOND CENTER for wedding bands. "How'd you find us?" the man behind the counter says.

"We saw all the stores and didn't know which one to choose," I say. "So I asked this man who looked as if he worked in the area 'Any one place carry only gold wedding bands?' He said 'Nat Sisler's,' who I suppose, from the photo there, is you, '4 West, down the middle aisle on the right. There are forty other booths there but you won't miss his. He's got the biggest sign.'"

"Just like me on both my office windows," my father says. "Biggest the city allowed for a dentist. If they'd allowed me to have signs to cover my entire window, I would've."

"Too bad you don't know this man's name," Nat says. "We always like to thank the people who refer customers to us. But he was right. We've nineteen-hundred different rings, so I promise you won't walk away from here without finding one you like. Anything particular you looking for?"

"Something very simple," I say.

He holds up his ring finger. "Nothing more simple and comfortable than this one. I've been wearing it without taking it off once for forty-five years."

"That's amazing," Magna says. "Not once?"

"I can't. I've gained sixty pounds since I got married and my finger's grown around it. Maybe he'll have better luck with his weight. He's so slim now, he probably will."

"More patter," my father says. "Then when you're off-guard they knock you over the head with the price. But remember: this is the Diamond Center. The bargaining's built into the price. Here they think it's almost a crime not to, so this time whatever price he quotes, cut him in half."

"Single or double-ring ceremony?" Nat says.

"Double," Magna says, "and identical rings."

"Better yet," my father says. "For two rings you have even greater bargaining power. Cut him more than half."

Nat brings out a tray of rings. "What do you do?" he asks me. "You look like a doctor."

"I teach at a university."

"So you are a doctor, but of philosophy."

"I barely got my B.A. I write, so I teach writing. She's the doctor of philosophy."

"Oh yeah?" he says while Magna's looking at the rings.

"Turn your ears off," my father says. "Next he's going to tell you you're a handsome couple, how great marriage can be, wish you all the luck and success there is, which you'll need, he'll say—all that stuff. Though they love bargaining down here, they love making money more, so act business-like. Ask him right off what the price of this is and then that. Tell him it seems high, even if you don't think it is. Tell him you're a teacher at the lowest level. Tell him you make almost zero from your writing and that she won't be teaching next year, so you'll have to support you both. Tell him any other time but this you might have the money to pay what he's asking, but now, even if it is something as sacred as marriage, you're going to have to ask him to cut the price more than half. And being there are two rings you're buying—"

"What do you think of this one?" Magna asks me. It looks nice. It fits her finger.

"You have one like this in my size?" I say.

"That's an awfully big finger you have there," Nat says, holding my ring finger up. He puts several ring sizers on my finger before one fits. "Ten and a half. We'd have to make it on order. When's the wedding date?"

"Ask him how much first," my father says, "ask him how much."

"The fourteenth," Magna says. "But I'm sure these will be much higher than we planned to pay."

"That a girl," my father says.

"Hey," I say. "You'll be wearing it every day of your life, you say, so get what you want. I happen to like it."

"How much are they?" she asks Nat.

He puts the ring she wants on a scale. "Seventy-two dollars. Let's say seventy. The professor's, being a much larger size—and they're both seamless, I want you to know. That means they won't break apart unexpectedly and is the best kind of craftsmanship you can get—is eighty-five."

"Sounds okay to me," I say.

"Oh my God," my father says. "I won't even say what I think."

WE GO TO THE APARTMENT of a rabbi someone told us about. His wife says "What would you like to drink? We've scotch, vodka, white wine, ginger ale—"

"Scotch on the rocks for me," I say.

"Same for me, thanks," Magna says.

"So," the rabbi says when we all get our drinks, "to your health, a long life, and especially to your marriage," and we click glasses and drink. He shows us the certificate we'll get at the end of the ceremony. "On the cover—I don't know if you can read it—but it says 'marriage' in Hebrew."

"It's a little bit gaudy for me," I say. "You don't have one with fewer frills? Oh, I guess it's not important."

"It is so important," my father says. "That certificate will end up meaning more to you than your license. And it's beautifully designed—good enough to frame and hang—but of course not good enough for you."

"You'll have to provide two glasses for the ceremony," the rabbi says. "One with the red wine in it you'll both be drinking from."

"Dry or sweet?" Magna says.

"What a question," my father says. "Sweet, sweet."

"Whichever you choose," the rabbi says. "You'll be the ones drinking it."

"A modern rabbi," my father says. "Well, better than a modern judge. Ask him what synagogue he represents."

"By the way," I say, "do you have a congregation? George said he thought you'd given that up."

"Right now," he says, "I'm marketing a wonderful little device that could save the country about five hundred thousand barrels of oil a month, if the public would just accept it. I got tired of preaching, but I'll get back to it one day."

"What he's not saying," his wife says, "is that this gadget will only cost three and a half dollars retail, plus a slight installation fee, and will save every apartment and home owner about fifty dollars a month during the winter. The oil companies hate him for it."

"I wouldn't go that far," he says, "but I will say I haven't made any friends in the oil industry. But the effectiveness of the device has been proven, it'll last without repairs for up to fifteen years, and someone has to market it, so it's almost been like a crusade with me to get it into every oil user's home. Wait, I'll show it to you."

"Wait'll he comes around to telling you the cost of his ceremony," my father says.

"The other glass," I say, after we've passed the device around. "Is that the one I'm supposed to break with my foot?"

"Scott has the most brilliant interpretation of it during the ceremony you'll ever want to hear," his wife says. "I've heard it a dozen times and each time I'm completely absorbed. Actually, except for the exchange of vows, I'd call it the highlight of the ceremony."

"Would you mind if we don't have the breaking of the glass? We've already decided on this. To us it represents the breaking of the hymen—"

"That's just one interpretation," he says, "and not the one I give. Mine's about the destruction of the temples and other things. I use biblical quotes."

"Wait wait wait," my father says. "Did I hear you don't want to break the glass?"

"It's also just a bit too theatrical for me," I say to the rabbi. "Just isn't my style."

"Isn't your style?" my father says. "It goes back two thousand years—maybe even three. You have to break the glass. I did with your mother and her father and mine with our mothers and their fathers with our grandmothers and so on. A marriage isn't a marriage without it. It's the one thing you have to do for me of anything I ask."

"I can wrap a lightbulb in newspaper if it's only that you're concerned a regular glass might cut your foot," the rabbi says. "But if you don't want it."

"If they don't, they don't," his wife says.

"We don't," Magna says, "but thank you."

"Then no second glass," he says. "It's your day."

"That's it," my father says. "Now you've really made me mad. That she's on your side in this—well, you must've forced it on her. Or maybe not. Anyway, I'm tired of complaining. From the man's point you'll be missing the best part of the ceremony, not the second best. I won't even begin to advise you about anything about the rabbi's fee."

"I know what your advice will be," I say, "and I don't want to bargain with him, is that so bad? Because what's he going to charge— a hundred-fifty? two hundred? So how much can I cut off it—fifty, seventy-five? What's fifty anyway? What's a hundred? And he's a professional. A professional should not only do his work well but know what to charge. You always let your patients cut your dental fees in half?"

"If I thought they'd go somewhere else, sure. Because if I wasn't working on them I'd be sitting around earning nothing in that time. But if your rabbi asks four hundred?"

"He won't. You can see he's a fair guy. And I'm not a complete jerk. If I think his fee's way out of line, I'll tell him."

"That's not the way to do it, but do what you want. I've said it a hundred times to you and now I'll say it a last time. Do what you want because you will anyway. But I'll tell you something else. Your mother didn't give you three thousand dollars of my insurance policy benefit to just piss away."

"That money was nine years ago. I didn't ask for a cent of it but she thought I deserved it because of the four years I helped her with you. And I used it to good purpose. I lived off it and worked hard on what I wanted to work on for one entire year."

"Oh, just pay anything he asks no matter how high. In fact, when he says his fee, say 'No, it's too little,' and double him. That's the kind of schmo I sometimes think you can be."

We're being married in Magna's apartment. The rabbi's talking about what the sharing of the wine means. My mother's there. My brother and sister and their spouses. My nieces and an uncle and aunt. Magna's parents and cousins and her uncle and aunts. A few of our friends and their children. My father. He looks tired and ill. He's dressed for the wedding, has on his best suit, though it needs to be pressed. He sits down on the piano bench he's so tired. The rabbi pronounces us married. I'm crying. Magna smiles and starts to cry. My mother says "What is this? You're not supposed to be crying, but go ahead. Tears of happiness."

"Kiss the bride," my sister says. I kiss Magna. Then I kiss my mother and Magna's mother and shake Magna's father's hand while I kiss his cheek. I kiss Magna again and then my sister and brother and brother's wife and my nieces and aunt and uncle and Magna's aunts and uncle. Then our friends and Magna's female cousin, and I shake the hand of her male cousin and say "Oh what the hell," and kiss his cheek and the cheek of my sister's husband and the rabbi's cheek too. I look over to the bench. My father's crying. His head's bent way over and he dabs his eyes with old tissues. He starts making loud sobbing noises. "Excuse me," I say and I go over to him, get on my knees, put my arms around his lower legs and my head on his thighs. He's sitting up straight now and pats my head. "My boy," he says. "You're a good sweet kid. I'm actually having a great time. And there was no real harm meant between us and never was, am I right? Sure, we got angry as hell at one another lots of times, but I've always had a special feeling for you deep down. It's true, you don't have to believe me, but it's true. And I'm so happy for you. I'm crying because I'm that happy. I'm also crying because I think it's wonderful you're all together today and so happy, and I'm glad I'm here. Your other sister and brother, it'd be grand if they were here too." I look around for them. "Maybe they couldn't find the right clothes," I say. I get on one knee and hug him with my cheek pressed against his and then he disappears.

How Aliens Think

"Rovera"

To die for the love of boys. What could be more beautiful?

MICHEL FOUCAULT, reported by D. A. Miller

Vera & baby Ian (2 wks.), arriving "Rovera."
That was her homecoming outfit, a butter-yellow pique two-piece: impractical for a new mother, but it *was* pretty. Vera stood under the rustic pokerwork sign, waiting while Robert backed and edged the car into the tiny driveway and feeling no impatience, just infinite gratitude for being home at last. Only when Robert came along the path, holding his Brownie camera, then her eyes brimmed. She tilted her head a little towards the baby and smiled for the picture. Blessedly, she had her body to herself again now, and this wee treasure too.

"Another quick snap, OK?"

The tears she blinked away weren't so much for the pain, or the awful, well, *immodesty* of giving birth, but two weeks on that maternity ward, with nineteen other mothers and their squalling bundles in cots at the end of each bed, had left her cruelly exhausted, and shocked to the heart. They were treated like—they *were* like—cows lined up in a milking barn. And what some of those women talked about, joked about, was not to be believed.

Never again; once was enough: she and Robby were in full agreement on that.

With Ian, in any case, they had all they needed. People said boys were harder, but this one was just a sweet little moaner compared to those bellowing bull calves in the hospital. She carried the baby upstairs to the back bedroom, which was fitted out with a chest of drawers and changing table (used, but Robby had sanded and painted them a pristine white), cot (new), and a rocking chair by the window where she could feed him. In half an hour she was settled there with her cup of tea on the sill and a clean nappy draped over the breast the baby was working on.

While he was so engaged, or when he was being changed and wiped, he was "the baby." Other times, as when propped up among cushions for a photo, he was their son, Ian, who would grow up to be a person (only without her nose, she hoped—too much of a good thing, there—or Robert's chin—too little of that, bless him).

With her free hand, she put aside the voile curtain to see how the Hockneys' summer house next door was coming along. They'd planned it for Dave, their twelve-year-old with TB, to be out in the fresh air. And what a pathetic affair it was! Six feet across at most, supported by rustic-style poles that a March wind could blow down, trellising halfway up the sides, and a pointy roof clapped on top. Today, the carpenter was wedged inside with his behind sticking out, fitting a couple of benches.

The baby pulled his mouth off her breast with a sudden pop. She looked down and laughed at those big eyes—he'd surprised himself, hadn't he? The door creaked—that was her Robert. He asked if he could come in before he put his head 'round, so humbly bashful about it, as if she and the baby were a kind of royalty. Like a St. Joseph in the Nativity scene—and in a way she liked that, but in another way, somehow not so much.

Robert tackling garden, Sept. '32

Every fine weekend he was out there, getting it under control, cutting back the overgrown hydrangeas and forsythia along the path. Back and forth he went with the secateurs and a rake, making piles at the back of the garden to burn; and Vera took Ian out between naps to watch his father work.

Afternoons, the baby could sleep in his pram outside, unless the wind blew the bonfire smoke towards the house. There was also a problem if the smoke blew towards the Hockneys', because the sick boy was parked out there in the summer house, wrapped in a blanket, even on overcast days. The sound of his coughing penetrated, like some irritating machine set to go off every few minutes: a cough, then another cough, and a rasping effort to clear the phlegm out of his throat. He had a little bowl to spit in, on the round table between the benches. She avoided looking at it, even from a distance over the fence. Mrs. Hockney would regularly hand him in something to drink, but Vera had yet to hear her say more to him than, "Here you are, Dave; don't forget your medicine." The father came out once in a weekend to mow the lawn, or just to look at it and tell Rob he wished the whole thing could be cemented over; then he'd stop by the summer house to tell the boy to "buck up there"—or words to that effect. They had a second child, Alice, named after the Princess Royal, who played only in the front garden or down the road with her friends.

Robby had mentioned before how it bothered him, Dave being left out there by himself all the time, with only a book or a jigsaw puzzle on a tray.

"I can understand it to an extent, their being worried about the infection. But wouldn't you think they could do a bit more for the lad?"

Vera agreed completely; and weekdays it must be worse, since he couldn't go to school. But you couldn't say anything. Even a friendship with these neighbors was out of the question: not only were they distinctly better off (Mr. H., who was with Internal Revenue, played golf on Saturdays), but they'd hung an expensive metal plaque over their porch, with "St. Ives" in Gothic letters, which made an unfortunate contrast with Robert and Vera's notion of melding their own names to make "Rovera." Nobody likes being shown up as, well, naive.

"To me, it's that you never hear him complain."

"No," she said, "you don't, do you?"

Once the garden was organized, Robert suggested to the Hockneys that he could teach Dave how to build a model aeroplane. Along with playing the violin, this had been a favorite hobby of his before his marriage. He'd pay for the supplies—balsa wood, glue, tissue paper, and so on—out of his own pocket, and he already had the tools. Once Dave got the hang of it he could amuse himself, perhaps. Mrs. H. jumped at the idea—no surprise to Vera, be it said.

By the time cold weather set in, Rob and Dave had built together a pair of Sopwith Camel biplanes. They had a test launching on a fine, windless day, with the Hockneys standing in a row outside their kitchen door. Vera held the baby up to watch, on the other side of the low hedge. Mr. H. had his camera at the ready.

Great aeroplane launch, Nov. '32
That was Dave, all wrapped up in two pullovers, a scarf, and a knitted cap, jittering with excitement on the summerhouse step, asking was it ready, could it go now? A sweet-looking boy, sensitive type. Vera appreciated the way he looked up to her husband. Robby was so goodhearted: you could tell, just watching them, what a wonderful father he'd be when Ian got a little older.

He put the ready-wound launcher into Dave's hands, set the biplane's angle, stepped back, and checked his watch. At his word Dave released the crank, the rubber band spun, and the red-and-white plane soared upwards to rooftop height, banking into a wide, elegant loop over the rows of gardens, orbiting there with a featherweight buoyancy, round and round, until Vera's neck got a cramp looking up.

"One minute, ten seconds so far!" Rob announced. The flight was already a triumph. Vera never saw such rapture as she did then on Dave's face. And still the plane flew on and on, in such perfect circles you could hardly tell it was gradually descending.

At one minute, forty seconds it was spiraling visibly tighter, down to a few feet overhead. Another turn, and it just missed the pear tree at the back of the Hockneys', came 'round again, and dived past Vera to clip her washing line loaded with nappies, tumbling end-over-end into the grass. Robert ran back through the alley to retrieve the plane, accompanied by a spatter of applause. He'd explained to Dave the hazards presented by the terrain—too bad they couldn't use the sports field yet. Even so, when he returned with the wing struts on one side hanging down broken, the poor lad was distraught.

"It's O.K., Dave, we'll fix it. Only take an hour."

He put his arm around Dave and gave him a quick sideways hug, but the wheezing only worsened into spasms of choked sobbing. Vera watched—she couldn't say a word—while Rob pulled out his handkerchief and wiped the boy's eyes, his messy face. It took all that time, she observed, for Mrs. H. to get over there and take the boy indoors. And then—Vera put a hand over her mouth, silently screaming "Where's the carbolic?"—Rob stuffed the handkerchief, loaded with germs, right back in his pocket.

For Christmas that year Vera made her husband a dressing gown: it was a lightweight wool plaid, half-lined in taffeta, with piping around the collar and cuffs. She was concerned there might be a misunderstanding between the two of them, Robert being so quiet. But when they'd agreed that one baby was enough, she never thought it meant they wouldn't make love again. There were ways to prevent babies, even she knew. She'd been back to normal three months now, Ian was started on the bottle, and still Rob kept to his side of the bed. Perhaps, if it went on like this, she should speak to Dr. McKechnie.

How to put it into words, though? So difficult—especially with a Scotsman who didn't waste words himself. Also, she didn't mean to complain, when Robert was so good to them, bringing home his weekly pay envelope and putting it right on the table for allocation according to their budget, with a small allowance for his lunches and cigarettes. He got up every morning without fail to take out the ashes and start the boiler. Put out the bins. Gave her an affectionate kiss on the cheek when he left in the morning *and* another when he came in the door at twenty-five past six. A truly devoted father, too, if awkward at showing it. The way he'd befriended poor Dave, anybody could tell. He even sent an extra Christmas card next door, specially for the boy.

Dec. 25, '32: Robt. & baby Ian, aged 6 mos.
On Christmas Day, after they got home from his widowed mother's house (every year Vera brought over the pudding and the mince pie, and every year it was no comment), she had Robert try on the dressing gown. The size was perfect. Did he like it? He said of course, it was beautiful, almost too good to wear for everyday. No, but he must wear it, that was what it was *for,* she said.

Vera picked up the camera, for once, put the baby in Rob's arms, and while Ian in that thoughtful way of his leaned back to study his dad's face, she took the flash picture. When the baby was in bed, she got a small glass of port for each of them, with biscuits, and took the tray into the lounge, where Rob sat leafing through a *National Geo-graphic*. She handed him the glass and stroked across his shoulders, meaning all the time: *See how I love you, Robby? Even besides going to your mother's every Christmas, and not to my own family (which always upsets them), because I know you need me to.*

There was more that she could have said. Wasn't it true that their marriage itself had been his idea—oh, very much so—when she'd been perfectly happy with her secretary's job in the city, being friends and going to concerts together? And now that she'd done it, become his wife, had the baby, and all—well, for the first time she really felt she *deserved* a husband. In bed she made one more try, reaching her arm over him as he lay beside her. He shifted onto his side, facing her, and put his free arm over hers. Their knees, clothed in flannel, bumped together.

"Oh, sorry," he said.

"'S all right."

She moved her hand gently down around his ribs, let it wait tact-fully there. A minute or more passed. She heard his breathing slow down, until finally he was asleep and his hand over her elbow relaxed and slid away. Why on earth had she said it was all right, when it wasn't?

Ian meets potty, Apr. '33

Dr. Truby King advised that toilet training should be accomplished by the end of baby's first year. So far, Ian sat on his potty-chair just to please her, without delivering the goods. It seemed an opportunity, when Robert came down with bronchitis, for Ian to be shown the use of the toilet by his Dad, after the worst of the infection was over.

The two of them went off to the bathroom together after break-fast, and sure enough Ian produced a small number two, right in the potty. *That* was a celebration! But only a couple of mornings later, Rob suffered his first hemorrhage. Vera heard him choking, from where she was fastening her stockings in the bedroom. She ran in, and all she could think to do was stuff a clean nappy to his mouth to catch the blood. Then she dashed next door to call the ambulance from Mrs. Hockney's phone, leaving him there on the toilet with poor little Ian beside him.

When she got back, Ian had managed to crawl to the top of the stairs, potty-chair tied to his behind, howling for her. And Rob was still on the bathroom floor, deathly pale, gripping for dear life onto the edge of the bath.

Rob was operated on in the hospital, and Vera's mother came to stay for that time. But there was no use trying to get Ian back on the potty; none of Dr. Truby King's ideas worked. The problem was he'd been put right off it, that was his Gran's opinion, and Vera was afraid she was right. They'd have to wait awhile and try it later, elsewhere in the house perhaps.

They told Vera the bad news: Rob had developed a virulent TB in both lungs: the one that was operated on couldn't be saved, but there might be a chance for the other, caught at this stage.

Easy to see how he got it, of course. If the Hockneys had only put Dave in the sanitarium, where he belonged! And if only Rob hadn't involved himself! But they hadn't, and he had, and no use crying over it. Back home, she went upstairs to Ian's bedroom, where he was napping soundly. Quietly she lifted the corner of the voile curtain and looked down at the summer house, where Dave was lying on two pillows, his head towards her. Mild sunshine lit up the blond hair, drooping uncut over his forehead. *I've got a husband in the hospital, lost one lung already because of you,* she thought, *and I've a child still in nappies. I could just strangle you, you young menace. And your blasted parents, into the bargain.*

Aug. '33: Postcard from Hockneys, Torquay, Devon
The Hockneys moved, at short notice: Internal Revenue habitually switched their officials to different regions every six years or so, to ensure honesty. When Rob came home after months of convalescence, he was disappointed to hear they'd left, and he asked how Dave was. Vera said, very shortly, she thought he was much the same.

But it was a shock to see the way Rob looked, creeping between bedroom and bathroom. For him to come downstairs once a day for supper was a heroic journey. Everything he touched had to be cleaned with carbolic, his laundry boiled. Vera's hands and arms up to the elbow became red and cracked, though she used Vaseline constantly to salve them. And the worst was that Ian, now a toddler, wasn't allowed to go closer to Rob than three feet. "Dad" signified for him this piece of human furniture, parked here or there in the house, kept off limits like the glass cabinet in the lounge, and about as interesting. Ian was an easy child, good as gold. Vera even caught herself using similar language about Rob to the new neighbors. "He's so good, such an easy patient."

She knew, though, watching Rob's eyes, that every breath he drew in frightened him, as if something might tear open inside. Nobody would tell her if he was right. He talked even less than before, mouthing the words so she had to lean over to hear. Reading the morning paper took half his morning; he unfolded it so slowly it maddened her to watch, then repeated the process for every page, painstakingly refolding and unfolding.

Since he'd been put in the little third bedroom, Vera thought about making it more attractive. Some photos on the bureau could make it up to him a little for being kept away from Ian. She went through her box for snapshots of father and son together. There were plenty of pictures of her and Ian, of Ian sitting in his high chair, Ian learning to crawl. But the only decent one she had of father and son together was the snapshot from Christmas, which she'd rather not see again.

She bought a frame set for three pictures: one of the baby sitting up, one of her holding him, and the Christmas photo, and set them on the night table. When they'd been there a few days, Rob asked her if she could put up the snapshot of him launching the plane with Dave. So she took the photo with herself in it out of its frame—as she told Robby, he could see her face any day of the week—and put the other one in. Mr. Hockney's was certainly a much better picture. Well, they could afford a much better camera, to start with.

Jan. '34 Rob't in his chair at the french windows
If he were a dog, the thought flitted through Vera's mind, alone in the kitchen boiling up milk, *we'd have to be thinking about putting him down.*

His mother insisted he had more color in his face, but any sane person could see that for all her efforts Rob was worse off than the day he'd come home. Fevers and sweating every night, and the flesh had melted off him: he wouldn't eat because his throat hurt too much. She made endless milk puddings—rice, custard, and tapioca—but whatever she made, he never finished a bowl. He was going downhill, didn't the doctor see, who came 'round every three weeks to prescribe cough mixture and Friars' Balsam inhalant? And the laundry was a nightmare—blood spots on the handkerchiefs and pillow cases leaving more and more overlapping brown stains, which eventually you couldn't bleach away.

It came to the point that Rob needed help getting out of the bath, even. He hardly ever came downstairs; his meals all had to be taken up. A grown man, to be this feeble? And good Lord, what miserable thoughts must he be thinking? He never said, so she didn't know.

The next time the doctor visited, she asked him to come into the front room for a minute. There she put it to him: Robert was losing ground, and she was at the limit of her strength, running between the patient and the baby.

"Well Mrs. Benskin," he said, "I've only been waiting for you to say the word. I'll put in a request tomorrow to the sanitarium."

July, '34: Robert taking the sun on terrace, Broadhill
His complexion was nicely tanned, his face had creased itself into a smile, although the body on the lounge chair was just a bony sketch under the striped blanket.

Vera came every Saturday, leaving Ian alternately with her mother and with Rob's. Since she couldn't drive the car, she took a train and two buses—over two hours each way for a one-hour visit. The bag she carried contained a box of licorice All-Sorts—because each time he'd ask her: *"Have you brought me my Spanish?"*—and the bottle of Sanatogen tonic wine that he liked before supper, and the other bottle, of Chlorodyne, for his stomach. The bottles were individually wrapped in brown paper, then put in a Chisholm's bag to disguise them, for the staff at Broadhill were strict as well as stingy with the medicines they handed out: mostly aspirin and bromides.

"It's no use complaining to them," Robert told her when she protested. "Look at it from their viewpoint: if they started making exceptions to the rules, they'd never stop."

But why shouldn't he have these little comforts, since he wanted them? For the first time, she'd begun to think about how much time he could have left. She took the photo of him then, for Ian's sake as much as for her own, and before she left, remembered the small square envelope that had come for him in the post. He drew his hands slowly out from under the blanket to take it, and edged a fingernail under the flap. Vera made a mental note to bring scissors and file next time, to cut those nails—and the toenails, too. The sheet of paper inside was lined and written on both sides in pencil.

"It's from Dave," he said, clearly pleased.

"Oh, is it?"

Of course she already knew, because of the Devonshire postmark. But why spoil the surprise? Now Robert was reading it, word by word, as she sat and passed her gaze along the row of immobile patients, all propped at a slight angle on their lounges, some apparently asleep, others being talked to by relatives (but the murmuring voices didn't carry in the open air, with the sound of a lawnmower going below the terrace, and farther away a tractor turning hay in a field). Robert turned the sheet over and read to the end.

"He mentions that Sopwith Camel we made, Vera. Says he still has it, keeps it in his room. He's in a sanitarium, too, near the coast. He's making friends, a couple of boys near his own age."

It was a long speech for Robert, and Vera mustered up enthusiasm: how nice of Dave to write, and by the way, did he want her to speak to the doctor about a transfer to somewhere pleasanter than Broadhill?

Robert thought for a minute and finally said not to bother: this was as good a place as any. He'd become friendly with a couple of the other patients—one fellow had been 'round the world twice, working his passage on the P & O liners, had many stories to tell. She said he should think about it anyway, and meanwhile it would be Ian's second birthday on Thursday, so she would bring him next time. Something to look forward to.

Before leaving, Vera checked to see that none of the nurses was around, opened the Chlorodyne bottle, and poured forty drops, counting, into the glass of water beside his lounge. He drank. She tucked the bottle into his carryall, under a book, and waited beside him till he drifted off.

June, '35: Ian on donkey rides, Sandown Bay, Isle of Wight

So many things to be grateful for, despite all. This holiday for one (the first they'd had since Rob became ill), thanks to the life insurance benefit so promptly paid up. Ian's happiness made her life worthwhile: things like feeling the excitement through his hand holding hers, coming up the gangplank onto the ferry boat. As soon as they got back, Vera would have the house sold—the estate agent was showing "Rovera" to prospective families even now—and her secretarial position at St. George's School (C. of E. endowed) would begin in late August. By that time she'd have a flat arranged within walking distance of her mother, who'd take Ian in the daytime till he was old enough for school.

Under the sun and the sea breeze, just cool enough to be comfortable, she felt an enjoyment that had been missing for so long, practically since she was a single girl. Ian, in his white floppy sun hat and swimsuit, was at work in the brown sand with his bucket and spade. Having a deck chair, too, that was well worth the sixpence a day. Vera shaded her eyes and looked down to the shoreline where a small wave folded over, made a small "plash!", thinning out into sand, followed by another, and another, out over a hazy sea to the horizon, and the plume of grey smoke from a steamer, and what was that big boat now, coming into view 'round the headland to the right? Even without binoculars you could see it must be one of the great liners, painted white, with many rows of portholes along the side.

Vera pointed it out to Ian and told him that liner was probably going to India—or Africa—magic names, her voice implied. She drew a big circle in the sand: here's where *they* were, three-quarters up on the left, and here was Europe to the right of them, Africa straight down, and India all the way over there, and he could go to India some day because it belonged to England, and so did a lot of other places.

Ian wanted to know the liner's name, but she couldn't see from such a distance, only guess that it might be a P & O boat. Which brought to mind the friend Robert had mentioned during his last months in the sanitarium who had sailed 'round the world, also the books he'd been reading: memoirs of travel in distant places. When Robert passed away in March without warning (the telegram arrived at eight-thirty A.M.), she went to Broadhill and packed up the few things from his nightstand. On top was *The Seven Pillars of Wisdom,* which he had asked for at Christmas. All the pages were cut, that was his methodical way; and tucked in about two-thirds through as a bookmark was the square envelope with the letter in it from Dave— no, there were two or three letters, so Robert must have had more correspondence with the boy.

Her first thought at the time was to keep the book for Ian to have, later; her second, decisive thought was to donate it to the sanitarium library. It would have had to be fumigated, in any case. The letters she dropped quietly into a waste basket under the nightstand, as none of her business.

For a while after Robert passed away, she would catch herself in a wicked hope that Dave had died of the disease, too. She even considered writing to the Hockneys to find out if he had. Fortunately she'd refrained, so that now, on this wide beach with Ian, she felt no shadow on this little life the two of them were making. When she imagined her mother, or another relative or friend asking her if she would think of getting married again, she absolutely knew her answer: Never. And if they pressed her, asking her why, she had the answer to that too: "I've already got everything I need."

On the Island

AFTER DINNER the Driscolls sat for a while with Mr. Soo, by the big windows looking out and down over the bay. There was nothing to close: they were just great oblong unscreened openings, with all that fantasy of beauty spread straight before them. Mary had not learned to believe in it, any more than she had learned to believe that the shadowy, bamboo-furnished, candlelit room behind them wouldn't be invaded by insects—even perhaps bats, or one of the host of hummingbirds. For storms, there were heavy shutters. But nothing ever seemed to come in; only the air stirred, faintly sweet, against their faces; it grew spicier and more confused with scent as the dark strengthened.

Mr. Soo, in his impassive and formidable way, seemed glad to have them; or perhaps he was only acquiescent, in his momentary solitude. The inn was completely empty except for themselves, Mr. Soo, and the servants. This was rare, she gathered, even in the off-season she and Henry had chosen—and, indeed, their room had been occupied, only the day before yesterday, by another couple. A party of six would arrive after the weekend. Being here alone was part of their extraordinary luck. It had held for the whole trip: in Port-of-Spain they had got, after all, the room facing the Savanna; on Tobago they had seen the green fish come in, the ones that were bright as fire in the different green of the water; they had even seen, far off, on the trip to Bird of Paradise Island, a pair of birds of paradise, dim and quick through a great many distant leaves, but unmistakable in their sumptuous, trailing plumage.

This still, small place was their final stop before the plane home, and just as they had planned it, it was beginning as it would end, hot and green, unpeopled, radiantly vacant. "It's the closest we'll get to real jungle," Henry said eagerly. And the jungle was no way away. The inn sheltered in cocoa bushes, shaded by their immortelles: Mr. Soo's plantation was a shallow fringe stretching for acres and acres, with the true jungle less than half a mile behind it. Mr. Soo, she felt sure, had never read one of Henry's books, but obviously was aware of his name; and this perhaps had led him to offer them brandy and sit by them in one of the gleaming, cushioned chairs, as they stared out to the disappearing sea. He did not look to Mary like a man whose pleasure lay in fraternizing with guests. Pleasure? His hair, in short, shining bristles, clasped his head tightly, giving the effect of pulling his eyes nearly shut by its grip. His face was the agreeable color of very pale copper; the mouth straight and thin, the nose fleshy. She and Henry had secretly discussed his age: thirty-eight? forty-four? thirty-seven? In the exhausted light he appeared now almost as though he had been decapitated and then had his head with its impassive face set, very skillfully, back upon his shoulders.

Mr. Soo had been born in Trinidad, but had come here to the island almost fifteen years ago, to raise cocoa. Mary was sure that the friends who had told them about the tiny inn had spoken of a Mrs. Soo, but she was not here and there was no reference to her. Arthur, the major-domo, had said only, "No Mrs. Soo," in response to an inquiry if she were away. Dead? Divorced? A figment of friends' imagination?

"Yes," Henry was saying, "like it's too mild; they can't wait to come again. They're very bird-minded."

Mr. Soo looked at him in astonishment. "Your *friends?*"

"Yes. Very. Why?"

"They seemed to me," said Mr. Soo, obviously shocked, "very nice people. Intelligent. Not bird-minded."

Henry now gaped, baffled.

"Bird-*minded,* Mr. Soo," Mary said nervously. "I think you're thinking of how we sometimes say bird-*brained.* Bird-*minded.* It means thinking a lot about birds. Anxious to see new ones, you know."

Mr. Soo still had an offended air. "Very intelligent people," he said,

"*Very!*" said Henry and Mary simultaneously.

A rush of wings veered past the window, in the new darkness. "Very few here on the island, intelligent people," said Mr. Soo. "Just natives. Blacks."

There was a short pause. A faint yattering, like the rapid clack of unskilled castanets, came dimly from the upper reaches of an invisible tree.

"Haven't you any Chinese or Indian neighbors?" asked Henry, noncommittally.

"Fifteen miles," said Mr. Soo, "is the nearest. I do not like Indians," he added. "But they are civilized. They come from civilized country. On Trinidad, all the shops, the taxis, all mostly Indians. They have an old civilization. Very few criminals. Except when they are drunk. The criminal classes are the blacks. Every week, choppings."

Oh, God, thought Mary, here goes our jungle holiday. Well, she decided immediately, we don't *have* to talk to him; we can go to our room in a minute. She caught Henry's glance, flicked to his wrist.

"Good heavens, it's after ten!" he announced like an amateur actor. "If we're going to get up early for the birds . . . "

Mr. Soo said quickly, "Lots of birds. Even at night. Pygmy owls. They fool the other birds," he explained. "That honey creeper, green honey creeper. The pygmy owl fools him. Like this." He suddenly puckered his lips and gave a tremulant, dying whistle; afterward, he smiled at them for the first time. "And you see cornbirds. Tody-tyrants, too. And motmots, with long tails . . . " He sketched one with a quick hand on which the candlelight caught jade. "They pull out their own tailfeathers. And the kiskadee. That's French, corrupted French. *Qu'est-ce qu'il dit?* Means, what's that he says? Over and over. The kiskadee."

The Driscolls rose, smiling. Are the birds part of the inn, like the soursop drinks and the coconut milk and the arum lilies?—or does he like them? It seemed to Mary that he did.

"There was a bird this morning," she said, "on the piles . . . "

"A pelican," interrupted Mr. Soo.

"No," said Mary rather shortly. "I know pelicans." (For heaven's sake!) "A little boy told me what it was. But I can't remember. Like 'baby' . . . "

Henry and Mr. Soo said simultaneously and respectively, "A *booby!* That's what it was, a booby!" and, "A little boy?"

"The *nicest* little boy," said Mary, answering Mr. Soo. "He showed me the fiddler-crab holes and all the live things growing on the big rock, on the sea side."

"What was his name?" asked Mr. Soo unexpectedly. He had risen, too.

"I haven't an idea," Mary replied, surprised. "No, wait a minute . . . "

"A black boy," said Mr. Soo. "With a pink scar on his cheek."

Mary was not sure why the words she was about to say—"*Victor,* I'm sure he told me"—seemed suddenly inappropriate. In the little silence, Mr. Soo surprisingly bowed. "I am sorry," he said with obvious sincerity. "He is, *of course,* not allowed there. He has been told. This will be the last," he said quickly. "I am *so* sorry."

"Good heavens," said Henry, rather irritably, "he was fine—we enjoyed him. Very much. He was a bright boy, very friendly. He showed us how he would fight a shark—imaginary knife and all, you know."

"He was in the *water?*" said Mr. Soo with a little hiss.

During this contretemps, Arthur had approached; his dark face, lustrous in the candlelight, was turned inquiringly toward them over the brandy decanter.

"No, really, thanks," said Mary. She managed to smile at Mr. Soo as she turned away, hearing Henry say, "We'll be back for breakfast about eight," and then his footsteps behind her across the lustrous straw roses of the rug.

LATER IN THE NIGHT she woke up. Theirs was the only bedroom in the main building except for Mr. Soo's apartment. Earlier, massed poinsettia, oleander, and exora had blazed just beyond their casement windows in the unnatural brilliance of the raw bulb fastened outside—now, by a round gold moon that was getting on for full, blue and purplish hues had taken over. The bunches of blossom were perfectly still.

She could see Henry's dark head on his pillow; he was spread-eagled with one foot quite out of bed. Very soon, familiar pressure would swallow them. Henry, even here, was immersed in his plots, manipulating shadowy figures, catching echoes of shining dialogue. It had nothing to do with happiness, or satisfaction, but she knew that increasingly Henry's mind veered from hers, turning in patterns whose skill she admired. Henry believed in his plots. His cause and effect, lovely as graph lines and as clear, operated below all things. This island, which seemed to her full of hints flying like spray, yielded itself to him in information of tensions, feathers, blossoms, crops. More and more, like a god let loose on clay, he shaped and limited. She loved him for this, too: for his earnestness and the perfection of his sincerity; but sometimes now, she knew, her mind seemed to him disorderly and inconsequential, with its stubborn respect for surprises.

A breeze had begun to stir. The blanched crests of blossoms nodded beyond the broad sill and there was a faint rattle of palm fronds. Also, something moved in the thatch.

I will go to sleep if I think of the right things, she said to herself, and she set about remembering the misty horses, galloping easily over the Savanna track in the Trinidad dawn; she'd stood in her nightgown on the balcony to see their lovely, silent sweep. And the fern banks on Grenada: hills of fern higher than towers, deep springing hills of fronded green. And the surf, the terrifying surf, when they'd launched the little boat off Tobago for the trip to Bird of Paradise Island. The turquoise water had broken in a storm of white over the shining dark bodies and laughing faces of the launchers, the boat tipping and rocking, flung crazily upward and then seized again by dripping hands. She'd felt both frightened and happy; Henry had hauled her in and they'd plunged up and down until finally they reached deep water and saw ahead of them, beginning to shape up in the distance, the trees which perhaps sheltered the marvelous birds. "Nothing is known of the breeding habits of Birds of Paradise," her *Birds of the Caribbean* said. She repeated this, silently, sleepily. Nothing is known of the breeding habits of Birds of Paradise. How nice.

Suddenly, she heard water, a seeping sound—though, on her elbow, she could see it wasn't raining. She swung her feet over the bed, but not to the floor. Luck had been good here, but in the dark she wouldn't walk barefoot and her slippers she kept under the sheet. She felt her way cautiously to the bathroom door. Inside, she lighted a candle—the generator went off at eleven o'clock. The bathroom was immaculate, but water shone by her feet and seeped toward the

depression which served as a shower floor. The toilet was unob-
trusively overflowing in a small trickle. Eventually the floor would
be covered and water would ooze under the door. What on earth
could they do about it tonight, though? Move in with Mr. Soo? She
began to giggle faintly. But it was a bother, too; in remote spots
things took forever to get themselves fixed. She put Henry's sandals
on the window ledge, blew out the candle, and closed the door softly
behind her. Henry hadn't stirred. She got back in bed, thinking: It's a
good thing I saw those sandals—they were *in* the water! The words
set off an echo, but, as she remembered what it was, she fell asleep.

By morning, the water was in their room, reaching fingers in
several directions; the heavy straw of the rugs was brown and dank.
When they came out into the pale, fragrant sunlight of the big room,
Arthur was throwing away yesterday's flowers from the two big blue
vases on the low tables. Henry, dropping his binocular-strap over his
head, stopped long enough to report their problem. Arthur looked at
them with an expression of courteous anguish and ritual surprise and
said that he would tell Mr. Soo.

When they returned two hours later, hungry and already hot, Mr.
Soo had come and gone. His small table, with its yellow porcelain
bowl filled each morning with arum lilies, was being cleared by
Arthur, who brought them a platter of fruit and told them that after
breakfast he would transfer them to Mr. Soo's room. They were
astounded and horrified in equal proportions. "That's absolutely
impossible," said Henry. "We can't inconvenience him like that, why
can't we go down to one of the beach cottages? Or up on the hill?"

Arthur, who at the moment represented all help except the invisible cook, did not say: Because I can't run back and forth and still do
everything here. He said instead, "Mr. Soo did tell me to move you
after breakfast."

Henry was anxious to talk to Arthur. Wherever they went, he
absorbed gestures, words, inflections, as a lock-keeper received water, with the earnest knowledge of its future use. He was very quick
at the most fugitive nuance; later it would be fitted into place, all the
more impressive for its subtlety.

Arthur had poured their second cup of coffee. Now he reappeared
from behind the red lacquer screen, carrying one of the big blue

vases. It was filled high with yellow hibiscus and he set it gently on one of the teakwood stands.

Henry said, in his inviting way, "You do a bit of everything."

Immediately, Arthur came to the table. "Only I am here now," he said. "And the cook. Two boys gone." He held up two fingers. "Chauffeur is gone."

On short acquaintance, Mary did not particularly like Arthur. He had a confidential air which, she noticed, pivoted like a fan. At present it was blowing ingratiatingly on Henry. "Mr. Soo had a lot of trouble with help," said Arthur. Mary saw with a rather malign amusement the guest's breeding struggle with the writer's cupidity. The victory was tentative.

"Now *we're* upsetting things," said Henry, not altogether abandoning the subject. "It's ridiculous for him to move out of his room for us."

"Won't upset Mr. Soo," said Arthur soothingly. "He can shut the apartment off, sitting room, library. Another bath, too, on the other side. Used to be Mrs. Soo."

Mary could see the waves of curiosity emanating from Henry, but he gallantly maintained silence. "There is a sleep-couch in the sitting room," Arthur went on. "Mr. Soo does want you to be comfortable, and so." He pivoted slightly to include Mary in his range.

His eyeballs had crimson veins and he smelled of a fine toilet water. "Mr. Soo is very angry with that boy," said Arthur. "Mr. Soo does tell he: Stay away from my beach, ever since that boy come here."

In spite of herself, Mary said irascibly, "But that's ridiculous. He wasn't bothering anyone."

"Bother Mr. Soo," said Arthur. "Mr. Soo is so angry he went last night to go to see he grandmother. Told he grandmother, that boy does come here again, he beat him."

"May I have some hot coffee, please?" asked Mary.

Arthur did not move. He swept his veined eyes from one to the other. "Mr. Soo does not own that beach," said Arthur. "Can't no mahn own a beach here. Mr. Soo's beachhouse, Mr. Soo's boat, Mr. Soo's wharf. But not he beach. But he don't let no mahn there, only guests."

"Why does he like this beach so much?" said Mary, for it was small and coarse, with plenty of sharp rocks. "The boy, I mean."

"Only beach for five miles," Arthur told her. "That boy, Vic-tor, come with he brother, come to he grandmother. They live top-side. Just rocks, down their hill. Very bad currents. Sea-pussy, too. Can't no mahn swim there."

"May I have some hot coffee?" Mary said again.

Arthur stood looking at her. At this moment a considerable clamor broke out in the kitchen behind them. Voices, a man's and a woman's, raised in dispute, then in anger. The woman called, "Arthur! You come here, Arthur!"

Arthur continued to look at them for about two seconds; then, without haste, he went away, walking around the screen toward the kitchen.

"All right, all right," said Henry, answering a look. "But you know perfectly well we can't come here for five days and tell Mr. Soo who he must have on his beach."

"It isn't his beach."

"It isn't ours, either."

Something smashed in the kitchen. A door banged viciously. Outside the window went, running easily, a tall, big boy. His dark, furious, handsome face glared past them into the room. He dived down the wooden steps past the glade of arum lilies. His tight, faded blue-jeans disappeared among the bushes.

"What was *that* in aid of?" said Henry, fascinated.

Arthur appeared. He carried the faintly steaming enamel pot of coffee, and coming up to them, poured a rich stream into Mary's cup. Then he said: "The big brother of Vic-tor, he's a bad bad boy. Daniel. Same name as the man fought the lion." He bowed slightly, thus reminding Mary of Mr. Soo, turned to the other teakwood stand, lifted the empty blue vase, and went off with it behind the screen.

" '*Fought* the lion'?" said Mary, inquiringly, to Henry.

"Well," said Henry, "I suppose Arthur places him in the lion's den, and then improvises."

That was the last of the excitement. They were transferred quickly and easily from their moist quarters; the toilet was now turned off and not functioning at all. Mr. Soo's room lacked all traces of its owner, unless a second bed could be seen as a trace. It had a finer view than their abandoned room, looking all the way down the series of long terraces to the small bright rocky beach.

GREENNESS TOOK OVER: the greenness of the shallows of the bay before it deepened to turquoise, of the wet, thick leaves of the arum lilies, soaked each morning by an indefatigable Arthur, of the glittering high palms, and the hot tangled jungle behind the cocoa bushes shaded by their immortelles. Mary had—unexpectedly to herself—wanted to leave before their time was up. She had even suggested it to Henry right after breakfast on that second morning. But Henry wanted to stay.

"It *isn't* Mr. Soo," she said, trying to explain. "It hasn't anything to do with that. It's something else. There're too many vines. Everything's looped up and tangled. The palms rattle against the tin and give me dreams."

"Don't be fey," said Henry rather shortly. "We'll be away from palms soon enough."

Mr. Soo continued cordial in his immobile fashion: he talked to them from his small table when, at dinner, their hours coincided. Once, he had Arthur make them each a soursop, cold and lovely as nectar, when they came in brown and sweaty from the beach rocks. But by some obscure mutual assent, there were no more brandies. After dinner, the Driscolls sat on their tiny terrace, watching the moon swelling toward fullness, and drank crème de cacao in tiny gourd cups provided by Arthur. They knew they were destined to share their final hours on, and their first off, the island with Mr. Soo. He too would be on the biweekly plane to Trinidad. Mr. Soo said he was going to Port-of-Spain to procure plumbing fixtures. Arthur said Mr. Soo was going to procure a number two boy and a chauffeur. Where on earth did Mr. Soo wish to be driven, over the narrow, pitted, gullied roads that circled the island? Through and through his plantation, perhaps. Arthur took no note of coldness in relation to his comments on Mr. Soo; also, Mary felt, the most ardent questioning would have led him to reveal no more than he had originally determined. His confidences went by some iron and totally mysterious autodecision. She was uncertain how his sentiments stood in regard to his employer.

On their last afternoon, the Driscolls went for a walk. Just before dusk, they decided to go deep along the jungle path. This was the hour for birds; all over the little island they were suddenly in motion. Almost none, except the hummingbirds with which the island fairly vibrated, flew in the golden hot midday, but at dusk the air was full of calls and wings.

Mary and Henry went along the middle ledge, above the lilies. Down on the beach, the fiddler crabs would be veering, flattening themselves, then rearing to run sideways, diving down holes into which fell after them a few trembling grains of sand. From here, the Driscolls could only see the white waves, leaping like hounds up at the rocks. They went along slowly, musingly, in the fading heat, up the steep path back of the garden sheds, below the giant saman, the great airy tree with its fringed, unstirring, pendent parasite world. With its colony of toe-hold survivors, it was like the huge rock on the beach, half in the tides, to whose surface clung and grew motionless breathers.

They turned up the small, dusty road toward the solid wave of tree crests towering ahead. They had been this way twice before; they remembered a goat tethered up the bank at eye-level, a small scrubby cow standing uncertainly in the ditch. They would pass a cabin, half up the slope, with its back to the bay far below, its straw roof smothered under rose-colored masses of coralita. They walked in intimate silence. The road was daubed with the fallen blossoms of immortelles and their winged pods. Once, two laborers passed, stepping quietly on their tough bare feet, the shadows of leaves mottling their bodies and bright blue ripped trousers, machetes swinging gently from their heavy belts.

Around a curve, they came on a dead, long snake, savagely slashed. Just before their path struck off the road, there was a jingle and faint creaking, and around a tangle of scarlet blackthorn rode two native policemen, their caps tilted against the sunset, their holsters jogging their elbows. They pulled their small horses, stained with sweat, into single file; one raised his hand easily in a half-salute and both smiled. These were the first horses the Driscolls had seen on the island, and the first police. Of course, there had to be police, but it was strange how out of place they seemed. When the hushed fall of the hoofs in the dust died away it was as though horses and riders had melted.

Later, sitting on a fallen tree in the bush, Mary thought idly about the snake, the laborers, the policemen. Henry had gone further in, but she had felt suddenly that she couldn't walk another step. She sat on ridged strong bark coursed by ants and thought about the policemen, their faces, their small dusty horses, on that peaceful, hot patrol. Surely there must be almost nothing for them to do. And yet the idea of violence, she realized, had come to the air she breathed. Not violence as she knew it in Henry's books, or in the newspapers at home—riot, rape, murder, burglary. This violence seemed a quality of growth—the grip of the mollusks on the wave-dashed rock, the tentacles of the air plants flowering from the clutched saman. It oppressed her with its silence, its lack of argument. Perhaps she responded in some obscure portion of her feminine heart. An ant ran silently and fast over her hand. She shook it off and stared into the green that had swallowed Henry. His preciousness to her appeared not enhanced but pointed up by her sense of the silent violence of growth around her, as if, among the creepers, windfalls, sagging trees, his face, clear to her love, defined itself as the absolute essential. Of the rest, blind accidents of power, and death, and greenness, she could make nothing. Nothing they might do would surprise her.

There was a wild cocoa bush not ten feet away, dropped into this paroxysm of growth—thin, tall, struggling for light. She could see the pendulous gourds in their mysterious stages of ripeness: cucumber green, yellow, deep rose-bronze, and plum-brown. That plum-brown was on the voluptuous poles of the bamboos, the great, breeze-blown, filmy, green-gold stools of bamboo.

She listened for Henry. There was provisional silence, but no real stillness; hidden streams ran with a deep, secret sound in the throat of distant ravines, and the air was pierced and tremulous with bird calls, flutings, cries, cheeps, whistles, breaks of song; response and request; somewhere away, lower than all the sounds but that of water, the single, asking, contemplative note of the mourning dove.

All at once, there was Henry. When she saw him, she realized that some portion of her had been afraid, as though, like the police on their little horses, he would melt into the greenness for good.

"Did you realize I'd forgotten my binoculars?" he asked, infuriated with his stupidity. "Of all idiotic times!"

Suddenly, she flung herself at him, winding her arms about his neck, linking their legs, covering his face with quick, light kisses. He held her off to look at her, and then folded her tightly in his arms, as though she too had come back from somewhere. "We haven't a flashlight, *either*," he said, "and, if we don't look out, we'll be plunging about in the dark, breaking everything."

On the way home, they went more rapidly. The birds were almost completely silent. Now and then one would flash in the tree crests far above them, settling to some invisible perch. We've left this island, Mary thought. There came a turning point—on a wharf, on a station platform, in the eyes of a friend—when the movement of jointure imperceptibly reversed. Now they were faced outward—to their suitcases, to their plane, to the Port-of-Spain airport, to Connecticut and typewriters. Mary began to worry about the dead snake, in the thick dusk; she didn't want to brush against its chill with her bare, sandaled feet. But, when they came to the spot, she saw it at once. It seemed somehow flatter and older, as though the earth were drawing it in.

As they rounded the bend to the final decline, a sound came to them, stopping them both, Mary with her hand digging into Henry's arm. They thought at first it was an animal in a trap, mistreated or dying. It was a sound of unhuman, concentrated, self-communing pain, a dull, deep crying with a curious rhythm, as though blood and breath themselves caused pain. "What *is* it?" cried Mary, terrified.

"It's a human being," said Henry.

He was right. Drawn close together, they turned the bend in the road, and saw the group from which the sound came; just up the steep slope to their left, in front of the cabin. Raw light from a kerosene lamp on the porch fell on the heads of the men and women, in an open semicircle. Around this space crawled on her hands and knees a woman. Her head was tied in a red kerchief and the light caught her gold earrings. She pounded the earth with her fist, and round and round she crept in short circles.

Dark faces turned in their direction, but the woman did not stop; on and on went the sound. Alien, shocked, embarrassed by their own presence, the Americans hesitated. Then Henry caught his wife's elbow and steered her, stumbling, down the path.

"Oh, Henry, *Henry* . . . " she whispered frantically to his shadowy face. "Oughtn't we to stop? Couldn't we? . . . "

"They don't *want* us!" he hissed back. "Whatever it is, they don't want *us*."

She knew he was right, but an awful desolation made her stumble sharply again. The sound was fainter now; and then, in a minute or two, gone. Below them, they could see the light bulb lashed to the trunk of the saman tree, like a dubious star.

LATER, MARY WAS NOT SURE why they said nothing to Mr. Soo. Neither, strangely, did they discuss it between themselves in their bedroom, showering, dressing for dinner. It was as though its significance would have to come later. It was too new, still, too strange; their suspended atmosphere of already-begun departure could not sustain it.

This sense of strangeness, and also, perhaps, the sense of its being their last evening, seemed to constrain them to be more civil to Mr. Soo. Arthur, bringing their daiquiris, told them there would be a cold supper; the cook was away. His air was apologetic; this was evidently an unexpected development. On the terrace, he set their drinks down on the thick section of a tree bole that served as a stand, and looked through the open casement window into their room, now transforming itself again into Mr. Soo's room: at the open, filled suitcases, the range of empty hangers, the toilet bottles on the dresser.

"You sorry to go?" asked Arthur. "You like it here, and so?"

"Very, very much," said Henry. "We hope we can come back."

"You know, one thing," said Arthur. A gong was struck imperiously. Arthur took his empty tray back through the room. The door closed behind him.

PERHAPS IT WAS too late for a more cordial response; perhaps Mr. Soo, too, felt that they were no longer there. Above his lilies in their yellow bowl, he was unresponsive. After one or two attempts at conversation, the Driscolls ate their cold supper, talking to each other in tones made artificial by several kinds of constraint. Over coffee, Henry said, "I'd better see him about the bill now—it's all going to be so early in the morning."

Mary waited for him by the huge open window-frames, where

they had sat on their first evening, discussing with Mr. Soo their bird-minded friends. The moon, which tonight was going to be purely full, had lost its blemishes of misproportion; it was rising, enormous and perfect, in a bare sky. She could hear very faintly the sound of the tide as she stared out over the invisible bay to the invisible sea.

Behind her, Mr. Soo and Henry approached, their footsteps hushed by the straw, their voices by the silence. Turning, she was confronted by Mr. Soo's face, quite close, and it struck her that the moonlight had drawn and sharpened it, as though it were in pain.

"I hope you and your husband have been happy here," said Mr. Soo.

"Very," said Mary. (Now we're in for a drink, she thought.) "The birds have been wonderful . . . " she began, but Mr. Soo was not listening.

"The driver from the airport will be here at six," he said. He turned and left them, walking slowly over the gleaming rug.

The moon hadn't reached their terrace. Arthur, arriving with the crème de cacao, had to peer at the tree bole before setting down the little cups. He did not go away, but stood and looked at them. Finally, he said, "Do you remember Vic-tor?"

"Of course," said Henry, and Mary added, "The little boy."

"He's gon," said Arthur.

Henry said with interest, "Gone?"

"Dead, gon." Arthur stood there, holding his tray, and waited for them to speak. When they still did not, he said, "He did go off those high rocks. Back down from he house, those high rocks. He did go to swim in that sea-pussy. Like he grandmother told he not to. He is gon, out to sea; no body. No body a-tall. He was screaming and fighting. Two men fishing, they tried very hard to grab he up, but couldn't never get to he. He go so fast, too fast. They will never have no body—too much current, too many fish. He grandmother told he, but that boy, he gon to swim. He won't even mind he brother, brother Daniel, brought he up," said Arthur, turning away and continuing to talk as he left, "*or* he grandmother, took he in. The cook is gon," said Arthur, faintly, from the distance: "Now Mr. Soo, Mr. Soo is all alone." The door closed.

Mary got up, uncertainly; then she went into the bedroom and began to cry very hard. She cried harder and harder, flinging herself on the bed and burrowing her head in the pillow. She felt Henry's hands on her shoulder blades and told him, "I can't think *why* I'm crying—I didn't even know the child! Yes, he showed me the crabs, but I didn't *know* him! It's not that . . . " She was obsessed by the mystery of her grief. Suddenly, she sat up, the tears still sliding down over her lips. "That was his grandmother," she said.

"It's a pattern," said Henry miserably. "We saw it happen all the way from the beginning, and now it's ended. It had to end this way."

She touched his face. His living body was here beside her. She slid her hand inside his shirt, feeling his flesh, the bones beneath it. The room was filled like a pool with darkness. She ran her fingers over his chin, across his lips. He kissed her softly, then more deeply. His strong, warm hand drew her dress apart and closed over her breast.

"I love you," he said.

She did not know when Henry left her bed. She did not, in fact, wake until a sound woke her. Her bed was still in darkness, but the window was a pale blaze from the moon, now high and small. It struck light from the palms' fronds, and against it she saw the figure on the ledge, in the open window. Young and dark and clear, and beautiful as shining carved wood, it looked against all that light, which caught and sparked on the machete's blade. It was gone; she heard a faint thud on the earth below the window. She raised herself on her elbow. In Mr. Soo's moonlit room she stared at Mr. Soo's bed and at what she now made out on the darkening sheet. It was Henry's dark head, fallen forward, and quite separate. His eyes were still closed, as if in an innocent and stubborn sleep.

FROM   1996

I Am Dangerous

Hemingway's Cats

I

When, on the first morning of their honeymoon, Antonia opened their door to let in some fresh air, an enormous cat sprang into the room. Mottled orange and gold, very quick despite its size, the cat leapt onto a chair beside the dresser and then toward Antonia, who recoiled and nearly fell backward, crying out in alarm. Next it went for the bed, bounding onto Antonia's dented pillow and into Robbie's lap, where it curled promptly into a ball and closed its eyes. Propped against his own pillow, half-sitting so he could see Antonia better—watching her dress, watching her move gracefully about the room—Robbie laughed hysterically at the sight of his wife crying out, jumping back into the room's dimmest corner. "Hey—hey, it's only a cat," he managed, but he could hardly speak for laughing, and certainly Antonia could not speak. In fact, Antonia could not move. For what seemed half an hour but was probably only two or three minutes, she stayed back, trembling, while her husband laughed and the cat slept.

Yet Robbie looked guilty, climbing out of the bed. The cat made a small disgruntled noise, then rearranged itself on Antonia's pillow.

"Honey, you're all right, aren't you?" Robbie said, in the solicitous bridegroom's voice he'd tried all during the night. Naked, he came toward her with arms outstretched. "I didn't mean to laugh, it's just that you looked so—so damn *funny*," he said, and he dropped his arms and started laughing again. "I'm sorry," he said. "It's just that squeal you let out, and that little jump backward—"

"I've got the picture," she said, though not bitterly, for seeing the incident through Robbie somehow helped. She felt her body loosen, and when Robbie embraced her, she felt again the wave of pleasurable emotion—gratitude? relief?—that had swept her into this marriage and changed her life so profoundly, in a dreamlike swift few months; had changed *her,* as she liked to think. (For she had lived a meager life, cramped and embarrassed and afraid. It was like her, she thought, to be afraid of an ordinary cat.)

"Don't be mad," Robbie said, rubbing her shoulders.

"I'm not mad," she said carefully. "I'm embarrassed that's all. For acting like such a fool."

"You were just startled," Robbie said, "it's nothing to be embarrassed about," and he turned back toward the bed, clapping his hands. "Shoo!" he cried, and the cat's tail stiffened with alarm, and in an instant it had leapt off the bed and out the door. The room was still.

"I don't like surprises," Antonia said, from her place in the corner.

"Don't worry about it, it's nothing," Robbie said cheerfully, heading for the bathroom. "It's something to tell Dad—you know, an anecdote. When we get home."

Robbie's father, Vincent, was paying for this honeymoon in Key West. He'd spent his own honeymoon here, in the mid-sixties, and every few years he went back again, telling his wife and children and friends that the island was "another world"—not exactly paradise, he'd say, but as close as *he'd* ever get. Vincent was a large, bearish man with a blunt, square face and quick-moving eyes, ice-blue. Antonia had met him only a few times, and he frightened her in a pleasant way; from the beginning she'd felt that Vincent liked her—which was, of course, very important to Robbie—and on the flight down from Atlanta, her husband had delivered the final judgment, in the off-hand manner Antonia knew he had copied from Vincent. "By the way," he'd said, turning a page of his magazine, "at the reception Dad drew me aside. He thinks you're terrific—that you're 'perfect' for me, in fact." He'd given a brief laugh; Antonia had felt that anything she said might sound tactless, so she murmured agreeably, gazing out the small blurry window. Down her arms and back went that shiver of apprehension she felt whenever Vincent's name was mentioned. She knew that he was, in his son's eyes, a colossus—a decorated Vietnam vet, a self-made businessman, an autodidact who knew several languages and liked to quote Nietzsche, an expert sailor and marksman. In short, any boy's hero. Learning that he thought well of her, Antonia had felt the permanence of her marriage far more acutely than at the moment she and Robbie had said, both of them quite meekly, "I do."

By the time Robbie came out of the bathroom, she'd made the bed and opened their drapes to a flood of sunlight. As she expected, Robbie kidded her for straightening the room—they were on vacation, for heaven's sake, the maid would be arriving any minute!—but she liked to keep busy; she'd never been the type to just sit. Nor did she enjoy waiting around for slower people, though of course she hadn't mentioned that to Robbie. Her mind worked quickly, her senses were keen, but if Robbie was a bit lethargic and had not quite mastered the details of everyday life, maybe that was an advantage: Antonia would have that much more to do, her days would be filled to bursting. Robbie was Vincent's oldest son but the last to get married, and had there been some tacit hope on Vincent's part that Antonia would assume the role of looking after him, keeping him on track? If so, maybe that only meant that Antonia had found herself; or, at the very least, had found a sort of refuge.

Man and wife, they went out into the cool morning air. Vincent had made a list of things they must not miss—not only tourist attractions, but restaurants and bars Vincent liked, little shops where they were to be sure to give the proprietor Vincent's best regards—and now, out in the sunlight, Robbie unfolded the list and stared at it, bewildered. "Dad's handwriting," he said, apologetically. "Somehow I've never been able to . . ." Antonia felt that he wasn't really talking to her, but she said pleasantly: "Here, let me try." Robbie gave her the list and immediately began fiddling with his camera. Antonia felt an obscure pleasure that she could read, and quite easily, Vincent's tiny, crabbed handwriting, which looked at first glance like some other language. Now her eye paused over one of the items on the list—"the Hemingway house." The address was across the street from their guest cottage, and looking up Antonia saw an enormous yellow-painted house, complete with columns and verandas, several out-buildings, a yard shaded by lime and banyan trees, and a red-brick wall separating the compound, in its dim-shaded serenity, from the sunlit noisy street. Squinting, Antonia saw that there were several cats perched along the wall, as though standing guard.

"Look, it's where Hemingway lived," she told Robbie. "We're right across the street." She didn't know why the fact should please her—she had never read a word of Hemingway—but somehow it did. She felt it might have been some clever signal from Vincent, who had arranged their Key West accommodations.

"Is that right? Hemingway?" Robbie said vaguely, pushing his glasses up his nose, lifting his camera. He snapped a picture of the house.

When they reached the front gate, Antonia thought she saw their intruder on the corner gate-post, stretched indolently on his side, eyes half-closed in the sun. Tawny-gold, tawny-orange, and really quite fat. Antonia had the impulse to lunge toward the cat, to frighten it, but perhaps the cat would not be startled. Perhaps it would not even move, and she would look foolish once again, and Robbie would start laughing uncontrollably. In any case, she resisted the impulse and followed her husband toward the house.

The cats, it turned out, had actually belonged to Hemingway. Every half hour there was a tour of the writer's house; and their guide—a tiny, angry-looking black woman in her forties—paused before one of the dining room windows, where a dainty tan-and-black kitten had perched on the sill. All the forty-odd cats on the property, she said, were descendants of Hemingway's own cats, and if anyone looked closely he would see that each cat's paw had six toes. They're all related, the woman repeated, all descended from Hemingway's cats. She spoke in a bored, precise voice. A man near Antonia and Robbie raised his hand to ask a question, but the woman was already leading them upstairs. Here they saw the writer's bedroom, though the bed itself had been roped off and could not be touched. The room had a musty, oaken smell. Spread out on the bed were several rare books and manuscripts of Hemingway's. The woman was reciting an anecdote about the friendship between Hemingway and Fidel Castro, but Antonia only half-listened—she had glimpsed something under the bed, a slender black cat hunkered down as though ready to spring, its huge gleaming eyes fastened on

Antonia. Once again, Antonia froze. Now the other tourists were shuffling out, the guide's voice was fading down the stairs, and Robbie touched her arm: "This is pretty interesting, huh? The room where Hemingway slept, somebody famous like that?" Antonia smiled thinly. She could not take her eyes from the cat, which had not moved, had not even blinked. . . . But Robbie took her forearm and pulled her away, mumbling something about lunch. Downstairs, it occurred to Antonia that she had actually become involved in a staring contest with a cat—a little black orphan of a cat that no one else in the room had even seen. Even worse, the cat had won.

Yet somehow the incident cleared the air between her and Robbie, or perhaps cleared a space in her own mind. She laughed to herself about the cat under Hemingway's bed, and then she could laugh about the first cat, which had frightened her so badly. One o'clock of her first full day as Mrs. Robert Kendall, and a great tension had been relieved in her. She and Robbie found an outdoor cafe right on Duval Street, they had margaritas and sandwiches made with pita bread, they talked and laughed for more than an hour. When their food arrived, Robbie had continued the theme that everyone in his family loved Antonia—literally everyone, and Vincent above all.

"The others take their lead from Dad," Robbie said comfortably. "If *he* likes you, then everyone does."

"But you just found out yesterday?" Antonia asked. She kept her tone light, flirtatious. "Before the reception, you didn't know—"

"If he *hadn't* liked you, I'd have known," Robbie said. "In fact, there wouldn't have been any reception."

Antonia sat for a moment, not eating or speaking.

"But wait, I didn't mean—" Robbie dropped his sandwich on the plate, swallowed his mouthful without chewing. "What I meant is, Dad wouldn't have sprung for everything if he hadn't approved. So it would have been a much smaller affair."

"The wedding, you mean."

"Of course I mean the wedding. What else would I mean?"

Smiling, Antonia took a tiny bite of her sandwich, her jaws nearly motionless as she chewed. Abruptly, Robbie laughed. He lunged for the camera, snapping the shutter before Antonia could duck away.

"I never know when you're kidding!" he cried, delighted.

"I told you," Antonia said, fixing him with a keen, motionless gaze, "*no* pictures. Not today, not ever. Now give me the camera."

Antonia's hand darted out, but Robbie had lunged again, pulling the camera onto his lap; she swatted him several times, making little grabs for the camera, and Robbie hunched over, giggling and jerking from side to side, almost upsetting the table. From the other tables, several older couples looked over and smiled. A pair of young, playful newlyweds, they might have thought. Lighthearted. Carefree.

"Dad *did* mention that," Robbie said, facetiously protecting the camera with both his arms. " 'She won't allow a single photograph?' he wanted to know. 'On her wedding day?' . . . He seemed suspicious," her husband laughed, "but I told him to send the photographer home. I said"—and Robbie doubled over, nearly hysterical—"I said that you were wanted dead or alive in twelve states, and to forget about the society page."

"The society page?" Antonia said faintly. "But I thought Vincent—I thought your father scorned that kind of thing." She pawed at Robbie's lap a few more times, but half-heartedly; she didn't really want the camera. If she decided to destroy the film later, she could.

"Oh, that's just a line of his. Actually, he gets quite a kick out of it. They plastered Tod's wedding all over the *Journal-Constitution*," and here his voice lowered, "but then he and Karen had twice the wedding we did. Not that I'm complaining, of course. It makes sense when you consider that Karen's parents—"

Robbie broke off, perhaps catching the implied comparison of Antonia to Karen, perhaps censoring what might sound like criticism—however mild, however indirect—of his father. Stuffing the rest of the pita bread into his mouth, he chewed somberly for a while. Quite often he went into these boyish reveries, as though bewildered by the sinuous windings and sudden pitfalls of even the most ordinary conversations. Delicately Antonia licked the salt around the rim of her margarita, not really alarmed. During these past months she had negotiated her way among the Kendalls as best she could, generally steering clear of Vincent, sending him from a distance the kind of demure but enigmatic smiles that appealed to such men. Brusque and theatrical, with a braying voice meant for whole rooms to overhear, Vincent had few enough occasions to draw her aside, and she had been careful not to create any real opening. His shrewd and watchful true self, she knew, was in many ways a slave to his persona, and after his booming queries received answers that were intelligent but so mild as to lead nowhere, he'd had little choice but to move along, or else to begin one of his monologues that soon had many others gathered around. The other Kendall wives were also intelligent, beautiful, and mild, though naturally rather than carefully so; and she lacked their sleek blonde beauty, not to mention their patrician carelessness. Yet gradually she had felt that she'd won Vincent over; Robbie's comments on the plane hadn't really been much of a surprise. Antonia's eerie containment, her expressionless dark eyes and the dark fine hair that curved along her jaw identically on either side, and of course the graceful but alert silence, if not vigilance, that she had developed throughout her adult years and that had charmed more than a few men—all this had snagged Vincent's interest, perhaps even more than his interest. She discounted Robbie's remark about the society page, after all. The real energies of such men lay elsewhere.

After the waitress brought their Key Lime pie, Robbie blurted out, this time not bothering to swallow, "I'm sorry, honey, I mean about suggesting that Karen—You know I don't *care* about that."

Antonia detested sweets, but she forked off a bite of her own pie. "I know," she said. "I don't care, either." As Antonia well knew, Karen had descended from Atlanta's higher social echelons to marry that upstart Vincent Kendall's youngest boy; soon enough, of course, he'd be far richer than any of Karen's family. "Actually," she said, "I sort of like Karen."

"I don't want to live like that," Robbie went on, not hearing. "I can't stand all the parties, and the pretentious house, and all the talk about their last vacation, their next vacation . . . I want something simpler, I really do."

Antonia laughed. "You've made a fine start, haven't you?" she said.

They spent most of the day following Vincent's list, checking off the items one by one. They bought T-shirts at Fast Buck Freddie's, stopped for a drink at Sloppy Joe's ("Hemingway's favorite bar," Vincent had scrawled), and rented bicycles and pedaled down to the beach, stopping at "the Southernmost tip of the United States," as a sign proclaimed, and gazing out at the calm, rather colorless sea. "Now I know why people love this place—why Dad does," Robbie said, shading his eyes against the sun-dazzled water, his mouth opened in delight. "It's so peaceful here, don't you think? So quiet and relaxed, with the palm trees and the warm weather, and nobody dressed up, nobody in a hurry . . . " Antonia had looked down, a bit self-conscious in her white linen dress and matching low-heeled shoes. Already she'd perceived that she was overdressed for this place, at least for the daytime, and vowed that tomorrow she would wear the T-shirt and pair of blue jeans she'd brought for lounging in their room. She didn't want to stand out, after all. She wanted to be part of all this. As they rode about the island, she'd paid less attention to the scenery than to her husband, watching him from the corner of her eye. Amazing that he seemed so comfortable, she thought, that *he* didn't notice if his wife were overdressed, her white straw purse dangling awkwardly from the handlebars; that *he* didn't keep checking to see was this real, was she really there, were they man and wife forever. He rode with his eyes squinted happily, tongue darting out the side of his mouth, pointing to a lighthouse in one direction—*look, Antonia!*—and a baroque church steeple in the other, *look at that!* Yet he didn't glance at her, and she felt that, yes, they were married, they were irrevocably bound together. Her calves had tensed with a sudden bright energy, and all at once she didn't care how she looked: "Try and catch me!" she cried, pulling her weight hard against the handlebars, and Robbie let out a whoop and began the chase, a wild, laughing pursuit, not of Antonia but of his wife.

She led him all the way to the bike shop and looked over her shoulder, head cocked, as he coasted into the shade where she had stopped, near the entrance. He was panting heavily, shaking his head from side to side; Antonia saw droplets of sweat flying off around him. "You're amazing," he said. "I'm practically worn out, and you haven't even broken a sweat. Your legs must be—your legs are great," he got out, still panting. "Thank you," she said, with a little mock bow, but in truth she *had* begun sweating; a thin film coated her face and neck, even her slender pale arms. For some reason she lifted her wrist and touched her tongue to it, remembering instantly the salt around her margarita at lunch, and she said, "Hey, what does a girl do to get a drink around here," and Robbie raised his eyebrows in a villainous leer.

"Look," Antonia said, "they're selling fruit drinks across the street—go get us one, will you?"

Her husband trotted off, while Antonia carefully parked the bikes, then took her compact out of the purse. Startled, she saw a mussed version of herself in the tiny mirror, her hair plastered against her throat on one side, sweat glistening along her upper lip like delicate whiskers. Quickly she daubed at her face with Kleenex, freshened her tawny-orange lipstick, brushed her hair in place with a few deft strokes. Then Robbie appeared beside her, panting, bearing two styrofoam cups with *Fruit Smoothie* printed diagonally along their sides; the cups held a frozen ruby-colored substance, ruby-colored straws. "Hey, there's a tour bus right down the street," he said excitedly, "it's just loading up. Let's go, Antonia! That way, we're sure to see everything!"

"A tour bus?" she said, and her first thought was how Vincent would disapprove—why follow the herd, why not strike out on your own? But Robbie looked so eager, shifting his weight back and forth like an overgrown kid, smiling. Her husband was past thirty, but Antonia knew he would always look boyish and that Vincent never had: his army pictures showed a stalwart, glaring youth of nineteen, ready to do battle with life. She could imagine him spitting the words out the side of his mouth—"oh by all means, *a tour bus*"—and then grinning or even laughing, but his eyes staying cold, contemptuous. After only four months, could it be that she knew Vincent better than his oldest son ever had?

But she said, "Good idea," and as they boarded the bus—which was actually an open-air trolley, several cars long, crowded with chattering, brightly dressed tourists—Antonia felt glad to do anything; that energy she'd felt when they were on the bikes kept returning in great ecstatic waves. She could hardly sit still, and when the tour guide maneuvered their attention from one side of the street to the other, Antonia moved her head quickly, obediently, as though watching a tennis match. Though really she could not have remembered what she saw. Much of the route she and Robbie had already covered on their bikes, and when they turned into a quiet, tree-shaded street, her legs tensed before she quite understood where they were. Then, just as she'd spotted the compound of detached cottages where they were staying, the tour guide reported through the microphone, with histrionic enthusiasm, "And here on our right is Ernest Hemingway's house, where he lived during the years 1931 to 1938, writing such works as *For Whom the Bell Tolls* and *Death in the Afternoon.* At that time Hemingway was married to Pauline Pfeiffer, a wealthy woman who enjoyed gracious living and who . . . " But Antonia stopped listening, her eyes narrowed as they surveyed the house, the spreading banyan trees, the red-bricked wall. As usual, several of the cats had placed themselves along the wall at random, cats of varying colors in varying positions. None was looking at Antonia. As the trolley passed, one of the cats jumped off the wall abruptly, and in her seat Antonia gave a little jump, too; but the cat had leapt in the other direction, toward the house. Now the trolley was in the next block; the tour guide was pointing out something else. Antonia sat back.

"Honey, is something wrong?" Robbie asked.

"No, nothing," said Antonia. "I'm just restless, that's all. I wish we could get off."

"Then we *will* get off," and before she could stop him Robbie was moving up the aisle, bending to the tour guide's ear. The trolley stopped at the next corner, and on the sidewalk Robbie said, bowing gallantly, "What now?"

She had to laugh. "I hope we didn't offend him," she said, sorting through her purse for Vincent's list. "But it occurred to me that Vincent wouldn't have approved—" The words were out before she could stop herself. She saw the flash of hurt in Robbie's eyes.

"But I thought—"

"Never mind," she said, looking from the scrap of paper to her watch. "Look, it's after six. Let's walk around a bit more, then go down to the Pier House for the sunset. Your father says it's not to be missed. Then we'll have dinner somewhere."

Briefly he'd lapsed into one of his daydreams, but he recovered quickly and soon they were back on Duval Street, pausing at art galleries and souvenir shops and open-air bars where folk musicians were playing. Already the air was cooler, the street atmosphere changing slowly from afternoon to evening. Now there were fewer children, fewer dogs; there were more young couples like Antonia and Robbie, some of them dressed casually for dinner after a day at the beach. Antonia felt relieved, her spirits lightened, and once again Robbie had the eager, slavish energy of a spaniel, loping inside a cafe to get ice water when Antonia said the fruit drink had made her thirsty, fetching a newspaper and postcards from a corner Rexall, then going back again when Antonia discovered she hadn't brought a pen or stamps. She wanted to send a card to the Lassiters, she told Robbie, and of course to Robbie's parents. Though perhaps *he* should write that card . . . ? And what about Robbie's brothers, and his grandmother out in Scottsdale? Since she hadn't been able to make the wedding, perhaps they should—

"Hold on!" Robbie laughed. "I only bought a couple of cards." He reached out and pinched her cheek, lightly. "Let's just write to our parents," he said. "That's enough, don't you think?"

So they went to the Pier House, finding a table at the edge of the sunset deck; they sat to write their cards. Or rather, Robbie studied his for a moment, then thrust it at Antonia and asked if she didn't mind. "Your wifely duty, after all," he said happily, sitting back and opening the newspaper. Antonia stared down at the cards. She sipped at the milky-looking drink Robbie had ordered her—a piña colada?— and addressed the cards in her girlish, rounded handwriting. *Mr. and Mrs. Vincent Kendall. Dr. and Mrs. William Lassiter.* Though her adoptive parents had missed the wedding—her father had pleaded an important medical convention, her mother refused to travel alone— she knew they would want to hear from her. After she'd left Birmingham seven years ago, only weeks after her eighteenth birthday, there had been a good deal of friction over Antonia's disinclination to write, to let them know where she had settled. Yet she never *had* settled, really, moving from Birmingham to New Orleans to Dallas; then back to New Orleans; then to Atlanta; then to Nashville and back to Atlanta again—working for a series of powerful men. "Assistant" to a state senator, "staff coordinator" for an agribusiness tycoon . . . She'd done well in these jobs, even if she'd been little more, really, than a glorified receptionist. A punctual, attractive presence in the morning; close-mouthed but alert all during the day, which her employers seemed greatly to appreciate without taking *her* very seriously; on occasion, a sympathetic listener at night, non-judging, non-committal. Yet she seldom stayed anywhere for more than a year, having a keen sense of when she was wanted, when she was not—the orphan's legacy. She did not want anyone saying she'd outstayed her welcome; there was always another city, another man who needed her. Another opportunity, as she liked to think.

Once her mother had shouted after her, *Go on then! I guess you can take care of yourself!* Mrs. Lassiter was sickly, a professional invalid; in a rare loss of temper, Antonia had remarked how much sense it made, her having married a doctor. The Lassiters had been a childless couple in their forties when they adopted the six-year-old Antonia; and now she thought, staring at the postcard, that she might never— was it possible?—see them again. When Dr. Lassiter had not been too busy, he had sometimes smiled at Antonia as though from a great distance, a rueful smile as though to apologize, to acknowledge that a mistake had been made, he hoped she would forgive them . . . ? When she turned eighteen, he informed her that there would be little money, perhaps no money; it would all be channeled into a research foundation, established in the Lassiter name. This time he *had* apologized, not quite meeting her eyes. By now, his daughter being a very mature eighteen, his wife's shouted accusation must have seemed the one absolute truth about Antonia—that she could take care of herself; that she would always "land on her feet," as one of her bosses would later remark.

I understand, of course, she'd said, lowering her eyes. You've given me so much already.

Now she wrote, in letters a bit larger than usual, *Having a wonderful time!* and then wrote the same message on the card to the Kendalls. She signed both her and Robbie's names and quickly stamped the cards and thrust them in her purse.

"Done?" Robbie asked, not looking up from the paper.

"Done," she said.

She tried to pay attention to the lowering sun—an enormous orange ball, poised above the watery dark horizon—but her gaze had returned to her husband's bent head. It intrigued her, the way her attention kept snagging on Robbie; the way she kept thinking *hus-*

band, rubbing the word along her tongue as though testing its meaning, its relevance to herself. As though feeling her attention—for how closely, how strangely she was watching him!—Robbie looked up, giving her a quick boyish smile, both happy and fearful.

He stretched his arm across the table, the hand upturned. "Antonia?" he said. "Is something—?"

Her heart had filled, and she felt a sudden catch in her throat, a loss of poise. Confused, she put out her own hand and Robbie grasped it, hard.

Off to the side, there was a sudden burst of applause and the clicking of cameras.

Startled, Antonia and Robbie looked over. A crowd of perhaps forty or fifty, many of them photographers, had gathered along the deck; the couple followed the crowd's attention out to sea, where the sun had just dipped below the horizon, sending brilliant orange and pink trails into the sky.

"The sunset," Robbie said, and quickly he and Antonia exchanged glances, and just as quickly broke into laughter.

"And I thought—" But Antonia didn't dare finish: the idea was so absurd.

"Me too," Robbie said, and they laughed again.

When the waiter approached and asked if they cared for another drink, Antonia was remembering the cat that had burst into their room that morning: so quick, insistent, full of life. She remembered how fearful she had been, her cartoonish alarm that Robbie had found so hilarious. Evidently the cat was one of Hemingway's, and evidently its paws had six toes; but the cat, after all, did not understand. The cat had not meant to frighten anyone. She remembered the way it had curled into Robbie's lap and gone to sleep, uncaring, as Antonia cringed against the wall.

I don't like surprises, Antonia had said.

Now the table was jostled, nearly upsetting Antonia's drink. When she looked up, she saw that Robbie had leapt toward the waiter and begun embracing him. "Hold on! Hold on!" the waiter laughed, pulling back from Robbie's ecstatic greeting. As Antonia watched, her husband kissed the waiter's cheek, the side of his neck; good-naturedly, the waiter kept pushing him away.

Then Antonia saw that the "waiter" was Vincent.

He had commandeered an empty tray, and one of the little red aprons; had approached their table with his head lowered and voice disguised, was there anything they needed, would they care for another drink . . . ?

An elaborate, funny ruse: very typical. His skill in making himself the center of attention, delighting his son, disarming criticism: very typical indeed. Antonia felt light-headed, though she was hardly surprised. Now Vincent winked at her, slyly, over Robbie's bobbing shoulder, as if they were conspirators. Oh yes, very typical: funny and charming, mischievous, certainly beyond criticism.

For Robbie, of course, this was the high point of the trip.

"Dad, you joker!" he cried in delight, falling back into his chair as Vincent took the seat next to Antonia. "When did you get here, anyway? Were you here for the sunset? We've been following that list you made out, all day long, but we never dreamed—Gosh, this is great! Isn't this great, Antonia!"

She gazed across at Vincent, her head lighter than air, feeling dazed in a half-pleasant way; but no, she felt no surprise, no alarm. She felt nothing. "Yes, this is great," she said without irony, not that Robbie was listening. He kept reaching across to cuff his father on the shoulder; he kept hitting the table happily, so that the glasses and silverware rattled.

"Now settle down, everybody," Vincent laughed, watching Antonia. He looked sunburnt, authoritative, his eyes a bright, sharp blue; he wore a tan polo shirt that stretched tight across his massive chest, and a tan nylon windbreaker, and white tennis shoes without socks. Dressed so casually, boyishly, he looked like a sportsman of some kind—an amateur sailor, perhaps. Out in the water, a few minutes ago, Antonia had glimpsed a sailboat going past, the sail billowing, tinted pink by the lowering sun. Now she glanced out to the horizon, but the sailboat was gone and the water had turned dark, choppy; dusk had fallen quickly, she thought, and craning her neck she saw that the crowd had dispersed from along the deck; most everyone had gone off to dinner, to their plans for the evening. . . . Antonia remembered that burst of applause, how it had startled both her and Robbie—the newlyweds, the lovers—and how they had

laughed, embarrassed and pleased to discover that no one had noticed, after all; that really no one cared. They were part of the world,
she thought, and why should anyone mind if they loved, or failed to
love?

Watching Vincent and Robbie, their heads bent close in conversation, Antonia understood that her life was over.

II

There are no surprises, she thought. After all.

The next few hours passed swiftly, or very slowly—she could not
be sure. It was true, she thought, that in dying you flung open a door
to your past life, your past lives; and again you lived them, quickly. Or
slowly. There are no surprises, she thought, because everything is
connected, leading in a zigzag chain back from the present moment;
leading back, finally, rather than forward. Attuned very lightly to
"the present moment," her expression blank, stunned, neutral—
vaguely she heard the scraping of chairs, vaguely she understood
that Robbie and Vincent were leaving, Vincent's arm across his son's
shoulders, their heads bent close together—she sat remembering the
cat from that morning, understanding how everything was connected, knowing with a pitiless thrill of certainty that there were no
surprises, after all. Only errors in perception.

Though the knowledge arrived, as knowledge usually did, too
late.

When someone spoke, using the name "Antonia," she looked up.
She fixed her eyes on Vincent settling back in his chair, Vincent
drawing something from the pocket of his windbreaker—a yellowed
newspaper clipping, a bulky white envelope—and Vincent finally
gazing back at her, his eyes a cold blue but not unfriendly, not really,
just frank and forthright. Now that Robbie was gone.

Instantly she knew the contents of both the clipping and the envelope.

"Another drink?" Vincent asked, almost gently.

She shook her head, *no.*

"I sent Robbie back to the room, Antonia."

And she nodded, *yes.*

She said, "But the key—I have the key, here in my purse. . . . "

"Don't worry, Antonia, he'll get the key from the manager. He can handle that much, don't you think?"

Vincent smiled, though his eyes didn't smile.

"Yes. Yes, of course."

But someone else was speaking in Antonia's place; someone else sat here prim and pale, hands folded around the icy drink as though anchoring her body to this table, this world.

"How did—how did you find out," she said, faintly.

She'd been afraid, for a while, that somehow her boss had found out, but he was a pathetic man, gossipy and embittered, and soon enough she'd dismissed him as a meddler. Those were satisfying days, after all, with the eldest Kendall son paying her such lavish attention, sending roses to her desk each morning, taking her to the same exclusive restaurants where her own boss took his clients. The owner of an accounting firm that had seen better days, her boss had two-thirds of his office space leased out from under him by the Kendalls and he spent much of his time gossiping about Vincent— that "heartless opportunist"—within hearing range of Antonia's desk, never failing to mention the two younger sons who were "sharks, just like their father," and that oldest boy who did well to find his desk in the morning. . . . Hearing this, Antonia smiled thinly; she signed for her flowers, she blocked two hours off her calendar for lunch. Why should she be afraid, after all? She'd never enjoyed such self-possession, such eerie poise. She'd never held such power.

Powerless, she sat watching Vincent as he examined the palms of his hands.

"I almost didn't," he said, trying to sound casual, trying to spare her, "and the man I had, um, looking into you, I'd paid him off the day before the wedding. He's an old gumshoe type, a real digger, and he seemed disappointed that he hadn't found anything. So he kept on, without my knowing—I guess he figured there'd be quite a bonus, if he could uncover . . . " Vincent was almost whispering.

He pushed the newspaper clipping in the middle of the table.

So she let her eyelids fall, let her eyes skim across the headline, ONE OF 'DAWSON'S GIRLS' KILLS SELF, DAUGHTER FOUND IN LOCKED CLOSET, but she said nothing. She felt nothing.

She remembered her own closet, back home. A locked closet.

She remembered how Mrs. Lassiter complained all during Antonia's high school years, why wouldn't she go out, why wouldn't she come downstairs when one of those nice young men dropped by, didn't she want to be popular, did she want people to think she was *odd?* There was no reason for this, absolutely no reason—she was so pretty, after all! Sometimes Antonia locked the door against her, she turned up the stereo or buried her head in a book, she felt her skin drawing tight along her bones, *no, no,* and soon enough the boys stopped coming around. Soon enough, her mother stopped worrying that Antonia would not go out at night, would not accept dates, would not lead the "normal" life of a high school girl. Dr. Lassiter took her side, saying to leave her alone; he'd always despised the slavish conformity of most teenagers; why shouldn't they admire Antonia's independence? Occasionally he would give her a twenty-dollar bill, or a fifty, which Antonia stored away. For the future. By her eighteenth birthday she had nearly three thousand dollars locked in her closet, in a shoebox thrust back into the closet's dimmest corner. Possibly the money would come in handy someday, for who knew what the future held, who knew?

"This is very awkward, of course, for someone like me," Vincent told her, "someone who has been brought up to respect women, to understand their needs. . . . " He nudged the envelope a bit further in her direction, and obligingly she picked it up, gauging its thickness with her sensitive fingers, as though taking the measure of Vincent's grief, or embarrassment, or pride.

"Yes, of course," she whispered.

"I want the best for my family, I really insist on that," Vincent said mournfully. "It's more than just money, you know. It's a name they can be proud of, proud to give their own children, and their grandchildren. . . . If there were some kind of blight, at this early stage—" Out of tact, he stopped himself. He gave her a pleading look.

"I understand," she told him.

Do you understand? Father Callahan kept asking, and Antonia knew she must say yes, always yes, and especially to this tall silver-haired priest to whom Mrs. Lassiter had presented her new child, her dark-haired lovely child, for instruction in the faith. Eventually the Lassiters had become "lapsed Catholics," and when they stopped

attending Mass, Antonia stopped; but at six she had received the
sacrament of baptism, followed the next year by her First Holy Communion, Antonia only one of a giggling horde of little girls in white
dresses and veils, interchangeable. She remembered feeling happy,
that day. She remembered feeling a vague sort of joy.

"Mrs. Kendall is very devout, of course," Vincent was saying, "but
an annulment won't be difficult, I'm told, and we have a story—a
rather carefully detailed story—which it would help a great deal if
you didn't contradict. Not to anyone. Not ever. I'd be very grateful,
Antonia. If you'll send your new address to my office, preferably an
out-of-state address, I'll see that you're taken care of. This is *my*
mistake as much as anyone's, and I don't intend for you to suffer
for—" Again, he stopped himself. He nudged the envelope a little
closer. "This," he said, "is only for now. I think you know that I'm a
responsible man. You know that, don't you? So there's no reason for
you to be angry or to feel—well, vengeful."

"Yes," she said, mechanically. "I mean, no."

And finally she'd answered Mama's question—What do you say to
Mr. Jones, sweetie, what do you say?—and Antonia stammered Yes,
I mean no, and while Mama and Mr. Jones laughed—she hadn't
known him as "Mr. Dawson" then, much less as "Senator Dawson"—
while they laughed she gripped her mother's leg, pressed her flaming
cheeks against the warm fleshy thigh. What, you don't like me? Mr.
Jones said again, grabbing Antonia's sides and hauling her into the
air. Is that it, huh?—but the question confused her, she didn't understand, she winced at the smell of his cologne and his breath reeking
of cigars and his eyes a bright hard blue in the fatty ridges of his face.
Is that it, Antonia? Well, next time I'll have to bring you something,
won't I? Maybe some jelly babies, how about that?—or a doll, one of
those new-fangled dolls that wets and everything? Or I could take
your picture, eh?—why should your Mama get all the attention?
Thinking yes, I mean no, she'd only nodded, and Mr. Jones and
Mama laughed again, and again they hugged each other in that slow
way, and Mama said in her husky voice, She'd rather have money,
she's just like me, and they laughed once more before he left. Mama
was so pretty then! And after he left they always hugged in the real
way, tight and wild and crazy, and Antonia said, What do I say,

Mama, I never know what to say, and Mama said, Honey, it doesn't matter. They don't listen anyhow.

"Antonia, I wish you'd say something," Vincent went on, returning the clipping to his pocket. Ready to leave, but wanting something more. "Listen," he said, "if it's any comfort, I think it's a shame what they did, letting that Dawson off, sending him back to Washington with a slap on the wrist . . . I was a young man then, and I remember thinking how unfair it was, how badly the system had failed. . . . What could be more sickening, all those girls stashed here and there, half of them on drugs, and just because some oversexed buffoon . . . Well, I shouldn't be bringing this up, but I wanted you to know—"

She reached across and took his hand; squeezed her fingers along his wrist, his forearm.

"Maybe it's not too late?" she said, hoarsely, her eyes vacant. "Maybe we can work out some kind of . . . arrangement?" she said. She smiled, thinly. "You like me, don't you? Robbie said you did."

"Yes—I mean, no," Vincent said, the first time she'd ever seen him stammering and confused; his eyes swerved away. "I'm sorry, but no," he said, taking a deep breath. He recovered. ". . . You look a little pale, why don't you sit here by the water, have a nice dinner," he said, and quickly enough the waiter was summoned, the order given; her food arrived only minutes after Vincent left.

Calmly, Antonia picked at the red snapper.

She picked at the roll and butter.

You're so pale, Mr. Jones said, taking off the seersucker jacket. Doesn't your Mama ever let you play outside? Not waiting for an answer he stalked around the little trailer, identical to the one on the other side of the park where Mama's friend Rita lived, Rita who had hung around all the time after Daddy left, bragging about how she never had to work, how modern these little trailers were, complete with little stoves and little bathrooms and even a closet for your clothes! And a TV. And a stereo. Rita hung around her trailer all day reading magazines and smoking Kools and taking little pills Mr. Jones gave her that made her feel airy and weightless, and happier than she'd ever felt in her life. C'mon, you've got to meet him, Rita said, and later Mama had been to Antonia and said, It's only for a little while, honey, till we get back on our feet, OK? There was a little

curtain to pull across Antonia's sofa-bed, for when Mr. Jones came to
visit, or Rita came with a bottle of Early Times to sit gossiping all
night with Mama, or even when Mama was home and Antonia just
wanted to shut out everything: she could draw the curtain, pretend
she wasn't there. But she couldn't pretend with Mr. Jones's heavy
presence in the room, his weight jostling the trailer as he stalked up
and down, looking into drawers, rifling through Mama's little closet.
Where is your Mama, anyway? he asked. Does she always go out
when she's not expecting me?—I'll bet she does, I'll bet she *does,* but
Antonia remembered not to answer; she just sat on the sofa-bed with
hands folded in her lap and waited, waited. When he got close
enough she could smell his breath, the same as Rita's when she
brought the Early Times, and he sat beside her and gave her a wobbly
smile and said, How old are you, anyway? Eight or nine by now, eh?
Antonia waited. She stared at the camera Mr. Jones had brought out
of the closet. What's the matter, kid, cat got your tongue? he said,
and something in his voice told her to answer and so she said, No
sir—I'm six, and for some reason Mr. Jones found that funny and
asked how long her mother would be gone, and Antonia said she
didn't know.

"Dessert, ma'am?"

"No," she said. "Nothing else."

Calmly she opened the envelope, extracted a twenty and put it
beside the check. Touched her napkin to one corner of her mouth,
then the other. Outside the Pier House she headed toward a taxi but
then hesitated, turned, moved out along the street instead. A mild,
fragrant night. All the shops and restaurants and bars were still open;
music drifted onto the air; people were strolling, laughing, in no
hurry. Antonia herself walked slowly, in no hurry. When she did
reach the cottage, the door was unlocked, and first she checked the
closet to see that Robbie's clothes were gone but hers were not. She
went to the window.

She heard someone opening the door, she heard footsteps just
behind her, and she tried to ignore her heart—it had begun to beat
fast, as though she had raced all the way home. Willing herself to stay
calm, she gazed out the window. She gazed across the street.

The windows in the trailer were too high, and she could not get to them; Mr. Jones was holding her down. In any case, there were no streets outside, no lights, nothing at all to help her. Only a few darkened trailers, placed about at random. It was quite late, Mama had gone with Rita and another friend to the movies, a double-feature, she had made Antonia promise not to go outside and *not* to answer the door, and to get in bed before ten o'clock. Of course, Mr. Jones had his own key. Of course, Mr. Jones had the habit of doing whatever he wanted, and now Antonia simply lay on her mother's bed, her legs twitching despite herself, pretending she was behind that curtain and fast asleep in her own bed, and then pretending she was outside, running, running, darting this way, that way! She did not feel the probing fingers, she did not hear the camera's clicking or see the dazzling flashes. She wasn't there, exactly, so how could she make a noise? But when she heard Mama's key in the lock (they decided not to stay for the second feature, Rita would say later: thank God for that, at least), she screamed and screamed. The other woman ran off, and then Mama started screaming, and Mr. Jones struck her across the mouth, but she kept screaming, and then she was crying, and by the time the police arrived Mr. Jones was crying, on his knees and crying, begging forgiveness. He came toward Antonia on his knees, begging, pleading, where she lay very still on the bed. And later, when her mother started screaming again, taking handfuls of pills and screaming at people not in the room at all, Antonia did not object when she opened the closet and said, Just for a little while, I promise—till Mama feels a little better. She went out for a moment—to the phone at the corner, it turned out—and rushed back in, sobbing, and Antonia heard more pills rattling out, and all was still until the giant yellow-haired policeman unlocked the closet door and said, Good Lord—

Motionless, she stared out the window and across the street. Her heart had calmed. Her legs had relaxed. Every minute or two she touched her cheeks with the palm of her hand. Robbie had spoken a few times, but had fallen quiet at last. He sat on the bed, behind her; or on the chair. He didn't know what to do, he'd wept—whether to go or stay. "Antonia, what should I do? I feel like I'm nothing inside, like I'm dead, I don't know. . . . Can't you speak, Antonia? Honey?" Outside, a car had honked: several quick impatient beeps.

She didn't answer. She would like to comfort him, she thought, but it was not in her nature; she hated emotional displays. In any case, she couldn't pay attention to Robbie. Her eye was drawn out of this room, to the house nestled in darkness across the street. She stared, stared. Yes, it was Hemingway's house, and along the brick wall she could make out soft dark clumps in the moonlight, the cats perched at random, vigilant, eternal. They were everywhere, she thought, covering the walls and the grounds and the house itself, guarding everything that was not theirs.

Robbie tried again. "Antonia," he wept, "I'll die if I lose you, don't you understand? Already I feel like I'm dying, like I'm nothing inside . . . you understand, don't you? Antonia?"

Outside, the car horn blared. Or was it one of those cats, sending its wail into the night?

"I don't mean to be cruel," she said at last, "but Robbie, you really won't. You really *won't* die."

Basepaths

THE FOUL LINES are crooked, the outfield too shallow, and the infield's in crying need of repair. But it's a diamond nevertheless, with the same ninety feet along its basepaths that Kenny has seen big leaguers run all summer.

As bullpen coach for the Kansas City Royals, his view has been somewhat oblique, not really close to the action until a guy rounds second and makes the turn to third. If it's one of his, Kenny cheers. If it's an enemy runner, he listens for the bullpen phone to ring or the pitching coach holler "left" or "right" from the dugout.

Here in Massachusetts he's finishing up a quick visit to Salem State College, taking a last look at the school's diamond from above as he sits ten rows up with the painfully young athletic director.

"It sure would be nice to have you with us," the kid is saying. "Ken Boyenga of the Cincinnati Reds."

"I'm with Kansas City now," Kenny tries to remind him, but all he hears is blather about those Reds teams, the last of which he'd rather forget. Didn't he spend nearly all his career with the Redlegs, the AD's now asking; wasn't he their rookie of the year?

"No, no," Kenny demurs. "I was a slow starter, a late bloomer, like they say. And I came up with the Cubs, not the Reds."

"Really?" The young man brightens, then tries to excuse himself. "I guess that was before my time."

There's a silence the athletic director fills with some chatter about how Ken would like coaching here. "In a year we might have some staff for you," he's told. "A full-time groundskeeper in addition to the guys from physical plant, and maybe even a pitching coach."

"Oh, really?" Kenny asks, trying to sound interested.

"Most of those guys you caught in Cincy are novice coaches now," the kid is saying, "just starting in JuCo or even prep. I know you were pretty good friends with Don Kruse and Jeff Copeland, and Copeland even put in for the job you're looking at now."

"No lie?" Kenny wants to say, but stops short. Knowing Kruse and Copeland doesn't make for a good set of references. But this potential employer of his seems to know all about his days with the Reds, even if his first three years in Chicago are a dark mystery. For his day and a half on campus all those wild stories never came up—but now, an hour before he leaves for the airport, he's getting a this-is-your-life treatment from someone who must have been a teenager at the time.

"Ken Boyenga," the AD's saying again. "Only catcher who could handle the mount that staff writers said was the craziest in baseball. You could handle our student athletes here, no doubt!"

"No doubt," Ken repeats, looking for a way to say goodbye and ask where's his ride.

"Do you mind if I call you Kenny?" he's asked.

"Nope."

"Was that the only nickname you had in pro ball?"

"Yep."

"Wasn't there some problem when Kruse, or was it Copeland, tried to change his name? I mean his real name?"

This is just the conversation Kenny doesn't want to have, so he ignores the question and asks if they shouldn't be thinking about his flight. It's an indirect one, routed through Chicago rather than directly to Minneapolis, where the Royals are starting a weekend series, thanks to the airline he'd rather use being on strike. He really can't be late or risk getting bumped. But the kid is still full of questions. Isn't there time for just one? OK.

"Have you considered managing in the minors? I shouldn't really mention this, but as one old Redlegs fan to another, the others on our short list have done that."

Kenny's not a Reds fan and never has been, he wants to clarify, but decides to give an honest answer. "Haven't before," he says, thinking how his baseball career has come to this or nothing, as he's been told

KC has someone else in mind for bullpen coach next year, an ex-Royal just released by the Yankees. "But to be honest with you, it's going to be that or this."

"I really do hope it's this," Kenny hears the kid saying, and is touched by his sincerity. Well, maybe he hopes so too, and takes a last look at this college diamond that despite all the work it needs still sparkles enough in the bright sunlight to make his eyes shed tears.

Back at the AD's office he retrieves his bag and is introduced to the school's driver who'll run him in to Logan. But today must be nostalgia day in old Salem, for the guy wastes most of an hour bringing Kenny into Boston the long way, past the river and through the academic area, where student traffic from three big universities slows them to a crawl. "There it is," the driver says excitedly and points to another field not unlike Salem State's. "What's that?" Kenny asks, forgetting why they've come this way, and is told that over there's the original diamond from old Braves Field. "Spahn, Sain, ad pray for rain!" the driver waxes, and Kenny notes that the day is crystal clear.

Great flying weather, but he gets to the desk just ten minutes before flight time and learns he's too late, his seat's been taken. Worried she'll be cursed, the agent assures him he's already been booked on a later flight with almost the same routing. "Almost?" he asks skeptically, and is told he's still set for a nonstop to Chicago that connects to Minneapolis–St. Paul. "Just one stop," he's assured.

"For Christ's sake, where?" he asks, wondering what's between Chicago and the Twin Cities.

"Mason City. That's in Iowa."

"I know," he says, recognizing the name. "We have a farm team there," then immediately regrets the reference, fearing another interview about baseball.

"That *is* a good place for young salespeople to start," she agrees. "Maybe some day they'll be selling out of Boston or Minneapolis like you!" She beams brightly, handing him his ticket and some coupons.

"What's all this?" he asks.

"Your flight doesn't leave 'til eight," she announces, and before he can complain adds that there are coupons for a dinner and complimentary drink at the airport VIP room.

"One crapping drink?" he blurts out and at once apologizes, but she's already smiling something more than her company-school smile and handing him a fistful of extra coupons.

"You didn't get them from me, did you," she advises with a wink, and Kenny says of course he didn't, he made them.

Feeling better than he should, he grabs a cabin tag for his bag and heads off toward where she's said he'll find the VIP club. But first a phone call to the Hyatt's desk in MSP, message for Marshall Adesman, Kansas City's traveling secretary saying he'll be late but ready to rejoin the team as promised. He's happy not to have missed a single game, easy as it seems they get along without him. What a way to end what should have been a dream career, he thinks: half a year on the Royals' bench, a boring winter back home in Cincinnati, and this spring and summer working as a bullpen coach, psyching out and warming up Kansas City's relievers. Now, as August ends, he's down to just two options: college coaching and minor league managing.

The one thing he won't do is coach in the minors. He's thought it over and there's nothing in Triple-A Tacoma or Double-A Chattanooga, let alone Single-A Sonoma, Mason City, or Charleston (not to mention the rookie clubs in Elmira and Bradenton) that could make him be anything less than captain of his destiny. Well, tonight he'll get his first look at one of the places he could be if Salem State doesn't pan out, at least as much as one can see from the airport.

In the swanky club he orders a surf 'n' turf, forks over a drink coupon, and counts the rest: over a dozen. Geez Louise, he mutters, and for the second time today thinks of Don Kruse and Jeff Copeland, for either of whom these would not have been enough. Well, maybe for Kruse, who swore he preferred to keep himself clean—for worse mayhem later. Damn that kid for bringing all this up. He heard about it when Kansas City picked him up and still must fend off requests for stories when the charter flights run late from the coast. Is it why they're not asking him back as bullpen coach? No, that makes no sense, since the minor league managing job they've teased him with is just as responsible, if not more.

Oh, what the hell, he muses, getting dizzy from the quandary. Fingering the coupons he knows he won't use, he nevertheless starts humming a line Jeff Copeland used to boom out on the charters from San Diego, Frisco, and LA after they'd been up for hours with many more yet to go: "It's all right, 'cause it's midnight, an' I got two more bottles of wine." Somebody must know the song, Kenny realizes with a start, for from behind him a voice is calling, "Cheers, fella!"

BY THE TIME they're in the air it's twilight, but Kenny doesn't mind. Always a nice view in the evening, the old city's population packed so tight that street lights cluster like a field of diamonds. The takeoff has sent them out across the bay; but now, as the jumbo jet swings back toward land, the urban map passes beneath as if it's moving and he's standing still. Dotting that map are reference points more focused than anything the natural landscape can offer: the gold-domed state-house, the huge bridge over to Cambridge, and—nestled along the Back Bay and named for the marshlands drained for its construction so long ago—Fenway.

Although the plane is several miles away and already five thousand feet high, Fenway Park stands out as the brightest of Boston's lights. Such white luminescence compared to the city's amber, whiter still for being banked off the green he can discern even from here. Several minutes later the amber's turned to blue, a blue that's fuzzing away in the haze, but the striking glare of the Red Sox' stadium can still be distinguished. To Ken's amazement it remains a distinct point, so much brighter and whiter than everything else that half an hour later he can see it poking through the gloom. I'm five miles up, he thinks in amazement, and probably two hundred, maybe two hundred and fifty miles away: I don't believe this! Now he keeps his eye on it, compulsively, craning around in his seat even as the lights of Buffalo and Toronto come into view ahead. If he didn't know it was Boston back there, he could never guess it, or even imagine that the one fine point sparkling in its dim smudge on the trailing horizon was Fenway Park.

Then, just as the last hint of it fades away, something else catches Ken's attention. The pilot has said they're passing over Toronto, and it is a rather nice looking carpet of light stretching right up to the sudden darkness of the lake. But up ahead he sees some dimmer clusters, probably London or Kitchener-Waterloo, and beyond them another sparkling island: Detroit. And at the Island's near edge he sees a point of light so much brighter than all the rest. He makes a bet that it's Tiger Stadium, Briggs Stadium as they called it in his youth and where, on a trip with his father, he saw the visiting Red Sox and Ted Williams beat the Tigers with a home run. For the next half-hour he keeps his eye trained on it, until they're over Windsor. He can see the international bridge, and follows the trailing lights of its off-ramp to the ballpark itself.

Thirty-two thousand feet, the captain says. That's over six miles high, Kenny calculates, and marvels that, directly over the stadium as they are, he can distinguish infield brown from outfield green. Can't see the bases, couldn't bet he'd see the players, though he tries. But from the shape of things, even so far away, he can visualize the basepaths. Maybe someone's rounding them right now, sweeping past second and aiming, for a moment, at one of those little cages down the lines they use as bullpen benches. God, how he hates sitting out there, and here's where the team is coming after their weekend with the Twins. But how he loves this old park.

He hates to take his eyes away from it, but steals a moment to open the USA Today that's been sitting on his lap unread the whole flight. Toronto at Detroit, starting time 7:30. Nine o'clock now, could be fourth or fifth inning. At takeoff the Red Sox must have been just getting under way; right, New York at Boston, 7:30 start. It amuses him to think that for twelve or thirteen games a year he's almost face to face with the guys down there, playing before the same crowds. He knows half the Detroit players and even some of the regular fans, aficionados with season tickets in the first row over the near-in bullpens. He looks down and Tiger Stadium's still there, glowing green within and white without. See ya Tuesday, he says with a nod, then figures he's been staring out the window long enough and turns back to his paper. But there's the pitching line for Minnesota at Chicago, and even as he's figuring where the Twins will be in their rotation for his game tomorrow it dawns on him that he just might see his third ballpark tonight.

What time? Seven o'clock start, and it's 9:15 now with well over an hour to go. No way. But Carlton Fisk calls the slowest game in baseball; the Sox are never out of there before ten. Who's pitching for the Twins again? Kenny notes the knuckleballer, thinks piteously of the catcher, and decides if the plane loops into O'Hare from the south and approachs the city before 10:30 there's a chance. Of course there is: he's gained an hour because of central time.

Looking back, Tiger Stadium's a harder dot to focus on than Fenway, given that the greater part of metro Detroit stretches past it to the west. But it's there, Kenny is sure. Then he wonders if he could have picked up Municipal Stadium across the lake in Cleveland; check the paper—no way, the Indians are out in Seattle. Maybe the Browns were having a workout tonight, it's their exhibition season. But who cares if it's football? And probably not, anyway, as he recalls looking south from Toronto where the lights would have been; if the ballpark were alight, right there on the southern shore, he would have seen it, an easier shot than he has at Chicago now.

And Chicago's there, he can see it, a string of lights running perpendicular to his course: the western shore of Lake Michigan. He traces the lights south and there, a little inland, is a spot so much brighter than the rest he has no doubts that it's Comiskey.

Please, he prays, as his ears pop and he feels the plane slow a bit and tilt forward: come in from the south. They're heading right for the Loop, and at the north of it he can see the John Hancock sticking up above the rest like black tinkertoys. Again, all the other lights are blue or amber, but Comiskey sparkles in pure whiteness. It strikes him that these are the three oldest ballparks he's seen tonight, lit like freight yards with hundreds of incandescents boxed atop metal towers. He's wondered how the new parks can be just as bright with half the power, and now knows why: all that excess wattage at Fenway, Briggs, and Comiskey is going straight up and out. He thinks of the bullpens at Chicago, stuck out there beneath that tiny bleacher section beyond the center field fence, and remembers looking up to count the floodlights on each pole. An even hundred, ten across and ten down. How many poles? He'll count those when they end the season here in five—what is it—five and a half weeks.

Suddenly the plane makes a steep bank to the left, sending Ken's glance straight down into the blackness of Lake Michigan, and he realizes he's in luck, the pilot's going to cruise along the lakefront before turning inland a couple miles south. Make it three miles and he'll see the park. Another bank to the right and the shoreline passes beneath. Cars on the Outer Drive, there's a college campus—ITT, a tough one. Geez Louise, they're coming right down Wentworth Avenue at about five thousand feet. Less than a mile up, and he can see a person, at least a figure, at a mile, if he knows where to look. Holy cripes, Ken's thinking, breathing fast and as excited as a child on a first flight ever. Things are rushing past and he no sooner sees the Dan Ryan and its heavy traffic than the ancient stands loom up and his vision pours into the outfield. White on the grass. Who's behind the plate? Unless he's been lifted, and he wouldn't be unless hurt, it's Carlton Fisk, a thousand miles from the park that made him famous but one that Kenny was looking at just a couple hours ago.

At O'Hare Kenny sees he's got less than twenty minutes to make his connection, but he darts inside a terminal bar where he sees a TV set aglow. A commercial's showing, but the channel light reads 32, not 9, so it's the Sox. The game's back on with a scoreboard shot they're holding too long, something about it being knotted in the tenth. "Who's catching?" Kenny asks the bartender. "Catching?" the guy asks in return. "Who the hell do you think?" and that's answer enough for Ken.

"What's the deal, fella?" he's being asked by the salesman he pushes past, hurrying from the bar, and Kenny has to ask himself what is—after all, he was standing fifteen feet from Carlton Fisk three weeks ago in Kansas City, and can introduce himself right here in Chicago on October first, second, or third. He could tell Fisk about the answer to a trivia question: Which ex-Cub did the White Sox trade to make room for free agent Carlton Fisk? For the year and a half they've worked in the same ballparks Kenny's never had the nerve to do that, but maybe he should, especially now that he can say he's seen him from an airplane as well.

From an airplane? I've been in this game too long, he thinks, as he lets the Mississippi Valley Airlines agent check his bag that's too big for carry-on in these different dimensions of commuter flying. Too long. It's what he's been thinking about all day, his day and a half the Royals let him have off between series so he could look into this college job. Professor Boyenga? What comes next, President of Yale? It really wasn't worth the effort. Nor does he find it worth the effort to look from the window of this small, noisy plane as it climbs westward from O'Hare and angles slightly to the north for Minneapolis. Can't look into the Humpty Dome, he tells himself; and besides, it's dark, the Twins are here and so is he. "There," he corrects himself, and leans back to have a last look at Chicago. But at this low altitude the city's out of sight.

HE SLIPS INTO a shallow sleep, then wakes with a start as the stewardess eases his seat upright. Minneapolis already? No, Mason City, and he realizes he'd forgotten the stop. This is what he's supposed to be looking at—one-in-five chance, really one-in-three he could be here next year if he tells Salem State to take a walk. He tries to focus out the window but sees nothing. Because there *is* nothing, he soon realizes, and waits for the lightless countryside to pass. Then some lights come into view, yard lights from farms, corners where sections meet, a small town way off to the right, and to the far left some lights that must be the interstate he presumes they'll follow to the Twin Cities. Then the edge of what might be considered suburban sprawl; they even have that here. Then a river he guesses will lead to town. And suddenly something so bright it actually hurts his eyes.

A ballpark. Jesus, four-for-four, Kenny thinks, realizing they're about to pass over the minor league field where the Mason City Royals, if that's what they're called up here, play. My God, it must be near eleven, midnight Boston time. Then he remembers how late his own games in the minors could go, ineffective hitting rarely able to break out in a lead and sloppy fielding letting those leads slip away. Or it could be the second game of a doubleheader; bet they have to make up lots of wash outs and cold outs from April and early May, the poor suckers.

His interest aroused, Ken pushes his face against the window to look down. They're much lower, yet not as fast as over Comiskey, and he has time to see not only that white's in the field, visitors batting, but that the bleachers are stone cold empty while what he can see of the grandstand looks pretty sparse. Maybe their start was four or five hours ago too, who knows. Anyway, in a moment the ballpark's gone, there are some open fields, a factory (Closed? No lights, so at least no night shift), some tract houses, and right away a runway. Nothing more to see, not even a view of downtown. Ten minutes on the ground and they take off, banking right before they join the interstate and follow it at twelve thousand feet to the airport south of Minneapolis–St. Paul.

Kenny cabs it to the Hyatt, gives the bellman a five to take his bag upstairs, and heads right for the bar. No players here, he knows; players can't drink in the place they're staying—bad image. Not even encouraged for the coaching staff, and their manager has a favorite place across town where Billy Martin once had a famous fight and baseball folks can still cadge a drink. But Marshall Adesman's here, and he wants to be sure the traveling secretary knows he's back in time, before midnight, to merit meal money.

That's on Adesman's mind too, as his eyes leave Kenny's face and dart to his watch, missing because he's left it in his room, and to the bar's clock, which is such a mess of colored lights he can't read it. But the cagey secretary tries a guess nevertheless.

"12:01," he says as a greeting. "No fifty-five bucks."

"12:01 bartime, 11:46 real time," Kenny answers. "Cough up." Realizing he's been tricked with his own shamming, Marshall pulls an oversized wallet from his jacket pocket and counts out two twenties and three fives. "So I'm tipping fives all night, huh?" Kenny objects, and Adesman tells him to stow it, he'll pay for drinks and cover the tip as well. Kenny feigns surprise and the traveling secretary demurs, making an elaborate wave-off motion while muttering. "Unless you've got your buddies Kruse and Copeland along."

"Hell," Kenny laughs, "they're my coaching staff at Salem State, where we're all professors of intercollegiate athletics," and Marshall cracks up at the line, never guessing how true it could have been.

Nor will Kenny tell him, for at just this moment he's decided he'll forget about college and start talking seriously about managing in the minors, even if it's in that godforsaken park they just dive-bombed in Mason City. Mason City, he realizes, is in the same chain with Royals Stadium, which he hasn't seen since Tuesday night, and Fenway, Tiger Stadium, and Comiskey, where he tells Adesman he's seen games tonight. Salem State sure ain't, he reminds himself. Let Copeland and Kruse have it.

"So you really saw old Briggs Stadium from the plane?" Marshall accepts the stories about Fenway and Comiskey, taking off and landing, but tries to argue that you can't see anything that small from that altitude. "Small?" Kenny protests, remembering how big the park looked when he was fifteen. "Maybe you thought you saw it," the traveling secretary allows, but this makes Kenny even madder.

They switch topics to Mason City, and Adesman asks if Kenny saw a pitcher there named Freddie Guagliardo.

"Huh?" Kenny asks, and is told the kid will be joining them September first in Detroit.

"Small world," the two friends agree.

The Safety Patrol

IF YOU LOOK ON PAGE 253 of the New College Edition of *The American Heritage Dictionary*, there, in the right margin toward the bottom of the page, you will find an aerial photograph of a cloverleaf interchange at Fort Wayne, Indiana.

Of the six cloverleaf interchanges in Fort Wayne, I am reasonably sure I know which one this is. It is not my favorite. That one is down the road. There, there was a small country cemetery right where the new interstate was going to go. I was on the citizens' committee that saved the place. You can still see it buried beneath the loops and ramps as they detour, twisted out of the way like a spring sprung. On some Sundays, I drive out there, drive around the place, entering and exiting. The interchange spreads for miles. I catch glimpses of the headstones—they're old, from before the Civil War—the patch of prairie grass and wild flowers, the picket fence. It is in the middle of the storm of concrete and cars. Saved. But there is no way to drive to it. All access limited, the site undisturbed. Like clouds the shadows of trucks sail over the plots, change the color of the stones.

The cloverleaf pictured in the dictionary is a perfect specimen. There has been no finagling with the curving lobes of the ramp as they coil from one dual lane to the other. If you look closely you can see snow in the ditch defining the mathematical berms, shading the grade, giving it depth and perspective. A beautiful picture, one the children are proud of.

When we do dictionary drills I include the word *cloverleaf* as a kind of Crackerjack prize for the students. They cut into the big book as I've taught them, into the first third. Some feel comfortable using the finger tabs scooped out along the edge. They turn chunks of pages, getting close, getting to C. They peel each page back, then read the index words *close call* and *clown*, saying the alphabet for each letter. And then, one by one, they arrive at the right page. Fingers go up and down columns. One or two gasp, then giggle. They point and whisper. They say things like "wow." They can't wait to tell me what they've found.

The cloverleaf is there with pictures of a clothes tree, a clown licking an ice-cream cone, a clover—the plant and its buds—the cloister of San Marco in Florence, Italy, an earthworm with a clitellum, and the clipper ship *Lightning*. The pictures seem to make the words they represent more important.

THE LIGHTS ON the television and radio towers are always on even during the day, when you can barely see the flush of the red lights. The newer towers have bright strobing lights, too. You see sharp simultaneous explosions all along the edges. There are revolving lights at the very tip. Guy wires angle down so taut as to vibrate the heavy air around the towers. There are a dozen at least now, and more going up. The neighborhood is zoned for towers.

I like to play games while I look at the towers. Which one is taller? Which is furthest away? Coming up State Street on my way to teach, I watch the towers as I drive. They are solid lines, the lights slowly coming into sychronization. I am waiting for a red light, watching over the cars ahead of me down the road. Each tower is beating its own red pulse. Two or three pulse together a time or two. Then they drift apart, align with other tower lights. I know if I watch long enough, if I am lucky enough and happen to glance at the right time, I'll see all the lights on all the towers switch on and off at the very same moment.

The closer I get to the towers, the lacier they become. The lattice is like a kid's picture of lightning shooting down the sides. I've been to the root of some of the towers, and they are balanced at a single point on a concrete slab. There the metal flares out in an inverted pyramid, then up slightly, tapered really, but coming together anyway past the red twirling light at the top of the lone antenna pointing to a distant vanishing point.

The closer I get to the towers the more air they become. They disappear. The red and white curtain of color where they are painted in intervals hangs in the air. The lights are nearly invisible in the sun. At that certain distance, when they disappear, it is like the red line of mercury in a thermometer held slightly off-center.

I used to worry about the houses that have been built beneath the towers. They are starter homes, small, shaped like Monopoly houses, the colors of game tokens, glossy blues and reds and greens and yellows, with a trim a shade darker but the same color. The trees are puny and new, fast-growing ginkos and Lombardy poplars quaking in the breeze and spraying up like the towers way above them. The houses are scattered and crowded into cul-de-sacs and terraces like an island village. The addition is called Tower Heights. The guy wires from the towers anchor in backyards in deadeyes and turn buckles the sizes of automobiles. They are fenced off and landscaped with climbing flowers. The lines of one tower can slip beneath the lines of another, over still another, so the houses and yards are sewn up in a kind of net of cables arriving from the sky.

My students say the towers groan sometimes in storms. The wires twang. They tell me they like to lie looking up at the clouds sailing above the towers. The towers move against the clouds. They sway and topple. On a clear day, the shadows cast by the towers sweep over the houses in single file. My students take to geometry, all the lines and angles, acute, right, obtuse, the triangles, the compass point of the towers, the parallel lines. When I pull the blinds up on the window of my classroom, there, off in the distance, are the towers and wires. The roofs of their houses are just visible, a freehand line drawn beneath the proof.

THE CHILDREN THIS YEAR have been very well-behaved. It is something we've all noticed and commented on in the lounge. The women think it's me. I am the only man. I teach sixth grade and take most of the gym classes. I have the basketball team. The Safety Patrol is my responsibility.

It is crazy but I am in love with all of these women in the school. Miss A, Miss B, Miss C, Miss D, Miss E, Miss F, Miss G, Miss H, Miss I, Miss J, Miss K, and Miss L, who teaches kindergarten. The principal,

Miss M. The nurse, N, who visits twice a week, I first met during hearing tests this fall. The children were listening to earphones, curling and uncurling their index fingers in response to the pure tone. The music teacher, Miss O. The art instructor, Miss P.

How did I get here? It is difficult to say. But with each it seemed natural enough. Each relationship has a life of its own.

There is a lot of locker-room talk in the lounge and during staff meetings. When we meet in a group I'm ignored, taken for granted, as they search around inside their brown bags for the apple, rinse the flatware in the sink. They talk about their boyfriends. In all cases that would be me they are talking about. None knows of my other affairs. When they yak about love they do so casually so as not to let on to the others, to tease me with this our inside joke. Their candor protects them, renders me harmless; their wantonness deflects suspicion from the room.

It is exciting. I share a preparation time with Miss D. We smooch for the half-hour in the lounge. The coffee perks. Our red pens capped. On the playground Miss C chases me playfully, jogging, then sprinting. The children are playing tether ball, box ball. They're screaming. She always almost catches me. When children from our classes are in the lavatory, I hold hands for a second with Miss G as we lean against the yellow tile brick in the hall. She turns her body around, presses her face against the cool wall. I haven't been compromised, because none of them wants to be discovered. If I am alone with one, the others leave us alone because the only time any one of them wants to be with me is when she can be alone with me. I love the moment when we all step out in the hall, look at each other and step back in the classroom, drawing the door behind us to begin teaching that day.

I am the only man, but I don't think that has much to do with the discipline of the children. Perhaps there is something in the air. It's history, I think. I like teaching history, geography, health, the big wide books that contain all of the pictures. You know the old saying about history: study history or you're doomed to repeat it. That's all wrong, I think. You study it *and* you are doomed to repeat it. Maybe even more so because you study what's happened. Get to know it and it's like it's already happened. It is the same story over and over. It is time once again for kids to raise their hands, part their hair, say "please" and "thank you," follow directions. That's all.

THE SAFETY PATROL is in the rain. The streets are slick with oily rainbows, pooled. The gutters are full, flowing. The rain is soaking, steady. They are wearing bright yellow slickers. The water sheets down them. The bills of their yellow caps are pulled down flat between their eyes, hard against their noses like the gold helmets of heavy cavalry. The snaps are snapped beneath their chins. Their chins are tucked into their dryer chests. The flaps cover their ears, cheeks, necks. The claw fasteners shimmer down the fronts of their coats. They've polished them. They wear black rubber boots over their shoes. They stand in puddles, take the spray from passing cars without moving, their arms fixed at the proper angles, holding back the antsy students pressing to cross the streets into school.

The belts are orange, cinched tight over the shoulder, tight across the chest, over the heart, all buckled at the waist. The pools in the street turn red with the traffic light's light. The orange belts ignite as the headlights of the cars strike across them. For the instant it is just the belt floating without a body like the belt is bone in an X-ray.

The bells ring. We close the doors. Outside the Patrol stays on the corners in case someone is tardy. Their heads pivot slowly checking all directions. Their faces sparkle. There are worms everywhere on the sidewalks. The towers' lights are juicy. Then from somewhere I can't see, I hear the clear call of the captain. "Off do tee." He calls again in the other direction, fainter. "Off do tee." Each syllable held a long time. Then the lieutenants at the far ends of the school repeat the same phrasing. The patrols leave the corners one by one, covering each other's moves as they all safely cross the wet streets and come into school.

EACH YEAR I DO a sociogram of my class. It helps me get a picture of how it all fits together, who the leaders are, who follow, who are lonely or lost, who are forgotten. I ask questions. Who in the class is your best friend, your worst enemy? Who is most like a sister, a brother? Who would you never tell a secret to? Who would you ask for help? Who is strongest? Who would you help? If a boy and a girl were drowning who would you save if you could only save one? Who would you give part of your lunch to? Who would you pick to be on your team in gym class? Who would you want to pick you? Who makes you laugh? Who makes you mad? If someone told you a secret and told you not to tell it to anyone in the class, who would you tell it to? Who do you miss during summer vacations? Who would you want to call you on the telephone? Who do you walk home with? Who would you walk home with if you could? If you could rename the school, who would you name it after? If you are a girl, which boy would you like to be just for a little while? If you are a boy, which girl would you like to be just for a little while? If something has to be done in class, who would you ask? Who would you want to do your homework? Who would you want to teach you a new game? Who ignores you? If you ran away, who would you send a letter to? If you were in the hospital, who would you want to see most? If you were afraid and by yourself in the dark, who would you call out for? The children like this test because they know the answers. They sneak looks at each other as they work. Their pencils wag.

I collect the data, assign values, note names. I graph responses, plot intersections. I never question their honesty. I can map out grudges and feuds, old loves, lingering feelings, all the tribal bonds and property disputes, the pecking order, the classes in the class.

And then I have conferences with the parents. We sit on the down-sized chairs. I cast out the future for their son or daughter in the language of talk shows. I dissect the peer pressure, explain the forces at work. The parents want to know about change. Is this set in stone? Can my son be a leader, a professional? Will my daughter grow up to like men? I tell them that it's hard to say, that the children are all caught up in a vast machine of beliefs and of myths. It is of this group's own making. These responses are almost instinctual now, I tell the parents. Each class has its own history, its own biology, its own math and logic. I'm just presenting what's what.

I know now who leads the class and who operates in the shadows. I know where the power is and the anguish, who shakes down who, what favors are owed, who might turn a gun on his friends, on himself.

I ask these same questions of myself. I answer Miss A, Miss B, Miss

C, Miss D, and so on. Who do I trust? Who would I save? Who would I want to go home with? I wish I could ask the women as well, but the results would be skewed.

There is no place to stand, no distance. Skewed.

THE SAFETY PATROL IS in the hallway of the school before and after classes and at lunchtime. Inside, they wear the white cloth belts they launder. A bronze pin, given by the Chicago Motor Club, is attached where the belt begins to arch over the shoulder, the collar bone.

There is no running in the hall. The Patrol patrols up and down, one stationed every two or so classrooms. Stay on the right side of the hall. There is a red dashed line painted on the floor. The Patrol stands at ease, straddles the line. The small children move along cautiously, try not to look around. There is a bottleneck near the piano on rollers that moves from classroom to classroom with the music teacher, Miss O. The piano is pushed keys first, against the wall. The bench is flipped on top of the upright. The legs point up like a cartoon of a dead animal. Handles are screwed on the side for easier moving. Something spills out of the intercom which only the teachers can understand. Loose squares of construction paper stapled on the bulletin boards lift and fall as kids pass by.

A Safety Patrol will speak. "What's your name?" and everyone in the hall will stop. "Yes, you," the Safety Patrol will say. Each member of the Safety Patrol can always see at least two other members. Their bright white belts cut across plaids and prints. They are never out of each other's sight.

They have arrayed themselves this way on their own, without my help. The captain and his lieutenants have posted schedules, worked out posts and their rotation. The Safety Patrol is on the corners of Tyler and State and on the corners of Tyler and Rosemount, and one is at the crossing on Stetler with the old crossing guard who has the stop sign he uses as a crook. A Patrol walks with a passel of kindergartners all the way to Spring Street, almost a mile, to push the button on the automatic signal. He eats his lunch on the corner and walks the afternoon students back to school. A lone Patrol guards the old railroad tracks that separate the school from Tower Heights. There are Patrols at each door into the building. They are strung through the halls. There, I've seen them straightening the reproductions of famous paintings the PTA has donated. They watch over the drinking fountains. They turn lights out in empty classrooms. They roust stragglers from the restrooms.

I WANT MY STUDENTS to copy each other's work. It is a theory of mine. I've put the slower ones in desks right next to the ones who get it. I've told them that it is all right by me if they ask their neighbors for the answers, fine also for the neighbors to tell.

They want to k iow if they own their answers.

They want to know what happens if they don't want to tell.

Fair questions. I see them covering their papers with their hands and arms as they go along, turning their backs on the copier.

"What are you protecting?" I ask them. Students can't break the habits they have of cheating. They look out of the corners of their eyes. They whisper. They sneak. They drop pencils on the floor. They don't get this, my indifference. My indulgence. If they would ask me I would tell them the answers but it never occurs to them to ask me.

We are doing European Wars. The Peloponnesian. The Punic. The Sackings. The Hundred Years. The Thirty Years. We are studying an Eskimo girl and a boy from Hawaii. Our newest states. We are doing First Aid. We are doing the Solar System. We are doing New Math. We spell every Wednesday and Friday. We read "A Man without a Country."

We have taken a field trip to one of the television stations to appear on the "Engineer John Show," a show that airs in time for the kids coming home from school. Engineer John dresses like a railroad engineer—pin-stripe bib overalls, red neckerchief, crowned hat, a swan-necked oil can, big gloves. Really he is the other type of engineer who works with the transmitters, the wires, the towers, the kind in broadcasting, during the rest of the day. As a personality, he is cheap. He introduces Sergeant Preston movies and Hercules cartoons and short films provided by the AFL-CIO called *Industry on Parade,* which show milk bottles filling on assembly lines or toasters being screwed together. There are no people in the films. The students love the show, especially the factories of machines building other machines. They think Engineer John is a clown like Bozo, who is on another station, because they don't know what the costume means. To us in the studio audience he talked about electricity while the films ran on the monitors. He talked about the humming we heard.

Later, we wound through the neighborhood in a yellow bus dwarfed by the towers, dropping students at their houses. I sat in the back of the bus next to the emergency door with Miss J, holding her hand and rubbing her leg. We both looked straight ahead. Squeezed.

The Safety Patrol made sure the windows did not drop below the lines, that hands and heads and arms stayed inside. The captain whispered directions to the driver. The stop-sign arm extended every time we stopped. All the lights flashed as if we had won something.

EVERY YEAR THERE IS a city-wide fire drill. All the schools, public and parochial, evacuated simultaneously. An insurance company provides red badges for the children, the smaller children wear fire hats. They are sent home with a checklist of hazards and explore their houses. Piles of rags and papers. Pennies in the fuse box. Paint cans near the water heater. I know they watch as their parents smoke. They inventory matches. They plan escapes from every room, crawl along floors. They touch doors quickly to see if they are hot before they open them. Extension cords. They set fire to their own pajamas.

In school they discuss their findings with each other, formed up in circles of chairs. They draw posters. They do skits.

On the day of the drill a fire company visited. Their pumper was in the parking lot gleaming. A radio station, WOWO, broadcast messages from the chief and the mayor and the superintendent. These were piped through to our classroom. A voice counted down the time to the moment when a little girl in a Lutheran elementary school this year would throw the switch and all the buzzers and bells in every other school would ring. Of course, this drill is never a surprise. That's not the point. Usually the alarm just sounds, and those assigned to close the windows close the windows. They turn out the lights. They leave everything. My students form into single file, are quiet for instructions, no shoving, no panic, know by heart where to go, what area of the playground to collect in, how to turn and watch the school, listen for the all-clear or the distant wail of sirens.

I ARRIVE AT SCHOOL in the dark. The Safety Patrol is already sowing salt along the sidewalks. Their belts quilt their heavy overcoats. They are scooping sand from the orange barrel that is stored at an angle in a wooden frame on the corner with the little hill. The captain watches over the dim streets as others spread the sand in sweeping arcs. Going by, the few cars crush the new snow. In the still air, I can clearly hear them chopping ice and shoveling the snow.

I GAVE ALL the women sample-sized bottles of cheap perfume I bought at Woolworth's. Their desks were covered with tiny packages wrapped in color comics and aluminum foil, gifts from their students. I smelled the musky odor everywhere in the school for months later.

Miss J sent me a note one day. A fifth-grader, one size too small, handed it up to me. It was on lined notebook paper. Three of the five holes ruptured when she pulled it from the ringed notebook. In the beautiful blue penmanship many of the women have: *Do you like me? Yes or No.* She had drawn in little empty squares behind yes and no. The fifth-grader waited nervously just outside the door. My class in the middle of base two watched me as I filled in the *yes* square and folded up the paper. I sealed it with a foil star, sent the child back to the room. My own students watched me closely. I knew they were trying to guess the meaning of what I did.

I thought I saw them all blink at the same time. I couldn't be sure, because I can't see all the eyes at once, but it was a general impression, a feeling, a sense I had, a moment totally my own in my classroom when what I did was not observed.

In the lounge the smell of the perfume is strongest, overpowering the cool purple smell of mimeograph, the gray cigarette smoke, the green mint breath, the brown crushed smell of the wet Fort Howard paper towels.

Miss A has drawn our initials, big block printing, in her right palm, stitched together with a plus sign. Her hands are inscribed with whorls and stars, marks against cooties and answers to problems. If I just touch her she thrills and titters, runs and hides, rubbing her body all over with her streaked hands.

IN FORT WAYNE we say there are more cars per capita than in any other city in the United States except Los Angeles. I believe it when I am caught in traffic on State Street. Up ahead are the school and the axle factory and a little beyond them the towers. We creep along one to a car through a neighborhood built after the war. All the houses have shutters with cutouts of sailboats or moons or pine trees.

I drive a Valiant. I shift gears by pushing buttons on the dash, an idea that didn't catch on.

In the middle of the intersection I am waiting to turn across the oncoming lane. The Safety Patrol watches me, knows my funny old car. It has no seat belts. The way they hold their hands, their heads, it's like a crucifixion. Their faces are fixed.

I am stopped again by the crossing guard in the street. He leans heavily on the striped dazzling pole. I have seen him swat the hoods of cars that have come too close. The Safety Patrol is behind him, funneling the children along the crosswalk of reflecting paint smeared in slashes on the street.

The guard has told me a story that may be true. He says when he was a boy he saw his kid brother die at the first traffic light in Fort Wayne. The light had no yellow, only the green and red flags snapping up and down. The boys knew what it meant, crossed with the light, but the driver came on through, peeled the one brother from the other. It was a time, the guard has said, when signs meant nothing.

He has played in the street. When he was a boy, he told me, he played in the street, Calhoun, Jefferson, highways now, throwing a baseball back and forth with his brother. They didn't have to move all day. He drove cattle down Main Street, cows home to be milked twice a day, then back out to pasture.

He remembers when all the land the school is on and all the land around was a golf course, and before that a swamp. All of this was a swamp, he says.

I like old things. I like the old times. It doesn't take long for things to get old. Everything seems to have been here all along but often it is not old.

Our principal tells us one day there will be no students, the neighborhood is aging, running out of babies, but there is no evidence of that. The school is teeming every year, spontaneous generation. We do that old experiment each year in the spring. The cheesecloth over the spoiled and the rotting meat grows its fur of maggots. The children love this.

Getting out of my car in the parking lot I am almost hit by something. It zips by my ear. Something skitters across the pavement. Nearby Miss F flings acorns my way, Brazils, cashews, mixed nuts. When we're alone she pinches me long and hard, won't let up, kicks me on the shins. She bites when we kiss. She says she likes me, she doesn't mean to hurt me. She wants me so much she wants to eat me up.

THIS IS AN elementary school. The sprawling one-story was built in the 1950s with Indiana limestone, a flat roof, and panels in primary colors. Its silhouette is reminiscent of the superstructure of the last luxury liners—the SS *United States,* the *France*—streamlined with false ledges and gutters trailing off the leeward edges, giving the illusion of swift movement.

The Safety Patrol makes a big deal of raising and lowering the flag. Three or four members and always an officer parade out in the courtyard. There are salutes and an exaggerated hand-over-hand as the flag that flew over the nation's Capitol goes up and down. They fold the flag in the prescribed way, leaving, when done properly, that pastry of stars which one of them holds over his or her breast.

Finally, you can never be emotionally involved with any of this. That's a fact, not a warning.

This is an elementary school. The children move on. I have their homeroom assignments for junior high school. It's all alphabetical from now on. I come to the school believing it is some kind of sacred precinct. Teachers are fond of saying how much we learn from the children, how when we paddle it will hurt us more than it will hurt them. Tests test what? What was learned or how it was taught? Children are like any other phenomenon in nature.

The first steps in the scientific methods according to the book are to observe, collect data. An hypothesis would be an intimate act. All the experiments would be failures. I know my job. I am supposed to not know more than I do now. No research. I repeat each year the elemental knowledge I embody, the things I learned a long time ago.

I watch the seasons change on the bulletin boards. I take down the leaves for the turkeys and the pilgrims, and the leaves leave a shadow of their shapes burned into the yellow and orange and brown construction paper. The sun has faded the background. The stencils and straight pins, colored tacks and yarns, the cotton-ball snow, the folded doily flakes, no two alike. The eggshell flowers are in the spring. The grass cut into a fringe on a strip of green paper is curled bluntly through the scissors. The summer is cork.

THE SAFETY PATROL FOLDS its belts like flags. At the end of the school day they are sitting at their desks folding their belts to store them away. The other children have already been ferried across the streets. It is like a puzzle or trying to fold a map. The trick is to master the funny angle of the crossing belt, the adjusting slides, the heavy buckle. It's like folding parachutes. They leave the packets in the center of their desktops, the bronze pin on top of each.

I go home and watch the "Engineer John Show." There are so many kinds of people that exist now only on TV—milkmen, nuns in habit, people who live in lighthouses, newsboys who yell "Extra." Engineer John arrives with the sound of a steam engine.

We know that when tornadoes happen they are supposed to sound like freight trains. It is spring and the season for tornadoes, which Fort Wayne is never supposed to have according to an old Indian belief, still repeated, that the three rivers ward them off. We will drill. The students sit Indian-fashion under their desks, backs to the windows. Or in the hall the bigger children cover their smaller brothers and sisters.

During our visit, Engineer John told us about the ground. How electricity goes back to it, finds it. I thought of the towers as a type of well. These pictures gushing from the field, a rich deposit. The electrons pump up and down the shafts.

In storms, the children say they watch the lightning hit the towers.

They turn their sets off and watch. The towers are sometimes up inside the clouds. The clouds light up like lampshades. I think a lot of people watch the towers, know which windows in their houses face that way. They sit up and watch when the storm keeps them awake. Or when they can't sleep in general, maybe they stare out at all the soothing, all the warning lights.

THE SIXTH-GRADE GIRLS are gathered in one room to watch the movie even I have never seen. I have the boys. They are looking up words in the dictionary. I tell them that dictionaries have very little to do with spelling but with history, with where the word comes from, how long it has been used and understood.

Miss K calls me out in the hall. The doors are closed and she leads me to the nearest girls' restroom and pulls me inside. I always feel funny in the wrong washroom, hate to open the door even to yell in "Hurry up" to my girls, who are just beginning to use makeup and are dawdling over the sinks and mirrors.

We cram into the furthest stall, and Miss K unbuttons her dress, which has her initials embroidered on her collar—AMR. We have played doctor before in the nurse's room, where there are screens, couches and gowns. There are even some cold metal instruments ready on a towel. She is in her underwear when we hear the doors wheeze, and someone comes in. A far stall door clicks closed and we hear the rustle of clothes and the tinkle. Miss K worms around me, crouches down to look beneath the partition. Elastic snaps. The flush. We hear hands being washed in the sink, dried on paper towels.

When we're alone again Miss K finishes undressing. She clutches pieces of her clothes in each hand, covers her body and then quickly opens her arm. She lets me look at her, turns around lifting her hands over her head, clothes spilling down, taking rapid tiny steps in place. She tucks her clothes into the wedge of her elbows, hugging the bundle next to her breast, her bronze nipple. She reaches down between her legs with her other hand, watching me as she does so, trying not to giggle. Then she shows me her hand. There is some blood on her fingers, she thinks it is so funny. She couldn't sit through the movie.

Perhaps all of the women in the school are bleeding at the same moment, at this moment, by chance or accident, through sympathy, gravity, vibration. It's possible. It could be triggered by suggestion, by a school year of living out blocks of time, periods of periods, drinking the same water, breathing the same air. And what if it had happened, is happening? Would it be any worse if the planets all aligned or if everyone in the world jumped up in the air at the same time? The school, a little worse for wear a few days each month, tense, cramped, even horny, a word my students always giggle at. And now that some of them are alone with dictionaries I know they are looking up all the words they've never said and know they should never say.

THE BRIGHT YELLOW tractors are back cutting the grass around the school. The litter in the lawn is mulched and shot out the side with the clippings. The driver takes roughly a square pattern, conforming to the shape of the lawn, the patches fitting inside each other. The green stripe is a different shade depending upon the angle of the light—flat green, the window of cut grass and the bright lush grass still standing. The tractors emit those bleating sounds when they back up, trimming around trees.

I see all of this through my wall of windows. The Safety Patrol on their corners cover their ears as the tractors come near. I can see them shouting to the other children, waving at them, yanking them around. Their voices lost in the roar of the mowers. They mean to take the shrapnel of shredded branches, stones, crushed brick, the needles of grass into their own bodies. An heroic gesture they must have learned from television.

THE WORD carnival means "the putting away of flesh," according to The American Heritage Dictionary. I feel as if no one knows this as I thread through the crowded school halls.

Parents and neighbors and high-school kids have come to the carnival. We're just trying to raise money for audio-visual equipment, tumbling apparati, maybe buy a few more trees. The students are here, many with their faces painted like clowns, one of the attractions. Some fifth-graders are following me around since they have learned I'll be their teacher next year. They're drinking drinks that a fast-food place donates. Their lips and tongues are orange or purple or red or a combination of those colors. Underfoot a carpet of popcorn pops where we walk. The floors are papered with discarded spin art and scissored silhouettes. People are wearing lighter clothes, brighter clothes. They form clots in the hall, push and shove. Children are crying or waving long strips of the blue tickets above their heads, hitting others as they go by. It is a job, this having fun.

Each room has a different game run by the teachers and room mothers. I am floating from one place to the other, bringing messages and change, tickets and cheap prizes. One room has the fish pond. I see the outline of Miss B working furiously behind the white sheet, attaching prizes to the hooks. Children are on the other side of the sheet holding long tapering bamboo poles. In another room is the candy wheel. Another has a plastic pool filled with water and identical plastic ducks. There are rooms where balls are tossed at hoops and silver bottles. There is the cakewalk. One room is even a nursery where mothers are nursing or changing their babies. In all the rooms are the cards of letters—Aa Bb Cc Dd Ee, some in cursive Aa Bb Cc Dd Ee with tiny arrows indicating the stroke of the pen. There are green blackboards, cloakrooms, the same clock, the drinking fountain and the illuminated exit sign over the door.

In the cafetorium adults are having coffee. Children are rolling in the mats. Pigs in blankets are being served, beans, Jell-O. Up on the stage behind the heavy curtains is the Spook House. Four tickets. There is a long line.

In the dark you are made to stumble and fall. Strings and crepe streamers propelled by fans whip your face. There are tugs on your clothes, your shoes, your fingers. There are noises, growls, shrieks, laughs. Things are revealed to you, such as heads in boxes, spiders, skulls, chattering teeth. All the time you can hear the muttering of the picnic outside dampened by the curtain, the thrumming of conversation. And your eyes just get used to the dark when you come upon a table set with plates each labeled clearly: Eyeballs, Fingers, Guts, Hearts, Blood, Brains. You can see clearly now the cocktail onions, the chocolate pudding, the ketchup, the Tootsie Rolls, the rice, everything edible. The tongue, tongue. Someone is whispering over and over "touch it, touch it." And it's hard to, even though you know what these things really are. Or you want to because you know you never would touch the real things.

I go outside up on the roof, I have the key, to sneak a smoke. The Safety Patrol is out in the parking lot. The towers are sputtering off in the distance. For a couple of tickets you take a couple swings with a sledge hammer at an old car. The car looks very much like mine.

The glass is all removed, the sharp edges. It only looks dangerous. The sound reaches me a heartbeat after I see the hammer come down. People like the thin metal of the roof, the hood and trunk, the fine work around the head and taillights. The grill splinters. The door that covers the gas cap is a favorite target.

The Safety Patrol rings the crumpled car, holding back the watching crowd a prudent distance. Their belts together are a kind of hound's-tooth pattern. In the moonlight the metal of the car shines through the dented enamel and catches fire. The car has been spray-painted with dares and taunts. A blow takes the hammer through the door, and there is chanting. Again. Again. Again. And the Safety Patrol joins hands.

FROM   1985
Crazy Women

Haunted by Name
Our Ignorant Lips

I

Well, the first thing you're going to have trouble believing is Birdie
Braine herself. Almost six feet tall, with a back straight as an Indian
warrior and hair just as black. A wealth of bosom, and handsome
dark eyes.

That's right, "Birdie Braine." Christened Bertha by her old daddy
(Wendall Braine) and her mother (born Fern Clay, that's right, too,
earth to earth and ancient, because Fern's family have lived in this
valley for almost two centuries, as Wendall's copy of Dell's *History of
the Wyandotte Valley* will attest). Christened Bertha, but slipping very
quickly into "Birdie" by all the schoolboy wits, as if humorless old
Wendall had cunningly figured it out long beforehand.

Wendall once owned six hundred acres of good dark bottom land,
but he began to get strange cautionary signals and started to sell it off
near the end of his life and stash the money away in unlikely places, a
stack of twenty dollar bills stuffed behind the painted cherry wain-
scoting in the dining room ("What'll you do if there's a *fire!*" Fern
would shriek at him in public, when she thought he'd be obliged to
pretend to listen to her, at least; "Do? I won't do *nothing!*" Wendall
shouted back at her, pounding his knee with a palm as big as a Ping-
Pong paddle. Wendall was six feet six and weighed two-ninety in his
prime—that's where Birdie got her height, everybody said); but near
the end, he got wary and tired, and took in his flesh. And that's the
way it looked—tucked in around his starched collar in soft leathery
tan folds, little gray bristles sticking out here and there (so women
wouldn't caress him, he said; they'd get their hand pricked if they

did), his black eyes turning softer and shallower (as if filling up with strange memories), and their sockets going deeper all around, like two perfectly symmetrical balls-and-joints carved from light walnut.

Fern was in her grave now, no longer nagging. Wendall Jr. had run away from home, stopping an inch short of his daddy's six and a half feet and flunking out of college, in spite of a basketball scholarship ("He wasn't first-string material," his high school coach, Jerry Frick, always said; "too slow."). Then Wendall Jr. floated around the country, getting hooked up with an oil driller, and phoning the old Braine place twice or three times a year to ask for money or find out how they were.

Fern was dead. Buried in the family plot back of the old Clay mansion (red brick with white stepping-stone borders up the roof— built in 1846 by Fern's great-great-granddaddy, who'd live to muster a regiment in the War of the Rebellion and die of swamp fever in Mississippi. Capt. Clay, with a southern name, come south from Ohio in a passionate but murky cause, to die south of his Kentucky heritage).

But the Braines were Ohio and, more specifically, Wyandotte Valley, through and through, and had Creek water in their veins. Wendall reached the age of sixty-seven (his weight slipping clear down to two-hundred) and then he passed away one Sunday night in his chair during a National Geographic special. Birdie figured this out, because she phoned her daddy at nine o'clock that night and not getting any answer, went right on over there and found him slumped way back in his chair, his face hard and turning purple around the mouth and eyes, the television going on channel twenty. He looked like he'd been dead about an hour, she told people. And so far as anybody can tell, he had.

Old Wendall had built his darling Birdie girl a nice little brick ranch house at the edge of town, where she lived alone and liked it. That's what she said to everybody in that smart alexandra voice of hers. Just like back in school, when she'd introduce herself to a stranger, she'd say, "Birdie Braine. You know: cheep, cheep." Then she'd laugh, hah, hah, hah, staring curious, but a little cold-eyed, at the other person to see his reaction.

Yes, that is Birdie, all the way. She'll go wading a hundred yards through briers and poison ivy to embrace her fate. If everybody else had forgotten that silly nickname, Birdie would have kept it alive by her own reference. Birdie Braine, cheep, cheep, hah, hah.

But if anyone showed the least flick of interest, Birdie would say, "It's an old English name. They settled the Wyandotte Valley in log cabins. Had to shove the Indians aside with their elbows just to have room to swing the axe."

Of course, her last name was strange enough, without the birdie part. But she herself was strange enough to eclipse both of them, once you knew her. I know, because Birdie and I are the same age and have gone through school together all the way, except for her college and my college and law school. But neither one of us could stay away. We knew where our destinies were (I'll tell you something: I've waded through some briers myself), and we came back to the Wyandotte Valley, the old ancestral home, the little white village nestled sleepily between the long sloping hills, where nothing public (or public relationally) happens. Yes sir.

Birdie has never married. No man big enough to hold her, maybe. Who knows? She's sure as hell a virgin (I tell you, I know her almost better than anybody ever *should* know anybody else), but who knows what dreams she has? Or, in the obtuse, uncaring public way of the world, who the hell cares?

But never mind that. This account is for people who care. Or who *can* care, who can see the little things happening that make up the brick and mortar of our days, while we keep reading crazy maps made by distant organizations (not men) that presume to define our realities.

Birdie Braine was and is like no other human being who has inhabited (or does or will inhabit) the earth. Birdie is county recorder, has run for county offices off and on for fifteen years, her own little personal women's lib movement. Birdie won't stand still for men's ways. Don't get the wrong idea: Birdie is no fashionable Lesbian Libby, or any other kind of addled ad-libber; has no unnatural affection for women's bodies (this much I know about her dreams), and if she has lusts for men, she has never even let *them* show, beyond sentimental gestures and occasional remarks.

Then there was old Wendall. What kind of stories did they tell each other? What sort of games did they play? I've often wondered.

The night he died, George Sickles (the constable, who used to shoot baskets in our driveway with my kid brother) phoned and broke the news to me.

"Birdie says you're the lawyer," George said in an official voice. This was ridiculous, because everybody *knew* I did all of Old Wendall's legal work (and that included Birdie, too) and such didn't need mention, but I went along with his tone and said, "Yes, I'm the man. How is she holding up?"

"Birdie? Oh, she's doing pretty good. Maude Fulmer's here, and old lady Smith from next door. I think there'll be some others here before long. They just took Wendall away. He was sure dead. His face looked like them lead soldiers we used to make out of molds when we was kids. The same color."

"Yes," I said.

"His heart," George said.

"Well, I guess I'd better come on over."

George agreed, and I hung up the phone.

"Who was that?" my wife called from the kitchen, where we have our television set. We've put it right back by the window, and she and I have two antique Boston rockers placed right before it, and we sit and watch it every evening. My wife says that I cuss once for every time the rocker comes forward, because of the silly drivel they have on television. But I watch it anyway. She says I love to hate it.

"That was George," I told her. Then I waited about four steps and two swings of her rocker while I walked into the kitchen and I said to the back of her head, "Wendall just died. He called to notify me."

My wife stopped rocking and turned around and looked at me. "Wendall?"

"Yes."

"Oh, that's too bad," my wife said, after a long pause. She turned around and looked at the dark window above the television set. Beyond the window, there's a stone birdbath and my wife's flower borders. Beyond that, the old shed in back, and then the garage. Beyond that, a vacant lot, then another street with only three little houses on it, and then the wooded hills in back. And then, of course, the sky. Which you couldn't see, now, because the kitchen was lighted.

"Well, I'm going over to see Birdie and see if there's anything I can do," I said.

"This will kill Birdie, too," my wife said, shaking her head.

"I don't know whether it will or not," I said. Then I got on my coat and hat and walked out the side door, where my shiny new Oldsmobile sat waiting for me.

II

The immediate problem was Wendall Jr. and how to find him.

I asked Birdie where he'd been when they'd last heard from him. Birdie paused and thought. She was wearing a gray pant suit and sitting in a big stuffed chair with her arms on the sides. Her face was dry and composed, but there seemed to be a strange light in it, as if something had just exploded deep inside. (But then, maybe that's my imagination; who can tell?)

"The last time he called, he was some place in Arkansas," she said, leaning her head back in the chair and staring up at the ceiling.

"What town," I said.

"I don't know," she said, "But we've got to let him know. I mean, I just can't stand the thought of that phone ringing some time when I least expect it, you know, and it'll be Brother, and I'll have to tell him."

That's what she always called him: "Brother." There was something primitive, elemental about it. And yet, I don't think the two even *knew* much about each other, let alone understood. Brother was four years younger than Birdie.

I was thinking this right then, and she must have heard what I thought, because she said. "When we were very small, I used to hold him on my lap. You know, at that time, he was my baby, my doll. And yet I have no more idea what he might be doing right at this minute than if he was a man from another planet." She shook her head at the thought.

"What town was it he called from?" I said. All business, because somebody has got to be.

"I honestly don't know," she said.

"Well, you're not much help. I can't call every number in Arkansas and ask if Wendall Braine's there."

"No, you can't do that."

"Would you know the town if I said it? Did he tell you where he was calling from?"

"He talked mostly to Dad," Birdie said. "Only I happened to be here at the time, helping Dad with some things. Dad did say where he was calling from. But I can't remember."

"Little Rock?" I said. "Fort Smith?"

"No," Birdie said, shaking her head. "I'd remember it if it was one of those."

I gave a big sigh and stood up. Old Wendall had a big library across the hallway, so I went in there and went to his shabby gray U.S. atlas, big as the top of a nightstand. I brought it back into the front room, where Birdie remained seated motionless in the chair, staring up at the ceiling with throat exposed.

I opened the atlas up to Arkansas and began to read off the names, one by one. Birdie closed her eyes and listened her way through Augusta and Batesville and Crocketts Bluff. When I got to El Dorado, she opened her eyes and said, "I think that's it. I think that's what Dad mentioned. Only he pronounced it 'El Do-ray-do.' "

I told Birdie that maybe they pronounced it that way down there, and then I went to the telephone, dialed information, and asked for Wendall Braine.

"He probably isn't there any longer," Birdie said. "It was two or three months ago that he called. He's always moving around. Not only that, I don't know what name they would have. They just stay in motels, I imagine."

The information operator couldn't help with Wendall Braine, so I told her this was an emergency and that I needed the phone numbers of every motel in El Dorado. She hemmed and hawed a little, but then she gave me the numbers of seven and I phoned then one, two, three. At the fourth, when I asked if a Wendall Braine or any oil drillers had been there, the woman at the desk said Oklahoma S. & L. had been there until last week. No, she had no idea where they had gone from there. Yes, one of them was a big tall man with dark hair and dark eyes, only she didn't know the name of Braine.

"Well, he has evaporated, it looks like," I said to Birdie.

She took a deep breath and said, yes, they were always leaving her. All of a sudden. She was all that was left.

I didn't ask her what she meant, but I had a pretty good idea. The first was Fletcher, who drowned one winter in Wyandotte Creek, when the ice broke. He was only eleven years old—a year younger than Wendall Jr. and five years younger than poor Birdie. Maybe she was a little crazy after that, too. Of course she was. Although she had never said so I knew damned well that she had rocked little Fletcher on her lap, too, pretending he was her baby, her doll. Yes, Fletcher had been the first. Now, old Wendall, her daddy. And now, in a manner of speaking, Brother. They had all left her in the valley. Outside, snow was beginning to fall.

It was almost midnight when I backed my Oldsmobile out of the Braines' long winding driveway. Near the road, there was a big Indian mound, with a hundred-year-old sycamore tree growing out of its ear. When my car backed out on the country road, my headlights passed slidingly over the mound like a marine beacon.

I'd almost forgotten about this old mound. One evening long ago when our family had visited with the Braines to play bridge, I'd gone to the window and looked out in the darkness, wondering mightily upon this mound. I could almost see the dead warriors sitting around it in a circle, their bones all mashed into the heavy clay, their eyeless sockets faced out toward the stars and moon, only two or three feet away from the air.

When I asked Birdie why they didn't dig into the mound for relics, she said, "Oh, no. That's against the law. Not only that, the mound is their graveyard, just like Mt. Clemens is ours."

Mt. Clemens is the Methodist Church, back up on Route #146, where everybody used to go to church years ago. Even then, when Birdie said this, there was a newer church and a newer high school. Why she'd mentioned Mt. Clemens, I'll never know. But she always did have a gift for the spooky, the remote, the out-of-the-way. If I'd asked her, she might have said, "Mt. Clemens is where my dreams live when I'm not having them."

She was crazy enough to do that sort of thing. I know. Don't think I don't.

III

We have two grown daughters, my wife and I. One (Nanci) is married to a complete fool who is so totally and commitedly a fool that he'll never be able to suspect that he is one. He and our daughter live in a Chicago suburb, and he works as a clerk in a men's clothing store in one of the big shopping centers there.

My wife and I have visited them several times, but so far as I am concerned, I'll never go back. When our daughter married that son of a bitch, it was like she committed suicide. The fact is, she was a smart girl—really smart and talented—except for this one thing of mistaking this straggle-faced idiot for a man. The tragedy is, she could have sacrificed all her other talents if she'd been able to see through him, and she'd be ahead. It's enough to break a father's heart.

This half-wit sits around and reads the paper and comments on world affairs, and she waits on him hand and foot, thinking everything he says is luminous with truth. He picks his ear with his index finger. He makes two hundred dollars a week, more or less, at his clerking job, and she makes half again that much as a secretary, but neither one of the damned fools seems to consider this a barrier in his assuming omniscience on any topic having to do with worldly success . . . and any other kind of success is as beyond his comprehension as Aztec phonology.

Anyway, we have another daughter (Marilee) who's smart enough, and makes a pretty good living as a lab technician in Pittsburgh. But she lives alone and wears men's sweat shirts and tennis shoes. She wouldn't be bad looking if she could unsquint her eyes (she wears the expression of someone bare-faced in a wind storm) and understand something of the implications of her gender. She's not a dike or anything (I honestly believe this, because you can be sure I've wondered); she just doesn't seem to give a damn for men as men, or women as women. One way or the other. I mean, the poor looney little bitch just bops around, living in a world of *people.* Neuters to be nice to and take an interest in.

I bring this up for a reason. This information is *material.* My wife and I sit side by side, rocking back and forth, watching television (I sometimes get a flick way back in my mind of old Birdie, watching the same things, maybe rocking right in tune with us), wondering where in the hell we went wrong in raising two girls like these. Just what in the hell did we *do?* Or what did we *neglect* doing, that we should have?

No, there's no hope of grandchildren, either. The damn fool son-in-law comes from a family that is riddled with everything from mental illness to premature senility, from diabetes to hickies and glaucoma. They are a race of idiots and dwarfs and nonachievers. Somewhere, deep in the back of his lineage, I sometimes get the echo of laughter at the fact that they've secretly conspired to empty the sewers of their blood into ours.

So far as I'm concerned, they've stopped my heritage, that blood, as with an embolus. Killed my line, because (I swear, through no fault of mine) our other daughter will never conceive, or even conceive of the desirability or even possibility of doing so. This pontificating half-wit has done it. He's had the minimal sense to have a vasectomy, and I sometimes hope out loud that our daughter gets knocked up by an itinerant genius (hush, my wife says); but the poor dumb girl has been insidiously schooled in fidelity, if in nothing else, and our line ends in a pompous whisper, mocking my ancestors who *achieved,* goddamn it, and *built this valley.*

You think this is irrelevant to the issue (yes) at hand? Oh, no. You do not listen, if you do. Or you do not forehear (as in foresee, but a subtler, more elusive art).

What a vicious, unconscious revenge for what an inscrutable crime!

Do you hear, now? For the Braines were coming to an end, too! Yes. This is the fear that dear Birdie felt rising like floodwater in her life. Old Wendall had possessed dynastic prejudices, without doubt. Old Wendall named his son in his own image (like God naming man with the jealous egocentric impress of selfing form). Wendall continued the madness, repeated it. Be thou me, my son! Take unto thyself mine own name. (Yes, I can hear it as plain as day.)

IV

Brother did not call. Could not be found, anywhere. I phoned the headquarters of Oklahoma S. & L., but they said Wendall Jr. was freelancing, now, according to the last report they'd gotten. At any rate, he was not in their employ. (They sniffed the lawyer in my voice, and thought I was about to garnishee his wages. I could tell; I sniffed their sniffling. But they wouldn't have lied to me; merely felt indelicately and obviously comfortable in telling the saving truth.)

Silence.

Old myths arise in my mind and are reenacted. Birdie was class president of our graduating class (Wyandotte High, 1941); I was valedictorian.

Birdie had written a poem in her senior year, and Miss Rumbacher had pinned a copy above the entrance to the English room. When it was taken down, Birdie made another copy by hand (her handwriting going straight up and down and as even as the stitches of a sewing machine) and gave it to me.

"I think you can understand something of this," she said. For once, she was not joking. She blushed and hustled away from me in the hallway, the sturdy calves of her legs rubbing together with each step (I had followed her up the stairs many times and had often witnessed this miracle).

I told her I had liked the poem, which was a lie because I hadn't read it after hearing Miss Rumbacher praise it so highly and refer to it a dozen times.

Later, though, I read it. Then read it again and again. Birdie was strange beyond understanding. Already, she was practicing madness. The rotting bodies of those Indian warriors had been radiating dark juices of romantico-philosophic-weltschmerz from the mound; poisoning the Braines' well water. (Killing poor old Fern and affecting old Wendall's mind; driving Fletcher to any icy suicide, according to Birdie's gradually evolved sense of things.)

The poem itself:

OLD WYANDOTTE

Hark, hark to the falling leaves
Shuddering down from the highest limbs.
Summer pleases, but light deceives,
Autumn is truth as the light dims.

Most the world is past, is past!
We the flurry of small moments.
Join we soon the eternal cast
Attired eternal in earth's garments.

Now our civilized confusion
Into the present valley seeps;
But the ancient Indian nation
Haunts by name our ignorant lips.

Wyandotte, oh Wyandotte!
Lost land of forgotten folk!
As your Fate, so our lot;
For we are teamed in the ghostly yoke!

Birdie's mind (after all these years, still) flies up into the high branches of that sycamore tree and chirps hoarsely, a raven of madness.

Her eyes darken. She does not talk as much; never jokes. Birdie Braine. (No cheep, cheep, no cheap joke, no hah hah. Silence. Brother is being awaited. The longer gone, the more mythic. He grows another inch; still another. He is taller than daddy, and he frowns down out of a rain cloud, roiling the creek where poor little Fletcher drowned so long before.)

"I wouldn't spend too much time with that woman," my wife said in the kitchen. I was rocking in my Boston rocker. She was behind me, shining her copperware with Brillo pads.

"What woman?" I ask, knowing full well what woman.

"Birdie. She's always been strange. And now . . . well, now there's really something wrong with her. I think poor Wendall's passing away was too much."

I turned around and stared at the woman, watching her hand make little circles in the copperware. Her eyes were distant; her lips pursed with the comfort of the power to reject, the salubrious safe bloodletting of the sick.

I growled into my cigar and lit a sulphur match. The flame pulsed at the tip of the claro cylinder.

"She passed right by me today and didn't speak," my wife said.

"Well, you've gotten even with her now," I said.

"Just what do you mean by that?" she asked. "All I'm thinking about is your own good. People like that who have problems . . . well, it's best to leave them alone."

"Unquestionably," I said.

"The woman's *never* been right, and you know it."

"No doubt about it."

"Her hair was hanging loose down her back. Clear to her waist. She had a crazy little hair ribbon hanging as crooked as could be at the back of her head. And wearing that awful gray pant suit she's always wearing."

"Birdie is a client," I said.

"Oh, you make me sick when you talk like that."

"The expression wasn't invented for the purpose of making people comfortable. Maybe people in the long run, but not particular people at particular times."

"I don't know what you're talking about."

"Not only that," I said, "but I've got my eye on some of that walnut furniture her daddy has stored in the attic. I can hardly wait."

"We have enough antiques already to open a shop," my wife said comfortably, having arrived at a formulaic complaint that helped her order her life.

"I will be the executor. Everything above board. Birdie will need liquid assets more than old chairs and tables. Unless she finds some of the money old Wendall has hidden around the place."

"I don't know what you see in that stupid woman."

"Stupid she is not and never has been," I said, waving my cigar in the air. It is little gestures such as this that relieve people of the responsibility of taking my words seriously. They think I'm funning, play-acting, pontificating. They regard me as a vestige of an old Chautauqua preacher, even though they know not the word and little of the truth it expresses.

"Crazy, then," my wife says, conceding an old point, in which she has often been forced to concede. (But never understanding how important it is that her diction be pure for her mind to be clear.)

"Often in school, Birdie Braine was singled out for her remarkable memory, her truly uncanny gift at certain kinds of mathematical computation."

"I said crazy," my wife cries, stabbing her Brillo pad in my direction.

"I was always a better speller," I said. "And I was more comfortable with abstractions and logic; but Birdie had an amazing computer in her head. You could throw out a two digit number and a three digit number and ask her to multiply or divide, and she'd come up with

the answer in seconds. Old Richards loved to make her perform for
visitors."

"It's time for 'Masterpiece Theater,' " my wife said, "At least that's
one show you don't grumble about."

"I am afraid for her," I said, "If Wendall Jr. doesn't call soon. She is
surely taking it hard."

"Or is that tomorrow night?" my wife asked. "Isn't this Saturday?"

"Of course, if he *does* call, it might be traumatic for her. I honestly
don't see how poor Birdie can win."

"It *is* Saturday. Honestly, I get so one day is just like another. I
sometimes think I'm as crazy as anybody."

"What will be, will be," I said, and snapped on the television.

V

Summer eased past in silence. A golden river of days, crossed by the
shadows of night.

What did Birdie do all this time?

God only knows.

I saw her several times in the way of business, and each time she informed me that Brother had not called. The last time was early in September, and I had to stop by the County office to check a deed. I came
across Birdie in the hall. She had just come out of the ladies' room.

"Well," I said, "have you heard anything?"

"No," she said. "Nothing at all. I'm afraid something has happened to him."

"I doubt it," I said. "The watched pot never boils."

"What is *that* supposed to mean?"

I stared at her an instant and had a shock. Birdie had suddenly, at
that instant, outgrown all jokes. (Oh what a fall was that!) There was
honest, sincere inquiry in her expression. What *did* it mean? (Right
then I knew: she would never cheep again. She had become Bertha,
harrowed and damaged and stuffy. Ah, but not to me; I would not
acknowledge it.)

Before I could explain, she clutched my arm and said, "Listen, I
have to talk to you, I've been thinking."

I patted her hand where it still rested on my arm. "Sure," I said,
"We'll make it soon."

Immediately, I despised myself for this action, for it had to seem patronizing.

But the fact is, it did not. Or did not appear to (did not appear to appear thus).

For Birdie's (Bertha's) eyes were distant, missing my ear and spiraling off into the dark corners of the hall. Her vision was crooked, inhabiting a crooked frame of space.

"You don't know how much it means," she said.

I wondered what she meant by that. But it would be some time before I found out.

VI

This was near Halloween. Some idiot of a boy put a cherry bomb in our mailbox and blew it clean off its stand. I remember standing out there in the cool darkness with my fists doubled up, looking this way and that up and down the street. I could smell apples in the air, burning leaves. The faint trace of carbons from cars racing in and out of the Dairy Freeze at the edge of town. And of course smoke from the burst cherry bomb.

It was then (as if in premonition, for the memory can only create that moment through the screen of subsequence) that I said half-aloud: "We do not have to celebrate the rise of demons from the earth into the world of men on a ritual October night. Oh, no. These boys are nudged and shoved forward by truly ghostly hands. They themselves are the demons, a profane and blasphemous heritage. I know them."

I went back in and my wife was walking toward me, saying, "It's Birdie on the phone. She wants you to come over."

The phone was still warm and a little damp from my wife's hand, and Birdie continued talking to me as if my wife and I were continuous.

"Yes," I said. "I'll come."

"I wouldn't," my wife said, when I hung up. "She wants you to help her look for old Wendall's money."

"Maybe," I said.

I went out to my Oldsmobile (older now, and filigreed with dust) and got in.

What I had not mentioned (but my wife's statement had implied) was that Birdie had said to meet her out at the old homestead, beyond the Indian mound. Where Old Wendall's ghost might still walk. Where the high-ceilinged rooms were beginning to soak up the coldness of the nights.

The moon was full, as it should be on Halloween.

The smell of that cherry bomb was still in my nostrils when I passed the Dairy Freeze on the way out of town. It had seeped into the car, in spite of its newness. Like cold. Like time. Seep, seep.

Everything was strange, transformed.

Birdie was an old woman, going mad. Brother had crawled down into the earth and would never come back again. Call him all you want. Call, call.

I had these strange hunches, deep in my bones. (Had been having them, more and more lately. Age transforms everything, it is the only medium of change. If the change is sudden, then time has passed. Absolutely. That day in the hall, I had seen twenty years flow through Birdie as if she was nothing more than a poor minnow seine, cold and frail in the terrible current that moves all of us eventually. All. Always.)

VII

The electricity had been shut off, the house sealed. A tomb coldness came out of the antique flower-papered wall. Birdie had ignited three kerosene lamps that radiated a dull heavy light only five or six feet about each of the Victorian tables they rested on. Beyond these circles, the rooms glided away from their touch—vaguely dark and ironlike in color, heavy with the burden of things accumulated.

Birdie had kept her fluffy white coat on, emphasizing her dark eyes. In that light, she was beautiful. It occurred to me that she had been born out of her proper time, for if she were young today, she would be considered stunning, majestic. Then, she had been merely grotesque, taller than most of the boys around her. She had, however, worn saddle shoes and walked straight, proud in her deviation.

"You're a lawyer," she said. "Tell me where Halloween pranks end and vandalism begins."

I lit a claro and blew smoke toward the ceiling. I have found that silence is inevitably the correct answer. Also, it gives you time to think.

"I suppose you think I want you to help me find the money," she said.

"Money was created by God," I said.

"That sounds like Dad," Birdie (veering toward Bertha) said.

"I couldn't imagine his saying anything like that."

"No, but it sounds like what he believed. It's what he *would* have said, if Mother hadn't made him wary of such talk."

"*Have* you found any?"

Birdie smiled tiredly. "Today," she said. "You'll never guess where."

"In the Indian mound," I said.

Her face dropped. She could never conceal surprise, and—more importantly—could never avoid its occasions.

"Where did you get an idea like that?" she whispered.

"The gods sleep there. Money belongs with the gods. Just an association of ideas."

"In the *chicken* house!" Birdie cried, indignant. "That's where I found it. A bundle wrapped up in an old chamois! It was stuck in a crack above the door."

"Golden eggs," I said. "How much?"

"Over a thousand dollars," Birdie said, lowering her voice again. A car raced by on the road, a hundred yards away. I could almost feel the pale headlights wash briefly over the Indian mound.

"Well, how much more is there, do you think?"

Birdie frowned and scratched her thigh with long fingernails. "I don't know. A lot."

"Have you heard from Brother?"

"No," she said. Then she sighed deeply, frowning at a kerosene lamp. "I was hoping he might be back here by Halloween, at least. We always used to have a big time at Halloween. In some ways, it was our favorite time of year. Even better than Christmas. The valley is beautiful in the autumn."

I nodded and blew smoke past my cigar. At that instant, there was a heavy adjustment of time, of the whole fabric of hours, minutes, days, years. It was like a great body turning over in its bed, shaking the walls and making the old photographs nod in their golden frames.

Birdie, Birdie. You are a child, cheep cheep. And so am I, for only this brief instant. The demons outside, speeding in radical patterns outward from the cold hellfire of the Dairy Freeze, were only as tangible as the conjured memories of our own past could make them. We have been left, abandoned by our children (both those we did and did not have) and by ourselves.

Where are you, Brother?

"We are alone," Birdie was saying, agreeing, nodding, fondling the money. Alone. She wanted me to take it and count it with her. She wanted me to stay all night with her in the house, and we would pretend we could hear the Indians singing from the mound.

Ridiculous. But thinkable, therefore something *like* true. Something conceivable.

"To think," she said, "that we would someday, you and I, be sitting here in this room, talking about such things!"

"It's a scary thought," I said.

"No. Not that. Not exactly. I mean, not *completely*."

"No, not completely."

Neither of us could say what was happening inside. I know this as surely as you know the image you see in the mirror is yourself turned around to face your need to know yourself. And thereby mock.

Why was she not known to be beautiful and therefore desired? Why was she not covered with children, tugging at her bodice, snuggling for warmth and nourishment? Why had that bosom *not been used*? What ghostly, indifferent men moved in and out of her dreams, either here or in her antiseptic ranch house, made of brick and surrounded by a trim lawn?

Oh, Birdie. Oh, Birdie Braine! Sad jokestress of Time and Ideality.

She talked about the money. She spun theories about where it might be, all the intricate interstices of the walls and cabinets. All the walnut tables and desks and chairs, under whose laboriously handworked innards a soft chamois pack might be snuggled, suckling time from the darkening wood.

I expected my wife to phone, asking where I was. (Did she picture me snuggled into Birdie, infecting her with love and being in turn affected?) But the phone had been disconnected shortly after the time old Wendall's brains and hallucinations had been.

"What if the chicken house had burned?" I asked. "Chicken houses possess a powerful mortality, because the wiring goes bad in them. Bad risks, Birdie!"

"Was I talking about chicken houses?" Birdie inquired. (She was not, had not been.) "You never listen," she said.

"What's that?" I asked, cupping my hand around my ear.

"Oh, shut up. You've never grown up, after all these years. Why do you *act* that way?"

"What is there to grow up to?" I asked.

"Now you're sounding like me. Or the way I think."

"I always sound like somebody else," I said. "Or their thoughts."

"That is true of all of us," Birdie commented sadly. "But then, things come to an end."

"Isn't it nice to be present at the ceremonies?" I asked.

"I'm not sure. I'm not sure."

"Your dad was foolish for turning his money into cash and hiding it."

"He was crazy. Part of him left before he died. He had a stroke. Nobody knew about it, but I did."

Ah, but *you* are somebody, Birdie! "I heard tell he had one," I said.

"One day he started humming at the breakfast table and then he got up and did a little dance. I thought he was just horsing around, the way he did years before when we were kids. God forgive me, but I thought he was *playing*. I started to say, 'Dad, for Heavens sake, act your years,' but then I saw."

"You saw," I prompted.

"I saw the look in his eyes. He was drifting off and calling out to me. He was scared. If there had been something inside him to grab, I would have grabbed it with all my might and held on!"

She said this with her fists clenched and her jaw square and her eyes beautifully solemn. If I had turned this into a joke, she might have thought of killing me. But if I had joked, it would have been to catch at *her* heart and keep it from drowning. I could see poor little Fletcher breaking through the ice of his look, screaming out to God that he couldn't *understand*.

"Yes," I said.

"Yes," she said, nodding. "Then he sort of glided or waltzed or something into the front room, and I helped him lie down on the sofa. I was just visiting, that day. I used to come out here pretty often, though. Almost every day. Somebody had to sort of look after Dad.

Brother was out somewhere, in the world. He had left for parts unknown."

"He only wanted to live," I said.

"What?"

" . . . his own life."

"Yes."

"Which brings us to the Indian Mound."

"Oh, shut up. You scramble my thoughts like an egg beater."

"Tell me more," I said. (A request that few can resist; the question itself would, if used more liberally, compulsively, automatically— quite independent of any real concern—would obviate eighty percent of the lawsuits and therefore, by implication, most of the trouble in the world. But of course, I was firm in my desire to know. And honest.)

She talked, then. On and on. A bottomless supply of suspicion, terror, love, ideality, wistfulness, and tenderness of memory. For after all, memory is something achieved, like mind. It is something larger than ourselves, which we yearn to grow into and understand, which is to say, comprehend.

Birdie said none of this, but it was the unwobbling pivot upon which her ideas turned. Saying, saying. Cheep, cheep. Her mind sighed over me like a forest. ("Will you find words for me?" it asked. I said yes, and therefore now say these things.)

Bad dreams. Bad dreams. Birdie was sleeping too much these days, practicing death. Alone. Alone.

Behind the old family house, there was the trace of a road—long since abandoned. You could see it faintly adumbrated along the fence of the cornfield, under the cold distant shadow of the hills, and then you came upon the old abutment of a bridge that had once crossed a dried-up creek. The cement was gray, soft-looking—like dead mastodon bones clotted in the tangled slaw of winter grass.

No one called. The phone was dead.

Fletcher and old Wendall were as distant, now, and as mythic as the dead Indians who eased themselves ever deeper, rain by rain, into the earth. The cemetery at Mt. Clemens gave forth noises at night. You could hear the thub-dub, like a heart or drum, clear to the edge of lights radiated by the Dairy Freeze.

While she talked, I could almost feel the glow of those packs of money hidden by crazy old Wendall. (I knew that Birdie had only started to look; Wendall couldn't have hidden them so cunningly that *she* wouldn't find them.) The packs, wrapped in soft old chamois, glowed in my mind, burning bright like lumps of coal. Or little Dairy Freezes, the light of our hopes and comfort and ceremonial need for foods so that we can remember and predict and hope.

No one called, except for Birdie. No one heard, except for me.

Wendall's ghost sighed and stumbled along the hallway upstairs, asking for a drink of water.

Birdie is an old woman, going slowly, easily mad. Slipping. Her sigh flutters and falls away.

Rain is falling. My wife dials her phone and hears a recording.

Birdie does not exist. She has died four years ago. Time gallops over our faces and we gasp for light.

My children drift off, down separate rivers, remembering and/or forgetting my prayers and admonitions.

Blood flows into death, one river, one way.

Fletcher drowns inside us, each time his memory rises to the surface. No one remembers a single word he has spoken, therefore he is eternally silent. And after all these years, *has not existed,* as if by cosmic decree.

This thought is enough to kill poor Birdie. Cheep, cheep. The chicken house turns over in its rising grave.

At Mt. Clemens, where Birdie's dreams live when she is not having them, I start up my new Oldsmobile and ease it out into the soft gravel, and down it's slipping (like the back of an old man's neck), toward the moonlit valley and the lights of town.

A dog stands on top of the Indian Mound and barks in the mist.

Birdie reaches behind the attic door and feels the soft fold of chamois. But it is too late. The house is closed up. Forever. Brother is gone. He will not come back.

Birdie has gone, too. The two of them teamed in a ghostly yoke.

I speak her name. Birdie. Birdie.

JEAN MCGARRY

FROM   2002

Dream Date

The Last Time

I.

Gertrude Stein wrote all night and I sleep all night and most of the day. When I get up—slowly, grudgingly—what do I do? Nothing. Gertrude is in the kitchen making fresh pasta and I'm stretching out on the divan, tired from brushing my teeth with that special brush whose nubs are mohair and fold right down to the ebony stick so nothing but fluff touches my sensitive whites. On the divan I study the pattern of the ceiling and all the time that's gone by since this style of ornament—fruits and plants and curly-headed boys—was in fashion, long before Gertrude's day, and Alice's too. Alice is typing last night's pages. Typing doesn't irritate me, so the door to the tiny study is left open and she can see me and I her and we exchange signals and reports on Gertrude's latest infamies. But all of it done with a wink and sweet smile.

Soon the *déjeuner* is ready and Gertrude sets the table under the canopy on the terrace. We eat from the five food groups and drink from the sixth group, wine, and sometimes the seventh, coffee. For the eighth, we just smoke, careful not to blow directly into each other's faces.

Gertrude is just thirty-five and has all her hair and Alice never looked worse or better. She has a suit on and sits low in her chair, although her legs are actually very long. She kneels for pictures and tucks the long shanks under her suit skirt. Gertrude is not tall, nor is she fat. That's another trick. Once they've served me and I've eaten my fill of farina, polenta, noodles, rice and had my aromatherapy, I settle in the leather armchair to look at pictures. I'm fond of two artists, neither of whom became a household name. But all their paintings they gave to me and Gertrude had them bound in these large books, so I could while away the hour between lunch and *café* flipping through the canvasses, or unraveling them if I feel like it: just pulling a string and, over time, there's nothing left. Our days together are long and fruitful. After pictures, I'm dressed in my pure silks, and fine pumps are put on my feet, a green umbrella or a pink parasol, depending on *le temps fait beau* or *mal,* and a small corsage is purchased on the street corner. Gertrude ties it on my left wrist and takes my hand in hers. Alice walks behind us and does the marketing.

Five full days pass before our next visit with Picasso, who comes alone. He's an irritable guy and we're all—me included—walking on eggs until he's taken off his cap and ironed out some of the wrinkles that hatch his face.

"Mr. Picasso," Alice says, "a cup of tea or a drop of wine?" That gives him something to think about while we skitter about picking our chairs, and last one gets that low stool near the fireplace.

"I don't know," he says and looks around the room until he finds me sitting up straight in a ladder back chair. "Who's that?" he says.

"As if you didn't know," I say so fast that the words are like arrows on their target before they even spring the bow.

"What did she say?" he asks in Spanish, the only language I don't have, or so he thinks. He eyes me, but my face and narrow form, much sought after by Mr. Klee and Mr. Miro, are just popular filler to him, although perhaps—in the back of his mind—a thin cat.

Trouble begins to boil. The two ladies offer Mr. Picasso fifty dollars so he can buy his own lunch and rent a studio on Avenue des Pompiers for the next ten years, so he's satisfied, in a sense, and doesn't go away angry or empty-handed, but of course, he fails to say goodbye to me, or even salute me for my birthday, which is next week, so I curse and swear in every written language until Gertrude comes with the syringe and gives me my first shot of Evening in Paris.

It turns out Gertrude has to pay them all, and more now that I'm here, big as life, a fly in their ointment.

"Why," I ask Alice after we both hear Hemingway wiping his feet on the doormat, ready to knock with that ham fist, "am I a fly in their ointment?"

"Shh, darlin'," she says. "Wait now." And that day, I do, tucking my feet under my skirt which covers my legs just to the ankles.

Hem comes alone. He's in uniform but the war's been over for five, six years. In he comes with thick boots and a big, toothy smile. "*Miracolo,*" he says. And that means, Alice whispers in my ear, another sentence has been written, pulled like a tooth rooted in the jawbone, or even in the ribcage, or rooted in the feet, for that matter.

"Okay," I say. "Celebration." And we take a colorless, odorless liquid of a lethal proof and each drinks to art, to grandeur, to manhood and to the three ladies of the rue de Fleurus, with their pink faces and easy ways, especially the ways of Alice, whose fingers curl around mine to boost my spirits. Hemingway has never liked me and his big mug shows the ugliness of his feelings as soon as he sees that I'm not going anywhere. I can count the fleas on his collar and the hairs on his head, if I felt like it, and in a game of marbles or tic-tac-toe, he'd eat the dust. Hangman is my true sentence. But I'm nice, I'm friendly, I ignore the puss with its strained, false smile that he puts on just to keep Gertrude from sinking her teeth in his neck. Gertrude and Hem have been at war since '06, which may be why he wears the uniform. It's up to Alice—it's always up to Alice—to make the peace.

We each give the writer and telegraph artist a ration ticket—mine is actually an old chance in a turkey raffle—so Hem can buy the can of milk for Hadley's brat and a night of peace in that hovel, so Hem leaves, saluting the chief and wearing his welcome very thin indeed by a sneer toward me that comes in range of Alice's strong eyes.

"To hell with him," I say, as the door slams shut.

But Gertrude is wild and throws over her shoulders her velvet writing garment—even though the Paris sun has not set on the '20's—and begins a little earlier that day to drain the ink tanks of Western Europe and then on to the carbon pencils and eat all that paper, too, while she's at it.

That's the spell that Hemingway, the old fraud, casts on our house, or fog maybe I should say, or plague. The sky darkens and Gertrude thinks it's nighttime; factory whistle blows and the mill must be turned.

Thank heavens, at that moment, Ez Po and Bill Williams show up with hotdogs and cupcakes, enough for all, and the Chinese characters to go with them.

"Hi, Bill," I say. "Hello, Mr. Pound."

"Hiya, Betty," says Bill, but Ez's head is all beehive and he's praying to the seventeen god families of known history for a blessing on the canto of tomorrow; a curse has clearly dogged the canto of today and we know about last week and a month of Sundays before that.

"I said hello, Professor Doctor Pound," but Gertrude cuts me off, proffering a silver salver of confetti, those delicious stale almonds packed in a coat of sugar, and EP fills his pockets. Bill sits down beside me, but without a word. We shake hands, kiss cheeks, punch shoulders, pat backs and rub each other's forearms. I take a hotdog and break it in half.

"Take. Eat," I say.

"Thanks, Pal. Don't mind if I do," is his reply and with it, Ezra's eyes pop open.

"Hot dog!" he says, and sits, eyes burning, with fifty ideas slotted behind them. Happy to be filled in the head, he eats his fill of dogs (Where had they gotten them? The *patisserie?* The *boulangerie?*) while Alice's busy hand peels the papers on a couple of black-and-white cupcakes, the kind you can get up around Boston and Fall River. We eat in peace, although Gertrude doesn't touch the stuff. Pickled onions for her and a quarter of a pickled egg for my darling Alice, with wine in those dirty flasks.

Once filled, we circulated papers. (It was so nice not to be despised.) Essays, poems, a libretto, four tiny short stories, a recipe, and blank page from me. We read, first silently, then with closed eyes, shut tight. Ezra read from one of his indoor screens, a canto or a little bit of rubbish that collected there. Bill had his banjo and everything with us was American fourth of July, for fifteen to twenty minutes, until—pooped—the two men of letters left and the three of us (mostly Alice) were left to clean up the mess and backbite, which was the chief fun for all the work of the rue de Fleurus.

II.

Some days no one came. The rain fell, the sun shone. Gertrude wrote all night until her blood collected in her feet, stuffed into *pantoufles* like the bros. Goncourt wore. Then she passed out. Alice was there, pushed up in a chair next to Gertrude's to take that heavy head on her shoulder. The picture I have in my mind! I was never jealous because I had four or five cats, a litter from Colette's favorite, unnamed pet, stuffed into the cracks between me and the wall. In that way we never felt like a threesome, a sore-pointed triangle. I gave them their space because Alice's love was complete. She was made for love, where Gertrude was made for greatness and I for sleep.

This is compatibility of a sort, and very easy for the folks who visited us, trying to make their way, or bull their way into history. We offered (even Gertrude) no resistance. Why not Gertrude? She salivated for glory, but she also had money, and Alice—don't forget—so these punies who came by, with their crayons and their worn-out Fabers and their flat hats, they did her no harm. Alice had kept the fattest coat of love wrapped around her Gertrude—tough as a walrus skin, thick as a church wall and roomy, for Gertrude was growing, right under our eyes, and under tout Paris, for that matter, or under that part of it that came knocking.

One day, though, and sadly, it all changed. Life is like that; it doesn't tolerate perfection or contentment, even what they had, and what I could get from Colette's cat's litter, and keeping an eye on the pair, and letting them take care of me, an American in Paris.

It started here. One very simple day, the car broke down and overhead, there was a flight of migrating birds ("ducks," I said; "geese," said Gertrude, and "no difference," Alice said, whether she believed it or not). In fact the flying birds or fighting tigers were pigeons from Sacré Coeur on their way to Ile de la Cité for the leavings that were always choicer. At the time, no one understood the meaning of this sign, but more were coming. We hopped a tram, but without tickets, and boy-o-boy, the fur did fly when the trouble started. Down at the station where we were—I want to say "escorted," but arrested and cuffed is more the speed of it—none of the given bracelets quite fit around the meaty bone of Gertrude's fighting arm, so they took her left, which threw everybody off; *flics* and prisoners were all in a foul mood as the paddy carried us, siren-screaming, to the lock-up, a holding pen, I guess it was.

"Name?" asked the desk sergeant.

"Ha!" I said out loud. "Wait'll he hears."

"*Attendes,*" he said to me, "*tais-toi.*"

"Name?" He turned to Alice, and together she and Gertrude did the great thing, true American Yankees: they shut their traps tight.

"*Kein Deutsch,*" little Alice said.

"A-la-la," the chief man said. "*Attendez, tout le monde,*" and out he went looking for what we didn't know.

Let me put it in a nutshell. Held all day for questioning until every language cop in the capital had been jerked out of his hideyhole to come translate the three madams until finally the chief inspector, a real character, thought to ask the arresting officer what we had done, what all three did to need the people of Paris's police apparatus, beloved institution, to undo it, to get justice or repairs. No one could remember; it hadn't even been written down.

How could it be, since there was no confession, no name, no street address? All was general puzzlement, or the beginning of a dangerous kind of irritation. I had stood that whole time stone silent, my mug all tucked up without its usually juicy expression that gave everybody the bright idea that I could be read like a book, and who knows what kind of book. Well, then I spoke, I said my piece, first words I wasted on the French *flics* or any French.

"This," I said, pointing to my left where Alice stood, tall and Sapphic, "is Gertrude Stein, who owns half of America, and this," I said, pointing to Miss Stein, who still had the car crank in her hand, "is Missy Toklas."

Fine, sure, they said in their own language, but who are you?

"What do you mean who am I? Who are they? Aren't you going to check? Check it out."

They didn't like the tone, I guess, because, in a minute, the pair of sapphs were ushered out the main door, toodle-o, didn't even think to say goodbye, going straight to the *Tabac* to buy a thousand tickets, or as many as they thought they'd need between now and the end. For me, it was different; it was always different.

But I served my time. I saw the butterflies on Devil's Island; I marched in a striped suit to the Bastille. My legs were too skinny and weak for the big ball, so they found a child's ball. (That's what they do in France.) It was pretty but heavy and I carried it in my own arms and wept bitter tears of auld acquaintance be forgot, but by the end of the first month, Mr. Camus showed up. He'd gotten wind of it and thought to spring me by offering the name and address of someone they really wanted. So out I went and off I trotted. Mr. Camus, a tough-guy—no pulp in him the Algerian ragazzi hadn't beaten out of him—squired me up to the flat he kept with Beckett's ex and put me up for a few days till I stopped crying and could lap up some chocolate, because I was so meatless by then it sounded like bones dropping when I fainted dead away two or three times *par jour* from sheer inanition. Mrs. Beckett, a nurse, tried to pep me up, feeding me with an eye dropper from her own cup, chocolate with a stinger of Armagnac. Little by little, I pulled what I had together and rose off my litter at the foot of Mr. Camus's own litter, and sometimes right next to his, and sometimes pulled over so there was no difference between what was his and what was mine. (And Mrs. Beckett was in bed, too, or out on call.)

"Alice and Gertrude," I started to say when I found my voice, but so weak it was that it barely crossed the barrier of my soft teeth.

"Alice and Gertrude what?" said Mr. Camus, lighting my and his cigarette. We smoked like fiends.

"Do you mean," I said, "what is their last name or what was I going to say about them?"

But his eyes glazed over. Something was eating him. His hair was turning white, just individual hairs, but I could count them when he pressed me to him so tight that his hair was in my eyes, and being me, I opened them.

"My sadness," I said, "my cutie," because we were in love, "what ails you?"

He lifted those oily eyes, mud-color, to shine on my still-emaciated face and said, "*Au jourd'hui—*"

I stopped him dead. "I've already heard that one before," I said.

"*Maman,*" he went on, as if the words were putty in his mouth, but then he stopped because he could tell that I *did* know it.

"Etcetera, etcetera," he said.

And we took the day off—a boatride up the Seine, *une piquenique,* a little music and boozing. He carried me home in his arms, just a pile of bones I was, with a bocce ball. This was not the life for me, too heroic, so I packed a few things—nothing, really—in a baggage and traced my steps back to where it won't surprise you to hear I was going.

Love was fine, but I'd gotten my fill of it. I left Mr. Camus a suicide note, so he wouldn't come snooping, a tip for Mrs. Beckett (her life was hard), and hoofed it over to rue de Fleurus. Gazing up at the windows, I saw a TO LET sign. What I didn't know—or didn't know yet—was Paris was yesterday. Alice and Gert had started out for the south with Picasso and Fernande and that trip was just the first in the slope toward the end. I sat on the doorstep. Little by little, no one came. Hem, a little bird told me, was in Spain; Bill and Ez had parted company, and even Mr. Fitzgerald was less frequenting the Ritz bar and had pulled in his horns for the nonce. The work had really started, the fun was over. For me, the fun was just beginning.

Nighttime had not yet fallen on Lutèce, but Jean Rhys came clicking by to look me up. A laugh a minute she wasn't, but at the Brasserie Lipp, where her connections were, she led me to Fordie, to Joe Conrad and, on off-days, to Eddie Dahlberg and Mr. Miller. Such were the joys. The end was in sight, just the three chimneys of the *Queen Mary,* or maybe it was the *Lusitania,* but over I went with steamer trunk of memories. I was delivered with the rest to the bottom of the sea, five fathoms, and here I lie, my father's eyes are still my eyes, my time is now my own. I think of Alice, and for a long time before going to bed early, I know she thought of me.

ROBERT NICHOLS

FROM   1991

In the Air

Six Ways of Looking
at Farming

I

The Lalumieres were anticipating the auction with dread. The farm
was to be auctioned—buildings and equipment. Here is a typical
newspaper notice:

February Specials

> 316 acre dairy farm—155 tillage, 100 pasture, 220 × 36 comfort stall
> barn, 109 stalls, 20 × 70 and 20 × 50 concrete silos with unloaders,
> 110 milkers, 23 young stock, full line of modern equipment.
>
> Stocked and equipped—$425,000
> Bare—$350,000

The Lalumieres had seen such notices for a long time; only now it
applied to them.

Let's not describe the auction itself. The household items are sold
off: these have been collected and stored on the porch, and are sold
for small amounts to random buyers who might take a fancy to such
things—let's say, an old music box. Equipment: tractors, mower-
conditioners, seed drills, balers, and silage choppers. These go to
other farmers and equipment dealers. Then the herd itself . . . by now
the crowd has moved inside the barn, glad to be out of the rain. A
good holstein with calf in her going from $900 to $2,000. The land.
Then finally the farmer's debt to the moneylender is paid off. The
crowd has left. It's stopped raining. The family is sitting on the porch
looking out at the empty yard where the flowers have been tram-
pled, at the empty equipment bays, at the empty barn—but with
enough cash to keep going.

It is the Lalumieres sitting here. The story has already taken us beyond the bare words of the auction notice:

"February specials. 316 acre dairy farm . . . 155 tillage," into the zone of sadness. The family is sitting on the porch together. Each feels it in a different way. It's all over, the noisy theatricality of the public event. At their backs is the emptiness of rooms. A lilac bush crowds on the porch railing. It reaches out toward them . . . its blossoms still wet, deepened in scent and color, hanging in their weight.

2

Some months before, Ed and Therese Lalumiere were sitting at the kitchen table. The old man was in a characteristic pose for him— with his head down resting on his arms, fists pressed against the temples. He was short, his barrel chest pushed against the table edge, his arms like butcher blocks. Next to the fist, a pocket calculator. Therese stood behind him, her back to the refrigerator, half an ear toward the grandson napping upstairs, glad that his volcanic energies were for the moment sleeping.

The financial papers were spread on the family dinner table— account books, copies of tax forms, paid bills, bank statements, etc. Sheets in piles clipped together covered the surface as solidly as plates.

This is what they amounted to:

EXPENSES: Food and household expenses, transportation, utilities, phone, medical.

Grain, herbicide fertilizer. Equipment maintenance. Insurance, veterinary, seed.

Taxes. Repayment of loan.

INCOME: Twice-monthly milk check. Logging. Trailer rental.

Market value of farm listed—40% of equity in loans.

Overall zero or minus income.

The point was: there was no way out.

No need to think about it. No need for the two to speak to each other of blame, failure, of fortitude, resilience, of cunning calculation, of hope. This is what the figures added up to. They had been gone over a thousand times.

The old man's pose—short stocky frame, head resting on arms, fists to the temples, etc.—not of despair but simply the posture of a man with emphysema. A way to relax the tension of the neck and give some room for breathing to the lungs.

The point was, there was no way out. No matter which way one moved, nothing would give an inch—as if the landscape: trees, fields, every blade of grass were made of iron.

Therese with her back to the refrigerator, looking out the window at the big maple, from whose limb was suspended by a chain a car engine.

Business of the farm continuing as usual. The daughter-in-law in town working. The son—repairer of the engine—now in the barn milking eighty cows. And the grandmother looking after the grandson.

She's listening for his waking, ear tuned to his stirring and shouting, his step stamping downstairs. Already she feels his hand inside hers pulling and tugging this way and that in childish circles, dragging her—the willing captive—on one errand or another.

3

One day the farmer had passed a group of Haitians picking apples in his neighbor's orchard. The men worked speedily on ladders, arms reaching upward through the leaves, twisting, dropping the fruit into bags tied to them. The gang moved down a row of trees stripping them of fruit.

Later Ed Lalumiere was able to observe two of these imported laborers in the supermarket. The language, of course, was incomprehensible to him. What struck him most was their shirts: blue, faded, worn through and many times mended. In the aisle, sheltered by the walls of canned goods, they chattered volubly. But they became silent and guarded. And going through the checkout counter, they couldn't answer questions but stared dumbly.

As Lalumiere passed by the orchard, one picker—a man the same age as himself—was standing by the fence pissing. The Haitian, who had his front teeth missing, was only a few feet from him.

Behind him the gang of apple pickers performed their task in the orchard aisles among the trees. They worked rapidly, chattering among themselves with a raucous and surreptitious air. They were like a flock of crows.

The squad of laborers, imported by the Immigration Service, came from overseas. They lived in dormitories and were all men. The pickers, who were all bone and sinew, who could work all day in the air without stopping . . . whose hands were coal black and whose eyes were slightly bloodshot . . . seemed to Lalumiere immeasurably strange.

4

Therese had read a story about a farm in the west. It was foreclosed and about to be sold at auction, and the neighbors prevented bids from being taken. It was unclear whether their farmer-neighbors had guns. The farm was being auctioned off at the instigation of the bank. Undoubtedly there were buyers, but due to the feeling of solidarity among the crowd of farmers, their sense that what was happening was unfair and wrong, it was not possible for the auctioneer to begin.

There were a number of conceivable happy endings to the story. But simply reading the story—that such a thing should happen—gave Therese joy. She had showed the item to Ed—who was tickled.

This item of news contrasted to her own nightmare. She had dreamed they were having an auction. It was their farm that was being sold off by the local auctioneer, a man named Pratt. Everyone knew Pratt. A jovial man, he had relatives in town. For years they had gone to Pratt to buy and sell cows. But in the dream he was wearing a frock coat.

Pratt was speaking in a strange language, or his patter was unusually garbled. Though it seemed he was speaking to her, she couldn't understand a word of it. One of the townspeople explained that he was saying this auction was special, it would be held under a unique set of rules. There was of course a money price on the farm, corresponding to what was bid. But also the work done on the farm by the Lalumieres would count; that is, it could be reckoned in a dollar figure—the years the family had spent living there for four generations and the value of the farm to the town: its beauty, its open fields and woods. For all these, the Lalumieres would receive a cash credit.

"But these things—everything we put into it—don't count," Therese objected. "It don't work out that way."

"It's true, they have only a symbolic value," the neighbor told her. "But so has money only a symbolic value." She assured her that the townspeople would stand as witnesses for the Lalumieres. And so they would be able to enter the bidding.

She had been told that the prospective buyer of the farm was there, or the buyer's agent. Therese looked for him but couldn't find him. She kept looking for this person, whom she imagined as a foreigner, some hostile power. Somewhere there must be this baleful figure.

The bidding began, but the unknown buyer had not materialized. Instead, Therese realized, it was the neighbors themselves who were bidding against her. As in all auctions, bids were made by signs, a nod of the head or the flick of an eye, traced by the auctioneer. She was scanning the faces. The audience remained more or less expressionless, the eye of the auctioneer merely traveling over them as his lips moved, traversing the faces and picking up the secret signs.

The bidding had begun. The townspeople and neighbors were all familiar. It was all ordinary. That's what made the dream more terrifying.

5

As he drove the tractor, Jack Lalumiere could turn his head and watch the baler, pulled by the tractor, extrude the bales of hay onto the large flatbed wagon, which was pulled behind that. On the bed, a farmhand caught the bales as they came off and swung them onto a pile in back.

The helper was a Vietnamese or Thai laborer, a man twice the age of Jack. He was agile. Due to his short stature, the man had difficulty piling the bales. He had to stand on his toes to reach the top, to position them on the structure which was slightly quaking.

At the barn, when the wagon load was full, the bales of hay would be lifted by conveyor to the second-story loft.

There were woodchuck holes in the field. Where it had been cut, the field showed a mat of brownish white against the uncut green. With the large tractor and rig two men could harvest thirty acres of hay in a day in the June heat.

The tractor's path, parallel to the hedgerow, continued in a straight line in slow motion through the grass. It was as if it were a ship: Jack at the wheel was the pilot, and the farm laborer—with his wispy patriarch's beard and rope sandals, feet spread and bracing himself—was a deckhand . . . moving through seas of green.

Jack rarely looked back. The laborer concentrated on his task. The driver's attention was on the window, the swathe of hay being taken up by the machine, in front of which swarms of grasshoppers were flying up and moving out to the sides in silent waves. The tractor puttered along dreamily.

A flock of crows lifted from the field, circled, cawing and scolding, and disappeared over the wood. The wood seemed to be the true kingdom of the crows.

The hedgerow extended the length of the field. It had once been a line of fence but had grown up to shrubs—alder and buckthorn, and more substantial trees—so that it was now a dense barrier, a bulwark of impassable shadow. Beyond it could have been woods or wilderness. In fact, at the bottom could be seen chinks of light, crossed by an occasional strand of barbed wire. The openings could have been made by some animal browsing there. Jack remembered it as once being a pasture with cow-plop and purple thistles. There had been a gate somewhere. Several years ago he had looked for this entry point but had failed to find it. Jack remembered they used to go through the fence somewhere. That was long ago. They had walked through the field, he and the neighbors' children, with their bathing suits, and at the bottom there was a river and pools. After swimming they would lie on their backs on their towels, arms behind their heads, looking up at the sky.

That time was far away, forever inaccessible. What was barred by the impassable hedge was not so much a place, but a time. It was the territory of childhood.

6

The three men were bathing in the pool. The river entered after a stretch of rocky shallows, and left the place over a lateral shoulder of rock the water had smoothed. The river made a long curve around the hay field, forming several pools. The deepest and coolest was this spot where the men were bathing, splashing the water with their arms or buoyed up and half floating, balancing on the bottom with their toes.

Ed Lalumiere's body was the most compact, like a block of wood. The Vietnamese, also short, was thinner and frailer, his skin paler in the moonlight. The Haitian floated on his back half submerged like a black tree that had fallen in and the current was carrying along.

The bathers' pool insisted on its own quiet. It was night. And perhaps the flowing water did their speaking for them. Or it was enough for the moonlight to tell a plain story written on the newly mown hay field, which glowed like a piece of paper. The alfalfa stems gave the field a stippled effect.

The moon didn't seek out the church steeple or any number of metal roofs of houses. Or if it did seek them out they were merely points of light glancing off the sleeping town.

At some point in the night the bathing West Indian, who was tall and rangy, would have clambered up on the stony lip, his arms dripping, and edged his feet ahead warily so as not to slip, and bent down, like a heron fishing. Lalumiere may have sat back against the mud bank which rose vertically, his eyes open wide because in the night freshness he was able to expand his lungs fully. And the Vietnamese farmer would have simply floated, hardly moving, his head tilted back, like a petal, not so much submerged in the water, as in memory.

He had been soaping himself, rubbing the dust of the day's work and hay chaff off. He smelled sweet. So perhaps it was a woman's body he was remembering.

All of the men submerged in memories. Or they were floating above their memories hardly conscious of them. They had drifted down, sunk below the illuminated surface, into the dark. They were no longer bitter or sweet memories, light or dark, but confused sediment at the bottom, and the bathers were swimming over them.

If it had been daylight, the three would have been stretched out on top of the bank sunning themselves. They would have been talking with each other about soils, the merits of different feeds, the cost of fertilizer and seed, what price a cow or goat would fetch at the market. Of the tricks and dodges of bankers and moneylenders. Of how farms could be lost through debt.

They could have talked about all of this as they lay drying on the banks. If the glare of the sun behind the eyelids had not been too red. Or the sky had not been too blue. Or the sun's heat reaching through their pores had not made them too sleepy.

But now it was night. They were swimming, disembodied in the pool. It was moonlight. They had floated beyond the bank's shadow.

They were refreshing themselves. The day's work was over. The townspeople were in bed. The field was full of sleeping grasshoppers. The woods were owned by owls. The river, as it slipped by, had its arm around the waist of the fields.

"Comme s'bon s'baigner," Lalumiere whispered, in a language long since forgotten. It had been the language of his grandmother . . . which now came up into him through his toes. Good to swim, to be floating in the cool water, to be refreshed, to be with companions. "Comme s'bon s'baigner," Ed Lalumiere repeated, thrashing with his arms and propelling himself forward in the direction of the Haitian.

Who reared up at him laughing and repeating with a shout, "Oui. C'est bon se baigner!" Recognizing it was his own language but a different patois. He spouted water at Lalumiere through his teeth.

"S'bon s'baigner. Comme t'dis," the Vietnamese murmured, his eyes crinkled at the corners and sweeping his arms forward at the pleasure of the strangeness being broken by words.

West Baltimore

"SAY A PRAYER FOR ME," Eight-thirty, half-toothless fat Margaret on the hot sidewalk, dark Italian lunes under sharp eyes, white hair in a shingle. "I don't go to church (why should I lie?) except for the lunches. The nun's from the south, I love her accent, she's nice." West Baltimore and Margaret born ten blocks from here over a grocery her parents ran, ten blocks and sixty-two years.

"But say a prayer for me anyway, Larry. My landlady said she's sold the house. Drove up yesterday in her big car. I told her I didn't know about the Sadanas—you know, the family from India that lives on the second floor. I said I didn't know about them or about Punky and his ma on the third floor—you know Punky, Larry. His ma don't get out I said I didn't know about them either but me, I understood I could stay a year, so I said I aimed to stay for the seven months I got coming. I pay my rent. You want to be my lawyer?" Larry smiles, in a hurry to get to his summer-school law class. Eight-thirty, sidewalk already hot. "I been up since five, I always wake up early."

Marg's Tippy always wakes up first and waits for Margaret to, like this morning at five, just light. Marg puts on her housecoat and slippers and goes back through the kitchen to let Tippy out in the yard. Tippy does her business down next to the garbage cans and then comes back to be let in. Likes it in the house better, some dogs are like that.

"Fred here's Tippy's friend." He was a straw, pitiful when Marg started giving him a piece of bread now and then. "He's big but he's nice. Two or three times a day he comes around to say hello to me and Tippy." Marg doesn't have the teeth for a real ef. *Fred* in her mouth is a blurred *Pred*.

"Ever hear of a praying cat? Man up the street had one. Every morning it'd jump up on the chiffonier in front of the crucifix and cross its paws and close its eyes and pray. Lucy saw it, you know Lucy up the street."

Marg's been up since five. Fed Tippy, ate a piece of bread and drank a cup of tea looking at the TV and trying not to think about the landlady. The air wasn't real hot yet. Then she got her pail and brush and went out front to scrub her stoop. The paperboy said hi when he passed by, and he had an extra for Margaret today. The stoops always look nice and fresh after you scrub them in the morning. "I scrubbed Larry's this morning too, his and his wife's. I don't mind working, it gives me something to do."

Marg's father came from Sicily, worked stevedore five years, went back for her mother and brought her back. When Marg was growing up they lived over the grocery. Momma raised all the children to be honest and good. No steal, somebody don't have to eat, you give— talked broken. Some of the brothers and sisters are dead now. Vince lives in Baltimore, used to be a captain on the police force. George is dying in a hospital in Florida.

You don't want to look too closely at Marg's legs. All sorts of things, blue, yellow, stuff that'd be covered if people still dressed the way her mother did, if Baltimore was Sicily. Stoop dry now, Marg has a look at the paper. "Tippy listen, what's her name got married again. There was a bad earthquake. There was some people in a prison over in Africa—didn't say if they was colored or white. The jailers got tired of killing 'em, said okay, youse kill each other. The Taliaferros' girl's boy's in jail for stealing a car. Vince said if he'd only stole twenty he'd've had a suspended sentence. Dagwood never changes."

Another fire already? No, it's an ambulance this time tearing up Lombard Street. "Tippy don't howl at them like some dogs. Good thing, she'd be howling twenty times a day here. Fred must've come from somewhere off this main artery though 'cause look, Tippy, Fred's throwing his head up, will he howl?" No, he's learning.

Marg walks out to the curb. She can see straight down Lombard to downtown. Before they had cars, and before they had so many tall buildings, it was a pretty view down to the harbor. Marg was last down there when she lived up on Hollins Street. She and that nice lady that lived under her used to take a bus downtown almost every Saturday to do some window-shopping. What was that lady's name? It wasn't Teresa. It wasn't Carolyn, what was her name. It wasn't Anna Maria. Sighting down the wide dirty street is like holding those tall downtown buildings between the tips of Marg's lashes. No more ambulances for now.

When she's done with the paper Marg brings out her stepladder and her bucket and rag to wash her front windows. "If we wait long enough maybe somebody'll come along to help us, Tippy. I climbed trees when I was a kid but with my legs like they are now I don't know if I'd do any better with that ladder than you would, Tippy."

Street-level rowhouse windows in this part of Baltimore have crowds of dolls looking out, artificial flowers, stuffed animals, palm trees and cars, Jesuses and fruit arranged between the glass and the lace to make the house prettier and cheer up people that walk by. Lots need cheering up in this part of Baltimore. Marg used to put nice things in her windows when she'd be on the ground floor. She had a ceramic tree limb with three fat bluebirds on it. For a while she had a liquor bottle shaped like a fiddle. She bought it at the Goodwill store—Marg never touches a drop. Once she had a perfume bottle from the Goodwill too and it was a Spanish lady. She had them all in her window, the fiddle on one side and the bluebirds on the other, like they were making music for the lady.

In a while sure enough out comes Punky and offers to help. "Punky, *please* be careful. I'd never be able to look your mother in the face if you fell and hurt yourself washing my windows. You'll under-stand what I mean when you have kids of your own."

"That'll be never," says Punky.

"Stay out of Punky's way, Tippy." Tippy's small and looks as if she has some collie in her, always looks sleepy. She stands on the stoop and tilts her head, watching Punky wash Marg's windows. He's a good boy, sixteen, knows everybody in the neighborhood. "Punky, how's your mother this morning? What are youse aiming to do if that landlady sells the house out from under us? I told her I didn't aim to move till my lease was out."

"Lots of luck," says Punky.

"Thanks, Punky, those windows look real nice. Don't they, Tippy."

Vince doesn't drink either, none of Marg's brothers and sisters. Their parents used to drink wine with their dinners, but that was in the old days. They talked Italian with each other. Strict, wouldn't let their children drink wine or smoke. Vince smokes but Marg's never smoked a cigarette. In the old days there weren't so many bars and taverns either. Most of the ones you see now used to be grocery stores (they call them confectioneries). Now they're bars, some of their windows are bricked up.

Outside in the two o'clock heat the marble of the clean steps feels cool under Margaret. She fans herself with one of the fans she got two for a nickel at the Salvation Army store around on Pratt Street. Stiff paper stapled to wood like a big Popsicle stick, and shaped sort of like a Popsicle too. A pale green orchid with rays like the sun and a pale ad for a mortuary up on Baltimore Street, says courteous service in every price range, air-conditioned. Tippy lies in the shadow beside the steps. Up and down the sidewalks, in gutters and in the street broken glass sparkles in the blaze of heat. Marg shades her eyes. Who's that skinny lady crossing the street up there? Is it Lucy?

Lunch was good at the church, beans and franks, slaw. They're not supposed to let animals in the church but Tippy's so good and quiet the nun lets her stay in the vestibule. Today Marg couldn't eat all her beans and the nun let her scrape the plate off in the alley for Tippy.

When the weather's nicer Marg and Tippy take a walk after their lunch but today they just came on home. The pavement was burning Tippy's feet so after a while Marg picked her up and they came the rest of the way like that. Most ground-floor bedrooms are in the back but sometimes an old person has to live in the apartment and they give her the front room, or people watch their TVs in the living room during the day, so sometimes an air conditioner sticks out right over the sidewalk. Water drips out of it and that's good for the dogs and cats, but the air blowing out of it is even hotter than the air in the street. Loretta across the street said her kid brother said some of the new people that are moving into the neighborhood now and buying whole houses and fixing them up and living in them one family to a house like in the old days, said some of those new people have their whole houses air-conditioned. Must be behind their houses, they have the fronts fixed up nice. That'd be nice to have the whole house cool in the summer. Of course you heat up your backyard while you cool down your house, and some of that extra heat could get into other backyards where people don't have air conditioners and have to keep their windows open.

With Tippy under her arm like a purse Marg came on back down Pratt. Both the crab stores were full of people. The Lithuanian bar still has windows and some people were in there, old ones and young ones, drinking beer. It must've been air-conditioned. They must've been talking Lithuanian.

Yes, that is Lucy, bowlegged and skinny, looks like some kind of comedy bird. You can tell Lucy's Irish, there's still some red in her hair. You wouldn't guess she was fifty though. Marg waves, Lucy doesn't see her yet. Irish sticks together as much as Lithuanians but they talk good English. Colored sticks together too. One of Vince's boys drives a city bus and he said there's places that's all colored, don't no white people live there.

"Here, Lucy." Marg gives her the other fan. It's round and more colorful. Lucy says hi to Tippy like they were both arriving at work at some factory and Lucy didn't have time to say more than hi. Tippy didn't wag her tail even when she was a pup.

What was that lady's name though? It wasn't Teresa, it wasn't Catherine. It wasn't Ramona. She wasn't Italian or Irish either. Wasn't Lithuanian or Polack either. What was her name though? It wasn't Leona.

"Hi, Larry. Tippy, say hi to Larry. Lucy, this is my neighbor Mr. Larry."

Colored people live in the house in the alley behind Marg's. Usually Marg doesn't notice them but last Friday they had a picnic in their backyard, barbecued something and for a while in the afternoon it was nice to hear them over the fence when Marg was hanging out her drawers and nightgown she'd washed in the sink—they were having a good time just like a bunch of Italians except you couldn't understand most of what they said. But after dark they got loud. They were drunk and they'd laugh and then they'd get mad and yell out things. You couldn't say anything or they'd break your windows. Mostly they're quiet though. Hi Larry. Lucy, this is my neighbor Mr. Larry. Tippy, say hi to Larry.

Larry back from his law school pats Tippy's head. Him and his wife are nice people. He's a law student, she's a nurse at Mercy. One of their friends lives with them. They all help each other and they mind their own business. Lots of people around, you mention something and before you know it it's in the next block. They'll start rumors on you too. That lady across the street's the worst. Not even married to that man that lives with her. Sits under that tree—only house in the block set back from the sidewalk—all day in her nightgown and one fancy robe or another, eats melon and watches everything like it's hers and then talks about people and if she don't see something for gossip she'll make it up. Just because Marg ain't married and her best friends are women, that lady started a rumor Marg *likes* women. Marg first heard it around the corner, halfway down the other block. She was mad—came back and let that lady know what she thought of her loud enough for plenty to hear. They haven't spoke since. Loretta that lives upstairs next to that lady can't stand her.

Once that lady put a armchair out for the garbagemen to pick up. Loretta and her kids was taking it to use in their place and that lady come out and tried to stop them. She's a pain in the you know what.

Marg likes Larry but once this old man was walking up the street. Walking with canes and he was sick. Marg said rest on my steps a while. Larry comes out and's getting in his car, and Marg says, can you give this man a ride just three blocks up? He's sick and this sun's enough to make anybody weak. Let him take a cab, Larry said. He wasn't himself though, he'd spilled boiling water on his arm and scalded it. Once Marg tipped a cup of coffee onto her and the only thing she could think of was to cool it with cold tap water. The doctors said that was the best thing she could have done. It was like she knew what to do.

But Larry's nice. Sometimes he gives Marg a ride out to the supermarket. Don't worry, she treats him if he lets her, a Popsicle, a bar of soap. If she has to move he'll help her. It makes a difference if you know people you can ask for help.

Most of the people here's always been Lithuanian or Italian. Some Irish and then the colored people. Larry you know the lady youse bought your house from was Lithuanian. She was my landlady. Oh I wish I'd known youse so I could have set you wise. Youse shouldn't've paid fifteen thousand, but how could you know. I remember she came in all excited. Marg glances off toward the sky. Her eyes widen, she leans forward atremble with hope and rubbing her palms together. Big money, oh big money.

"Hi, Miss Margaret."

Hi Teresa, hi Donna. "Girls, this is Mr. Larry. He's gonna be a lawyer. You get in trouble with the law someday, he'll be able to get you out. Violence is one thing, but a woman don't have enough money, she steals a pretty pink dress for her little daughter, how can you hate her for that? Aw, I know it's not sure you could get these girls out but I know you'd try. Larry's Italian. My landlady's Italian though and she don't treat me any better. Oh she had me fooled at first, said Margaret I know you're on welfare. Acted like a friend. Fooled me. So just because you're Italian don't mean you're good. Ain't no guarantee."

Once Loretta from across the street spilled a pot of spaghetti down her legs. She was small then, it was in Highlandtown right after she and Darrel got married. She was wearing short shorts, had to go to the hospital and everybody looked at her with spaghetti all stuck to her legs. Healed up nice, but sometimes when it's cold the spaghetti marks show. Loretta's forty pounds heavier now. Darrel's that much or more. He works, and that lady across the street has started a story Loretta's doing things with some man when Darrel's at work.

"Say hello to the mailman, Tippy. I bet you wish all dogs was as nice as Tippy. I didn't think there'd be any mail for me. I don't guess you remember if you left Lucy anything. Tomorrow everybody'll be waiting for you. Say, if you got sick on welfare-check day would they send somebody else? I know it's against the law to put your hand in somebody else's mailbox, Lucy, but a lady I knew over on Bentalou Street, somebody stole her check right out of her mailbox while she was putting a Band-Aid on her grandchild that had cut itself. I gave her a piece of bread out of every loaf I bought that month. I dieted some that month, you wouldn't know to look at me now. Tippy, be still. Lots gave her bread, I wasn't the only one. I know you're hot Tippy, we'll go in a minute."

Here comes the donkey cart with fruit and bells. Tippy knows better than to get close to that old donkey. Leroy's the boy with the cart but it belongs to old Mr. Santoni. He's from Naples, not Sicily. Look at the pretty red panaches over the donkey's ears.

"It's too hot to sit on the stoop, Lucy, come inside."

Lucy's husband drinks, Lucy comes down two or three times a day to sit with Marg. Fifty-one, doesn't look forty, skinny, bright red lipstick, vacancy in her eyes from the life she's had. Lucy's none too strong. If Marg moves maybe they won't be seeing each other so much. "What's the matter with your ear, Tippy? Hold still, oh I see it, it's a tick, there, I should have thrown it out but I dropped it on the floor and I trod on it. Merv Griffin was good yesterday. He had a nice singer, looked like Julius LaRosa."

Lucy's voice sounds like a little kid's and she talks fast, says, "I saw Johnny Carson last night. I couldn't sleep, I don't know why, he was snoring to beat the band. I took the TV in the kitchen. I didn't turn no lights on, just opened the windows. There was some air." Talks like a windup toy, never looks at you.

Since Marg was the baby she stayed home longer than the others, helped her parents and then her mother with the house and grocery. Vince was already started in the police. George and some of the other boys worked in the rail yards and all the girls except Cecilia and Marg were married and raising families already. In '37 they had to sell the grocery. Marg cared for her mother when she fell ill with misdiagnosed cancer. Vince and the other boys arranged for the funeral and said Marg should have what furniture and stuff was left. By then she was too large for most of her mother's clothes so she sold them to people she knew would get some use out of them. Same for the jewelry she had to sell after that. Vince got her a job at a fish stall over in the Hollins Market. The pay wasn't good but she lived on it nine years. Sometimes she'd go to the picture show with one of her girlfriends. That job was hard work but she had a good time. Then the stall owner sold and the new one had children to give the work to. Marg worked nights as a cleaning lady in one of the new buildings downtown. The work was harder and the pay wasn't as good but she did it three years. But by then it was already getting dangerous after dark downtown. One night when she and another cleaning lady were waiting for their bus back to West Baltimore they were robbed by juvenile delinquents. Vince made her quit after that. He tried to find her some other job, in the daytime and closer to home, but they wanted younger people. Marg moved to a cheaper place in Ridgely and sold all the furniture that was any good. There was a bed from Italy. In '67 she got on welfare. By then she'd been living in places near Union Square for some time.

"If I'd've held onto that bed awhile it would've been worth more, I might've got me some teeth. Once, it must be fifteen years ago and it was summer, one morning down on Ostend Street I was going to sit with a lady I knew lived on China Street, her husband was a glazier. I was walking along and a girl comes out of a corner bar, like to run into me, had a baby under her arm, barefoot, had on cutoffs and a halter and around her neck was one of Momma's necklaces I'd sold to a lady that had died. A chain of butterflies. When Momma dressed up and put on that necklace she'd say, from Firenze, from Firenze. Best *oreficere*, Firenze. Her brother'd bought it for her when she was three.

"If the landlady kicks us out though Tippy we won't have to sleep in the gutter with Fred. A lady two blocks down, off Pratt Street, I saw her today at the lunch at the church and she said she was looking for somebody to rent her top floor. We could live there. It's the house next to the one that has that ad for Country Club Soda painted on the side of it, the one with the different kinds of fruit all in pretty colors."

AFTER SUPPER Margaret walks Tippy and Fred comes along too, into Union Square, a park the size of a block. Tippy heels naturally, Fred runs around more. It's still light out.

Back when Marg was a girl some evenings Poppa and Momma'd bring the kids walking up here through this park. Had real gas street lamps. Poppa said the kids should see how rich folks lived. Then after a while the people with money moved away, kept the houses or sold them, poor people moved in to rent. Now real-estate people have started to buy up houses. They pay more than anybody here could, then sell for twice that to strangers, people like Larry and his wife. They're not bad people but when they move in, those that lived there before have to go. Like that poor Puerto Rican family up the street, four kids and a baby on the way, all on the ground floor, been there going on three years. They fixed the place up, taped pictures on the walls, she made flowers out of colored tissue paper.

Lucy's home frying up a chop. Her husband's at the table. "I'm glad we have our house," she says. "Hope we can keep it a while, maybe we can. Marg's supposed to be out of her place at the end of the month. I don't know if I could live like that. It's not exactly her fault though. But still."

Larry's wife has washed her hair at their kitchen sink. Afternoon light comes in over the rooftops. Larry's at the table reading a law-book article about a poor lady that sued a canning company. Their friend's at the supermarket buying dinner. It's a pink sky with a trail from a jet, still hot. Some people start to get off work and then some are waking up and getting ready for night jobs. Larry's wife's drying her pretty brown hair in a towel, leaning against the water heater. Larry turns over his book and starts talking. His wife smiles.

In Union Square Marg's aquiline glance rakes the park and catches Fred finding a place to do his business. Seems like they're keeping up the grass better than they used to. Done with absorbing heat for the day, concrete and brick now need only sigh it back through another short hot night. "Tippy, see that house with the boy leaning out of the second-floor window? I used to live there, I loved looking out at the park. What was the lady's name that lived under me there? It wasn't Inez.

"Hi, Mrs. Anderson. She remembers me from when I used to live next-door to her there, always waves. She and Mr. Anderson own their house since 1927 but they didn't get it all paid for till the Second World War. He keep the rooms on the second and third floors locked, she ain't been in some of them in twenty years. She's too old to do anything but put up with it now. Face like a prune. I used to feel sorry for her. He'd take a chair out on their back porch, put a sheet around him and sit there and smoke a cigar and yell at her while she cut his hair. Had to cut the hairs out of his nose too. I don't see how she did it with that cigar smoke blowing in her face. Her eyes was already bad too, looked milky.

"Hey, Fred, I bet you're glad this ain't New York City—they'd put you in jail for doing that.

"If we do move to that upstairs apartment though Tippy we'll still come back up here sometimes for old times' sake." The new people are changing the houses around the square, sandblasting peeling paint off the brick, washing fanlights, restoring. They strip pilasters and architraves, the cornices with their block modillions, and paint them new colors other than black, new olives and bisques. "I'll have to see that upstairs place before I decide, though. There ain't a real backyard, it's all concrete, but there's two big clotheslines. It's on a alley but it's all white people. The rooms would be smaller but then they wouldn't get so cold in the winter. I'd be saving twenty dollars a month, that's five dollars a week. That's better than half a dollar a day, Tippy. I think I'll do it, I don't need to stay where I'm not wanted. Larry'll help me move, and Mike that lives with him and his wife. Punky'll help. Lucy'll help me get things ready to move and help me put things around in the new place. Hey, Fred, will you come down there to visit me and Tippy?

"I can still climb stairs. Good exercise." Slowly, her bulk filling the well, negotiating the turn.

The longest stair Marg ever climbed was to the top of the shot tower over east of downtown when she was ten. It was a Sunday afternoon, summer like now but not such a heat. Momma and Poppa took Margaret. The tower's like a big smokestack with a stairway inside. It had been built for some war, not the Great War but an earlier one. From the top you looked down inside and saw how they let molten lead drip and fall all that way down and into tubs of water to make ammo.

You could also look out over Baltimore, see the harbor and the boats at the docks, the different churches, the train yards, the parks including Union Square surely. Of course it mustn't have been as big as now, but it was so much bigger than Margaret had expected, she felt as if Sicily, Ireland and Lithuania must be out there beyond Fort McHenry. Poppa pointed toward Nanticoke Street, said see, Margaret, there's our house. She'd nodded but she really hadn't seen it, it was too small, there were too many houses, she tried but she couldn't. Poppa'd said wave, Margaret, wave to our house, maybe Vincente's looking out the window. She couldn't find the house so she'd waved to all the houses.

Most of the Union Square trees are ginkgoes. Once many varieties grew across North America and elsewhere, but the last ice age rendered them extinct, all but the one variety that survived in China by human intercession, venerated and tended in temple grounds through the centuries. These here are descendants of those Chinese ones. They are tall and seem to strain upward in the hot dusk.

That old man on the bench lives next to the Andersons. His story's a long one, but then everybody's is. Marg waves to him as she moves through the parkpast the dry fountain, talks a minute with somebody on the corner. All these people have their different stories. The rowhouses have stories and stories reaching back to before Marg was born and farther, and Marg knows many of those. What was the nice lady's name though? It wasn't Ramona, it wasn't Thelma. Around Union Square the houses stand in twos and threes like forty Andrews Sisters singing cheek to cheek for Margaret and Tippy and Fred under the tall ginkgoes in the last night.

History

WHEN I THINK of our brief marriage twenty-six years ago, before freedom rides and busing, it is like recalling pages out of a history book. In photographs Marcus, with his scalp-short hair, the part properly shaved, his shoes shined to a mirrory sheen, looks like a member of the Southern Christian Leadership Conference. I, with my open, white-girl smile, long bundle of blond hair, and dirty toes in California sandals, am a caricature hippie.

In 1960 all the newspapers in the nation's capital listed housing under White or Colored. Wherever I call, the landlords' first question always was: White? Both, I'd answer. We are both. Immediately, on the other end, there would be a sudden intake of breath as if I were a crank call or obscene or had let loose a big, bad snake into the wire which was inching forward, making its way up the wire to bite off an ear, pinch a nerve. They would let down the phone that carefully.

"My husband is white," Mrs. Trakled had explained over the phone, and she brought it up again when she was showing us the upstairs apartment she had available. She and the Reverend lived downstairs. It was an immaculate rowhouse in a nice Negro neighborhood with clipped lawns, rosebushes, and green and white awnings unfurled over freshly painted porches.

"The thing is," Mrs. Trakled said, "is that I am picky about my tenants." She looked at Marcus approvingly. "I understand you are studying to be a doctor at Howard University. My, my, a medical man." Marcus had worn a three-piece suit for our interview, carried an umbrella and looked quite the Englishman—from the colonies.

Mrs. Trakled was in purple. It was a plum dress for the Grand Tour, with pleated handkerchiefs springing clusters of violets pinned to her shoulders. She looked like Mercury on errand, wings at ready-alert. "And you, my dear," she said turning her motherly gaze on me, "working for the *Post*? I'm a professional woman, too."

Mrs. Trakled's sign hung in the front yard:

The Reverend Mrs. Trakled
Lessons in the Piano for Young Ladies

"Actually," she continued, "my husband is white-white. A man of the cloth."

I imagined ghost. Marcus gave me a look like Ku Klux Klan, but rabbit was more like it. The Reverend, who mysteriously materialized when we signed the lease across the grand piano, was albino and just about as old as Methuselah, with blinking, pink eyes and an embarrassed, bashful smile.

"The Reverend, once one of God's chosen orators, is now a man of few words," Mrs. Trakled explained. "We are from Mississippi, you see, and, would you believe it, we couldn't get married down there, had to ride separate cars up to D.C. and here we are."

"It sounds like the Underground Railway," I said.

"What say?" The Reverend shuffled forth, leaning in toward me.

"They are newlyweds, Rev.," Mrs. Trakled giggled.

"UNDERGROUND RAILWAY, really Joanna." We were packing like mad to make the move to the Trakleds'. I could hardly wait.

"Can I help it that I was a history major?"

"Yes indeedy."

"Can you hug me, Marcus, in Virginia, where you come from?"

"Are you crazy?"

I was. It gave me leeway. But Marcus was Mr. Rational. In Control. It took me five minutes to stuff my meager belongings in my straw suitcase. We were staying at his ex-roommate's. Marcus folded all of his stuff neatly, arranging it in piles before putting it in his trunk. I noticed the letter from his mother. Back in Virginia, half a step out of Washington, she did not approve of me. Her letter had left enough space between the lines for me to evoke the whole scene, one Marcus had once described—the rickety front porch of the P.O. boasting a bevy of overalled, tobacco-chewing Guardians of Justice. On the side of her house hung an iron washtub, and under the one tree in the yard was an old carseat with a spring sticking out like a corkscrew. Marcus said his mother made him wear a clothespin on his nose every Saturday and that he was scrubbed Saturday night hard enough to bleed (read bleach). Yet she didn't like me, I, who was a natural.

My mother, at home in California amid her cats and dusty pottery, dashed off a quick note (more later) stating that she knew I would always marry somebody interesting. What she had in mind, I knew, was somebody larger than life—a Paul Robeson—John Henry type, a Byron or a Browning. Somebody dark and dangerous, and definitely *très beau*.

Marcus and I had met at Howard University, E. Franklin Frazier's course, "Negro in the United States." It was a history course and I felt pretty historic myself, for I was the only white person in the class and, from what I could see, on campus, save one exchange student from Oberlin who assiduously avoided me.

"How do you like Howard?" Marcus and I were upstairs in the library, late spring, fans already set up on the long, lacquered tables. Outside the open windows, the air was still and dense even though it was eight o'clock at night.

"Fine," I answered, moving my long hair out of my eyes, giving the man a good look. He wore wire-frame glasses. Nobody did then, and he had an old-fashioned, professional look about him.

"Be honest." His wrists were thinner than mine and his fingers were long. You could play the harp in heaven, I thought.

"I'm always honest," I lied. Downstairs in the lobby there was a portrait of General Howard, blue eyes, no left arm. The old Union general had gone from freeing slaves to killing Indians. The first students at Howard were not freemen, but Chinese. It was a place full of contradictions. Yet, familiar.

"It's like a white school," I said. Every afternoon, light-skinned sorority girls linked arms and sang on the quad. It was like *my* college.

"So we're disappointed, are we?" He had a condescending, slightly humorous way of looking at me over the top of his glasses. He made me feel amusing.

"Surprised," I said.

"We," and he gently put one of his long, brown fingers on my wrist as if feeling for the pulse, "are human just like everybody else. Not morally superior, particularly wise. Just people. Suffering is not a good teacher, all publicity to the contrary."

I should have listened to those words, for they would have provided a key to the language of our marriage. Instead, at that time, I didn't see how prim he was and only noted how different he was from my counterparts at the bookstore where I worked, those pale and pasty male versions of myself. Marcus was older, a hundred times more interesting and, of course, mysterious as Egypt. My heart did a fast flutter-butter, and I knew I was done for. Once before I had been in love, during college, and that had been pure disaster. He was Oriental.

"I'm going to New York next week." Strains of the A.K.A. song wafted up. A sorority sister was passing by. The fans moved left and right on their stiff necks like sunflowers following the sun. I knew it was presumptuous to tell him I was going away, that is, as if he were interested, but I took the risk.

"I'll visit you," he answered. "I mean it." And we exchanged names and addresses. His handwriting was small, elegant, a stylized code.

"Joanna Kandel," he read. "And where is this in New York?"

"The Village."

"Ah, of course."

"No, really, it's just a cheap sublet, I can't let the opportunity . . . "

"Of course not."

"Are you laughing at me again?"

"Good gracious no." He raised his hands in surrender. "Why would I do that?"

THE JOB I FOUND in New York was worse than the one I left in Washington. Not a bookstore, which is all a B.A. in History from Mills College netted me in Washington, but at a Discount China store. I would say discounted discount china and narrow as a ship's galley with place settings, each one an extraordinary bargain, rising to the ceiling like the Leaning Tower of Pisa. A stroll to the back of the store provided seasickness, and the bathroom was always at high tide.

"*Qué pasa?*" Some cute Puerto Rican guys worked as packers in the storeroom. I had to go by them all on the way to the bathroom.

"Degeneration of values in the western world, *hombres,*" I'd answer, picking out a handy strip of Japanese newspaper from the packing crate. I read: "'Likewise the eastern world.' Nobody committing harikari anymore, what *is* this world coming to, yen for life reported on all fronts."

They'd stare at my hairy legs and armpits as if they had never seen such before and give me the old thumbs-up. Yes, we understood each other. Ditto the other salesperson, with whom I had a deep rapport. She was an Argentinian, refugee from the Peronistas, and had hopes of meeting a dentist in America, moving to Queens. I told her a little about Marcus. Not all, of course.

Friday nights and the city still baking a good 92°, I would do the rounds of the air-conditioned bars, few and far between in 1960. I especially liked the ones with aquariums, green bubbling, sea divers, startled sea horses. But no sooner would I get comfy on my stool than some lech would hunker up from the shadows, rest his chin on my shoulder. Oh yes, lust was the sawdust under our feet in those good old days. And I knew for sure somebody had to save me, for here I was in New York, New York, and I wasn't even having fun, couldn't even go for a decent drink. Sunday afternoons I spent in Washington Square Park watching city kids in scuba masks and flippers explore the briny depths of the three-foot fountain while I ate my Good Humor bar. Sometimes I went swimming at the Carmine Street swimming pool, where all the sleek lovelies stretched out on the rough concrete like numbers on some celestial clock.

One Friday night I was sitting on my chipped kitchen chair in my living-dining-kitchen wondering what to eat next when I heard a knock at my door. Only one person in the whole world knew where I lived.

That weekend we only went out for food and air. That was the time he told me about the P.O., Saturday baths, and the statue of the Confederate colonel in the town square. I told him that as kids my sister and I jumped on our bed until it broke and then we slept in a heap at a slant until one of my mother's boyfriends tied it up again with twine.

"Those chaotic days are over," he said. I wasn't sure what he meant, what new regime was in store for me, and I had never thought of my childhood as particularly chaotic, just fun. But I did think better of telling him about the time my mother, my sister and I drove through Mexico, the time we picked up a hitchhiker who dropped dead in the back seat of our car. When we drove back to the little seaside town near Ensenada where we had picked him up nobody knew him, wanted to claim him, so we buried him ourselves on a promontory overlooking the beach. We made a cross, since we figured everybody in Mexico was a Catholic, and my sister said a few words just as she had when Stravinsky, our pet beagle, died.

Coming home from work on Monday after our weekend, knowing that Marcus was waiting for me in the apartment, and watching the other working people in the subway with their bags of groceries, tired feet, I felt that at long last I had joined the human race, the real people. I was also going home, had my own bag of groceries and a bouquet of daisies for Marcus, who after all was from the country. Climbing the stairs to the apartment, I expected the door to be open but, from down the hallway, could see that not only was it closed but that somebody had pasted something to the door. At a distance, it looked like the Declaration of Independence, with lots of fancy signatures on it. Up close, I could see that it was a petition and eviction notice. All the mothers of the building, not the Ritz by any stretch of the imagination, alleged that I was a prostitute. Quietly, I unglued the document, stuffed it in my purse, and went inside. Marcus was packing, not because of the sign, which apparently he hadn't seen, but because he had to go back to Virginia, return to his job as a janitor.

At the train station, Marcus said, "I've been accepted at Howard Medical School." People were looking at us standing together, and this was New York.

"I love you, Marcus." I thought I should set the record straight. It was true. I had all the symptoms. Dry throat, clammy hands, etc.

"Do you think we should get married?" he said.

"I don't know." But I wasn't shocked at the idea. Love in my book did not necessarily mean marriage, but I was vaguely aware, even then, that Marcus's book was different. And I also knew, given the world, we had to be serious, all or nothing.

"I have GI benefits," he said. "Also, I've saved. It's been proven that married men do better in medical school than single ones."

"I would work, too."

"Until I finish," he added.

Marriage *was* a thought. After a rather haphazard upbringing, I had gone to a girl's college where everybody on my floor was engaged by senior year. Alumnae notes were full of tidbits about illustrious husbands and accomplished children. Marriage with Marcus would not be tame and ordinary. It might very well be the grandest adventure of all. I could see myself plucking burning crosses from our front yard with my bare hands. Insults from ignoramuses would bounce off my strong chest. I would be a moral Paul Bunyan, showing them all, showing myself. It would certainly be better than living alone in New York, or whatever else I could think of at the moment.

A BAPTIST PREACHER married us in Washington. Miscegenation was illegal in Virginia, and we didn't have the money for California. Marcus's former roommate stood up for us, looking zonked out of his mind. I laughed through the ceremony—cosmic joy, I told Marcus, who was miffed. I wore a paisley dress my mother had done up in a hurry, sent off. It was from an Indian bedspread, a pattern on the bottom of orange elephants trekking East. On my long yellow hair, I wore a wreath of laurels. Marcus was in his three-piecer, the one he wore for interviews and on Sundays for church.

Our bedroom overlooked a wonderful tree, and toward November the yellow leaves plastered themselves to the window like large, yellow hands, splayed fingers. They made me think of children's drawings of fall you see in school windows, and yes, I wanted children, a whole slew of them. They would be beautiful, brown Gauguins and I would be the Pied Piper leading them along the beach. Not Virginia Beach, natch. But some beach, somewhere. Marcus wanted two children, a boy and a girl, after he had finished medical school, his internship and residency.

November and the afternoons turned very dark. I'd come home

from my job at the *Post* to find a hallway of little girls waiting for their piano lessons in Mary Janes and braids so tight their eyes would slant up. On Saturdays, when Marcus was studying in the library, I swept the leaves off the front porch, helped the Trakleds put in storm windows, learned how to make sweet potato pie and Mississippi mud cake. I took the Reverend's damp tobacco wads, lined up on the porch banister, inside. They looked like frozen bonbons. When Marcus came home he'd shower for hours it seemed, eat quickly, and then fall into bed, rucking up into a tight ball like small armored bugs who curl closed at a touch. My job in the newspaper morgue, where I clipped and filed stories all day, was more tedious than the china shop. At least there I had the Puerto Ricans, the homesick Argentinean. In the morgue, we were all disgruntled history majors, English majors. It was the bookstore all over again.

Around Christmas, Marcus and I were invited to a party. Finally, I was going to meet his study group, talk to some folks. Remembering my mother's parties featuring wine, good talk, I dressed in comfortable slacks, a bulky sweater and my long scarf of many colors. I was prepared to spend the evening on the floor arguing about Marxism, music, Richard Nixon. Marcus wore his suit, as always. Marcus was Marcus. Cuddling up to him on the streetcar going down Georgia Avenue, I thought of when we would be coming home that night. We'd be a little tipsy. It would be like New York again, that weekend, our courtship. But he inched over ever so slightly.

"Anymore and you'll be out the window," I said.

"Joanna."

"I know." He hated public displays of affection, considered them in bad taste. I moved back to my side. The trolley jiggled and jangled, careened around corners. (The tracks are all dug up now. And the trolleys are in museums.) I looked ahead. Washington at night was empty. You could not tell what part of the city was segregated except in terms of buildings. There were good buildings and bad buildings, those with doormen, those without.

"I'm thinking of taking some courses again," I said. "At night, when you're not home."

He didn't catch the hint.

"More history?"

"I won't make that mistake again. Maybe psychology." I knew what he thought of psychology. Not much.

"I'm going to have a lot of papers next semester," he said.

"Meaning?"

"I was hoping you could help type them."

"Ah." But we had arrived. We got off the trolley, crossed the street, entered a dingy, unkept building.

When the apartment door was opened, though, I could see that I was way out of my depth. All the furniture was creamy white, soft and modern. Huge baskets of ferns hung from the ceiling. The lighting was subdued, the music jazz—cool, subtle jazz. The drinks were not jug wine, paper cups, that sort of thing, but a full bar, J&B, a real bartender in uniform, obviously hired for the occasion. People were drinking martinis. The hors d'oeuvres, while not plentiful, were hot, complicated, on silver trays. But the very worst part was that everybody except me was dressed to the teeth in clothes with style and cut, the kind of thing you see in fashion magazines. Marcus should have warned me. I wished I could have just fainted right there on the spot so that I could be removed, on a stretcher, with a blanket thrown over my body. My only claim to class at the moment was my hair, which was the color of gold, and Marcus, but when I turned he was not there. He had vanished into the crowd.

"Scotch on the rocks," I requested of the bartender.

"Hello there," a voice said behind me. I turned around. The woman was in a sarong-like dress, pleated at the hips. The drape was perfect and the color was shades of green.

"My name is Casey," she said.

"Joanna." Her hair was in a Billy Holiday upsweep, but, instead of a gardenia, she wore a spray of mistletoe over her ear.

"I'm Marcus's wife." She would know Marcus, surely.

"I know." Her complexion and smile were reminiscent of Lena Horne. I couldn't believe this glamorous lady deemed me worthy of a conversation.

"What I've been wondering," and she arched her penciled eyebrows, "is don't they have men where you come from?"

I looked about in a panic searching for rescue, comfort, something, realized I was very much on my own.

"Excuse me, Casey." I was trying hard to hold the tears, keep some semblance of dignity. "I feel sick," I said.

"Then I ducked into the bathroom." I told Mrs. Trakled the next day over tea, candied violets. "I wanted to stay in there forever."

"Oh," Mrs. Trakled huffed. "Those high-brown Louisiana girls think they are something. Just jealous is all. Just jealous."

Mrs. Trakled's relatives looked down on us from their oval frames. They lined the dining room wall, daguerreotypes, in high-collared dresses, watch chains, struck poses. There was nothing of the Reverend, no trace to the past. Sometimes I thought of him spawned spontaneously in some backwoods swamps, a Mississippi grub, pale and translucent, turning in a single lifetime from worm to man, cell to angel. Actually, Mrs. Trakled told me, he had been a preacher doing revivals when she met him. She was called in when the white pianist failed to appear.

"Do you think I should tell Marcus?" I hadn't. Not a word.

"Good heavens, no. Don't tell him a thing."

That night Marcus and I were seated across from each other, a late dinner, eight o'clock. I had the oven on and open for added warmth. The wind was whistling outside, and our bedroom windows were freezing up on the inside.

"Sometimes I wish I was in California, Marcus. Both of us."

"You act like it's my fault you're not." He folded his napkin.

"No I don't."

"Yes you do."

"Like hell I do." It slipped out.

"I hate vulgarity in a woman." I knew he did.

"I hate cruelty in a man," I replied.

"Oh, you people." He sighed, stood up.

"What people are you referring to, Marcus? California people? Other people? White people? For your information, I am *your* people."

"Joanna, what are you talking about?" He sat down again.

"Attitude. Yours."

"You are the one with an attitude."

"I am the one with a sense of family, the only one. Marcus, we are kin. You can't say, 'Oh, you people' to me. It makes you sound like that woman at the party."

"What woman?" He got up, leaned against the sink.

"The one who asked me if there weren't any men where I came from."

"Who said that?"

"Casey."

"She didn't mean anything."

"She meant plenty. Don't defend her. It was a mean thing to say."

"It didn't kill you, did it?"

"That's even meaner. Whose side are you on?"

He sat down, looked absolutely disgusted with me.

"I take you to a party," he said wearily. "I thought you would like it."

"I hated it."

"Great, that's just great."

I picked up his dish, took it to the sink.

"You know, Joanna, those are my friends, the people who help me, the people who would help you. If anything happened . . . "

"Marcus," I turned around from the sink. "Those people would not help me off the sidewalk if I was dying and you know it."

"So what about your friends? Tell me, what they would do for me?"

"My friends don't live in Washington," I said meekly.

"Where *do* they live, Joanna? Anywhere on earth?"

I couldn't tell him what people at work said when I showed them pictures of my husband. I hadn't even told him about my experiences in looking for an apartment. He didn't know what had happened to my world, that it was more than divided, that it had simply fallen away.

"I didn't see your mother sending us any wedding presents," he continued, "or your sister."

"My mother made my wedding dress."

"That Halloween costume?"

I had to sit down at that. "At least my mother congratulated me," I offered. "Congratulated *us,* which is more much more than your mother did. Remember your mother's letter, Marcus? And I quote: Are you doing the right thing, Marcus? Unquote. She thought I was pregnant or something."

"You could have been. Easily."

"I'll let that go. The point is that you side with the woman at the party."

"There is a serious shortage of Negro men, so that when a white woman . . . "

"Has one of their own . . . "

"Do you know what people think of you, of me, Joanna?"

"Do *you* know? Anyway, I don't care what people think."

"I do."

"You care too much, that's your problem."

"We have to live in society."

"We are society, Marcus." I felt strong enough to get up again, start the dishes. Usually I let them soak, but Marcus recently had explained to me how unsanitary that was.

"The world out there, Marcus, is full of hypocrites and chickenshits."

"It doesn't solve anything to say that."

"It puts it in perspective, Marcus, lets us know what is important, that we are more important." I looked over at him, remembering how I had felt that first time in New York when I opened my door to him. It was instant recognition, as if my door was really a mirror I was looking into. I had felt that close. Now, looking at Marcus, I felt a chill go through me, and it was like being confronted with a blank wall.

"When I become a doctor, Joanna . . . "

"The world will stop."

"You can make fun of it if you want. But do you know what one of my professors told me? He said that when he was doing his internship in a big-city hospital, a northern city hospital, a woman came into the emergency room bleeding to death, but she would not let him stick a needle for a transfusion into her. She would rather bleed to death."

"Did she?"

"No, of course not. He got a nurse to do it."

I sat back down in the chair, put my head in my hands. I knew what was coming. "Tell me about Charles Drew, Marcus, isn't he the one, the one who discovered blood types and then bled to death on some southern road because the nearest hospital was white? Tell me all the stories, tell me all about it."

"You act like those things don't matter."

"I know they do, but *I* am not your enemy. And you can't play it both ways." The wind rattled the windows. "You seem to *be* like the woman at the party, like your mother, people who are outside but want to be inside, yet you hate the inside."

"And you?"

"I am an outsider, too, can't you see that?"

"No. If so, by choice."

"It's not just color, race." I felt outside of everything at that moment. But from my distance I could see that to Marcus I was an insider and that maybe it had been part of my attraction, and that I had taken him for an outsider, but that really in his heart he wasn't. "I'm on the fringe of things, Marcus, of all things, of your things, too; you should be proud of me. I need some company, can't you tell?"

The bare limbs of the tree were scratching against the window like skeleton hands trying to gain entrance. I looked down at Marcus's elegant hand, the one that would cut and snip, sew back up. Formaldehyde from anatomy lab had pinched up the little pads at the end of the fingertips. His knuckles were wrinkled. With a surge of affection, I reached for it. But Marcus drew his hand back.

"For God's sake, Marcus, I don't want to cut it off."

Yet I felt like it suddenly. I could have. Instead, I ran into the bathroom and with two big swipes, using the scissors brought all the way from California, I cut off two feet of my hair, which had taken me since junior high to grow. Then I marched back into the kitchen.

"See," I shouted, putting a fistful of hair before him. "A hair sandwich, how do you like them apples? See what you made me do? Happy now?"

"Joanna." He shook his head as if I was beyond all hope.

"I present you my hair." I tried to make it sound victorious, but my voice began to wobble and my whole body was shaking. Lying there on the table, my hair looked like a prone animal, like a complete supplicant, a totally defeated, dead beast.

"You are so crazy, Joanna. You make everything so damned hard."

"You make it impossible." I was feeling light-headed as if, like

Samson, my strength resided in my hair. My neck felt cold, naked; my face was exposed. I was out there, stripped. Like a collaborator.

"You don't care," I wailed. "You don't even care."

"Shh," he said putting a finger to his lips, but not rising from his chair to hug and soothe me. "You'll wake the Trakleds."

I wailed all the louder. A line of roaches streaked out from the crack by the side of the table, took note, waved their antennae.

"Shut up, Joanna."

Then I really let loose, and in a few seconds there was a light tapping at the door.

"Joanna, honey, it is I, Matilda Trakled, are you all right?"

I went to the door, opened it a little.

"Mrs. Trakled."

"Oh child, you've gone and cut your beautiful hair, your crowning glory."

"No, it's all right," I said, sniffing. "Your hair is short, Mrs. Trakled."

"That's different. I'm an old woman."

"No you're not." I noticed that her bathrobe, like all her clothes, was a variation on violet.

"Do you want to come down and watch wrestling on TV? Gorgeous George is on."

Gorgeous George was our mutual favorite. Nights when Marcus was not home and the Reverend retired early, Mrs. Trakled and I stayed up for wrestling and mint juleps.

"Maybe some other time." I closed the door gently.

"Toodle-oo," she called, descending the stairs.

"You woke them up," Marcus accused.

"They were up." I looked at the African violet on top of the fridge. It was a gift from Mrs. Trakled, part of her collection, which she kept on a white teacart. Music was her vocation, she explained to me, and horticulture her avocation.

"You've wakened them," Marcus persisted. "Two innocent people."

"They are not that innocent, Marcus." In fact, Mrs. Trakled told me that the Reverend liked to put a pillow under her hips, hike her up. And during the train trip north, he bribed the porter and he and Mrs. Trakled, then Miss Gibson, got together on one of the top bunks in the Pullman. It was a metaphysical experience, I said to myself, their double-decker coupling, a preacher and his accompanist.

"You know, Joanna, I sometimes wonder," Marcus said.

"Me too. I wonder too, Marcus. Tell me." He had never said it, not once, not on our wedding night, never. "Tell me, honestly, do you love me?"

There was a moment of silence between us, a long moment, too long. I could hear the tree scraping and skittling along the baseboards, the roaches, lots of them, or mice. Another moment passed. I thought I could hear the plant on top of the fridge growing or at least straining toward us, its petals attuned to nuance, all hairs standing straight up. Then Marcus cleared his throat.

"Well?" I was waiting. That was it.

"I married you, didn't I?" he said.

He looked up at me, for I was still standing, and I read such fear in his eyes that I wanted to comfort him, tell him it was all right. Because I knew then that there was no point, that it was all over.

FROM   2001

The Book of Lost Fathers

Hard Times

WHEN I WAS TWELVE the war was still in its first year and Jimmy Barraclough, who had been our paperboy for as long as I could remember, enlisted in the navy and went off to fight.

"How could that happen?" my mother said to my father. "He can't be more than sixteen if he's a day."

My father shrugged. He was hidden behind the *Evening Express,* probably reading yesterday's Red Sox totals for the third time—he also read them in the Boston Post and the Portland *Press Herald,* both morning papers, as if he thought his re-readings could multiply the Sox's success when they won, undo their failure when they lost—and the shrug was not seen but telegraphed in the movement of the newsprint.

"Only a child," my mother said. She looked at me, sadly, and reached out to brush my hair away from my eyes.

"He looks old enough," my father said. "That's all a recruiter cares about."

My father had been in the First World War; he enlisted in the army out of college and was sent to officer candidate school at Plattsburg. His view of Jimmy's enlistment was doubly brusque, first because he had some experience of wartime, and second because he thought my mother was too sentimental to exercise good judgment in such a matter.

"I think it's a shame," my mother said.

My father lowered the newspaper to look at her. I never got used to that look; it combined aggravation and pity and scorn, and though I had seen it many times before, it always shocked me. When I was very young it had frightened me because it seemed to say that there was no more affection between them, and I wondered what might become of me, left alone in a hard world by loveless parents. Now that I was older, the fear had only turned to confusion. My mother seemed to displease my father, but he did not become angry or abusive; he simply looked at her, so.

"Well, it is a shame," she repeated. "What if he's killed?"

"He won't be killed." My father disappeared behind the *Express*.

"I hope not." She kissed me gently on the brow. "Think of his poor mother then."

EVEN THOUGH Jimmy Barraclough had no mother—she had "run off" with a man she worked with in the payroll department of the Scoggin textile mill, Jimmy told me—I shared my own mother's hope that he would survive the war. I felt I owed him a lot, for though he was nearly four years older he was a sixth grade classmate of mine, and I was one of the few younger boys whose presence he tolerated. Jimmy was waiting to be sixteen so that he could legally drop out of school, and I think my size—I was tall for my age—had something to do with his tolerance. Everyone else made him seem out of place, a giant among pygmies, and he must have felt singled out and oafish in that Edison School classroom presided over by Mrs. Florence Hardy.

In matters of true wisdom, matters unrelated to arithmetic and Palmer Method penmanship, Jimmy far outdistanced me. He had taught me to swear; he had introduced me to the vocabulary of human anatomy, particularly the female; he had taught me snappy comebacks—if somebody said, "Got a match?" you might say, "Yeah, my feet and your breath"—what my father would have called "smart remarks," worth a cuff across the face if he ever heard them.

Once Jimmy had actually shared a cigarette with me—a Lucky Strike—and, though I could not then appreciate the pleasure of inhaling, the dark green Luckies pack with its red-disc bull's-eye symbolized for me the world adults lived in and enjoyed. For all her compassion, my mother would have been horrified to know how much, and for what, I admired Jimmy Barraclough.

At the end of April, when Jimmy lied about his age and went away to the navy, I took over his paper route. The inheritance was unexpected. True, I had helped him—or he had let me follow him on the route—many times, especially on Fridays and Saturdays, collection days, and I think it was not only that my arithmetic skills were useful to him, but that I could be more patient with his slower-paying customers. All but one—a Mrs. Ouellette, who lived on the first floor of a yellow tenement house on Riverside Avenue—he seemed relieved for me to attend to.

There was no Mr. Ouellette. Mrs. Ouellette was a divorced woman, small and plain, whose apartment smelled of something spoiled. She had at least two small children—we saw them or heard them whenever we knocked at her door; they were forever bawling—and she wore a pink housecoat and pink bedroom slippers coming apart at the seams. Rarely did she have the money to pay Jimmy and me. Sometimes she would fetch her purse and make a show of looking through it for the thirty cents she needed, but more often than not she would simply look helpless and ask us to come back another day.

"Come back Sunday," she would say. "I'll have it for you then."

She must have known that Sunday was the most awkward day for Jimmy or me to call—though for a long time, call we did. Eventually, Jimmy seemed to write her off. "Never mind old Ouellette," he'd say. "I'll collect on my way home from the Y." The YMCA was on the third floor of the Masonic Building, but the basement was occupied by Scoggin Square Billiards and Bowling, and that's what Jimmy meant when he referred to the Y. It had five pocket-pool tables, one three-cushion billiards table, four candlepin alleys, and it was the high school hangout, the place where "the bad boys," as my mother referred to them, played Baby Eight—a nickel on the three and five, a dime on the eight. Sentimental like my mother, I used to worry that he might be distracted enough to stop delivering to her, but he kept her on his books, and then I imagined that some of my own patience had rubbed off on him.

I ALREADY HAD a sort of job, stopping by the Western Union office in the Hotel Belmont after school, delivering whatever telegrams had come in that day, but I was paid only a dime for each telegram and I could never count on a tip unless I brought especially good news to somebody. Taking over Jimmy's paper route gave me new status at home, and the extra money was a large part of that status. My father was a schoolteacher—he had gone to Amherst and gotten his master's in history at Harvard, and for a year when he and my mother were first married he had taught at a famous prep school in New Hampshire—but now he was practically unemployed. He did substitute teaching in the local high school, but mostly he kept the books for Tony Apollonio, a Greek who owned two novelty stores— we called them "fruit stores"—and operated a small trucking business between Boston and Portland. He was no trained accountant, my father, but he had a head for figures, a neat hand, and a polite but abiding interest in dollars and cents. I supposed he was good at his job for Apollonio. When I was younger, if I visited him on a Wednesday or Friday, days when he worked on the books, it seemed to me he was happy—that he was more accessible to me, more relaxed with me, than at home.

My mother was a telephone operator all through the 1930s and 40s. She never worked full time, except in the summer when the regular operators took their vacations, but she worked frequently and probably earned as much as my father did. I was terribly proud of her. Sometimes when she was working the day shift I would stop at the telephone office just before five o'clock and walk home with her. She let me sit in a high, caned chair beside her, watching her work until her relief arrived, and I would admire her competence—how she responded to the rows of pink and white lights on the board in front of her, drawing from their storage holes the snakey cords with brass plugs and punching them into the holes under the lights. She asked for numbers in an exaggerated, telephone-operator voice—"Number puh-leze"—and when she was making a toll call she recited numbers to other operators in Portland or Boston or New York in such a way as to deny any mis-hearing: "I'm calling thuh-REE, NI-yun, NI-yun, Jay-as-in-James." If I ever had to call home from school, I would mimic my mother, telling the operator "one, FI-yuv, thuh-REE, M-as-in-Mary," and feeling a kinship that is impossible in modern times. "Is that you, Stevie?" one of them would say. "Your mother has to work till six today, so she wants you to go straight home."

WITH JIMMY BARRACLOUGH'S paper route, of course I inherited Mrs. Ouellette, and I was determined from the start that I would not permit the kind of postponement of payment Jimmy had been willing to tolerate. After all, I told myself to justify my determination, Mr. Bradbury, the town's newspaper distributor, gave no extensions to me. I would be exactly as hard with Mrs. Ouellette as Mr. Bradbury was hard with me.

For a few weeks I heeded my own advice and was as persistent as I knew how to be in collecting Mrs. Ouellette's weekly thirty cents. If she didn't have the money on Friday, the usual collection day, I stopped again on Saturday, and if on Saturday she put me off, I was on her porch, knocking on her screen door, on the following Monday. I think my doggedness shamed her; she always blushed and made clumsy apologies when she finally brought out her purse and gave me money. "I'm awfully sorry," she would say. "I don't want you to think I'm a piker." I would duck my head and mumble that I didn't think anything bad about her. "Sometimes my check is late," she'd say. "Sometimes I don't get to the bank to deposit it before Friday comes." I didn't know what might be the source of her checks, or if indeed there were checks, but I began to imagine Mrs. Ouellette might be a widow, not a divorcée.

This possibility softened my attitude toward her later on—widowhood being acceptably tragic, free of the taint divorce carried in that small New England town—and after a couple of months I returned to Jimmy Barraclough's pattern. If Mrs. Ouellette had no money one Friday, I let the matter go and hoped she would pay me the next. Sometimes she did. More often when she came to the door she looked at me sheepishly—the blue of her eyes was pale, like ice, or like the coarse crepe ribbon my mother bought to decorate our parlor when the telephone operators had a baby shower—and put me off again. "I don't know what's wrong with the mail," she would say. "My check's late again."

Through all of my visits the two little Ouellette kids were in the kitchen, crawling on the linoleum floor or tugging at Mrs. Ouellette's ratty-looking housecoat; their faces were always dirty, and even if they weren't bawling there would still be a greenish smear of snot shining under their noses. The kitchen was too warm and smelled of kerosene from a heater in the corner; something was always cooking on top of the gas stove—soup, I thought, or some kind of fishy-smelling chowder. Mrs. Ouellette herself looked tired and sad to me. She was never really dressed; if she wasn't in the housecoat, she was in an old blue men's bathrobe that was out at the elbows, and her hair looked as if it hadn't been washed or combed in weeks. Now, looking back, I realize she was a prettier woman than I gave her credit for at the time—even-featured, with melting blue eyes and a sweet, generous mouth—but in that first full year of the war I believe I simply wasn't wise enough to see past her weariness. To a twelve-year-old, appearances are everything.

FAIRLY EARLY in my administration of Jimmy's paper route I noticed that Mrs. Ouellette was pregnant. Even despite the looseness and chenille coarseness of the pink housecoat, the swell of her stomach became more and more obvious, so that by summer's end she could not have hidden the fact of the child she carried even if she wanted to. I knew it was wrong for women without husbands to have babies— never mind whether the women were widowed or divorced—but it didn't occur to me to condemn her. I only felt sorry for her, picturing a third runny-nosed child crawling on the kitchen floor and imagining the stink of dirty diapers added to the unpleasant atmosphere of her tenement rooms. All the more reason—or so I must have thought—not to press for the weekly thirty cents she owed me.

It was not entirely one-sided, this leniency between us. As time went on, Mrs. Ouellette changed in gestures and actions toward me. She was less apologetic about her failure to pay for the newspaper, more sociable and outgoing toward me when I knocked at her door. Sometimes she offered me lemonade or Moxie or, once in a while, iced coffee—which I always refused because coffee was a drink for adults. We sat at the kitchen table, the two of us—the Ouellette children squalling around us—as if we were at an afternoon tea party, and we talked about the men in our lives. She told me about Mr. Ouellette, who was not dead, and about his abandonment of her just before their second child was born, and I talked at some length about the difficulty of living up to my father's expectations of me. Probably I was boring company for her, but she never said so.

It must have been in the course of these Friday afternoons in Mrs.
Ouellette's kitchen that I began to see that she was not as plain as I
had thought. Perhaps it was the pregnancy that helped transform
her, or it may have been the further sympathy I felt for her being
rejected by her husband. In any case, her face seemed different—the
features livelier, the eyes brighter—during our discussions. It might
have been our subject matter; I had begun to wonder about the
relations between married couples—how they seemed to leave each
other in the lurch at crucial moments of their lives—and I remember
one day confessing to Mrs. Ouellette my fears about my parents. She
seemed amused by me.

"They sound pretty normal to me," she said. "If that's the worst
he gives her—that dirty look—you're in luck."

"I wouldn't want to live by myself," I said.

"No, you wouldn't," she said. "It's no fun, unless you have something to look forward to."

That was the one time she touched me: reached out one hand—it
seemed terribly small, the fingers pale and delicate, not a strong hand
at all—and brushed the forelock of hair out of my eyes the way my
mother sometimes did.

"Hope," she said to me. "We live on it, even when there's nothing
and no one else."

JIMMY BARACLOUGH had been gone only a little more than four
months—it was September of 1942—when the telegram came saying
he'd been killed in the Pacific. I delivered it.

It wasn't the first telegram from the War Department I'd seen and
handled. I'd brought missing-in-action messages to three or four
families since the start of the war, and a couple of wounded-in-
actions, and I'd even had an earlier killed-in-action that I delivered to
a house on Ridgeway Avenue, a neighborhood where some of the
wealthy mill executives lived. But until the telegram about Jimmy, I
hadn't personally known the people affected. Also, I'd always put the
bad news into the hands of the mothers of the soldiers and sailors—
the fathers were at work in the afternoons, and in Scoggin the
mothers didn't begin to do men's jobs in the textile mills or the shoe

factory or at the Navy Yard in Kittery until later in the war—so that if I wasn't exactly comfortable with their moaning and weeping, at least I knew what to expect, and I didn't stay around any longer than I had to. Once they'd signed for the telegram, I was away, leaving them alone with their grief.

Because Jimmy's mother had gone off with another man, the address on the telegram didn't include her name. The news came to "Mr. Frank Barraclough, c/o Miller," Miller being the last name of the woman Jimmy's dad had moved in with after Jimmy went off to enlist.

Frank Baraclough was a local hero. When he graduated from high school he'd had a tryout with the Red Sox, signed a contract with them for a bonus that was rumored to have been a thousand dollars, and actually played in the minor leagues for a couple of Sox farm teams in the late 1920s. In his last year with the Sox, he played for their Pawtucket farm team, but halfway through the season he was hit in the face by a pitch. After that, he was a changed man. He'd been a sensational shortstop—my father told me all this as we sat outside Apollonio's store during his lunch hour, on one of the rare occasions when he and I found ourselves interested in the same topic—and he was famous for his ability to go to his right and make miracle throws to first without planting his feet. "Fancy" was his nickname; he was a cinch to be called up to the majors the following year, my father said, "if Fate hadn't intervened."

"Fancy Frank" Barraclough played ball for Robertson's Ready-Mix Concrete & Cinder Block Company—"Robertson's Raiders," for short—in the Scoggin Twilight League. He was close to forty, old for baseball—though this was wartime and even the major league rosters included players nearly as old as Frank Barraclough—and short-stop was no longer his position. He was in left field that year, batted sixth in the lineup, and had already told the sports editor of the *Scoggin Tribune* that he was giving up baseball at the end of the season. "I don't see the ball like I want," he was quoted as saying. "It looks kind of fuzzy to me around home plate." But he was still a popular player in the league; he had a strong arm, so opposing base-runners were cautious on fly balls hit to left, and though he struck out more often than not, when he connected he had more than his share of home runs—big, booming drives that had been known to clear the Johnson's Chevrolet scoreboard in dead center field, 415 feet away.

IT WAS THE middle of the afternoon, the Tuesday after Labor Day— the first day of the new school year—when I stopped at the Western Union office to see if there were telegrams to deliver. There were two: the one for Frank Barraclough and the other for Mr. Gowen, who owned a jewelry store on School Street. I delivered the Gowen telegram first—it was from his sister, telling him what time her train from Boston was arriving in North Berwick the next day—because I knew what the Barraclough message was. I wanted to postpone as long as I could—which turned out to be a mistake, because postponing gave me a lot of time to think about Jimmy being dead.

It was the first time I had confronted the death of someone close to me. A couple of years earlier Billy Roy had been crushed and killed by a freight elevator at the mill. I knew who Billy was, and I went to his funeral, but only because he was the older brother of René Roy, a classmate of mine. Jimmy was different: he had been a friend, and his dying raised a multitude of questions. How had he died? was one of them. And was there a body, or had he gone down to the bottom of the Pacific Ocean with his ship, never to be brought home, like the men on the *Arizona*? If there was a body, and the navy sent it to Jimmy's father, would there be a church funeral, and would the casket be open for all of us to look at Jimmy's corpse, and would I be able to bear to see it? I wondered too if Jimmy had done anything heroic, as if heroism—earning a medal—would justify the loss of his life. By the time I got to the Miller house on Kilby Street, I was crying; I had to wipe the tears off my cheeks with the back of my hand before I rang the doorbell.

It was nearly five o'clock, and when Frank Barraclough came to the door he was already wearing his Twilight League uniform—pale gray and pinstriped, with the words *Ready-Mix* across the front of the blouse in dark red script.

"Telegram," I said. My voice cracked on the word. I held out the yellow envelope with its glassine window, and Jimmy's father took it from me.

"Thanks, kid," he said. "Sit tight for a second and I'll get you something."

I never knew what he planned to give me for a tip, a dime or a quarter or what. As he moved down the hall away from me— number 3, the same as Jimmy Foxx's, on the back of his jersey—he was opening the envelope, and right away he saw what the telegram said. I heard him curse, saw him stumble and put out his left hand to steady himself against the nearest wall.

"You'd better scram, kid." He said the words hoarsely, but not unkindly. He didn't turn around to look at me—didn't let me see his face—and I scrammed.

UNTIL JIMMY'S DEATH I had thought of myself as the caretaker of his paper route, working and profiting from it only until his return from the battlefields of World War Two. Now that it was truly an inheritance, I began to feel the full weight of the responsibility the route carried with it, and I began to see some of the work I ought to do if I was to make it mine.

For one thing, I decided I should enlarge the route, add new customers, treat it as a living, growing enterprise. Jimmy had left me with eighty-six customers, and I still had the same eighty-six. Now on weekends, I knocked on the doors of people I didn't already deliver to, selling them on the idea that—especially with a war on—they needed the day's news brought to them regularly and on time. I even called at the Lemieux Funeral Home, never mind my timidness at banging the brass knocker and following old Mr. Lemieux along a carpeted hallway past something called a Slumber Room, where a pale gray-haired woman—a dead woman—lay face up in a casket of glossy dark wood. It was my second view of a corpse, but this one was a stranger; the sight didn't bother me, and in any case it was incidental to my signing up Mr. Lemieux. Within the month I had ninety-nine customers.

My second decision was purely financial. That first Friday after I'd delivered the telegram to Frank Barraclough I told Mrs. Ouellette she would have to begin paying me each week, or I would stop delivering her paper. I said I was sorry, but circumstances had changed. I told her about Jimmy being killed in action in the Pacific.

"I don't believe it," she said. Her expression didn't change; she simply looked straight at me, her blue gaze solemn and unblinking, her white hands working at the belt of the pink housecoat, and waited for me to unsay what I had just told her.

"It's true," I said. As it happened, the *Evening Express* I held in my hands contained the story—and his picture—of Jimmy Barraclough's death. I opened the paper to his obituary and held it out to her.

She didn't look at it. She struck the paper down with her right hand, tearing the page almost in half, and ran out of the kitchen.

I sat down in one of the kitchen chairs and waited for her to return. One of the Ouellette kids was on the floor in front of the stove, nose running and mouth open, looking as startled as I felt, and then he started to cry. I didn't know what to do. When Mrs. Ouellette stood up to leave the room, the front of the housecoat had parted and I'd been able to see she wasn't wearing anything underneath—her skin was creamy white and I could see the swell where she carried the new baby, and the hair, like cornsilk, where her thighs came together. I was dizzy with ignorance; I had scarcely any notion of what was happening here, except I knew I had witnessed something I had no right to see.

I was sitting, confused, trying to refold the torn newspaper, when she came back into the kitchen. The child went quiet when she appeared. Mrs. Ouellette was calm; there was no sign of agitation on her face; it didn't look as if she'd been crying. The pink housecoat was closed and the belt tied. She took the newspaper out of my hands and held it against her chest.

"I'm awfully sorry," she said, "but my check is late again."

"Well—" I said. I had no idea what I was going to say to her.

"I know you want to be a good businessman," she said, "but I wonder if you could give me a few days grace. Just till Monday. Just this one last time."

IT WAS AN EVENTFUL month, that September of 1942.

It was the month when my father was offered—and accepted—a

permanent job at Scoggin High School, teaching history and civics, which meant that he was able to stop keeping the books for Tony Apollonio's fruit store. His change of fortune pleased my mother, who was forever wary of anyone who spoke English with an accent— not only the Greek Apollonios, but the town's large, blue-collar French-Canadian population and, finally, the Edelsteins, an elderly Jewish couple who lived across the street from us.

It was the month I left Edison School and moved up to seventh grade at Emerson. The change from grammar school to junior high was important to me; it enhanced my opinion of myself, made me self-important in a way that Jimmy Barraclough might have appreciated, even if he couldn't have expressed it.

It was the month of Jimmy's funeral, a simple ceremony that took place in the Congregational Church on Main Street without the dead sailor's presence. His ship, a destroyer, had gone down in the Coral Sea with few survivors, so there was no body, no casket, no object to be mourned. Two strangers, uniformed naval officers with white caps tucked under their arms and uniforms that carried cords and stripes and jewelries of gold and silver, sat in a front pew while the minister praised Jimmy and "this young man's impatient desire" to die for his country. Frank Barraclough sat in another front pew, far from the officers, and listened to this praise with his head lowered; he looked like a stranger—in street clothes, with no name or number on his blue suitcoat—and I noticed the gray of his sideburns and the bald spot forming at the crown of his head. I had thought perhaps here was an occasion at which I would see Jimmy's mother for the first time, but she seemed not to be in the church. The one woman who was at the service was Mrs. Ouellette; it was the first and last time I ever saw her dressed up.

And it was the month, September of 1942, that I lost her as a customer.

I KNOW NOW that there's a lot of paraphernalia associated with death, especially death of an unnatural sort. Ambulances and doctors, police with their cars and their blatting radios, ordinary cars that belong to curious neighbors and other gawkers, and people—lots of people standing around in groups of two and three, talking in subdued voices, watching every movement around the scene of the dying.

A couple of days after Jimmy's funeral, that was what I saw when I arrived at Mrs. Ouellette's. The street was a chaos, with cars parked every which way and uniformed policemen—state troopers as well as locals—trying to get the curious to go on about their business. Red and white lights were flashing from the tops of the cars and the one ambulance parked nearest the porch steps. The door to Mrs. Ouellette's flat was open; I could see people moving around inside, in her kitchen, but I couldn't get close enough to see what they were doing. One of the front windows was broken out, and shards of glass were spilled all over the porch. Up on the third floor some stupid little brat was hanging over the railing, trying to look down, and his mother was hauling him back by his belt before he fell. While I was watching, one of the ambulance men came out of the flat carrying something wrapped in a brown blanket. He put it inside the back of the ambulance; then he went into the kitchen again and came out with a second blanket that also went into the ambulance. Finally he and his partner carried a blanket between them and loaded it after the others. Then they got into the cab of the ambulance and drove away, the siren making slow, soft whirring noises to warn people to move. There was no way I could get close enough to deliver Mrs. Ouellette's paper, even if I'd wanted to, so I decided to finish my route and come back later.

Nobody had told me Mrs. Ouellette was dead, but I knew she was, and so were her two poor little dirty kids—they were all under those blankets loaded into the ambulance. I didn't know why or how; I think I knew it had something to do with Jimmy Barraclough being killed in action in the Pacific, but I couldn't have explained the connection if you'd asked me at the time. All I was really sure of was that it was a shame, this business of dying for something that had no size or weight or shape: for democracy, if that's what Jimmy died for; for love, if that was Mrs. Ouellette's reason—which is what Doc Ross was saying when I got back to the tenement.

"Some people are too young to die for love," I heard him say. He didn't know I was there in the kitchen, and the man with him, the Scoggin chief of police—I recognized him from the picture on fliers he'd passed around for the coming election—raised one eyebrow and gave a slight nod in my direction. Doc Ross was our family doctor— J. Watson Ross was the name on his office door, but nobody ever called him anything but Doc—and when he made house calls he carried a small black valise filled with pills, wooden spatulas and gauze bandages, a rubber hammer, and his stethoscope. "Pink pills for pale people," he would say when he opened a vial and poured a few of its pills into a tiny white envelope.

Now he turned to look at me. Everyone else was gone; the ambulance men, the police directing traffic, the lookers-on—they'd all vanished. It was just the three of us in Mrs. Ouellette's dingy kitchen, the door of the gas oven wide open. There was more glass on the linoleum inside the door, a dirty white towel tossed under the table; the lace curtains stirred in the breeze that blew in through the broken window.

"What are you doing here, boy?" Doc Ross said.

"She was my customer," I said.

"Customer?" He took a step toward me, squinting at me in the half-light of the room. "What kind of customer?"

"On my paper route."

I think he recognized me then, for he smiled, and then he laughed—a short bark of a laugh. "Better she yours," he said, "than you hers."

"Yes, sir," I said, though his words had made no sense to me.

"What do you know about this business?" the police chief asked me.

"Nothing, sir."

"Nothing?"

I hesitated. "Is she dead?" I said. "Are they all dead?"

"All three," the chief said. "And the one she was carrying."

Doc Ross put out one hand as if to stop the chief of police from talking. "Do you know who the man is that made her pregnant?" he asked me.

"No, sir."

"No idea at all?"

"No, sir," I said. "No idea."

He gave me a long look, then shrugged and straightened up and put his hands in the pockets of his suitcoat. "I don't guess there's anything else to be done here," he said to the chief.

"Guess not," the chief said. He went over to the gas stove and checked all the knobs to be sure they were off, closed the oven door, carefully, so it didn't bang shut. "You'd better skedaddle," he said to me. "Your folks'll be waiting supper."

I TRIED TO TELL my parents what I had seen—the deaths, the broken glass, the police and Doc Ross—but my mother stole my thunder.

"I was on the switchboard when the calls started coming," she said. "It was about three o'clock. First it was Mr. Wiggin, from the flat just above Mrs. Ouellette, calling for an ambulance. He was the one who broke all the glass. First he had to smash the windowpane in the kitchen door, so he could reach in and turn the lock. Then when he got inside the kitchen the gas smell was so strong he had to use a chair to break out the window."

"He could have just opened the window," my father said. The evening paper was folded lengthwise beside his plate; he'd seemed so interested in it, I was surprised he'd been listening to my mother.

"He was in a hurry," she said. "I imagine he really thought that if he could let in fresh air—if he could do it soon enough—he could save the poor woman's life."

My father shrugged without looking up.

"Then it was Todd Emery, at the fire station, calling Doctor Ross," my mother went on, "and then, later on, it was the doctor calling from the flat. He wanted police to come, to make people move out of the street. 'Get these damned ghouls out of my hair,' I heard him say."

"What's a ghoul?" I wanted to know.

"Somebody who enjoys the company of dead people," my father said. "Are you enjoying this?" he asked my mother.

"There was a dirty towel on the kitchen floor," I said.

"It was against the door. She didn't want any of the gas to leak away," my mother said. "She wanted it all for herself—and for her little ones." Her voice trailed off; I thought she was going to cry.

"Dot," my father said—my mother's Christian name was Dorothy—and I knew my father had pronounced it that way as a warning, though the tone of his voice was a gentle as it was firm.

My mother stood up as if she were about to clear away the supper dishes, but for a moment she paused behind my chair, her hands resting lightly on my shoulders. "How terrible," she said, "to be poor and all alone."

My father opened the paper and gave her a sharp look above its pages. "That's enough," he said.

I understood why my mother was excited by her inside information about the deaths of Mrs. Ouellette and the children, and in some imperfect way I understood how her intimacy with the facts could upset my father, for whom history needed to be distanced—reported in the papers—before it was worth his attention.

But I didn't get to tell what happened just after the police chief told me not to keep my mother and father waiting supper for me—how I already had my left foot on the bike pedal, about to swing myself up to the seat and ride home, when Doc Ross called my name.

"Stevie," he said. "Just a minute." He came down the steps toward me. "She owe you money?"

"Yes, sir."

"How much?"

"Three weeks," I said.

"How much is that?"

"Ninety cents."

He took a dollar bill out of his wallet and gave it to me. "Keep the change," he said.

"Yes, sir. Thank you."

He looked up at the police chief, who was just locking the door to the dead woman's flat. "Now she's square with the world," he said.

Afterword *Jean McGarry*

While composing his biweekly Ramblers, Adventurers and Idlers, Samuel Johnson had little time for editors. A chronic procrastinator, he was often still writing while the copy boy was waiting at the door to deliver that day's pearl to the printers. Still, he seems to have understood the tensions inherent in the relationship of writer to editor. He certainly grasped the agonies of the author, who, "full of the importance of his work, and anxious for the justification of every syllable, starts and kindles at the slightest attack."

Johnson divides editors into two camps: the eager beaver, who "brings an imagination heated with objections . . . considers himself obliged to shew, by some proof of his abilities, that he is not consulted to no purpose, and therefore, watches every opening for objection, and looks round for every opportunity to propose some specious alteration."

In the second camp is the leisurely soul "with no intention than of pleasing or instructing himself; he accommodates his mind to the author's design; and, having no interest in refusing the amusement that is offered, never interrupts his own tranquility by studied cavils, or destroys his satisfaction in that which is already well, by an anxious inquiry how it might be better."

Fiction writers might think they prefer the supine version to the beaver, but in reality, we need them both, delivered in the right order and at the right dose.

In my experience, the editor of this series, John T. Irwin, has found the formula for dealing with writers. First of all, he's a genuine reader, who willingly goes where you want to take him. Judging from the stories gathered in this volume, he was as glad to show up in a surf shop as to visit Paris in the twenties, and he seemed to have enjoyed a sweltering, fractious family picnic as much as the armchair dreams of a philanderer. He's open to the sound of different voices, male and female; he can skim class divides and is as hospitable to an author with an old-fashioned yarn to spin as to an experimentalist who serves up his people straight, no chaser.

Oddly, it's in his passion for reading that John Irwin fulfills the duties of critic (Johnson's editor number two). If he likes the work, he enters into its spirit, locates the best of it, the gist of it, the sound of it, and clears the debris away. Not with the acid Pound applied to dissolve poetic debris word by excess word, and not with the scalpel Gordon Lish used to fleece his writers of rhetorical nap.

Irwin's method is less surgical but just as efficient. I remember receiving my first manuscript back from him after a tentative decision to publish it in this series was given. Each story in the collection had a single word penciled on its first page: "good," "maybe," "no," a couple of "excellents." I also remember the compacted half-hour of critique I received when I asked what was wrong with the "maybes" and the "no." In amiable terms, graciously laid on, these offerings were rendered to their bare outline and dismissed. The writer, "full of the importance of his work, anxious," etc., might well have struggled with this veridct and I think we all did—at first. Why did we eventually come around? Well, to my mind, if an editor is a genuine reader and appreciator, who can afford to ignore an informed judgment that one's piece isn't up to a standard set solely by oneself?

To those writers less easily shamed, Irwin proves gently resistant to continued pressure. Yet his patience is such that renewed efforts to push his hand never produce (to my knowledge) that editorial nuke: look, you stupid cluck, this story/poem is lousy!

Many of the authors gathered herein returned to the Johns Hopkins University Press with their second books, some with their third. It was at this later step that Irwin's editorial guidance meant the most to this author. With the aid of an uncanny memory (for the contents of the last book) and a comprehensive grasp of the genre, he was able to see where I was going in the new work, and why. He encouraged fresh ventures and offered valuable advice—the kind we might well offer ourselves were we able see the work through the wrong end of the telescope, where it's consolidated and condensed. Advice at the second- and third-book stages proved (to me) insightful, ingenious, and immediately useful.

In 1986, when I handed Irwin a collection of prose poems (never his cup of tea), he read them without prejudice, and even liked them, but suggested I write a realist novella as a setting for these bright bits. I did, and a new book emerged in 1987. Looking back, I see that that book was fueled by collaborative creative energy. For an editor— who is himself a writer—to make this kind of contribution to another writer's work is artistic generosity of a high order.

To intervene in this way over the long haul of a writer's career is so rare, apparently, that the names of such generous souls—Perkins, Pound, Howells, Heap, Ford, Weaver, etc.—are legendary. And deservedly so.

Contributors

ELLEN AKINS, a graduate of the film production program of the University of Southern California and of the Writing Seminars at the Johns Hopkins University, is the author of the novels *Home Movie, Little Women, Public Life,* and most recently, *Hometown Brew.* Her first collection of stories was *World Like a Knife.* She lives in Cornucopia, Wisconsin, with her husband, Stephen Denker, and their son, Will.

STEVE BARTHELME is the author of *And He Tells the Little Horse the Whole Story* and, with his brother Frederick, the memoir *Double Down.*

GLENN BLAKE was born and raised in Texas where the Old and the Lost rivers meet. His stories are set around those swamps, bayous, and sloughs. *Drowned Moon* is his first collection, and every previously published story in it was nominated for a Puschcart Prize. He teaches creative writing in the English department at Rice University.

JENNIFER FINNEY BOYLAN is the author of nine books, the first of which was *Remind Me to Murder You Later,* published in 1988. She lived and published under the name James Boylan until 2001. Her memoir *She's Not There: A Life in Two Genders,* was published in 2003. Other works include the novels *The Planets* (1991) and *Getting In* (1998). Jenny graduated from Wesleyan University in 1980 and worked with the original cast of *Saturday Night Live* as managing editor of *American Bystander Magazine* in the early eighties. She also worked as an editorial assistant and production editor at Viking Press/Penguin Books and E. P. Dutton, Inc. She received her M.A. from the Writing Seminars of the Johns Hopkins University in 1986. Since 1988 she has been a professor of American literature and creative writing at Colby College, in Maine, where she is currently co-chair of the Department of English.

RICHARD BURGIN is the author of ten books, including the novel *Ghost Quartet* and four short story collections, the last two of which, *The Spirit Returns* and *Fear of Blue Skies*, were published by the Johns Hopkins University Press. Four of his stories have won Pushcart Prizes and eleven others have been listed as among the year's best by the Pushcart Prize editors. He is a professor of communication and English at Saint Louis University, where he edits the literary magazine *Boulevard*.

AVERY CHENOWETH'S novel-in-stories *Wingtips*, from which "Powerman" is reprinted, was shortlisted for the Library of Virginia Prize for Fiction. His nonfiction work includes *Albemarle: A Story of Landscape and American Identity*. His forthcoming book on the creation of national identity in Virginia will be made into an hour-long PBS documentary film for 2007. He lives in Charlottesville, Virginia.

GUY DAVENPORT, a poet, critic, translator, and artist who lived in Lexington, Kentucky, published most recently *The Death of Picasso: New and Selected Writing*. His essays are collected in *The Geography of the Imagination* (1981) and *The Hunter Gracchus and Other Papers on Literature and Art* (1997), and his short stories are gathered in several volumes. He said of the story reprinted in this collection, "I wrote 'A Field of Snow on a Slope of the Rosenberg' as a farewell to writing fiction. Hugh Kenner saw straightaway that it was symbolically autobiographical (unintentionally). Another critic said that it was one more story by a mentally disturbed narrator. Another congratulated me on inventing an imaginary Swiss writer (Walser lived from 1878 to 1956, influencing both Kafka and Thomas Mann. I first heard about him from Christopher Middleton in 1948 at Oxford). John Irwin published it in *The Georgia Review* and accepted the book in which it appears, *Da Vinci's Bicycle*, sight unseen. My farewell was premature; I've published eight more collections of stories since. My feeling that I was making an ending comes from my sense of using up all available material when I write a story." Guy Davenport died in January 2005.

TRISTAN DAVIES teaches fiction in the Writing Seminars at the Johns Hopkins University. His first collection of short stories, *Cake*, appeared in 2003. In 2001, he received the Alumni Excellence in Teaching Award at Johns Hopkins. In 2004 he was awarded a Maryland State Arts Council Award as well as a Fiction Fellowship from the George and Eliza Gardner Howard Foundation.

STEPHEN DIXON has published twenty-four books of fiction, twelve novels, and twelve story collections. His latest book is the novel *Old Friends*, published in October 2004. Four of his story collections have been published by the Johns Hopkins University Press: *14 Stories, Time to Go, All Gone,* and *Long Made Short.* Altogether, about five hundred of his short stories have been published. He has been teaching in the Writing Seminars at the Johns Hopkins University since 1980.

JUDITH GROSSMAN is the author of a novel, *Her Own Terms* (1988, 2002), and a story collection, *How Aliens Think* (1999).

JOSEPHINE JACOBSEN was the author of seven books of poetry, two works of criticism, and three collections of short fiction. From 1971 to 1973 she served two terms as Consultant in Poetry to the Library of Congress, a post now called Poet Laureate. Her many awards included a 1994 Academy of Arts citation, the Lenore Marshall Poetry Prize, a fellowship from the Academy of American Poets for service to poetry, and the selection of *On the Island: Short Stories* as one of the five nominees for the PEN/Faulkner fiction award. Other honors include an award from the American Academy of Arts and Letters and eight inclusions of her stories in the *O. Henry Prize Stories.* Her volume *In the Crevice of Time* was a finalist for the National Book Award in poetry in 1995. She died in 2003.

GREG JOHNSON is the author of eleven volumes of fiction, nonfiction, and poetry. His most recent books are the novel *Sticky Kisses* and the story collection *Last Encounter with the Enemy.* Johnson lives in Atlanta and teaches in the graduate writing program at Kennesaw State University.

JERRY KLINKOWITZ was a minor league baseball owner/operator for seventeen years and is the author of *Short Season, Basepaths, Own-*

ing a Piece of the Minors, and many other books. During the off season, he is a professor of English and University Distinguished Scholar at the Univesity of Northern Iowa.

MICHAEL MARTONE'S new book, *Contributor's Notes,* is a collection of contributor's notes he has published in literary magazines. *The Blue Guide to Indiana* was published in 2001, and *The Flatness and Other Landscapes* won the Associated Writing Programs Award for Creative Nonfiction.

JACK MATTHEWS has published fiction, poetry, and essays. His most recent book is *Schopenhauer's Will,* recently translated into Czech but yet to be published in English—possibly because it's not a novel, biography, or philosophical tract but a combination of all three. His most recent book in English is *Reading Matter.* He and his wife live in the country where they collect antiques, American primitive oil paintings, and antiquarian books. He is Distinguished Professor of English Emeritus at Ohio University in Athens.

JEAN MCGARRY has published six works of fiction: two novels and four collections of stories. Her last book, *Dream Date,* was published in 2001. She has new stories in *Boulevard* and *Yale Review.* She has taught in the Writing Seminars at Johns Hopkins since 1987, where she is a professor of fiction and, since 1997, department chair.

ROBERT NICHOLS was born in Worcester, Massachusetts, in 1919. He practiced as a landscape gardener and construction worker for many years. He lives with his wife Grace Paley in Vermont. His first book of poems was *Slow Newsreel of Man Riding Train.* He has also published a fiction tetralogy, *Daily Lives in Nghsi Altai;* a collection of short stories, *In the Air;* and *From the Steam Room: A Comic Fiction.*

JOE ASHBY PORTER is the author of the novels *Eelgrass* and *Resident Aliens* and the collections *The Kentucky Stories, Lithuania: Short Stories,* and *Touch Wood: Short Stories,* as well as scholarly works on Shakespeare. Among his honors are Pushcart Prizes, NEA/PEN Syndicated Fiction awards, fellowships from the National Endowment for the Arts, Pulitzer nominations, and a 2004 Academy Award in Literature from the American Academy of Arts and Letters. He has taught at Duke University since 1980.

FRANCES SHERWOOD was raised in Monterey, California, graduated from Brooklyn College, received her M.A. from the Johns Hopkins University, and was a Stegner Fellow at Stanford University. She is the author of a short story collection, *Everything You've Heard Is True*, (1989) and of four novels, *Vindication* (1992), *Green* (1995), *The Book of Splendor* (2002), and *Betrayal* (forthcoming). Two of her stories have been included in O. Henry Award collections (1989, 1992), and one story was published in *Best American Short Stories* (2000). Twenty-four of her short stories have been published in magazines, most recently in the summer 2004 issue of *Zoetrope*.

ROBLEY WILSON'S second novel, *Splendid Omens*, was published in 2004. His third, *The World Still Melting*, is scheduled for the fall of 2005. He was editor of the *North American Review* for more than thirty years and now lives in Florida with his wife, novelist Susan Hubbard, and a herd of adopted cats.

FICTION TITLES IN THE SERIES